RUBY ISLAND

STEPHANIE RUTH

D1694381

Tī Kōuka

PUBLISHING

ISBN 978-0-473-59942-3 (Paperback)

ISBN 978-0-473-59943-0 (Epub)

ISBN 978-0-473-59944-7 (Kindle)

ISBN 978-0-473-59945-4 (Digital Audiobook)

Cover design by Tī Kōuka Publishing

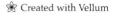 Created with Vellum

RUBY ISLAND

First impressions are hard to shake...

Big-headed ex-rugby star, Daniel Dante, refuses to believe a word celebrated ceramicist Kanako Janssen says, though why her new landlord's opinion bothers her so much is anyone's guess. She has enough to worry about, with her soon to be ex-husband refusing to sign divorce papers, Daniel's dog appearing regularly to freak her out, and an exhibition date looming.

Kanako is everything Daniel isn't, and nothing he's used to. Commitment doesn't come easily to a player who's been burnt so publicly before, but if he can't learn to trust this fresh-faced, quirky artist, he could well lose her altogether.

Like the swallows, Kanako's only in Otago for the season. But willing or not, the self-proclaimed introvert is being slowly absorbed into small town life on the lake, and she's in grave danger of falling in love with it.

For Josie,
who recognised me within the pages,
and liked this one best.

And for Nippon,
from a gaijin you welcomed with open arms.

Arigato gozaimasu!

CONTENTS

1

TWO MISTAKES

"There are only two mistakes
one can make along the road to truth;
not going all the way, and not starting."
- Buddha

Kanako Janssen had an hour to kill before her arranged meeting time, and though she was habitually early, a full sixty minutes was just plain ridiculous.

The mechanised voice of the sat nav observed her deviation off-course in Japanese, as she turned towards the lakefront.

"Put a sock in it," she muttered in response to the suggested U-turn, leaning across to switch the device to mute.

The unsealed off-road was flanked by slim-trunked silver birches and towering conifers, but it was the willows and poplars further along the shoreline that really drew her in. Already taking on the golden hues of early autumn, the trees blazed and shimmered in the late morning sun, like a fresh kiln-load waiting to be unpacked.

A young family shared an early lunch of fish and chips on a picnic table, the newsprint wrapping flapping lazily in the breeze, and a man on the pebbled beach threw a large stick for his dog. His lobs arced high and long, the canine nothing more than a blur of black and white as it streaked along the shoreline.

Kana parked, re-checking the exact location of the dog before climbing out of her SUV.

Simply deepening her breaths eased the majority of tension from the long drive.

The air was different this far south, like long, cool sips of mineral water. Her senses were waking, emerging from the ingrained pollution of the city.

A step towards something fresh, something new. Better to look at this upheaval as a beginning, rather than an end.

Taking her thermos and regional-map book with her, she settled at a vacant picnic table to sip her green tea, the action and taste winging her thoughts to Honshu.

What would Obāchan be doing now?

Kana opened the multi-city app on her phone. In Hiroshima, it wasn't yet eight o'clock.

Still too early to call.

She imagined herself in Obāchan's traditional farmhouse instead, enveloped by the scents and sounds she knew so well. If her grandmother was still sleeping, snow-white hair would be fanning across her *futon* like a heron's tail. But if she'd risen with the hens, her hair would already be tortured into a no-nonsense bun, and there'd be fresh eggs to crack over their morning *gohan*.

Kana sighed. Turning her face towards the sun, she lifted her sunglasses and closed her eyes. The daily ritual of missing her grandmother took on a physical ache, and the artist within her imagined it manifesting as a tangible gap under her ribcage.

Visible to casual observers? Probably not…

The dog's sharp bark startled Kana's eyes open.

So close.

Temporarily blinded by the glare of light off the water, she dropped her sunglasses back onto the bridge of her nose and spun around. She hadn't been paying attention, and it took a moment to re-orient herself.

A friendly-faced animal could be just as dangerous as an openly hostile one, in her experience. Thank Buddha this one was now on a leash.

Man and beast had left the shore, heading directly past her towards the farm ute, and the dog had dropped its well-chewed

2

stick near her foot, issuing a clear invitation. It crouched low and barked again, making her jump, and upend her tea.

Kana scrabbled to right the thermos, splashing liquid over herself in the process.

"Sorry. Forgotten his manners. Are you alright?" The man removed the stick and chucked it back towards the beach, his sheepdog responding with a high-pitched whine, straining at the leash to go after it.

Kana nodded, eyes still glued to the animal, and all those gleaming teeth.

Piping hot when she'd prepared it in Dunedin, her tea was now only tepid, lacking the heat to burn. Surreptitiously wiping the back of her hand off on her jeans, she tried to get her head together.

"Quiet. Heel." The soft commands took immediate effect, the border collie slinking against its master's jean-clad leg, silent.

The man had height, with a broadness about him that shouted RUGBY. The slightly crooked bridging of his nose—possibly an old break—helped cement the image, as did the black beanie pulled down over his ears. He wore muddied work boots, well-worn denim, and a checked cotton shirt.

Tricky to place his age with a good week's worth of dark stubble. More than thirty, less than forty, give or take.

But he wasn't moving off, as she'd hoped.

"Ah…" Kana was unsure how to politely tell the man to bugger off, having been wary of dogs since childhood. Ridiculously frightened, even by the smallest of breeds, she certainly didn't want anything to do with this relatively large one—well behaved or not.

Sliding her sunglasses down her nose, she narrowed her eyes at the two of them.

"You're not from around here." It was a statement, not a question. The dog owner motioned to Kana's open map book, just shy of the tea-puddle. "Are you lost?"

Mild irritation snapped, enough to make Kana forget the canine for a moment. She was beyond sick of being mistaken for a tourist in her own country. It hadn't happened for a while, but seemed to be ingrained in the story of her life.

Pure force of habit had her slip into the dismissive, slightly barbed old high school trick.

3

She spoke in Japanese.

"Sumimasen, Eigo wa wakarimasen."

Erecting a language barrier was the perfect conversation killer for this occasion. Rugby's cue to smile, take his dog, and get lost.

That threw him.

Daniel had assumed the woman was a Kiwi, with some Eastern heritage thrown in. She looked in keeping; at peace with the landscape. Her almond eyes and colouring would be very unusual in Japan. Autumnal—glowing like the trees lining the lakefront.

It was also uncommon for a Japanese woman to travel on her own in Aotearoa, especially without a basic grasp of English. Those less linguistically inclined tended to travel within groups.

Safety in numbers.

Glancing around himself, Daniel took stock of the surrounding area, and the distinct lack of anything resembling a tour.

He hadn't been expecting to hear anything other than English, so it took a moment to change gears. Reaching into his memory banks, he dragged his meagre Japanese to the forefront. Tenses, and the more difficult pronoun choices had always been an issue. Prepared speeches were fine, but some of the off-the-cuff conversations he'd attempted in the past had been disastrous.

"Gomen'nasai. Kiwi ja nai desu ka? Nihon-jin desu ka?" He was pretty sure that equated to 'My apologies. You're not a Kiwi? You're Japanese?' He then went on to ask if she was lost.

When he'd lived in Japan, the locals had fallen all over themselves to be helpful. The least he could do was try and reciprocate in some small way.

It had nothing to do with the fact this particular female was incredibly easy on the eye.

When she'd had her sunglasses on and was jumping out of her skin about the dog, he'd assumed she was younger. But though she was just a slip of a thing, this was a grown woman, not a girl.

A stunning woman.

Her eyes, though still appearing nervous, caught the light and radiated soft amber. Infused with a chilli-chocolate, the hair glossing

4

over her shoulders was even more intriguing due to its sheer mass, making his fingers itch to reach out and measure the weight.

He introduced himself as Daniel, and established her name was Kanako, all the while searching for any sign of recognition on her part.

Nothing. Not a single flicker.

The relief of being incognito washed over him, as welcome as a cool breeze off the lake, making him realise how rarely he experienced either nowadays. It turned the tables, making him slightly uneasy in his own skin. He'd become obtuse to the signs, unable to get a clear reading on other people's gut responses to him.

If he was just a man—any man—how would this woman perceive him?

Could he actually charm, merely by being himself? Or was it all in his reputation; his notoriety?

Disconcertingly, when Kanako smiled up at him from her lower position, her face upturned, it was Daniel who felt vaguely weaker. Almost as if the wattage she was using to turn on her sweet magnetism was somehow connected to his power source.

An unsettling thought. One he didn't care to analyse.

Mr Rugby, or Daniel, as he'd introduced himself, was adept at *Nihongo*. Not exactly fluent, but quite capable, with a decent grasp of the correct pronunciation.

Kana was left gaping, more than a little embarrassed. Her little tongue-in-cheek snub had just backfired, and bitten her firmly on the butt.

She squirmed.

Daniel was waiting for her to answer his latest halting question, and she was acutely aware she wasn't behaving as a Japanese tourist would; delighted one of the locals was well studied in her native tongue.

"I'm not lost, just taking in the view and having a break at the same time," Kana replied in the language of her mother, sticking to the simplest verbs and studying Daniel even more warily. He used his hands when he spoke, and his eyes when he listened, concentrating fully on her lips and expression.

They were an honest hazel-green, which made her squirm all the more for being so *dis*honest.

Daniel continued in Japanese, asking which part of *Nippon* she hailed from, and how long she'd been in New Zealand. He was an intriguing contradiction of a man, all burly and gruff, with impeccable manners.

"Hiroshima," she finally offered. Answering the where, if not the when, and remembering her own manners enough to ask which areas of Japan he'd travelled through.

Daniel had spent five years in Kansai. Osaka City—a huge industrial metropolis, topped only in size by Tokyo, and swarming in rich trading history. Far too urban for her own taste.

He'd played rugby for one of the large corporation teams.

Kana gave herself a mental pat on the back for that. She'd called it at first sight.

Daniel now helped trial and coach new players, and drew in internationals for the top Japanese league. He must've been a decent player himself to gain such a position. Not that Kana followed rugby. It struck her as a needlessly violent game, but she politely withheld that particular opinion from the man standing in front of her.

She hadn't forgotten about the dog, or the fact Daniel was a total stranger, so didn't invite either to sit. But it did feel good to speak Japanese, and to hear someone use her full given name.

No one called her Kanako now except Obāchan. It always got shortened to Kana, which she didn't mind exactly. It just seemed... *less*.

When Daniel left, he gave a polite bow and said he'd enjoyed meeting her, then wished her safe travels around the South Island. He hesitated for a long moment before finally turning away, to the point Kana began to wonder if he wanted something more from her.

Something *other*?

His eyes said yes, but his actions, no.

After Rugby's dusty farm ute had left the layby, Kana let out a long, shaky breath.

The ridiculous situations she got herself into, honestly. Her father would be in stitches when she told him. Not due to the fact she was talking to strange men in laybys, but due to her innate ability to entangle herself in accidental muck.

Taking off her Ugg boots, Kana rolled up her jeans. No longer having a husband around to try and talk her out of it, or call her nuts, she was going to brave a paddle in the shallows... Even if it froze her toes off.

Up to her calves, with the shore behind her, Kana soaked in the colours and wide-open sky, wondering who'd planted all of these beautiful European trees along the lakeside, and how ancient they were. She would have to read up on it.

How at home they looked. Strange when you considered how far they'd been removed from their original rootstock.

Just like herself.

"In the sky, there is no distinction of east and west; people create distinctions out of their own minds then believe them to be true," Kana murmured one of Obāchan's favourite Buddhist quotes under her breath.

If she were to emulate these particular colours in glaze, the poplar leaves would be mid-fired Abbots Dune through to Rimu in their graduated golds. The wind across the lake was chopping up patches of silver Chun over a thinly applied blue... Perhaps her modified Celadon in a high firing? And the deep, glossy black of Tenmoku would best match the far mountain peaks, with an added measure of iron oxide to slide it into the brown hues on the lower slopes.

Kana found herself assigning the colours she used on her stoneware to almost every view. It was an unconscious action, but this particular palette had her enthused about the six month artist-in-residence gig she was about to embark on. The backdrop of Lake Wānaka, diamond of the south, was nothing if not inspiring.

It took some time and a bit of stamping to be able to feel all ten of her toes again afterwards, but the dip was definitely worth it. It suited Kana's mood to baptise her travelling feet, uplifting the corners of her mouth.

Her hour was almost up, and she was more than ready to go and meet her patron.

2

WHAT MATTERS MOST

"Every morning we are born again.
What we do today is what matters most."
- Buddha

As instructed, Kana drove directly up to the main farmhouse to pick up the key for the annex and barn. But creeping the SUV at snail's pace gave her the opportunity to peer down the fork in the shingle driveway, checking out the low lying buildings she would be living in and working out of over the next six months.

The corrugated iron of the barn was painted a dark, forest-green, a bank of willows and toetoe screening it from the narrow access road. The annex beside it faced the view up to the old homestead.

Kana recognised the scene from the advertising and enrolment information. Red Canadian maples lined the gravel driveway up to the well-maintained farm-villa, and there was a warm welcome waiting for her at the front door.

Poppy Dante was a bubbly woman in her fit fifties, or sixties. They'd been corresponding via email since Kana had been chosen out of ten applicants for the potter-in-residence position, and there was zero-reserve in the hug Poppy initiated. Conversation burbled out of the woman like a brook.

Poppy's wild hair was partially tamed by a silk scarf, and her earthy eyes took in every detail of her latest ceramicist.

Hearing a dog bark somewhere on the property, Kana looked furtively behind herself, mentally counting the steps back to her SUV.

"Nothing to worry about. He's a working dog, so usually kennelled unless he's out and about with one of us, or working the sheep." The older woman must've noticed Kana's nervous start, and clearly recognised the cause. "Not a fan?" The words weren't spoken unkindly, and Kana thought she sensed a deeper empathy.

"I know attacks are rare." She attempted a light laugh, but it came out a touch nervy. "But my brain refuses to listen. They put the fear of Hades into me. All those teeth."

"Ah, I see. My grandniece feels the same way, actually. The neighbour's old tomcat will be teasing him." Poppy flicked her chin in the direction of the hubbub, placing a calming hand on Kana's arm at the same time. "He wouldn't hurt a flea, that one, but I'll make sure he doesn't bother you down at the barn. How's that?"

"Great." Kana breathed a sigh of relief. "That'd be perfect, thank you." She should've realised there'd be a high probability of dogs on this rural property, but it hadn't crossed her mind in all the commotion of moving out.

On the short drive back down to the annex, Poppy filled Kana in on the workings of the converted barn-studio, and the gallery in town where her first ceramics showing would be. Her benefactor also insisted she join the family for dinner back at the big house after unpacking.

As Kana put away the few food items she'd brought with her, she found two bottles of wine waiting for her in the pantry—one red, and one white. There was a small note attached from Poppy, welcoming her to the farm.

Kana rarely drank, having gotten out of the habit during the time she'd spent trying to get pregnant, but she appreciated the gesture, nonetheless.

The evening meal up at the farmhouse was a casual, family affair held at the kitchen table, with lamb shank stew and freshly baked bread to dip into it. Kana hadn't realised how hungry she was until she sat down to share the simple meal.

Poppy's niece, Adele, had been invited over with her daughter, Saffy. The eight-year-old was a little chatterbox, just like her great-aunt. Her father must've been of African descent, because although they had strikingly similar features, Saffy was a much darker version of her fair-skinned mother. Her intensely curly hair had been woven into tight Dutch braids, but sprung out the end of her hair ties—pom-pom style.

Saffy talked excitedly about school, her friends, and someone called Uncle D. The little girl obviously saw him as a father figure, and Kana deduced he must be Adele's other-half.

She checked out the redhead surreptitiously.

With her pale corkscrew curls pulled into a loose ponytail, Adele looked incredibly youthful. She had an open, engaging smile and freckles across the bridge of her nose, but there was something classic about the contours of her cheekbones and eyebrows that Saffy had inherited.

Adele was good at digging out information. Her eyes were crystal blue, and slightly hypnotic. When pressed, Kana found herself opening up about her divorce—the reason she was so eager to get away from her hometown.

Aware Saffy could be listening in on their conversation, she attempted to keep her tone light.

Adele accepted the information with an understanding nod, then promptly changed the subject. "Poppy gave me a pair of your blue teacups for Christmas, and I just love them. It feels like you're falling into the Pacific when you reach the bottom."

"Oh! Thank you." What a sweet compliment.

Smiling, first at Adele, then Poppy, Kana picked up a tangible warmth radiating back off both women, and was finally able to relax about accepting this position.

Double-guessing her choices had become an all too common trait. One she intended to cull. Ruthlessly.

After Adele and Saffy left, Kana thanked Poppy for a lovely meal. "I can't remember another time I've felt so instantly at home in another person's house."

Poppy laughed. "Oh, bless you. The farmhouse isn't *mine*. It's true I grew up here, but the farm's changed hands a couple of times since then. Datsun bought it a while back, and I sometimes look after it when he's away. Not the land, you understand—that's leased to the neighbouring sheep farmer."

"Datsun?" Kana thought she must've misheard the name. Surely that was a type of car?

"Yes. My son, D. We have an arrangement with regards to the annex, and the artist in residence programme." Poppy looked around herself. "The farm's almost unrecognisable from how it was in my time. Goodness knows it was damn near falling apart when he bought it."

Saffy's 'Uncle D,' Poppy went on to explain as they walked side by side down towards the annex, was her eldest son. It sounded like he was away on business a great deal, which was a bonus. Kana's work wouldn't often be interrupted.

"The ceramics programme was actually set up in memory of my mother, Nona Reynolds. Everyone knew her as Nana Nona in later life. She had eight grandchildren, and was pleased as punch about that. Loved cooking, loved her garden, and absolutely adored ceramics. When I was a child, she had a cruddy old kick-wheel down here in the barn, and used to escape to pot whenever she could."

They took the annex drive, branching off from the main access.

"When D bought the property a while back, I wrangled control over the barn. Mum would've liked that." Poppy reached out to lay her palm on the corrugated iron wall as they arrived. "Real Kiwi grit, she had."

"It's nice to learn more about her. Although it's called the Nona Reynolds Grant, there was nothing in the information pack explaining who she was."

Kana waited, sure Poppy was about to say something else about her mother.

"Do your family approve of your vocation as a ceramicist? Your call to pot?" Poppy asked instead, her tone almost wistful.

'Call to pot' was an apt description. Clay was Kana's obsession.

"On my mother's side it's considered prestigious, once you've attained a certain level. My father's family is from Holland—long history of ceramics there, too. Though my Oma would've preferred I was into something a little, um… *cleaner*."

Poppy laughed.

Oma didn't like dirtiness in any form, and her home was always spotless. The look on her face when she'd seen the state of Kana's poky Christchurch studio a few weeks back had been priceless.

"And your ex-husband?" Poppy let the intrusive question hang.

"No." Kana met Poppy's look directly. "I wouldn't say there was a lot of 'approval' on that front."

"Mm. Right. Good."

"That's *good*?" The incredulity shot straight out of Kana's subconscious, and into the air between them.

Poppy chuckled again. "Sorry, I have a habit of saying exactly what pops into my head. I meant good for you, no longer choosing that path. You have an incredible gift with clay. Anyone who can't see that's either blind or stupid." She handed Kana a substantial set of keys. "So it's good you're here. Nana Nona would've been over the moon. Nau mai, haere mai, Kanako. Welcome."

Kana lay in bed on the cool, starless night, her body exhausted by the drive, but her mind busy. Poppy's earlier questions had her musing over her eclectic family.

Raised by her Japanese mother and Dutch father—stoically maintaining their respective eastern and western contingents—Kana grew up endeavouring to be one-hundred percent southern, instead.

Kiwi.

For the most part she'd succeeded in assimilating to the land of her birth, though sometimes found herself dreaming of escape to one culture, when drowning in either of the other two.

Too tall to be mistaken for fully Japanese, and with lighter colouring, she'd always been referred to as *gaijin*. Foreign.

Within the Dutch community, she wasn't the blond, blue-eyed norm either, although it was the language that alienated her most. She understood the majority of the Dutch her father and Oma spoke together, but didn't often attempt to speak it. The guttural vowels made her tongue clumsy in her mouth.

It was clay that had eventually melded Kana's three cultural identities together, creating something so much more than the dislocated sum of her ingredients.

Kana might've wandered sideways off the path for a few years, but thanks to Nona Reynolds, she'd just been offered a precious opportunity to regain ground; to feel more at home within herself. She wasn't about to squander that chance.

The morning dawned bright and pretty, and like a child waking on Christmas morning, Kana couldn't contain her excitement as she poured over every inch of the gift she'd been given. The annex and studio were hers for a full six months, and they were *perfect*.

The one bedroom self-contained unit was small, simple and functional, with the odd quirky detail. Sequinned stars graced the sofa in the form of cushions, and there was a carved wooden elephant holding up the coffee table. The large converted-barn studio was fully equipped with tools, wheels, kilns, and shelving, all ready to go.

Kana unpacked her few remaining boxes. She'd left all but the essentials behind, attempting a clean break. It felt surprisingly good to be back to necessary (and truly precious) items.

Even more telling, it felt *great* to be free of the other junk—soon to be ex-husband included.

Coming to the last box, labelled Opa's Plates, Kana unwrapped more carefully, placing each piece on the teak sideboard in the annex. There were six in all, and looking along the line on completion, she smiled.

Her new living quarters may've been small, but with Opa's ceramics proudly displayed, it really did feel like home.

Kana took to her new solitary routine like a gecko to sun.

No one in the annex to plan around, or pander to. No schedule, other than the one she loosely followed in wedging, throwing, and turning her work.

Her own choices and her own space was a welcome change, something Kana had needed for the longest time, and her body and soul eased into new patterns with a sigh of relief. That wasn't to say she was alone, because as the week crept forward, she found herself more and more absorbed by the curious community.

People popped into the studio or stopped her on the street to introduce themselves.

With her own potting wheel delivered along with half a pallet of her favourite clay, the bank of shelving in the studio began to fill with tableware of various shapes and sizes. The two sturdy electric kilns looked serviceable, and had a proven track record, but Kana wouldn't truly relax until after her first successful bisque firing—still a week away at best.

Each morning Kana woke to a discernibly deeper autumn and practiced yoga. Poppy had given her wandering rights over the whole farm, so she ventured outside in the open if the weather permitted it. She'd discovered an old grove of fruit trees the first day she'd gone exploring, finding true calmness amongst the largely untended plot, and Poppy came across her there on Thursday morning before breakfast.

"Don't let me interrupt you. You look so peaceful, doing your thing."

Kana had chosen the flat, paved section under the grape arbour, bringing up two mats to combat the hard stone. Pressing down, she arched her back into a full cobra position before meeting Poppy's gaze.

"This was one of my favourite places as a child, though the orchard was producing then. Great view, isn't it?"

"Stunning." The lake was glassy and beckoning this morning, promising long, peaceful walks. Kana breathed in steadily through her nose, held it for the count of four, then released the air evenly as she eased her head and shoulders back down to the mat.

She heard the rustle of Poppy's supermarket bag.

Three enormous lemons had arrived in front of her mat when she eased into the same backstretch.

"Lemons," she stated unnecessarily, the tangy scent from their deep-yellow rinds filling her nostrils.

"My mother's Meyer is still going strong." Poppy indicated the direction with the wave of her hand. "Help yourself, anytime."

"Thank you. Lovely." Kana smiled back into her mat. "I'll have a slice in my tea."

"Actually, I'm glad I bumped into you. I have a proposition for you—a call for help, really." Poppy waited until Kana was in a raised position again. "My book club's supposed to be meeting tomorrow morning for a lakeside walk, but the weather forecast is atrocious. How would you feel about running an informal yoga class for us down at the Community Centre?"

Kana forgot to measure her breath, and it all came out in a hot puff.

"There'd be six of us, including Adele," Poppy raced on. "They're *very* nice people," she added hopefully.

Kana manoeuvred herself into a seated lotus, blinking up into Poppy's expectant face. The woman had practically saved her life with this ceramics gig.

She gulped. "Sure. I could do that. What time?"

———

Poppy's book club met at the Community Centre the next morning, resembling a flock of noisy geese. Though nervous, Kana tried to spend a minute with each one before the class, getting to know them —and their aches and pains—on an individual basis.

The women had pulled together a hodgepodge of scrappy yoga mats, but even with Kana's spare mat in use, two of the ladies were practicing on beach towels.

When the class finished an hour later, the participants came up to say how much they'd enjoyed it.

"Somehow, I feel taller! Is that normal? Where do we leave our koha?" Carissa, one of the chattier older women (lower-lumbar pain) held up a banknote.

"Oh, no. You don't have to pay." Kana waved the cash away, embarrassed. She was doing this as a favour to Poppy.

"But we always pay koha for community classes." Sally, the ex-hairdresser (wrist issues) seemed slightly put out, turning to Poppy for confirmation.

"First class is a free trial. Next week we pay."

What? Kana's eyes snapped to Poppy's.

Noting the older woman's raised eyebrows, she deduced the remark was being angled as a question, rather than a statement.

Her teaching was incredibly rusty, as Poppy would well know from her resume, but overall it wasn't a bad idea. It would force Kana out of the studio and into the social sphere at least one morning a week, and give her a little cash in hand.

"First class is free," she agreed slowly. "But if the room's available next week, you could each bring five-dollars."

"Ten," Poppy countered.

Kana looked around at all the eagerly nodding heads.

"Okay, ten. But I'll provide the mats."

As soon as she got home, Kana ordered a set of yoga mats online.

3

THE TRUTH

"Three things cannot be long hidden:
the sun, the moon, and the truth."
- Buddha

"I'll be with you in just a second!" Kana called towards the knock on the door, covering the mouthpiece of the phone so Samantha didn't get an earful.

"Hey, Sam? Gotta go. I think my porcelain delivery's here." She was opening the door as she spoke, laughing at her Christchurch neighbour, who was pretending to be huffy at being blown off for 'stinky mud.' "Don't be ridiculous. I'll call you right back." She listened to the ER nurse whine for a moment more about wasting her precious sleep hours waiting on phone calls. "I *swear*, ten minutes, tops."

Kana smiled vaguely at the visitor, her free hand reaching up to smooth her hair off her face.

Not a delivery guy.

The man on the doorstep was dressed in a dark suit, and tie. The cut looked expensive, though the fabric was a little on the crumpled side. He was clean-shaven, and broad, but had a rakish shag to his dark hair.

Sexy—like a well-dressed pirate.

Although his hazel-green eyes held a glint of something a little dangerous, he seemed familiar, somehow.

Very familiar. His nose…

Oh, *hell*. Kana's stomach dropped.

Mr Rugby.

He looked so different without the beanie. Without the beard. Without the friendly smile. Moving on autopilot, she hung up on Sam.

Was there any chance Rugby hadn't heard her burbling away in English?

Nope. Not a hope in hell going by the hostile look on his face.

Bugger. How were they going to play this?

"Um, hi." She went to slip her phone into her back pocket, realising belatedly she was still in her yoga gear, and therefore pocket-less.

"Good afternoon."

Looked like they were going to play it cool, then. *Glacial*, even.

"I just came to introduce myself, but I believe we've already met. Down at the lake." He thrust his right hand out, and Kana fumbled with the phone again before offering her own to shake.

"Daniel Dante, from up at the farmhouse. A pleasure to meet you. Again." Rugby's voice wasn't what you'd call friendly. Not in any way, shape, or form. All the words were in the right place, but he ground them out with a gritty bite.

It was like discovering the man she'd met at the lakeside had a dark twin.

He gave a firm handshake, squeezing a smidgen too tight. Kana felt the zip of temper through his palm, but held strong, refusing to shirk from the pressure until they'd both let go.

"*You're* Datsun?" she croaked. "D? My landlord?"

Poppy's son. Adele's other half. Saffy's Uncle D.

"Daniel. Yes." He made like he was going to leave.

"*Ugh*," Kana groaned, taking a step forward and reaching out with the intention of touching his arm. "Look, I'm sorry. I owe you an apology."

Rugby looked directly at her, *through* her. Kana imagined herself about an inch tall.

Changing her mind about touching the man again, she dropped her hand.

"Not at all. You don't owe me anything. Except, perhaps, rent?" Her landlord raised one eyebrow before turning to stalk back to the white, late model sedan. He didn't speak again until he'd reached for the door, and this time his voice was edged in sarcasm. "Congratulations on your language retention, though. Seriously. You've become extremely adept in a remarkably short time, and your Kiwi accent's impeccable."

Crap.

She'd just landed herself right in it, hadn't she? And shit had a habit of sticking.

Fuck it.

Stunning woman. Talented liar.

Not what Daniel needed on his doorstep right now, topping off a bloody exhausting day.

Fourteen hours in the air had made him cranky—all cooped up and too big for the seating. He'd just wanted to get back to the lake, back to the farm, and back to his own bed.

His right knee was aching like hell from the old injury, only adding to his foul mood.

The flight from Osaka had been uneventful, but he'd spent the time moving restlessly along the aisles checking on the five young rugby players he'd brought back with him, encouraging them to speak English amongst themselves.

The Japanese youths were being passed off to carefully vetted homestay families in Auckland, but not before a welcoming ceremony and lunch at the rugby clubrooms. Speeches that went on forever—smiling, being affable, and signing a never-ending stream of rugby balls and godforsaken T-shirts.

Then the domestic flight... At least he hadn't had to hold much of a conversation through that one. Though the perky flight attendant had seemed more than willing to tell him all about herself, she'd let him sleep when his eyes drooped.

He'd woken on descent with his jacket spread across him like a blanket, and a doozy of a headache.

Not being able to get a direct flight home, he'd hired a rental car and driven through the range from Queenstown, instead. The best leg of the trip, scenery-wise, but time he'd rather have spent sleeping.

Then the annex tenant—what had possessed him to drop in there unannounced?

Of all the fucked-up fates, it had to be the woman from the lake proving him a total idiot. The woman who'd infiltrated his dreams these past two weeks, making him wonder if he'd been wrong to walk away without any likelihood of ever seeing her again.

Well, he'd seen her now, and the surreal magic of that afternoon before his flight out of the country had been well and truly blasted to buggery.

Why had she told him she couldn't speak English? It had to be some kind of prank at his expense. Had she planted herself on the lakeshore to lure him into the ruse? To what purpose?

He didn't even want to know.

It was early evening when Kana's cell phone rang, just after she'd talked herself into leaving the annex to pick up a treat of fish and chips, and maybe eat them down by the lake.

Obāchan rarely called without a set reason, and this was no light catch-up.

Kana's old pottery teacher's wife, Yukiko Tanaka, had passed away. She'd been ill for a long time, but regardless of expectation, the old woman and Kana's grandmother had been close friends since they were schoolgirls.

The loss for Obāchan was huge.

It wasn't mentioned, but both grandmother and granddaughter knew that as the years passed, Obāchan would be more and more alone in Hiroshima. Her generation was thinning out. Dying off.

After she hung up, Kana sat on the front step of the annex until the ruru flew, hooting their calls through the inky night. She was no longer hungry.

On an annual—dead-boring—trip to Japan with her mother, Kana had been twelve when Obāchan had first taken her to Tanaka-sensei's pottery studio.

Obāchan revered, collected, and used Tanaka-sensei's pieces in all her tea ceremonies, and was practically a sister to his wife. She'd thought the busy studio and kilns might appeal to Kana, and she'd been right.

On the walk back to Obāchan's terraced plot, Kana had enthused about the colours, the smell of the wet clay, and the heat of the kilns. She'd asked incessant questions her grandmother hadn't been able to answer.

"Where do they get the clay? Can we get some? How do you learn to use the wheel? Can we get one? How do they make such incredible colours, and paint such clever designs? Can I try it? Please, Obāchan!"

Tanaka-sensei had been a master potter. To honour a favourite old customer, and because he'd said Kana's enthusiasm and foreign energy had charmed him, he'd agreed to give her lessons. Two mornings a week for the remaining month she'd been in Japan. Not *one word* of English to be spoken.

Those lessons had awoken an obsession in Kana. Not only her love affair with ceramics, but also with Japan. *Nippon*. The country that had eluded her affections for so long was suddenly revealed as a wonderland of art, inspiration, and history. The archipelago belonged in part to her, if not the other way around.

Her relationship with Obāchan had blossomed into more than just obligation that winter. Friendship, understanding, and mutual respect began to grow. Kana's Japanese language improved as she became greedy to learn, needing more formal language and adjectives when learning from Tanaka-sensei. The potter demanded and deserved the utmost respect.

Kana had cried fat tears when they left Hiroshima to go home that year, and never complained about their annual trip again, though it invariably cut a huge chunk out of her New Zealand summer.

Tanaka-sensei was not given to public displays of affection, but Kana knew he'd been fond of her, and proud of her progress. The winter she'd been fifteen, he'd presented her with a small trinket box in porcelain as a farewell gift. It had a delicate swallow, hand-painted in cobalt, on the lid. As simple as a single *kanji* character, the bird was perfect.

Flocks of swallows flew from Hiroshima each year, only to return and nest under the wide arcs of the bridges the following spring. Not unlike Kana's own pilgrimage.

That was the last time Kana had seen Tanaka-sensei, and now Yukiko was gone too.

Kana didn't sleep that night, though her soul was tired. Her creative fingers felt the need to work, and a half formed idea began to concrete the instant she started wedging clay.

The slabs she rolled were huge, and she padded out wooden blocks with newsprint to brace them in position as she worked features from memory.

The two busts should fit together as one piece, but she'd need to fire them separately.

She also needed more wood, and a ton more paper.

Daniel slept like a rock gathering moss. His body knew it was home, blissfully comatose in its own bed. Waking on Saturday morning and blinking at the clock, he was amazed to see he'd managed twelve hours straight.

A new jet-lag record.

Halfback was over the moon to be let out of his run, and curled himself into circles with his tail whipping frantically. Daniel had missed the border collie's enthusiasm, not to mention company, and gave the dog an extended belly rub before his biscuits.

After making himself a leisurely coffee, Daniel wandered down to the main gate with his steaming mug, Halfback loping backwards and forwards beside him. The sun shimmered off the lake in the distance, and the air was crisply clean.

It felt damn good to be home.

The one thing he needed to make this morning perfect was to get his hands on the sports news. Where the hell was the morning paper?

Daniel hunted high and low around the mailbox, as the rolled newsprint occasionally ended up in the toetoe after being hurled from the 4-wheeler. He finally gave up, surmising it either hadn't been delivered yet, or they'd bloody mucked up his subscription again.

It wasn't until he was walking back past the annex that a third option presented itself.

The new annex tenant's fire-engine-red vehicle, smack-bang in front of the barn, reminded him he wasn't alone on the property. One of his mother's art projects was in residence, quite possibly with her nose in his morning paper.

Daniel was tossing up whether or not he should risk another interaction with the woman, when the potter in question burst out of the barn, the hinges screeching in complaint as she heaved the door back. About to call out, he was surprised into silence to watch her perform a gleeful little stomping dance.

Then she threw both hands up into the air and shook them, as if summoning Rā.

Absolutely bonkers.

Halfback thought so too—but in a good way. He gave an excited little yip, and bounded over to include himself in the fun.

The dog did *not* get an excited yip in response.

Daniel belatedly remembered Kanako had been a bit freaked out by Halfback on the beach, but that was nothing compared to her reaction when the dog approached at full speed.

She was up on the bonnet, then the roof of the SUV in seconds flat.

"Heel!" The bloody fleabag was having a ball, making so much noise circling the SUV he didn't hear the command. Daniel whistled long and low instead, and Halfback slunk back with a hangdog expression, tail between his legs. He knew damn well he was supposed to have gotten permission before he left.

"You *sit*, and you *stay*," Daniel growled.

Shit, shit, shit!

Kana's heart was ricocheting off her ribs.

Where had the beast come from? More to the point, *where was it now*?

She swivelled, and saw the man striding towards her down the annex drive, the dog in question sitting calmly up at the T-junction with its tongue lolling out.

Sweet Buddha. Of course Rugby had a dog.

Of course he had a bloody rabid, woman-eating dog!

Kana scrambled to get down off the roof before her landlord reached her, catching the back of her shirt on one of the antennas and hearing the cotton rip as she slid to the ground, less gracefully than she would've liked.

"He's supposed to be on a lead!" she squeaked as Rugby got within spitting distance, embarrassed the man had seen her on the roof of her car, and incensed the dog had been allowed to come after her. She took a step to the side and double-checked behind her landlord's hulking frame.

The animal hadn't moved.

"Nooo." Rugby drew out the word, looking at her with cool detachment. "This is *his* property, so he's allowed to run free."

"Run *free*? He's allowed to…" Kana swallowed. "Poppy said she would keep him away."

"Did she now?" Her landlord waited a beat. "Well, Poppy isn't here." His voice held no trace of apology.

"Poppy isn't here," she repeated stupidly, blinking up at him before checking on the dog's whereabouts again.

"She's gone back to Dunedin for the weekend." Rugby flicked his chin back towards the dog. "He won't move."

"I don't believe that," Kana blurted.

Assuming the cool breeze on her left shoulder was an indication she'd torn her shirt, she shimmied backwards towards the barn.

Rugby followed, his brows drawn together. "Halfback wouldn't hurt you."

She laughed a little hysterically at that. "I don't believe *that* either." Slipping inside the barn, Kana tried to muscle the door shut between them. But when her landlord saw her intention, he placed his hoofing great boot in the way.

"One more thing, before you disappear." Rugby's voice was as smooth as stainless steel. "Do you have my morning paper?"

Kana was caught off guard by the unexpected request, easing the door open to him a smidgen more.

They stood—he in the sun, she in the shade—and contemplated each other. Her landlord smelt deliciously of coffee, and Kana noticed for the first time he carried an empty mug.

She licked her lips.

God, but she was tired all of a sudden. She needed some caffeine, or a really long sleep. She rubbed a knuckle into first one eye, then the other. It'd been a long time since she'd pulled an all-nighter in the studio, and her body wasn't used to it.

"The paper?" Rugby prompted, a little less aggressively.

Kana's brain clicked back to the early morning, when she'd heard the local boy go past on his 4-wheeler, and had celebrated his 'perfect timing.'

She felt her cheeks glow warm.

The Saturday newspaper her landlord was after was scrunched and stuffed into two enormous clay busts, now sitting, slow drying, in the barn. Still more of it was covered in slurry and muck on the workbench, and the weekender section had been soaked in water and used to moisten the bases of a couple of pots that'd dried out a touch too much to turn.

"Ah, no?"

Rugby raised one articulate eyebrow and said nothing, which made Kana a little more nervous. It was an unfortunate mix on top of guilty and exhausted, and against her better judgement she began to yabber.

"I'm afraid I can't help you there. Because, um… I don't actually read it. I never… I don't like all the doom and gloom. It's awful, isn't it? How they sensationalise…" she trailed off.

"Right." Her landlord watched her for a moment more, until she was sure her cheeks were flaming, then turned on his heel. "Halfback won't bother you down here again." He threw the words over his shoulder as he strode back towards the dog, and it sounded like a clear dismissal.

Well, good. Anything more to do with that particular man *or* his dog would be a bad idea.

4

HEART AND SOUL

*"Your purpose in life is to find your purpose
and give your whole heart and soul to it."*
- Buddha

Kana woke disoriented. Blinking at the unoccupied pillow on the other side of the queen bed, she wondered vaguely if Ken had already gone to work. She hoped he'd left, so she didn't have to draw up the energy to fight again.

Slowly becoming aware she wasn't at home, this wasn't her bed, and she was nobody's debate partner, Kana let out a shuddering sigh.

Thank Buddha.

The annex, that's where she was—her own boss, on her own path. She rolled onto her back, feeling a little stiff, and realised she was still fully clothed. She rarely slept during the day, it made her so muzzy-headed.

Hadn't there been a dog? She sat up abruptly.

No. The dog had been outside.

Padding downstairs, she glanced at the clock on the microwave. Three p.m.. No wonder she was so out of it.

Making up a large bowl of cereal and yogurt, Samantha's anytime go-to, and a habit Kana had picked up over the last

26

couple of months living with her, she headed back out to the studio.

This time she even remembered to double-check for random canines before setting foot outdoors.

Perhaps due to her thoughts on waking, Kana mulled over her relationship with Ken as she worked through a set of salad bowls, turning their leather-hard bases with a wire tool. A therapeutic activity—peeling off unnecessary clay to mirror the true curve of each interior, and morphing each vessel to purpose.

They were unable to have children, Ken and herself, and maybe that was a good thing considering how everything had turned out. Though the acknowledgement felt anything *but* good on a personal level.

Even as a child, Kana had wanted to be a mother, and as she'd grown older, the vague, indistinct plan had become an all-consuming ache.

It wasn't to be. Not this time around.

Maybe in the next life, if she lived this one well? Obāchan certainly believed so, though Kana herself wasn't entirely convinced.

She'd been given this window of time to lick her wounds and regroup, and it was imperative she knuckle down and deserve this residency. Her studio work last night on the two sculpted pieces was a good start, setting the standard. She'd have to churn out a bunch more of those if she was going to front up with the money she owed Kenneth, though.

A stylised swallow had been Kana's stamp since Tanaka-sensei died. His widow had insisted. Now Yukiko-san was gone too. Kana pressed her potter's mark into the base of each bowl with some sadness, but also a degree of pride. The little migrating bird was an honour to carry as her signature, conducting itself with stamina, adaptability, and grit.

Carefully transferring the bowls onto the green shelf, Kana missed the sound of the approaching vehicle, but the creak of the barn door easing open was unmistakable.

It was Adele and Saffy who squeezed through the entrance, and Kana caught Adele whispering to her daughter, "Don't touch anything, Sweet-pea."

Saffy put her hands under her opposing armpits when she got close to the workbenches, and Kana hid a smile at the gesture. She would've felt the same temptation on visiting a studio like this at Saffy's age.

"Would you like to try?" she asked Saffy after welcoming the pair in, her hands busy wedging a fresh kilogram of Nelson white. "I have a spare apron." She looked across at Adele to get confirmation it was okay to involve the child.

"Yes, please." Saffy grabbed the apron and tried to get it over her head before her mother could say no.

"Only if we're not in your way." Adele looked pointedly at the back of Saffy's head as she tied the apron strings. "And only for half an hour. We need to get to rugby sign-up by four-thirty."

Kana moved over to a clear piece of bench, handing Saffy a smaller block of clay and showing her how to wedge.

"We're working out any little bubbles," she explained as she worked the clay methodically into a ram's-head shape.

Saffy watched carefully, attempting to follow the action.

"If there's a bubble in the clay, the moisture held in there can cause an explosion in the kiln." Kana smiled encouragingly when Saffy's movements faltered at that information. "It's also a good way of working out your frustrations." Thinking of Rugby and his blasted dog, Kana gave her own ram's-head a couple of hard slaps, and caught Adele's amused chuckle.

Kana taught Saffy how to make two pinch pots and join them together with cross-hatching and slip, sealing them closed.

"Now you have a…" she left the sentence hanging.

"Ball!" Saffy enthused.

"Yes, or a…?"

"Bubble?" Adele guessed.

"Exactly. A big bubble." Kana smiled. "So what would happen if I fired this in the kiln, just as it is?"

Saffy's eyes widened. "It'd explode?"

"Probably," Kana agreed. "Taking a few things on the shelf with it, no doubt. But I'll show you what to do to combat that."

They shaped the first ball into an apple, then fashioned a deliberate hole in the base to allow the air to circulate. Saffy began shaping her second, larger 'bubble,' into a round-bottomed pear.

"Some mail arrived for you, actually." Kana spoke in an undertone to Adele as she washed up in the corner tub.

"Oh, did it? Thank you." Adele took the envelopes Kana pointed towards, wedged behind the studio phone, and rifled through them. "It's been over two years since we moved out, but the odd bit of mail still slips through."

"You lived in the annex?"

"We did. For just under a year until we found our own place in town. Daniel's generous, but we couldn't bum off the poor guy forever." Adele smiled, looking around the studio with a definite softening in her eyes.

Mm-*hmm*. Clearly stronger feelings than pure cousin-love going on.

"So, your ah... your cousin owns all of this?" Kana glanced around the studio too, the sight of the expensive kilns intensifying her discomfort.

"Yes, though Poppy actually runs the ceramic programme, D's the main patron. We shared Nona as a grandmother."

"That's *very* generous of him," Kana muttered, feeling a ton worse. The word 'patron' came across as a bit confronting when assigned to Mr Rugby. "Mr um... Mr Dante mentioned when we... when we met yesterday..." She stumbled over the words, because it was strange to use his actual name, and they hadn't met yesterday.

They'd met two weeks ago down at the lake, under totally different circumstances, as totally different people.

Kana swallowed, suddenly remembering her first impression—honest hazel eyes, and careful manners.

"I believe I owe him some rent? I couldn't find the amount due in the information Poppy sent me. I was wondering if you knew how much, since you lived here?" She wasn't about to tell Adele about her botched attempt at impersonating a Japanese tourist, or the fact she'd completely misinterpreted the deal when she'd been offered this position, thinking the annex came free with the studio.

She was ninety-nine percent sure her studio usage was free...

Oh, shit. What if it wasn't?

Though Kana was no longer living in her shared Christchurch house, she was still expected to cover half the mortgage payments until it sold. She wasn't sure if she could scrape together a hell of a lot more after that.

Adele laughed. "Oh, no! He would've been joking. It's fully covered by the trust."

"Joking," Kana repeated in disbelief. "Your cousin? Mr Dante?"

"Yes, Daniel." Adele brushed aside Kana's incredulity, pinning her with a strange expression. "He's a very funny and affectionate man, once you get to know him."

Possible. Though not exactly plausible.

It *was* true when Kana had first met him, he'd appeared a thousand degrees warmer.

She shrugged noncommittally, vowing to never venture close enough to answer that one definitively, one way or the other.

"D's been like a father to Saffy. Knowing what it's like not to have one around, he's made it his business to make sure Saffron never wants for anything. You've got the coolest Uncle in the world to take on school camps and invite to your rugby games, haven't you, Saff?"

"What?" Saffron looked up from carefully skewering an air hole —which she'd re-named an 'anti-explode hole'—into the base of a robust pear.

"You love your Uncle D," Adele reiterated.

"Yes. He's lovely," Saffy agreed with cheerful childishness.

Lovely?

Lovely to *look at*, maybe. All rough, and unapologetically masculine.

Adele held both hands out, palms up as if that proved her point, then frowned as Kana struggled out of her double apron.

"What happened to your shirt?"

"My shirt?"

"Turn around. You've scraped your back on something." Adele grabbed Kana's shoulders and repositioned her. "Ouch. That looks sore. Does it hurt?"

It really hadn't, until Adele ran a finger over the welt.

"We should get some antiseptic on that, the skin's broken. How did you do that?"

"Oh." Kana had almost allowed herself to forget the whole up-on-the-car scene. "Just clumsy, I guess." She grimaced at the half-truth.

Before Adele left, having played nurse, she invited Kana to join their family pizza night on Friday evening, up at the farmhouse. Poppy would be back from Dunedin, and Kana could meet Clem, the sheep farmer from the neighbouring property. The way Saffy bounced up and down at the prospect, Kana didn't feel she had any real option to say no.

Hopefully, Adele's 'funny and affectionate' cousin would be away on business again.

When the mother and daughter pair left, Kana went back to working on the two small orbs she'd made as examples for Saffy. She spent some time reshaping and adding to them, morphing them into the two swallows she'd envisaged sitting on the busts' shoulders, beaks reaching out towards each other. They were too wet to attach yet, but she carefully removed the plastic off the leather-hard busts to check the size, angle, and fit.

Touching her fingers to the familiar features of the taller likeness, she whispered the name, "Tanaka-sensei."

Moving half a step sideways to repeat the action, she stroked the more feminine jawline of the second face, too.

"Yukiko-san." Kana's voice broke on the name, and she didn't attempt to speak again, re-wrapping the busts carefully in their plastic.

"This one's good. Actually, it's perfect. I'll take ten of these." Kana tested the weight of the brush again, swinging it by the long handle. It was a good shape, and wouldn't leave any sediment at the bottom of the glaze bucket.

"Ten!" The hardware store staff member eyed her suspiciously. "How many toilets do you *have*?"

"Oh, just the one." Kana paused, maintaining a straight face with some difficulty. "But it's *very* dirty."

She purchased ten 'perfect' toilet brushes, and ten huge buckets with lids from the bemused sales assistant. While she was in town with a vehicle, she also stocked up on non-perishables. She usually walked in along the lakefront, but had been reluctant to carry too many cans in her backpack. They seemed to somehow double their weight on the trek home.

Craving sushi, though it was barely eleven, Kana bowled into the local store, and straight into her landlord's solid chest.

He was on his way out, and smelt *amazing*. Almost edible. Nutmeg? Beeswax? Something warm and biscuity, with honey on it.

"Oh, sorry!" Kana anchored her hand on his arm to steady herself, then dropped it like a fresh-baked potato.

He was all muscle and hot skin.

Rugby hesitated, staring down at her. "No problem," he murmured. Then, seeming to come to his senses, he stepped around her and out the door.

"Like shit on his shoe," Kana muttered to herself as she went over to peruse the pick-and-mix cabinet, fingers still burning from the unexpected brush of skin on skin.

"Pardon?" the woman at the counter said.

"Oh, nothing. Just talking to myself." It was becoming a bit of a habit.

Kana chose two each of salmon *nigiri*, fresh tuna, and egg roll.

"Exactly the same as Dante D!" The woman beamed at her. "With extra wasabi?"

"No. You can keep your extra wasabi," Kana returned somewhat waspishly. Then, humbled by the woman's surprised start, she checked herself. "I mean, no. No, thank you. That's plenty. Does Mr… ah, D come here a lot, then?"

"Yes, he does." The shop owner's smile appeared a little less friendly. "Are you a fan?"

"Not even close," Kana muttered under her breath as she shook her head, managing to keep both her words and saltiness to herself this time.

Paying her total in coins from her change purse, she pledged to check for any sign of Rugby's car, his farm ute, or his person before careening in here next time.

Kana told Adele the 'how many toilets do you have' gag when the young mother popped in for a cup of tea the following afternoon, making her laugh. Adele had arrived at the same time as the overnight courier with all of Kana's new glaze ingredients, and it was all she could do not to rip the package open, right then and there on the kitchen table.

Due diligence.

Tanaka-sensei had taught her better.

She'd be wearing industrial grade gloves and a top of the range mask, and be nowhere near food preparation when she went through this order, as some of the oxides could be really toxic.

Kana didn't mention running into Rugby, because Adele seemed to be under the impression the sun shone out of her cousin's butt. Respecting the fact there might be a bit more than kinship going on, Kana minded her Ps and Qs... and Ds.

Adele talked a lot about Saffy, but never once mentioned her daughter's father, so that gave Kana another excellent topic to avoid. They *did* talk about money though, or more to the point, laughed about their collective inability to earn any decent amounts of it.

Kana had spent a lot of cash on clay and glaze ingredients recently, and would have to watch it for the next fortnight—at least until the Dunedin gallery paid for their latest consignment. It'd be fine, as long as Adele was right, and Kana wasn't supposed to be contributing to the annex costs. When Poppy arrived back, Kana would double-check the large electrical bill from the kilns was covered, too.

"I'd love to own a little place like this one day, run it as a B and B and work from home." Adele gazed out the kitchen window, daydreaming. "Maybe even write a book."

"What kind of book?" Kana leaned forward, intrigued.

Adele wrinkled up her nose. "A collection of short stories. Love stories." She cleared her throat and readjusted her ponytail, discounting the idea firmly by adding, "It's just a pipe dream."

"Aren't they the best ones?" Kana smiled.

"No one wants to read romances by someone who doesn't have any in their life."

Huh. Did that signify a *no-go* on the cousin-love?

"*I* want to read it," Kana insisted, meaning it. But Adele merely laughed.

It was nice having someone to talk to. Kana had begun to think of herself as a bit of a loner while living in Wānaka. She'd always been somewhat of an introvert, recharging her batteries when she was on her own, but given too much non-social time she'd go completely nuts.

She missed Samantha, and the cosy shed she'd leased off her neighbour as her ceramics studio. She missed the pottery club she'd belonged to in Christchurch—the monthly raku firings, if not group politics. And she was also missing going out at night and hanging with the other Japanese tutors from her night courses.

Kenneth had never approved—not of the Japanese tutoring (*the hours suck*) not of the pottery (*there's no money in it*) and not of Samantha (*the man-hater*). Ken hadn't approved of anything Kana was, really. Except being Japanese.

He'd been strangely excited about her Japanese-ness, one of the only things about herself Kana had absolutely no power over. In retrospect, she'd probably failed to deliver on his early expectations, being staunchly Kiwi in her views on sharing household chores.

When she looked at their relationship from this distance, she could see all too clearly how the demise of her self-esteem had coincided with the rise of her husband's. After a few years of hard slog and ass-kissing, Ken had moved up to sectional manager, then partner in his Civil Engineering Firm. All with a wife at home, amusing herself with 'the messy arts' until they started a family. A wife who was unable to conceive, as it turned out, proving Kenneth's unspoken but implied belief Kana was somehow unfit for purpose.

That hadn't been in the unwritten contract. *Not* the product he'd been promised.

Kana held back a snort. How had she not seen how unsuitable Ken was for *her*, until they were so far down the track it wasn't funny?

It hadn't always been bad; they'd made a decent team in the beginning. Left side—right side. Opposites attract. But that was before Ken had made manager, and began relishing the role of

34

Omnipotent-Boss-Over-Everything with a touch too much enthusiasm.

When Adele broke back into Kana's thoughts, asking if she'd like to join in on a quiz night the following month, she jumped at the chance to support 'little-rippa-rugby,' whatever that was.

Kana thought it prudent to keep to herself the fact the fundraiser fell directly on her birthday.

It would put her twenty-five dollars out of pocket, but it'd be worth it to go out and enjoy herself, taking her mind off the slightly freaky milestone.

5

ARRIVE

"It is better to travel well than to arrive."
- Buddha

Daniel knew Poppy would be back in Wānaka by early afternoon. That meant he had approximately—he checked his watch—four more hours to get a full plan in place for the trees in the orchard. He'd fobbed his mother off twice already, and knew he'd be pushing his luck if he tried for a hat-trick.

She wanted it done, he grumbled for a bit, then did it. That's how it usually worked with Poppy and himself, though she wasn't an unreasonable woman, and over the years it had become a roundabout kind of game. Especially after his father died.

Daniel's thoughts were on other things when he strolled up the hill with Halfback keeping him company, but as soon as he'd spotted the female form under the arbour, his focus was nowhere else.

"Heel," he murmured quietly to the dog as he stared at Kanako in a full balance pose.

She'd brought some kind of matting up to the flat area and stood on one leg, with the other folded like a crane; foot tucked high on her opposing thigh. As he watched, the pose moved fluidly. Her feet met, and the hands pressed together at her chest winged out either side. She leaned forward from the hips, arcing further down to fold herself neatly in two, both arms coming around to hug her knees.

The potter moved like a dancer, all graceful lines and flexing curves, and just like the other day at the annex, her close fitting workout gear hid nothing of her shape. She was athletic, with swimmers shoulders and toned legs.

Daniel swallowed, knowing he should announce himself, but unwilling to break the spell or interfere with the view. Moisture was evaporating off the long grass, suffusing the scene with a dream-like haze.

The pose moved again. This time Kanako spread her legs in a wide scissor-stance—one hand stretched in front, the other behind—as if she was preparing to throw a javelin. Then she eased slowly into a back curve, one hand sliding down the back of her thigh and the other reaching for the sun.

As Daniel moved closer, he could see Kanako's eyes were closed. Her face rested in peace, a slight smile playing on her lips.

Christ. His mother's latest ceramicist was sexy as all hell.

He cleared his throat. "Ah, what are you doing?"

Kanako's eyes fluttered open, her startled gaze moving swiftly from him to the dog.

"Oh, I'm sorry. Poppy said it was okay to practice here, but if you'd rather I didn't, that's fine." Kanako stepped off the mats and began to roll them together, all the while eyeing Halfback, who sat obediently at Daniel's heels.

Was it fear of the dog, or fear of *him* rendering her unable to meet his eyes?

Moving over to one of the arbour posts, Kanako took a long necklace off a gnarled spur, and slipped it back over her head. Daniel caught a glimpse of a gold locket before she tucked it into her fitted T-shirt.

Kanako seemed much calmer than the last time she'd met Halfback; much more in control, maintaining a cool, even tone though both dog and man were fairly close.

"I don't mean what are you doing here. It's fine for you to go wherever you like on the property. I meant, what is that you're doing? Aikido?" Daniel slid his hand down to pet the dog's neck, letting Halfback know he was being good—staying close. Reminding him not to move a muscle.

"No. Yoga."

"Stretching?"

"In a manner, yes." Kanako tucked the rolled mats under her arm, jammed her sneakers on, and made to move off.

"It wasn't my intention to interrupt." The words came out stiff and wooden, and Daniel shifted his weight off his bad knee in discomfort, not particularly wanting to come off as a pompous ass again. "You can carry on. I'm just meeting the arborist up here."

"No, that's fine. I'm done, now." Kanako smiled tightly, glancing at him only once more before she took off down the narrow sheep-path to the left.

Daniel kicked himself for having butted in on her practice. He knew it took some time to get into the headspace, no matter what the sport, and Kanako had obviously been in the zone when he'd interrupted.

He took a small treat out of his pocket and slipped it to his ecstatic border collie.

"Good boy. Stay away from her."

When Daniel answered the door that evening, he should've known to put a shirt on. None of his family members had manners enough to stand back on the verandah, let alone knock in the first place. They usually bowled in, announced their arrival at high decibels, and took over the place. But he'd been expecting Adele, and had just stepped out of the shower and yanked on his jeans, so hadn't exactly had time to contemplate the pros and cons of his actions.

The potter wore black pants, and a silky long-sleeved top that clung to her as she jerked back, no doubt confronted by his half-dressed state. She checked behind him in a move he was coming to recognise, eyes seeking the whereabouts of Halfback.

"How can I help you, Kanako?"

"Oh!" She blinked back at him. "I'm a bit early, sorry. It's a habit of mine." She offered a foil-covered dish forward. "I can go for a walk to buy some time, but I'll hand this over now, if you don't mind?"

"What is it?"

"*Okonomiyaki.*"

"You're kidding." Daniel peeked under the makeshift lid, and the mouth-watering scent of vegetable pancake wafted. "Why are you bringing me food?" She'd used his favourite Bulldog sauce, with Kewpie mayo and fish flakes.

How had she known? Must've done her homework. Maybe he'd listed it as one of his weaknesses in an interview at some stage.

Daniel resisted the temptation to dip a finger into the topping and suck the goodness off.

Just.

Women had tried the food angle with him before, but this didn't feel the same. Something about Kanako's demeanour pointed towards a very different mission.

Her nervousness was all wrong for seduction, and there was nothing at all coy or sexualised in the way she presented herself.

Daniel frowned.

Kanako looked elegant and somewhat aloof, and with her lips pursed together, was clearly avoiding looking anywhere below his chin. Not even a sneak-peak.

"Adele said not to bring anything, but I figured *okonomiyaki* is the Japanese equivalent of pizza. Plus, it's easy."

So, this visit wasn't anything to do with him?

Daniel's ego took another minor hit, sharp enough for him to growl, "Adele invited you to pizza night?"

The question should've never been aired aloud, and he watched like an idiot as a blush fired up his guest's face.

Kanako cleared her throat and reset her shoulders. "Yes, I'm afraid she did." She stepped back off the verandah. "But I'm happy to go for a walk and come back when the others are here."

She didn't look 'happy' about any of it.

"Kanako, you don't have to… I mean, ah, would you like to come in?"

Once, and once only, Kanako's gaze flicked to his bare chest before returning to his face.

"No, thank you," she answered haughtily, then strode off without looking back.

"Shit," Daniel muttered, watching Kanako retreat and knowing his mother and cousin wouldn't be pleased.

It wasn't entirely his fault, though. Someone should've bloody informed him they'd decided to invite the annex tenant to their weekly family night.

He inched back the foil to take another deep sniff, and smiled.

If the smell of Kanako's *okonomiyaki* was anything to go by, it hadn't been such a rotten idea.

It took some time for the embarrassment to fade from Kana's face. The cool air helped, as she took the road to the orchard and carried on uphill towards the boundary. The trees up here were natives, with a completely different atmosphere from the European ones on the lower slopes. Denser and loamier, their evergreen foliage created shade for the ferns to hide in. The faint scent of beech honeydew and sweet mānuka soothed her senses.

Turning to breathe in the view of the lake, she eventually calmed. Daniel Dante was a big man, with an undeniably gorgeous body, a massive ego, and a habit of making her feel smaller than her significant five-foot-nine inches.

Buggered if she'd let anyone take her down a notch, though. She wouldn't accept any more of that in this lifetime.

No. Thank. You.

It'd been a bit of a shock to the system to have her landlord open the door in just jeans, water droplets still glistening on his skin and darkening his hair. He was no side-line coach, clearly. The muscular definition of his torso attested to regular use. There was no point getting all steamed up over how the guy looked, though. How he *acted* was much more important. A man's body was just that—skin, bones, and muscle—even if this particular prototype was worthy of a few lustful thoughts.

Kana began downhill after a reasonable lapse of time, watching her footing in her slippery-soled sandals. She hadn't come out with the intention of walking a dirt trail.

Out of the bush, she could see one battered truck and another car had arrived at the farmhouse while she was away. Now officially late, which normally wouldn't sit well, she was more than happy to be tardy in this particular instance.

Seeing there was a shortcut through to the back of the house, Kana took it, manoeuvring around the farm's outbuildings and sheds along a well-worn path. She came up short when she realised the long, partially covered run was for the dog.

It lay with its muzzle on its paws—big, sad eyes watching her silently as she moved past.

Kana paused. "Are you in there because of me?"

The dog's tail thumped and it raised its head expectantly at the sound of her voice.

"It's Halfback, isn't it? Poor thing. Who named you that? Rugby? I guess you'd prefer I wasn't living down at the annex, along with your owner."

The dog cocked its head to the side and perked one ear up, making it look quite comical.

Kana laughed, and the tail started to thump again.

"Don't get any ideas. We're *not* friends."

Kana lifted her chin and walked around to the front of the house to the sound of the dog's heartfelt whine.

"Well, bless my soul. What a pretty one!" The older gentleman who answered the farmhouse door gave Kana such an unexpected reception, she just stood on the verandah and blinked at him. "Dan never said… Of course he *wouldn't* though, would he? Jammy bugger. And now I've clean forgotten my manners."

Poppy obviously thought so too. "Don't just stand there, move out of the doorway and let the girl in, you great Clydesdale." She shunted the wiry man firmly sideways with her hip.

For a small woman, she wielded a lot of clout.

"My apologies." The man seemed to take the dressing down totally in his stride, and extended his hand. "Clementine Jamison from the neighbouring farm. I was momentarily bewitched."

"Old flirt," Poppy muttered under her breath.

41

"Kanako Janssen, potter in residence. It's a pleasure to meet you, Clementine." Kana shook his hand formally, before being whipped away and enfolded in a quick hug by Poppy.

"Come in, come in," Poppy hustled, practically hauling Kana down the hall. "We're in the kitchen, picking pizza toppings."

"Slow down Poppy, my love." Clementine grinned and winked conspiratorially at Kana, seeming all too aware his words would rile.

"Don't 'my love' me, you old dog."

"Now I'm a dog, am I? I thought I was a Clydesdale. Pick an animal and stick with it Petal, or you'll give me indigestion."

"Give it a rest, Clem," Poppy huffed, but there was a smile in her voice, and the two appeared close.

Adele, Saffy, and Daniel Dante were all sitting at the large kitchen table, in what looked like a scene from a cheese advertisement. Homemade pizza bases were being stretched out and sauced, while toppings were sliced, diced, and grated.

"Sorry I'm late." Kana deliberately avoided meeting Rugby's eyes, instead aiming the apology at Adele, who laughed.

"No worries. We don't keep time around here, and you're not the last to arrive. How do you feel about taking over cheese grating duty?" Adele waved a block of Edam in her direction.

Kana washed her hands in the large butler's sink, then picked up where Adele had left off with the grater.

When the final pair arrived, Kana could see well before introductions were made that the younger man was her landlord's brother, albeit with a smaller frame and lighter colouring. His atmosphere was also less weighty. There didn't seem to be any of the rugby player's brooding intensity in the musician.

Cameron Dante smiled a lot, and slid easily into the eclectic group, teasing his mother about the state of her boyfriend's 'old dunger of a truck' and grabbing his giggling little cousin-once-removed for a spin around the kitchen.

Kana warmed to him immediately.

Cam's partner, Shal, was a bit more intimidating. Mostly due to the fact she was unnervingly beautiful, with the most unusual blue-green eyes Kana had ever seen. If she took Candice Black and overlaid it with Celadon, or perhaps a wash of Crater Lake in a slightly lower firing, she *might* be able to come up with something close as a glaze. All that depth of colour was like looking into cool, deep water.

Kana had a sudden, desperate need to get back into the quiet calm of the studio and try her theory out, somewhere far away from this tight-knit family group.

Poppy obviously held real affection for Shal. After squeezing the woman half to death, she was listening attentively to the description of their trip inland. The couple lived and worked on the east coast, and had driven across to the lake for a weekend away.

"We would've been here earlier, but Shal was constantly stopping to take pictures," Cam teased his partner, who rolled her eyes.

"Right. It had nothing to do with the half-hour conversation you struck up with a complete stranger in Lawrence about roofing options," Shal countered.

"Of course not!" Cam grinned, turning to his brother. "New owner in the old Post Office. They're doing the place up as a café."

Clementine walked back into the kitchen through the back door, holding a huge salmon by the tail. Going by the proud grin on the older man's face, Kana assumed he'd caught it himself.

"Fresh off the boat," he announced.

"Clementine! Get that fish out of here this instant," Poppy admonished, hastily handing him a plastic chopping board and filleting knife. "Outside sink," she ordered, every inch the matriarch, shoving the man in the small of the back until he was out the door.

Clementine's chuckle followed her back in.

"Oh, what I wouldn't do for some *sashimi* sauce," Kana lamented as she watched the fish disappear, not realising she'd said the words aloud until all eyes turned to her. She raised her chin a little. "Seems a shame to cook such fresh fish," she muttered.

"You won't think it's a shame once you've had it on pizza, with cream cheese and capers," her landlord returned sardonically, and heat crept up Kana's cheeks.

What was it with this man, and his mission to make her feel small?

Ignoring Rugby, she turned her focus to helping Saffy slice

tomatoes without taking a finger off. The little girl was fairly gung-ho with a knife.

Kana felt his looming presence move away, and was relieved.

"My Obāchan taught me to make a bridge with my fingers, see?" She spoke quietly, making an arch with her thumb and forefinger to hold the fruit steady. "Then the boat rocks under the bridge until it settles at the bottom of the river." She took the little knife and used a slight sawing motion until the blade reached the board. "And when the tomato falls on its face." Saffy giggled, the sound so infectious Kana followed suit. "We start again."

"What's an Old-Bear-Charm?" Saffy took the offered knife and tried the bridge herself.

Kana laughed. "O-*bā*-chan is my Nana."

"Why don't you call her Nana, then?"

"Because she's Japanese—don't cut without looking at the knife!" Kana squeaked as Saffy turned to size her up, still wielding the sharp implement.

"Are *you* Japanese?"

"Half."

"Really? I'm half, too. Half black." Saffy didn't look entirely pleased about it.

Kana could see a fissure of discontent in the young girl, and experienced a flicker of recognition from way, way back. In her own childhood, discontent had built into discord, then disconnect.

She scrambled around for the right reply, a little panicked.

"We're all made of two halves, aren't we?" Kana finally returned, keeping her tone mild. "Because it takes two people to make a new person. Sometimes the two halves are from the same place, and sometimes they're from far apart." She paused. "We're lucky, you and me, because we have such a wide history from our far away ancestors. If we take care to remember that, we won't ever allow ourselves to become narrow minded, like some people. That's very good 'boat rocking' you're doing there."

"When do we get to paint the fruit?"

Saffy changed the subject just as easily as she'd brought it up, indicating she was done with it, and Kana breathed a sigh of relief. It wasn't her jurisdiction to be talking parentage with this eight year old.

"We don't paint them, we glaze them. They have to be bisque fired first. It's a waiting game."

Saffy sighed.

"Next Tuesday, before your rugby training," Kana decided. "I'll talk to your mum." She got a beaming smile from the little girl, whose teeth flashed white against the smooth brown of her skin.

When the pizzas were all made up, and the first one was in the outside brick oven, Clementine took charge of the turning. The rest of the family, and Kana, sat close-by in the back courtyard with drinks. Daniel and Shal were conspicuously absent, but Kana didn't think anything of it until Shal came out of the kitchen carrying a large platter, and a handful of side plates.

A fillet of bright Salmon had been deboned and sliced very thinly, then arranged in petals around a central bowl of *sashimi* sauce.

"You made *sashimi*." Kana jumped up, delighted.

"No." Shal laughed. "I'm just the courier. But I pax the chair next to you, because I love it too." She settled the side plates and platter on the table in front of Kana, then returned to the kitchen for chopsticks and the reheated *okonomiyaki*, now cut up in small squares.

"Mmm. Japanese starters. What a great idea!" Poppy grinned at her eldest son as he came out of the kitchen with a beer. "When did you make this, D? Kansai or Hiroshima style?" Kana was surprised to hear Poppy referring to the two regions famous for the thick pancake as she helped herself to a piece, wielding her chopsticks with practiced ease. "Clem, come and try this!"

"No. Kanako made the *okonomiyaki*, and I'm assuming it's Hiroshima style?" Rugby turned to her, pinning her with those hazel eyes.

"Daniel's favourite," Poppy slid in quietly, making Kana start.

Was it really, or was his mother just saying that to be polite?

Did the partiality explain Rugby's heated look? He was staring at Kana as if he was contemplating taking a bite…

"Ah, no. Actually, it's Kansai," she murmured, having trouble peeling herself away from that hot gaze. "I thought it might be the more familiar of the two, because of your time there, and I don't have a hotplate down at the annex."

"Do you need a hotplate? I can get you a hotplate." Clementine jumped in, trying to angle his chopsticks for a second piece. Using the two utensils together like a shovel, he wasn't able to get a good grip and the chunk of food dropped back onto his plate, untouched.

Poppy picked up the portion with her own chopsticks, deftly popping it into her boyfriend's waiting mouth.

They were very sweet together, these two.

"Oh, no. I..." Kana spluttered. She hadn't meant to imply the annex was lacking in any way. She had everything she needed.

"You could have this one!" Cam hassled his brother by pointing towards the large barbecue, holding pride of place in the courtyard. It looked like an extremely expensive, stainless-steel model.

"Over my dead body," Daniel muttered darkly.

"Chill, Datsun. He's just trying to rile you." Adele intervened smoothly between the two brothers. "Are you looking for another concussion, Camry?"

Kana looked from one Dante brother to the other. Datsun and Camry? What was it with this family and their car names? There was definitely tension skidding around between the two unlikely vehicles that hadn't been there a moment before.

"*Sashimi*, anyone?" Adele continued on. "It really is a delicious fish, Clem. You'll make some lucky woman a very happy fish-wife one of these days." She slid her aunt a sly look that wasn't lost on the rest of the group.

"Get away with you!" Poppy blustered, as her family laughed at her expense. "I've no need for a man. Especially one who forgets to turn the pizzas."

Clementine let out an expletive and bounded towards the pizza oven, where the distinct smell of burning crust was wafting.

6

FORGIVE

"To understand everything
is to forgive everything."
- Buddha

Poppy cornered Daniel in the kitchen after dinner with the backstory she was helping him with the dishes, but it didn't take him long to figure out what was really bothering her.

"I want to ask you why you're acting like such an ass, but in a more subtle and motherly way, of course." Poppy waved her hand around airily, indicating the entirety of his person.

"Sorry, you'll have to be a bit more specific." Daniel swung the dishwasher door open and began loading plates. Every second one he put in, Poppy removed to rinse off again, then handed it back to be reloaded. "They're clean enough," he growled.

"Not by my standards. Baked on cheese is the worst," his mother countered. "The woman's lovely, D. Everyone thinks so. But other than playing host, you're treating her like some kind of disease to be avoided. I expected better manners from you."

So, he'd been cooler than he normally would've behaved towards one of his mother's artists.

Out of character, perhaps.

Not exactly affable.

"You should've told me I was expected to be on my best behaviour, I thought I was going to be hanging at home with family tonight."

Daniel had a love-hate relationship with his public persona, exercising excruciating manners when approached by all and sundry, any time of the day or night. It came hand in hand with being so well known. Public property. It was even more crucial he went along with it, playing his role to perfection, since he'd fallen so far from grace in the past.

Poppy had never shown anything less than full support for him, even when the shit had truly hit the fan. People liked to bolster up young sports players as if they were invincible heroes and heroines, but turned quickly on those who proved themselves less than worthy.

He'd found that out the hard way.

"Don't be ridiculous," his mother scoffed. "I'm not asking for the full Dante D treatment, but you could at least show an interest."

An *interest*? He'd found it damn near impossible not to trip over his 'interest' in Kanako this evening, and had been tempering himself since she'd knocked on his door with her bloody addictive *okonomiyaki*.

No. Earlier than that.

She'd held his intrigue since day one, when she'd straight-up lied to him, and every interaction *since* then, if he was being honest. Lycra wearing, sun dancing, car climbing, yoga practicing... It didn't matter if she was stalking away in a huff, or slammed up close and personal for a couple of seconds in a sushi shop.

The woman was untrustworthy, not to mention off limits, and he had no business wanting to get closer to her. But when she'd come back from her 'walk' this evening, she'd been wearing a sprinkling of tiny mānuka flowers in her hair, and Daniel was still trying to decide if the dainty white accessories were intentional, or purely accidental. Not having a clear answer was driving him nuts, summarising his overall inability to figure her out.

He usually trusted his own judgment, but when it came to Kanako Janssen he was all up in the air.

"Do you have a problem with my choice of potters this time around?" Poppy slid the question in deceptively lightly as she dried

48

chopping boards, knowing where everything lived and putting it away as she went.

The answer wasn't a straightforward one.

"No. You choose whoever you like, Mum," he answered in an even tone, not looking to publicise how confused his thoughts were becoming regarding Kanako.

"Yes, I do," Poppy agreed, putting a hand on his arm to gain his full attention before locking eyes with him. "But this is the first time in two years you seem to be uncomfortable with it." His mother's irises were the same hazel-green as his own, and right now they were calculating the hell out of him.

Hole in one. Uncomfortable in every way.

"I'm sure she's a skilled ceramicist." Daniel raised one eyebrow, and Poppy laughed.

"Yes. She certainly is. She also happens to be stunningly attractive, Datsun." By calling him by his old car model, Poppy was not-so-subtly alluding to a girl he'd dated, way back in high school.

The girl he'd fought Cam over.

His mother's subtext was clear. Don't do anything stupid, take your foot off the accelerator, and stop thinking with your nether regions.

Daniel hesitated, then puffed out an agitated breath. "Okay, I'll grant you that one," he murmured.

Did he even want to know where his mother was going with this?

Poppy reached out to run a finger over his brow. "You remind me of your father when you do that," she mused softly. "All scowley." Clearing her throat, she moved the same finger down to his sternum, and tapped there. "I'm asking you, Daniel. Straight up. Did you make a comment to Kana about paying rent? Because when she came to me this evening and offered to help pay her way, even though I happen to know she can't afford to, I got the distinct impression she thought it was expected."

That got his attention, hitting him square in the solar plexus.

Guilty conscience? Definitely.

"Seriously?" he blustered. "I said that in jest, after she'd pissed me off."

"Well…" Poppy wiped her hands on her apron before removing

49

it, every semblance of her smile and sunny demeanour now glaringly absent. "I don't know *what* that lovely woman could've done to *piss you off*, as you so succinctly put it, but she is *my* guest at the annex by invitation. So, if you have a problem with it? Talk to *me*."

"Come on Mum, don't get all snooty about it. I don't trust your little art project, all right?" Daniel raised both hands in a back-off gesture. "She's a liar."

Poppy, out of everyone, knew what honesty meant to him. What dishonesty had cost him. It just wasn't worth the potential pitfalls.

"I may be getting long in the tooth, Daniel, but I'm not deaf or blind. I can assure you she's the genuine article or I never would've invited her here, and I won't have you making her feel unwelcome."

"Then you shouldn't have invited her into my *home,* on a *family* night, without asking me *first*."

"I *didn't*, you great buffoon! Adele did. Your cousin has precious few like-minded friends here in Wānaka, and she and Kana get along. If you'd bothered to open your eyes, you would've seen that!"

Kana stood frozen, one hand on the kitchen door and the other holding the empty water jug she'd come to refill. She hadn't meant to eavesdrop, but had heard her name mentioned, then raised voices, and one thing led to another.

What was she supposed to do now?

She looked down at the offending jug as she backed away. There was a bathroom down the end of the hall, she remembered with relief, hightailing it there.

Kana schooled her features back to calm in the mirror as she filled the jug with cold water from the sink. It wasn't like she'd overheard anything she didn't know already. Her landlord didn't trust her, and wished she wasn't here.

All she had to do was get back in the lounge and pretend to be collected, and unaffected. No problem at all, apart from the fact she appeared to be sporting random bits of tree in her hair.

Groaning, Kana hastened to remove the offending flower heads, which must've been hitching a ride since her unplanned stroll in the native bush. All evening to be precise, which was just typical.

Her hand shook a little as she plucked at the debris.

Somehow it'd felt different to hear the words spoken aloud, and Rugby's condescending tone had reminded her of her ex-husband, nudging her nose further out of joint. He'd referred to her as his mother's little art project, as if her work meant nothing.

Blood, sweat, and tears, all brushed aside in one snide comment.

It was clear Poppy didn't agree with him though, or Kana wouldn't have been invited to fill this position in the first place. The only thing she could do about it was try and smooth things out between mother and son, then keep out of Rugby's hair for the remainder of her stay.

Achievable, surely?

Kana was relieved neither Poppy, nor her eldest son, had returned when she cracked open the door to the lounge. No one even looked up, they were so caught up in Saffy and Cam's rowdy game of Connect-4.

Refilling Shal's and her own empty water glasses, Kana placed the jug back on the antique table, double-checking the moisture wasn't leaking through the cane tray. The last thing she needed was to be caught damaging the man's property.

"Thank you, Kana." Shal turned to her. "Saffy tells me you have a Japanese Nana?"

"I do, Yes. My mother's mother. Obāchan still lives in…" Kana faltered as both Rugby and Poppy entered the room. "Ah, she lives in Hiroshima."

"Do you speak Japanese, then?" Ignoring the atomic bomb references the city's name usually elicited, Shal went with a more personal question.

"I do, Yes. Not very often though. Not anymore. I used to teach, but…" Kana broke off to chew on her lip, very aware of her landlord's eyes on her.

"Uncle D speaks Japanese!" Saffy piped up.

"Uncle D has *super powers*," Cam muttered with unadulterated sarcasm.

Kana's lips twitched.

Aware of the child's urgency for a response, she looked down at

Saffy's expectant face. "That's clever. It's a very difficult one to learn, apparently. I cheated because my mother spoke it at home."

"You grew up here, though." Shal stated, rather than questioned, but Kana answered anyway. Better to get this fiasco over and done with.

She took a deep breath and ran with it.

"Yes, I was born and bred in Christchurch. But like a lot of first generation New Zealanders, I'm sometimes mistaken for a tourist, or a foreign student, which is jarring. I used to play along and pretend I couldn't speak English." Kana paused, embarrassed to realise everyone in the room was now listening in. "It was childish, but usually had the desired effect." She turned to catch Rugby still staring at her. "Unless someone called your bluff," she continued doggedly, her tone as apologetic as she could make it, without actually issuing the words. "It could come across as a nasty trick, if you got caught doing it."

Clementine looked across at Kana from his position on the sofa, and gave her a broad wink. "Fluent in two languages, eh? Beautiful, talented, *and* smart."

"Oh, Clem. You're such a big flirt," Adele admonished, laughing.

"That's what *I* keep telling him," Poppy agreed.

"Oh, *shi*—sugar!" Shal clutched her chest and jumped up, snatching a handful of paper napkins before leaving the room in a hurry.

Kana watched Shal leave, then turned to Adele, concerned.

Adele laughed. "She's fine. Just forgot to express, I'd wager."

"Express?" Kana blinked. Express *what*?

"Milk," Poppy explained. "Shal's breastfeeding, but they're trying to wean Levi off. Hence the weekend away without him. He's one now." She turned to Cam. "How's the bottle feeding going?"

"He's taking it from me, sweet as. Even from Katie, or Rue. But as soon as he sees Shal, he screams bloody murder until he gets the breast." Cam grinned a little wickedly. "Can't say I blame him…"

Poppy doffed her youngest lightly across the head, making him chuckle.

Kana had been totally unaware the couple had a child.

Poppy nudged Cam, pointing to the mantelpiece.

He walked over and brought her back the framed photo she was after, then she slid over to show her grandson off to Kana.

"This beautiful wee bundle is Levi, Cam and Shal's little boy, and my first grandchild." Poppy wore her pride like a badge of honour. "They live in Dunedin, hence my manic back and forth."

Kana felt the familiar, though unwanted tug on her insides, and stoically ignored it.

"He's very sweet." She looked across at Cam while she held the photo. "He looks like Shal... but has your mouth." Careful to notice details, but not display too much clunkiness, she handed the photo back.

It was always a bit of a social dance in order to keep everyone comfortable when a childless woman was caught discussing babies in any way. Especially if that woman happened to be getting on in years.

Kana pasted a polite smile on to cover her bases.

Cam laughed. "Yeah, he does." He took the offered frame and studied it. "He's a handsome little bugger." He looked up and smiled fully back at Kana, giving her a moment's pause.

Her landlord's brother was quite something when the happiness shone out of his eyes like that.

"Trouble too, just like his dad." Poppy snatched the frame back and placed it next to an older one of a man in a light suit. She put a finger to his tie, a faraway expression on her face.

Turning, Kana caught Clementine's dejected look, and knew instinctively he'd taken Poppy's action to mean something against himself.

Was the dark haired man in the photo Poppy's husband?

Divorced? Dead? Or just... gone?

Adele had said her cousin knew what it was like to be without a father...

Kana didn't even want to imagine life without her own.

When Poppy sat, it was next to Clementine on the sofa, so maybe she'd seen his change in mood, too. And when the others stopped taking any notice of her, she slid her hand into his.

Adele stated it was time for Saffy to head home to bed, and bundled the complaining child into her work-logoed station wagon before handing out hugs all around.

The moment they'd gone, Kana explained she was due an early night too, and left.

Happy with how smoothly she'd been able to extract herself, Kana was partway down the drive, nearing the annex turnoff, when she heard the dog barking. Turning back towards the farmhouse, she saw a flash of black and white whip out from behind the outbuildings.

Halfback danced in crazy circles on the grass before spotting her, and bee-lining in her direction.

Standing stock still, Kana gripped the large—thankfully clean —*okonomiyaki* plate in front of her chest like a protective breastplate.

Every hair on her body stood on end, because there was absolutely nowhere to escape.

The dog reached her in seconds flat, and Kana clenched her teeth, bracing for impact. But rather than jumping up, it circled her twice, then lay down.

Rounding her up, like a lamb to the slaughter?

"Go home," she whispered, eyeing it warily. Then louder, "Go. Home!"

The dog gave a high-pitched whine and crept forward a little on its belly.

"*No*! Stay there!"

It issued one bark, then rolled onto its back, giving her a view of its white belly and lolling tongue as it eyed her sideways.

A high-pitched whistle issued from the farmhouse had the dog scrabbling up abruptly and taking off again, streaking wildly uphill.

Kana could just make out Rugby on the verandah, calling the animal.

Had he just sent his dog down the drive to see her off? That was downright *mean*.

Mr frickin' Dante had nothing to worry about; Kana had no intention of ever setting foot in his house again.

"Did you let the bloody dog out?" Daniel stormed down the verandah steps and aimed the question at his brother.

"I did," Cam returned mildly, bringing his and Shal's cases in from the car with Clementine's help.

Cam's partner travelled with enough luggage to sink the damn Titanic.

"Saffy's gone, and he was begging me for a run." Cam shrugged.

"Shit!" Daniel ran a hand through his hair.

"What's the problem?" Clementine asked, clearly bemused.

"Saffy's not the only one who's freaked out by dogs. Mum's new ceramicist takes exception, too. I said I'd keep Halfback off her case, but I'm pretty sure he just chased her home."

Clementine and Cam both laughed out loud at the imagined spectacle.

"It's not funny," Daniel grumbled, but his lips twitched with the irony of it.

7

YOU YOURSELF

*"You yourself,
as much as anybody in the entire universe
deserve your love and affection."*
- Buddha

Hearing the barn door creak, Kana looked up from the new bust she was working on to find the neighbouring farmer standing awkwardly in the doorway, twisting his hat around in circles in his hands.

"Clementine! Welcome! Come on in."

"You can call me Clem. Everyone does." The older man visibly relaxed, stuffing his fisherman's hat in his back pocket and moving forward. He was dressed for a working day with dark blue overalls and steel-toed boots, and moved easily, like a much younger man. "What's that you're working on?"

"A bust."

"*Oh*, I..." Clem stopped stock-still, his cheeks reddening.

Kana laughed, reading his discomfort loud and clear. "Not a nude bust, like breasts, if that's what you're thinking. A bust, as in a 3D portrait."

"Oh, a *bust*!" Obviously relieved, Clem walked around the workbench and peered at the towering hand-worked piece.

"The nose is bothering me… It's not quite right," Kana murmured more to herself than to Clem, as she added another pinch of clay to the bridge and worked it in.

Clem's first surprised hoot deepened into a real belly laugh.

"My God, that's a good likeness. You must have pissed the fella off good and proper to have him look at you like that."

"He *always* looks at me like that," Kana returned with a touch of snideness, only half joking. "I was thinking of naming it Landlord," she fibbed.

She hadn't seen her 'landlord' in nearly a week, and neither car, nor farm truck had been up at the main house, which suited her just fine.

The bust of Daniel Dante had come together easily. He had striking features and a large presence. Kana had caught him holding a severe expression, with heavy brows, a hard stare, and a frown deepening the furrows on his forehead. It was a stylised likeness though, and she doubted anyone other than those who knew him well would recognise him.

"It's one in a series of pairs. Come, I'll show you." Kana moved over to the bisque-fired shelf and unpacked the protective bubble wrap she'd put around the first pair.

Clem's brows rose. "My, but they're beautiful, Kana. Bless my soul. The little swallows are so life-like, and this woman's perfectly serene…" he trailed off, looking across at her. "Do you know her, or did you just make these people up?"

"No. I knew her. I knew them both. They were very special. This piece is called Marriage." She moved the two busts closer together on the shelf on their wooden bats—bit by bit, until they became one unit with the birds beaks almost touching.

"Well now, *that's* clever. I thought they were two, but like that, they look like they were made as one."

Kana grinned. "Yes, that's the idea. Two halves of a whole."

Clem scratched at his jaw. "Is there another half to Daniel's, then?"

"*Yeeees*." Kana drew the word out, her smile dropping. "But I'm not happy with that one, either. It lacks something." Returning to her workbench, she unwrapped the plastic around the other piece of greenware.

"Oh, that's fabulous!" Clem marvelled. "A dog."

"Yes, Halfback."

"Halfback?" Clem looked surprised, then turned to study the dog's head again, making a non-committal sound in the back of his throat.

"What's wrong?" Kana challenged him.

"Oh, nothing. It's amazing with all the detail on the muzzle, and the teeth." Clem hesitated.

"But?"

"Umm..." Clem shuffled uncomfortably. "But this is a much more aggressive dog, wouldn't you say? A fighting breed. Halfback's a border collie. He wouldn't bare his fangs at Dan like that. Not if he valued his hide."

Kana stared at Clem, then back at the bust.

"What do I know about art, though?" Clem backtracked, offsetting his opinion politely. "I'm just a farmer."

"A farmer who knows about dogs," Kana countered quietly.

"Yes, I do. That's the truth of it." Clem looked at her searchingly. "Actually, it was Halfback I came to talk to you about. I have him as my sidekick while Dan's away this trip, and I'm gonna be out on the drive laying down some new shingle with a couple of young fellas this afternoon." Clem glanced at the sculpted dog again. "Now, I know he's not supposed to be this close to the annex, but I thought maybe if you knew in advance, it would be alright."

"Where is he now?" Her eyes shot to the open door.

"On the back of my truck."

"Oh." Kana wiped her suddenly moist palms on the back of her jeans. "Tied up?"

"Well, no. But he's an obedient sort, and I told him to stay there." Clem watched her closely. "I'm not one to pry, but it seems to me you have a pretty strong fear of canines, and unless you're the kind to jump at anything—which frankly, you don't seem to be—you've had a trigger experience that makes you feel this way." He ran a finger around the collar of his overalls. "Now, you could tell an interfering old bugger to go take a hike, or you could let me in on why Halfback puts the fear of blazes into you."

Kana found herself smiling into Clem's blue-grey eyes. His

underlying kindness shone through, and he exuded 'easy company' from every pore.

"Let me just get the plastic back on this, then I'll see if I can rustle up a raspberry muffin and a cup of tea."

"Now you're talking." Clem grinned.

"These are quite something." Clem stood in the annex lounge beside the sideboard, running his hand over the only one of Opa's plates with a geometric design. The orange and yellow squares were outlined in black, and had always reminded Kana of children's building blocks, or Tetris—the way they were all slotted together.

Clem picked up the old dinner plate with careful hands and turned it over to squint at the impression on the back. "I assume the windmill means they're Dutch?"

"Yes. All from the same factory, and all by the same artist. My grandfather," she called through from the small kitchen as she removed the muffins from the microwave and plated them up with butter.

Clem looked up and caught her eye as she brought through the tea tray. "Is that so? They're all so different, one from the other."

"Yes." Kana smiled, and because he seemed genuinely interested, told Clem the story of how the plates came to be in her possession as they sat down to tea and muffins.

At thirteen, Kana had thrown a jug—her first attempt at a handle —and gifted it to her Oma. On her best behaviour, the old woman had politely failed to mention the lip was all wonky, maintaining it would make a perfect pitcher for custard. Kana remembered hoping like hell the handle was up to holding the weight.

Her grandmother had gone on to reminisce about the hot custard her own mother used to make in the 'old country,' served with spiced apple tart. She'd lived in the little township beside the canal, catering to the industrial centre one mile downstream.

Afternoon coffee always brought on nostalgia in Oma, but every now and again, she'd throw in a previously untold story.

"Your Opa used to paint ceramics too, in Holland."

"*Did* he?" Kana's attention had caught, and held. "Really? He was a potter?"

"No, no, he didn't *make* it. It was a big factory, you know?" The old lady's accent was still strong, even after over forty years in New Zealand, and she always used her hands to express herself.

"There was a large ceramic factory near the town we grew up in. They didn't make the pottery, they—how do you say it—casted it? Cast it?" She'd been clearly frustrated by the word. English had a myriad of rules, as any language did, but Oma often complained she'd never known another to snub its own regulations so often. "It comes through to them already made. They paint the same pattern all day."

"Opa was a ceramic artist?"

"Yes. A good thing to call it. Ceramic artist." Oma had sat back on her chair, clearly satisfied with the title. "He was a hard worker," she added, nodding. "And a good man."

Kana had never met Opa. He'd died before she was born. She'd heard many stories of course, but not this particular one.

"I thought he was a builder?"

"In New Zealand, yes. An apprentice first, then builder."

"But in Holland?"

"In Holland, there were many jobs. Delivery boy, bookbinder, ceramic artist… Many jobs."

"Do you have anything he painted?" Drawn in, Kana had perched on the edge of her chair.

"I *do*. Yes." Oma had placed her coffee cup carefully on the doily and pulled herself up to stand, then moved to the old-fashioned china cabinet.

The trinkets in the glass cabinet were small and fussy, stuck down in position with little balls of ageing blue-tack. But the plates Oma had pulled from the lower storage drawer were broad and practical. Uniform in size, the scuffed top-glaze attested to plenty of use, though each hand painted design was vastly different from the next.

"Every year the artists put their design in for the new seasons… line?" Oma had obviously thought it another frustrating word.

"They keep their own entry if there's no success. Nicholas worked for six years, so six plates. This one's broken, but still, I keep it." Oma had laid all six on the table, like the tidy pattern on a die, pushing the two broken halves of the damaged plate together to make a whole. "I would ask Nicholas to fix it, but he's gone." She'd shoved her chin up as if to prove her stoicism.

Oma was a pragmatic soul, and had no use for messy emotions. Nicholas was dead, and had been for some time, end of story.

"I love them!" Kana had clapped her hands in excitement. "This one's my favourite." She'd indicated the detailed gypsy-caravan design, with musical notes flying out the door. "Or maybe *this* one." Sliding her fingers over the split plate in reds, oranges and white, she'd stroked the poppies and daisies. "So, Opa's designs never won?"

"No. Not what they were looking for. Too fussy. But they're pretty, aren't they?"

As Oma had re-stacked the plates, she'd continued to tell Kana stories of Nicholas, her Opa. He'd been a young father, Papa three times over before he'd had time to fully grow into a man himself, but dead many years before Kana had arrived.

"He would've liked your spirit, your zest." Perhaps on a whim, Oma had placed the broken plate on top, and moved the full stack in front of Kana. "These can be yours now, as you like them." Taking Kana's chin in her hand, she'd tilted her face up. "And as you have some of Nicholas in you." Her pale blue eyes had searched without need for permission. "He was a hard worker and a good man," she'd repeated, this time adding with a touch of whimsy, "And *he* was full of light and colour, too."

Oma was usually a stickler for no-nonsense observations, so the conversation had stayed strong in Kana's memory.

Kana's father had repaired the broken plate carefully with clear glue, and she'd displayed the set in every room, flat, apartment, and house she'd lived in since then.

Clem was easy to talk to, and Kana was enjoying his company, so she thought nothing of telling him how her fear of dogs had come about. It wasn't something she often brought up, or even thought about, but the older man had such a practical, gentle manner about him. His salt and pepper hair was in disarray, and had been since the removal of his hat.

It made him appear almost boyish.

He definitely had the *energy* of a child, more so than that of an adult; mischief twinkling from his eyes as he spoke.

Kana wondered what Clementine's relationship with Poppy was, exactly. Cam had teased his mother about her 'boyfriend,' and Kana had noticed the fleeting touches and covert handholding. They were obviously sweethearts. Why not openly so?

"Jumping Jesus," Clem muttered, throwing back the last of his tea. "No wonder you don't want anything to do with canines."

As a child, Kana had witnessed her pet rabbit being ripped to shreds by a couple of trespassing dogs in her own backyard. She'd been right there watching. Screaming.

Fangs. Fur. Blood and guts. The scene had certainly stuck.

She shuddered involuntarily.

Not a scratch on her body, but the experience had left a deep score in her mind.

"Oh, I'm fine if they keep to themselves," she assured Clem, and herself.

"I had a horse once," Clem stated as he moved to the mudroom and began to pull on his boots. "I'm going back more decades than I'd like to admit, here." He looked up and winked, making Kana laugh. "He couldn't abide me wearing boots, because his previous owner used to kick the shit out of him." He cleared his throat, looking a little sheepish. "Ah... Excuse my language. So I used to ride him barefoot. Drove my mother mad. That went on for a couple of months till it turned to winter, but buggered if I was going to go bootless in the snow, so I had to come up with another plan."

Kana noticed Clem didn't apologise for the word 'buggered,' so he either thought of it as a lesser cuss, or had decided her equilibrium could deal with a bit of sheep farmer's language. She moved out onto the front step with him, caught up in the story.

"What did you do?"

"I took an old pair of my dad's boots and wore them into the stable. Rua, that was the name of the gelding, took one look at me in those boots and rolled his eyes, snorted. Carried on, stamping and champing like he was going to pummel me. So I let him have a good look and a good sniff, then I took off the boots and left them in his stall. Let him go for it."

"What happened?"

"He kicked the shi... Well, ah, he had a *whale* of a time. Ripped those boots to shreds. Hoofs, teeth, you name it. Made a couple of holes in the stall that were my responsibility to fix, but other than that? It was all smooth sailing from there on in. Poor old Rua just needed to get it out of his system."

Kana had been walking alongside Clem towards his truck, forgetting all about the dog until they'd nearly reached the front fender, and it yipped to Clem in welcome.

"Stay," Clem reminded Halfback in a low voice, and got a whine in response.

Kana shot Clem a look. "You did that on purpose."

"Did what?" Clem lifted his shoulders in mock confusion.

"Got me out here with Halfback."

"Well, it struck me you haven't been formally introduced." He put a hand on her arm. "Do you trust me?"

"Oh, absolutely. But I don't trust *him*."

"Well now, it's intelligent not to trust an animal you don't know, but I can vouch for this particular one. And you can stand behind me if you like." Clem's voice changed to authoritative as he addressed the dog. "Halfback, come!"

Kana sucked in her breath, but stood her ground as the dog bounded down, tail wagging.

"Slow!" Halfback slowed to a trot. "Sit." He sat immediately. "Lie down... Roll over... Sit... Shake hands... Getaway!" Clem accompanied every instruction he gave the dog with a hand gesture, and each time, Halfback complied with what appeared to be deep-seated enthusiasm.

With the 'getaway' command, he raced in the direction Clem pointed, black and white tail flying like a flag behind him.

Clem drew his right hand up to his mouth and whistled long and low, and the dog arced back towards them, running full tilt.

That's the only time Kana stepped behind the farmer.

"Tell him to go slow." Clem instructed as Halfback neared.

"Who, *me*?"

"Slow!" Clem commanded, taking over. The dog did as he was

63

told. "Low!" The slinking walk turned into a belly crawl. "*Waaaait*," he growled, and the dog stopped altogether.

Clem turned to her. "Now it's your turn. Use a big voice, and use his name. Can you wolf-whistle?"

"Yes." Kana cleared her suddenly dry throat. "But I need both hands." She held up her two index fingers and wiggled them.

"That's fine," Clem chuckled, looking quite chuffed. "Okay now. Tell that dog to getaway"

Okay, sure. Just a walk in the park.

"Halfback," Kana croaked. The dog looked at her expectantly with his head on the side and she cleared her throat again. "Halfback, getaway!" She pointed in the direction of the farmhouse and he took off. "Oh!" She turned to Clem, delighted. "He did it!"

"He did, indeed." Clem chuckled. "You're a natural. Now whistle him back."

"Right." She frowned, liking the idea of the dog running away much better than it coming towards her, but putting her fingers in her mouth to whistle anyway.

Halfback rounded the bend a little slower than the first time.

"Slow!" Kana commanded, frowning. "Is he getting tired?"

"Could be. He's been out chasing…" Clem coughed and looked at his boots. "Ah, out for a morning run already."

"Out chasing rabbits?" she guessed.

"Well, now." The tips of Clem's ears turned pink, and his hat got yanked out to begin circling in his hands again. "He can't often catch them, you understand. The little buggers scarper down their holes, and he's not built for digging far."

Kana glanced back towards the dog. "Sit!"

Halfback had approached so slowly and quietly, he sat directly in front of her, awaiting the next instruction with his tongue lolling out. She bit back the gut-response to demand he 'getaway,' and actually gave herself a moment to look at him. He carried a depth of intelligence in his eyes, not unlike the old farmer.

"Stay!" She dragged her eyes to Clem, heart thumping in her throat. "Should I get him some water?"

"I'm sure he'd appreciate that, if you've got a spare ice-cream container or something. He usually helps himself to the sheep troughs."

Kana slunk back into the annex in search of a suitable water bowl. When she came back out a minute later, container in hand, Clem was crouched down with the dog, giving him a good scratching.

"Good dog. You're a damn good dog. Well done, boy. You helped a great deal, I'd say. Just keep any rabbit carcasses well out of her sight, okay?" Clem let the dog get a quick lick at his face, then started when he realised Kana was coming up behind him. He rose quickly, cheeks a little more rosy than the effort warranted. "Pick of the litter, this one. Superb dog. I could kid myself it's all in the breeding, but he's been given the training needed to keep him in line, too."

Kana hid her smile, and for Clem's benefit pretended she hadn't overheard the rabbit comment. "I've only got this big yogurt container…" She placed it on the ground a little away from both man and dog, water slopping.

"That'll be just fine."

Halfback obviously thought so too, sitting to attention.

"Okay." Clem waited until Kana had stepped away to give consent, and Halfback jumped over to drink thirstily.

"Well." Kana put her hands on her hips and studied the flank of the sheepdog. "I never thought I'd say this, but that was almost fun."

"Good," Clem grinned. "So, it's okay if he's out here with me this afternoon, then? If he's a problem, you can tell him to getaway or find Clem, and he'll scarper."

"Find Clem? Okay. And how long is Rugby…?" Kana's less than diplomatic name for her landlord popped out of her mouth before she had time to swipe it back. "Um, how long do you have Mr Dante's dog this time?"

"Just two more days," Clem answered, watching her fluster. His eyes were a little *too* astute when he added quietly, "Daniel's a good man."

"Oh!" Kana laughed, but it came out sounding a bit skittish. "I'm sure he is, Clem. But we don't seem to see eye to eye."

"Some things take a little time."

"Hmm. Some things," she answered without an iota of conviction. This was *not* going to be one of those things.

Clem called the dog up onto the back of the truck. "You know Halfback, now. But if another dog ever comes at you, your best bet is to make yourself as big and loud as you can and pick up a stick or something to fend it off. Put anything between you and the teeth— bike, tennis racquet, whatever. They bow to the alpha, but they have to believe you *are* one. Back away from them and eventually you'll reach the border of what they think they're protecting." He winked at her again. "Dog Psychology, one-oh-one. Free lesson in exchange for that delicious muffin."

Kana smiled, and Clem grinned back, settling into the driver's seat with his arm winged out the window. The farmer had gone out of his way to be kind, and understanding.

She stepped forward and touched his elbow lightly. "Thank you, Clem."

"Don't mention it." He started the engine. "Before I go. You said you thought the bust of the dog was missing something? I think I know what it is." He scratched at the back of his head. "Call me a romantic, but in my opinion, it's love. Halfback looks at Daniel like he's the returning messiah, because he loves that man something stupid."

8

WALK THE PATH

*"No one saves us but ourselves.
No one can and no one may.
We ourselves must walk the path."
- Buddha*

Kana had set aside the next morning to load the two busts she was calling 'Hongi' into kilns for their bisque firing. She purposefully hadn't shown Clem this pair, as it'd be good to get a true gauge on his reaction when they were glazed and ready for sale.

When it came to the crunch, she wasn't convinced the thicker slabs on the female form were dry enough, and reluctantly pulled the plug on her plan. Each day of drying put her gallery schedule back another few steps, and she was dealing with less and less leeway on the calendar.

Kana loaded one of the kilns with regular tableware stock, instead. Plates, platters, coffee mugs, and teacups. A section of the top shelf was set aside for her new two-in-one cup and teapot design, where the base was the cup, and the teapot itself settled inside to warm the vessel. It was a tricky design to perfect, the cup and teapot base having to fit together perfectly, but there were three she was happy with, and a fourth she could use to experiment with her new glazes.

She'd almost finished loading the bisque when Adele phoned.

"I have an unexpected afternoon free. Would you be up for a lake walk?"

Kana jumped at the chance. "Yes, I'd love one. What time?"

"One, but bring a jacket, there's supposed to be a southerly change coming through."

Adele was right about the weather, they were partway along the higher shore track when Kana felt the wind turn.

She stopped to take her windproof shell out of her backpack and Adele rolled down the sleeves of her polypropylene.

"Four seasons in one day." Kana smiled across at Adele, suddenly remembering the phone message she'd taken down for her new friend earlier in the day. She patted her pockets. "I nearly forgot to pass this on. A man called trying to get a hold of you at the annex this morning."

Adele was halfway through tucking her hair back under her cap, but stopped mid-movement, her arms creating a diamond frame around her face.

"What kind of man?" she asked, voice cool and even, but eyes troubled.

"I'm not sure. It was a little strange, actually. He didn't leave his name, and I wouldn't give out your number, so we had a stalemate for a minute there." Kana finally located the paper and pulled it out triumphantly. "But he left a message."

She handed it over.

He'd been business-like, but aloof. And the message was clear, but intriguing. The Australian authorities had located Adele's jewellery, and if she wished to have it sent over, she should call the following number and inform the lawyers of her current address. If she wanted the jewellery liquidated, she should do the same, with confirmation of her current bank account details.

"He said a letter would come with the same information," Kana added.

Adele relaxed visibly on reading the scrap of paper, then looked up, clear excitement in her eyes.

"Wow. It's been so long since it went missing! I never thought… Never in a million years. Huh! Weird. The call would've been from James, my ex-husband. Or maybe his lawyer," Adele surmised. "Aussie accent?"

"Yes, I think so. Saffy's father?" Kana turned to resume walking, but Adele didn't move to follow.

"No." Adele was looking back at Ruby Island, both hands on her backpack straps. "I met James later. Saffy's birth father's name is Moses."

"Oh." Kana waited for more information, but Adele was still gazing lake-wards, trancelike, her mind obviously a million miles away. "Well, he must've been a good looking bloke, because Saffy's stunning."

When Adele turned to look back at her, Kana suddenly realised the other woman was fighting tears, and wished she hadn't spoken so glibly.

Adele's distress made Kana not know what to do with her hands. Pat Adele's arm? Hug her? They didn't know each other very well…

Kana went with a supportive hand on her shoulder for a second or too.

"Yes," Adele answered simply. "He was. And she is, isn't she?" She smiled a little shakily. "I wanted to talk to you about my sweet Sass-a-frass, actually." Again, they began to walk side by side. "I took today off work because there was some trouble at school, and I got called in to see the principal. Apparently, there's been some bullying going on, and Saffy was involved." Adele kicked a random stone out of her path. "I also wanted to thank you."

"Thank me? What on earth for?"

"For giving Saffy a comeback. I was completely unaware. I thought it was going *fine*. She's got a nice bunch of friends, and on the surface she's doing very well. But there's this *one* little girl who's been tormenting her—insidious like. A little bit here, a little bit there. You know what I mean?"

"Oh, believe me, I know." Kana's ire rose. Some things never changed.

"She calls Saffy 'Half.' It might've started out as a mild dig, because she follows her Uncle D around like Halfback does. But when no one else is around, this girl adds other stuff. Halfback, Half-*black*, Half-*caste*, Half-*dirty*…" Adele paused, seemingly unable to get enough air into her lungs. "Half-*nigger*," she whispered, her voice uneven.

"Oh, *shit*." Kana came to a dead stop, grabbing Adele's arm and squeezing tight.

"Yeah. I know. She's only eight, this little girl. Who's been feeding her that hate?" Adele blinked rapidly. "So, anyway, yesterday, Saffy was being called names, and she stood up and shouted in front of the whole class, 'Both of my halves are beautiful, and you will never come close, Paris Drayton, because you will *never* be anything but *narrow-minded*!' "

"Oh!" Kana's hand flew to her mouth, remembering her quiet conversation with Saffy in the farmhouse kitchen. "*Ohhh.*" her tone changed as she realised the implications. "*Saffy* got in trouble?"

"She did, yes. Yesterday she got a mild talking to from her teacher about speaking unkindly to others. But luckily, Paris Drayton went home to her parents and complained."

"Luckily?"

Adele smiled, but there was a grim twist to her mouth. "Yes, luckily. Because they called a meeting this morning—parents and children of those involved. So Saffy could apologise, I assume. The principal is a straight-up woman, and she wanted the whole story. When Saffy gave it to her, there was enough egg on those parents' faces to serve a whole girl-scout troop for breakfast. I've never been so proud of Saffron in all my life. She spoke like a little United Nations candidate. So, I wanted to thank you for giving her the words, and the self belief."

"Oh, I didn't—"

"Yes, you did," Adele interrupted, adamant. "Saffy told them she knew a clay artist who's half Japanese, and explained how we're *all* two halves of a whole. Then she told that little room of people just how lucky she was to have her ancestors spread so *wide*, so she'd never have to be 'narrow minded.' " Adele's eyes glittered. "I probably don't have to tell you I blubbed my heart out, and the principal had to scramble around and find me a box of tissues."

"Oh." Kana huffed out a breath on a shaky laugh. "Well, you're welcome. It was just a passing comment..." Adele lifted her eyebrows, disbelief clear. "But I'm glad it helped."

Maybe if someone had given Kana the same comeback at eight years old, school would've been a bit of an easier ride? And maybe not.

Noting Adele's hair was curling around her cap in the dampening weather, Kana looked skyward. "Uh-oh. I think it's about to piss down."

"I think you may be right."

They turned in unison and walked a little quicker back towards the farm.

The two women sat in the small kitchen drinking tea, as icy rain pelted the latticed windows.

"I can't say I've ever been much of a green tea fan, but with honey, and a slice of lemon, it's actually quite nice." Adele stretched her legs out under the table.

Kana would let Adele find out for herself, but the combo was even better once you got to the bottom of the cup. The honey settled to infuse the lemon with sweetness.

She took out her own fruit slice and sucked on it.

"Not to be a slob, but I'm almost relieved the rain came early. I was on my feet all day yesterday," Adele continued.

"Your cleaning job?"

"Yeah. Full schedule on Wednesdays, and my back's feeling it. The agency has a decent hourly rate, and I can work within Saffy's school hours, but my body doesn't always enjoy it. It's a far cry from sitting at a desk as a legal secretary."

"That's what you used to do?" Kana tried to imagine the sporty mum in a suit.

"A lifetime ago. That's how I met James. He was visiting a property lawyer in the same building, and we got held up in an elevator."

"Aw, cute."

Adele laughed. "No, not cute. Disastrous. I mentioned we're divorced, right?"

"Right." Something they had in common, though Kana was still waiting on the paperwork from hers. "That bad, huh?"

Adele snorted. "That *good,* unfortunately. The guy basically set my knickers on fire, rendering me totally useless as a rational adult. We married far too quick. I hardly knew him. It was doomed to fail from the start." She caught Kana's eye, hesitating a moment with her fingers worrying at her earlobe. "Saffy got the raw end of the deal in the fallout," she finally murmured. "She loves James to death, he's the only dad she's ever known."

"Bugger. Sorry."

"You live and learn." Waving her past choices away, Adele sighed before appearing to perk up a little. "But it sounds like I might be getting my jewellery back, so that's something, at least." Adele held up the teacup she'd been holding. "I've been thinking. People would pay good money to make something of their own they could actually use. Have you ever thought about teaching pottery?"

Kana made a noncommittal noise. "*Nge.* There are much better teachers out there than me."

"You were really good with Saffy the other day. She can't stop talking about it."

"It's different with children."

"Why not teach children, then?" Adele leaned forward, frowning. "I could fill your first class off the top of my head."

Kana shifted in her seat, uncomfortable under such intense scrutiny. "I'm not here for long," she reminded Adele, neatly stepping the original question.

"Well, if you change your mind, Saffy would love it. How much do I owe you for the fruit she's been making?"

Kana snorted. "Nothing. Poppy's adamant I pay nothing for rent here and nothing for power, so Saffy pays nothing to pot, considering my benefactors all happen to be members of your family."

"For your time, then."

"Don't even go there, she's a pleasure to spend time with." Kana turned to look at Adele directly. "You both are."

"Thanks. Right back at ya." Adele leaned back again, lacing her fingers behind her head. "We struck gold when Poppy chose you."

Sure, some of the family seemed happy to have her here. Poppy and Clem… Adele and Saffy. They'd all made repeated overtures of friendship. Even Cam and Shal had seemed welcoming.

But Rugby? No.

"Your cousin doesn't get a say in who Poppy plants on his doorstep, does he?" she queried lightly, trying not to advertise how pensive she felt about that particular member of Adele's family.

Adele laughed. "No."

"I could've guessed that, to be fair." Kana set her mouth in a grim line.

It shouldn't matter, but her landlord's continued animosity kind of rankled.

"He's not grumpy *all* the time. Just when he's jet-lagged," Adele placated.

Kana thought she could read a twinkle in her new friend's eye.

"Which is pretty much…" she left the sentence hanging with her eyebrows raised.

Adele laughed outright. "All the time? Oh, come on. D's not that bad! He does like his own space though, that's true. Because he's so recognisable, people think they know him personally. Bowl on up and talk to him as if he's their best mate. But he's quite a private person, really. I think that's why Wānaka suits him. It's a small community, so everyone knows everyone already. He's no different here than anyone else."

"Right." Kana smiled vaguely, though she was battling confusion. "Wait, why would he be different from anyone else?"

"Well you know, like when he's in Dunedin, it's sometimes hard to make his way down the street without signing a few rugby balls."

"Because he played rugby?" That didn't make any sense.

"Yeeees, for Otago, then the national team," Adele filled in the blanks helpfully, cocking her head to the side as Kana digested that bombshell.

"For *New Zealand*?" Kana's voice raised an octave, partway through her yelp.

"You don't follow rugby, I take it." Any drier, and Adele's statement would be burnt toast.

"No. Not at all." Kana blinked, taking the information on board. "But I thought I'd recognise player's names from the media hype."

"This was years ago, now. Twelve, thirteen? D played first five, but blasted his knee after two international seasons."

"The right one." It had to be.

"Yes, you remember? They used to call him Dante D. They still do."

"No. I don't remember, but I've seen him favour the left one." When he'd stormed off to his car, the day he'd heard her talking to Sam on the phone.

"God. Don't ever tell him that. The recovery was extremely hard, with all sorts of setbacks." Adele looked so sombre all of a sudden, turning again to gaze out the rain splattered window. "But he was bloody determined to walk without a limp."

The following day, when Kana was about to walk into the supermarket, she noticed a dog tied to the bars outside. Along with the usual prickle of awareness, she felt a strange sense of recognition pass between herself and the seated canine. The black and white border collie's tail began to thump the pavement, and he *smiled* at her.

She looked around hesitantly, but saw no one.

"Halfback?" she whispered, stealing a step closer.

The tail thumped harder, and his bum began to wiggle. She checked his collar again.

Definitely tied.

"Ah, hi boy. If you *are* a boy?" Her eyes dipped lower.

Yep. Unmistakably so.

"Clem says you wouldn't hurt me. Is that true?"

Halfback grinned with his tongue lolling out.

"That's a lot of teeth you've got there." She shook her head and wrinkled up her nose. "A *lot* of teeth."

Breathe in for four, out for five.

"I want you to be nice." Kana offered her request up to the universe at large, before easing her hand out, palm down. She almost chickened out before it was within the dog's reach.

Don't. Be. Ridiculous.

People did this all the time.

She remembered stepping out of the annex's door and seeing Clem hunkered down with the dog, their faces close together and Halfback lapping at the farmer's chin, and willed the image to calm her.

Halfback sniffed at Kana's offered hand with a wet nose, then gave it two solid licks before she pulled it away.

"Good boy," she whispered, only a mild shake in her voice. "You're a good boy."

The dog stood, perhaps assuming she was going to walk him.

"Sit!" Kana commanded, with much more authority than she felt.

Halfback sat. Immediately.

"Oh, you *are* a good dog!" She laughed, surprising herself. "I think that's more than enough for today though, don't you?"

Again the tail thumped, and Halfback lay down on the pavement with his muzzle on his paws, big eyes looking up at her longingly. Or possibly hungrily?

Kana pushed the unhelpful thought away.

"So, I'll see you later." She walked away with her knees slightly twitchy, but head held high.

Daniel watched Kanako from inside the glass doors of the chemist, where he'd just bought a jumbo-pack of paracetamol.

Something about the woman made him forget to breathe.

She was casual in worn jeans and a large sweater, several sizes too big for her. When her hand reached out toward the dog, tentative to the point of shaking, Daniel found he was clenching his fist so tight his knuckles creaked.

Halfback behaved impeccably, without barking or jumping, though going by the frantic tail movements he was over the moon to see the annex tenant.

Daniel thought he even heard the ceramicist laugh, and his shoulders released the static tension they'd been holding on to, bit by torturous bit.

After what Clem had told him when he'd picked up Halfback, he felt like he'd just witnessed a minor miracle.

9

AN IDEA

*"An idea that is developed and put into action
is more important than an idea
that exists only as an idea."*
- Buddha

"Hi Kana, beautiful day! Your usual?" The bubbly coffee shop assistant had very cute dimples, low on her cheeks, and it was impossible not to smile back. Kana was reminded of a golden-haired cherub every time she dropped in here for her new favourite non-caffeine fix; a soy turmeric latte.

"Yes, thanks, Maddie." She stood on tiptoe to get closer to the sweet-treat jars on top of the cabinet. "Make it a large one, and are these yo-yos any good?"

"Ohmygod!" Maddie rolled her eyes and giggled. "They're *divine*. Mr Kaihanga's family recipe. Passionfruit icing in the centre."

"Okay, you've sold me. One of those as well, please." Kana looked around herself. "You're pumping today."

"Yeah, the sunny weather pulls people out. Number forty-two." Maddie handed over the order number in the form of a painted river-stone. "Good luck finding a seat." She was already dimpling up at the next customer, getting ready to take their order.

Kana turned and almost collided with two of her yoga students,

Carissa, and her twin sister, Marianne, who were leaning down to peruse the cabinet food. The women were a strange mixture of likeness, and stark difference. Carissa's hair was pure white, while her sister kept hers stubbornly brunette.

After waxing lyrical about the weather, the twins got down to business, rallying Kana to put her name down for the Ruby Island Autumn Working Bee in a couple of days' time. Marianne and Carissa were in charge of volunteers, and on the lookout for new blood.

Kana had studied the little island on her shoreline walks, but hadn't the means to get out there. Its dock often had a speedboat, or kayaks tied up to it, and the lush greenery and small beach intrigued her. She'd been trying to figure a way to spirit herself there, so was only too eager to put her name down for the community service.

"Since you know Adele, I'll get her to pick you up." Carissa went a step further, and organised her ride as well.

They exchanged pleasantries for a few more minutes before Kana went in search of a table, realising belatedly the small café had filled up even more in the meantime. She could only see one seat free in the far corner. Unless the guy with the newspaper was waiting for someone?

She made her way over.

"Is this seat taken? Do you mind if I—" Kana nearly dropped her river-stone when her landlord slowly lowered his paper and eyed her over the top. "Sorry, I… I had no idea…" She backed off quick smart, almost bumping into her latte and yoyo as they were delivered.

Why did she always have to come across as so klutzy around this particular man? She was a poised, confident woman. There was no need to act like a bloody teenager whenever she was in his vicinity.

"Help yourself." Rugby indicated towards the empty chair, but she knew she was imagining the warmth in his eyes. There was no true welcome there.

"No, that's fine." Kana relieved the surprised wait-staff of her cup and plate. "I think I see a chair outside in the sun. I need all the vitamin-D I can get, these days," she prattled on to cover the obvious snub, bent on escape. "So much studio work, recently. Thanks for the offer, though."

Maddie was clearly surprised to see Kana back at the counter. The young barista's eyebrows arched up in perfect symmetry. "Is everything okay?"

"Yes, sorry. Can I get this take-out?" Kana slid her two items and her river-stone back onto the counter, keen to be somewhere else. Anywhere else.

"Sure! Did you say take-out? Sorry, I didn't register that. I just assumed you were dining in because you *always* dine in." Maddie's little dimples weren't showing anymore, and she looked quickly from Kana to Mr Bloody Rugby, who'd come to stand alongside her as silently as a large feral cat.

Kana jumped a full foot when she realised he was right there, at her elbow.

"No, my fault. I completely forgot to say," she mumbled.

"Take my table. I was just leaving," her landlord offered.

"Oh, that's kind of you, really." Kana chewed on her bottom lip, while Maddie efficiently transferred the yoyo into a paper bag and the latte into a take out cup. "But I'm going to head out. Too many people," she fibbed.

Then the man surprised her twofold, by turning as she did and holding the door for her.

Daniel had been minding his own business, relishing being back home and drinking a lazy coffee while reading the sports section. He rarely got to handle a real newspaper now he'd cancelled his on again/off again subscription, and there was an honest pleasure in the rigmarole of folding and manipulating the newsprint. It hadn't been his intention to hide behind it, just his natural reaction when he'd been eavesdropping on Kanako at the counter, and she'd suddenly turned to look towards his table.

He'd seen her come into the café, of course. She was hard to miss with her cascade of auburn-tinted hair, and musical laugh. All smiles and conversation.

Everyone seemed to know her by name, and she came across as friendly, bubbly and engaging.

From a distance.

Kanako had instantly transformed to stilted and cool when she'd realised Daniel was there, though—preferring to take-out rather than sit next to him in the last available chair.

That didn't just say something, it *shouted* something.

Daniel was loath to admit it, but his mother was right. He'd been acting like an ass. Kanako had tried to apologise, make up for, and explain why she'd lied the first time they'd met. But he'd insisted on holding the residual grudge... Possibly due to the fact his intense and immediate attraction to the woman scared him shitless.

It shouldn't matter to him if his Mother's latest artist in residence liked to fib her way out of potentially sticky situations. There was no justification as to why he'd been so furious about it in the first place. Except the first time he'd met Kanako, their lakeside introductions had been infused with a strange, almost magical quality. Conversing in Japanese had given him a taste of anonymous connection, no doubt the foundation for this unquenchable hunger he'd been battling. Inconvenient, and building in ferocity.

Unreciprocated, too, if Kanako's face when she recognised him in the café was anything to go by.

The mild case of bruised ego had brought Daniel to ground, and frankly, he wasn't used to the sensation. Lightly, and with good humour, Kanako had fleeced him. He'd bought her story hook, line, and sinker, and wasn't usually so unwitting. Then she'd proceeded to brush him off like bothersome lint. Multiple times.

Not that he was counting.

Kanako, and her striking golden eyes, had been dancing through Daniel's subconscious his entire business trip. With less physical rugby, and a lot more boardroom antics, the ensuing boredom had allowed plenty of scope for his mind to wander. Japan reminded him of the ceramicist in small, sensual bites; the graceful turn of a woman's head, the way a *takoyaki* seller handled her chopsticks with quick efficiency, the enticing scent of street-food, and the shy smile of a hostess—flowers woven into her hair.

Intriguing. He couldn't get past that. Kanako intrigued the hell out of him.

"Where are you heading?" Rugby was genial enough as they exited the café.

"I was going to walk down to the lake," Kana decided as she spoke.

"Mind if I walk with you?"

She turned to him in bewilderment. "Would you like to?"

"Yes," her landlord returned, the hazel-green of his eyes catching Kana's attention before she looked away.

"Help yourself, Mr Dante," she mimicked his earlier words as they walked, and wondered at his responding flinch.

Unsure why he'd opt to spend time with her, given his earlier coolness, she was still pondering possible reasons when he responded.

"Call me Daniel." It didn't sound like a request, but a command.

She thought about it for a full millisecond. "No. That's okay. You're my landlord, after all."

"Please."

"Please?" Again, she turned to him in surprise. Had he just said that? Had she imagined the beseeching tone?

"I was rude, at the café."

"At the café?" That was just his go-to demeanour. Rude. Entitled. Egotistical. "Forget about it." Kana decided to play magnanimously. She could do that, no problem. "Adele told me you like your own space, and don't enjoy people crashing your private party. I didn't mean to invade your bubble." She shrugged, taking a long sip from her take-out cup. "*Any* of your bubbles; café, house, hometown... I didn't know you were back." She skittered off topic, bending the truth a little.

Clem had said two more days. Not that Kana had been keeping track of her landlord's movements, but in the back of her mind she'd known he was due back at the farmhouse yesterday.

Rugby shocked her then by laughing.

Out *loud*.

His eyes crinkled up at the corners and he threw back his head, relaxed and full of mirth. The action made him appear more youthful, and suddenly, incredibly attractive.

Kana took a small step away from him, subtly widening the gap as they walked side by side down the sloped footpath. She did *not* want to find this man attractive.

Not even a smidgen.

"Adele means *fans*, Kanako, and I wouldn't put you in that category. Not by a long shot."

He always used her full name, and it shouldn't mean anything, but the timbre of his voice whenever he said it sent a shiver up her spine. A feel-good shiver. An *I-shouldn't-be-feeling-this* shiver

Though it was sunny, the lake was choppy and grey, churned up by the light wind. They sat at the stony water's edge, one stunted willow screening the township behind, and the lake stretching out in front. Kana pulled her knees close to her chest, feeling somewhat vulnerable around this man, and not particularly relishing the state.

"Are you planning on sharing that yoyo?" he teased, nodding towards the take-out biscuit bag at her feet.

Suddenly, she wasn't remotely hungry.

"You can have it if you like," she offered, handing it over.

Rugby studied Kana for some time before sliding the bag from her fingertips, and she felt a prickle of unease under his scrutiny—conscious of the scruffy state of her hair, and the dried clay on her jeans. She'd left the studio in a hurry, and hadn't put on a scratch of makeup.

"How about we split it? Saffy likes to do this."

Her landlord took out the sandwiched cookie and twisted the two halves apart, grimacing comically at the uneven result. There was much more icing on one side than the other.

He offered the two pieces up, and Kana's hand hovered, undecided.

"Take the icing. It's good."

She could hear the smile in his voice, but wasn't prepared for the softness in his eyes when she glanced up.

Was her landlord actually *flirting* with her?

Surely not.

A man like Rugby would be used to getting his own way, manoeuvring other people and their resolve. Kana didn't have to do what anybody else said, or cater for anyone else's master plan, no matter how attractive they might be.

She took the icing *light* half, maybe just to spite him.

Rugby startled her by grabbing her wrist as she moved it away, half-biscuit in hand.

"What were you thinking, just then?"

Kana forced a little laugh, her eyes flicking down to the band of fingers now holding her captive.

"I was thinking I've had enough sugar, recently," she hedged, pulling her wrist free.

"Liar," he negated, voice low.

"I beg your pardon?" Kana tried to inject the appropriate level of indignation, but came off sounding a bit out of breath.

Rugby laughed—and though Kana wanted to feel nothing, she felt a whole lot more than that. It wasn't just the depth of sound, but the warmth in his expression.

"Imagine I hold in my hand a small, but very potent syringe of truth serum…" Holding his thumb and forefinger a little apart, Rugby twisted his hand from side to side as if shaking up invisible contents "There's *just* enough for two doses." Flicking the veins of his inner elbow, he looked directly at her as he mimed the injection sliding into his vein. "Ahhh…"

The grimace of mock pain made her smirk.

When he loosened up, he was almost likeable.

Rugby put down his half-biscuit on the paper bag and held out his hand.

"Your turn."

"What? No."

"Don't you want to play?" he spoke with deceptive softness, eyes challenging.

Kana blinked at him, unsure where this was going, or why Rugby was putting in the effort to hook her into his silly game. She slowly extended her arm towards him anyway.

Expecting him to mime the injection sliding into her inner elbow, as he'd done to himself, she faltered when he took her wrist again, trailing one large thumb across the faint blue of the sensitive skin. She had just enough time to wonder if he could feel her pulse skitter in reaction to the intimate touch, before he plunged the imaginary truth serum into her vein.

"It takes a moment for it to kick in." Rugby continued with the pretence, releasing her arm as he leant back on his hands, out of her personal space but still holding her gaze. "Okay, here comes my truth. I find you very attractive. In fact, you're stunning. I haven't been able to stop thinking about you. Not since that first time at the lake, when you took off your sunglasses and scowled down your nose at me."

Seriously?

Kana stared at him.

Yup. Rugby appeared to be dead serious.

He'd been so much easier to deal with when he was wishing her off his property. This close-contact charm-offensive was much more focussed in its assault, and a lot more confusing.

"Ah, thank you, Mr Dante. Mr... ah, Daniel... D. Flattering, but—"

"Your serum should be taking effect about now," Rugby interrupted, somewhat grim.

"Right." Kana hugged her knees to herself again.

No point in hanging back. If she were upfront and honest, it'd clear the air and perhaps get their landlord-tenant relationship back on an even playing field.

She looked sideways at him. "I don't want to be attracted to you."

The statement had the opposite effect to what she'd been expecting. Rugby broke into a slow and beatific grin.

"*But...* you are."

"That's not what I said," Kana negated, realising belatedly it was exactly what she'd implied, and to be honest, exactly how she felt.

"I'm just out of a long-term relationship, and not looking for any complications."

"Who said I was aiming for complicated?"

"Just telling you where I stand." She rose with purpose, grabbing her empty cup with her free hand. She hadn't made it two steps when Rugby blocked her path. "What are you doing?" she snapped, agitation mounting.

"Did you know who I was when we first met?"

"No." she shook her head to confirm. "There wasn't any mention of a landlord on the application information."

"On the application…?" Rugby shadowed her speech with a frown. "The artist in residence form?"

She nodded.

The confusion on Rugby's forehead began to clear. "No, I meant did you *know*… You know what? It doesn't matter. I think you just answered that. Why did you pretend to be a tourist?"

Kana drew a big, dramatic sigh. "I tried to explain this already. *You* made out like I was a tourist."

"I did not. I asked you if you were lost. Polite-local-guy helps woman-with-open-map. Woman thinks, who *is* this hot guy?" Rugby grinned. "It was a very simple plan."

"Well, I *wasn't* lost," Kana muttered, a little incensed he was finding this funny.

"But you *did* think I was hot?"

There he went with his big ego again. She moved to step around him.

"One more question. Did you take my Saturday newspaper?" The words were softer this time, like they meant more.

Kana hesitated only for a moment. "Yes. Sorry. I used it for clay without thinking."

"You read it first, though." It was a statement, not a question.

"No. I don't read the paper. It's too depressing. I needed it as stuffing for a hand-built piece." Kana frowned, thinking back. "There's one bit I remember though. A headline. *'Doctors Fail To…'* I don't know what they failed to do, because I'd already ripped that piece out and used it. It's bugged me ever since."

"Has it, now?" Rugby considered her with an intent gleam.

"It has. Yes."

"There's something *I've* failed to do." The corner of Rugby's mouth tugged back up into a smile, and Kana was conscious of a faint warning bell going off in her head. There was something very unpredictable about this man. "One more minute of your time. I've been wanting to try something out…"

His hands moved to her shoulders and rested lightly, and Kana could've pulled away from him when she realised what he intended to do. Those hazel eyes told her *exactly* what he was up to.

Instead she stood stock-still as Rugby's head lowered, and his lips slid softly atop hers.

He was so *warm*. Heat radiated off the man in waves, awakening her mouth and firing up her pulse as she took in the scent of him. He smelt of the lake, and the trees at the farm... beech honey, and the twisted roots beneath their feet.

Everything earthy, and alive.

One hand left her shoulder, easing behind her neck to tangle into her hair, drawing her head inexorably back. Kana sighed as she opened her lips to the gentle caress of his mouth.

Great Buddha, he was good at this, and it'd been a long, long time since she'd gotten so lost in a simple kiss.

Kana didn't know when her hands had come up to rest on Daniel's chest, but that's where she found them—complete with half a crushed yoyo biscuit and slightly crumpled take-out cup—when the man pulled back by slow degrees. He was smiling down at her when she opened her eyes.

He should smile more often. It softened all his hard edges.

Daniel. Her landlord. Mr Rugby. Dante bloody D.

"Still not attracted to me?"

"Nope. Don't think so," Kana lied, barefaced, as she blinked up at him.

"Truth serum worn off, then?" Daniel teased.

"Maybe." She allowed a small smile in return before stepping back, out of Daniel's reach. "But I think your minute's up, Mr Dante."

"Call me Mr Dante again, and I won't be held responsible for my actions," Daniel called after her, but there was a smile in his voice, and he didn't make any move to stop her as she left.

Kana could feel his eyes on her as she slipped away, slightly kiss-drunk and brushing crumbs off the front of her sweater.

What the hell had she just gotten herself into?

10

HEALTH OR DISEASE

"Every human being is the author
of his own health or disease."
- Buddha

The Ruby Island clean-up day arrived crisp and sunny. Although Kana knew she had a day of potentially gruelling work ahead of her, she was also excited—itching to get over the water and explore.

Sitting down to her breakfast cup of tea on her front doorstep, she found the cancellation text from Adele.

So sorry! Have to pull out. Tummy bug going around school & Saffy threw up in the night. Keeping her home today. I'll arrange someone else to pick you up at eight, and get you to the wharf. Is that okay?

Kana texted back in the affirmative.

When Clem arrived, right on time, it was a relief to see someone she knew, rather than a stranger.

Kana climbed into his beaten up farm truck with a genuine smile on her face. The older gentleman was a pleasure to talk to—quick to tell stories or crack a joke.

Her smile faltered when Clem nosed the truck away from the main gate and up towards the farmhouse.

"Is Poppy back?" she hazarded.

"Nope. We're giving Dan a lift down to the dock as well. Hope you don't mind a bit of a squeeze?" Clem threw her a sideways glance. "It's not far."

Kana looked down at the front bench seat in the snug cab. Clem wasn't a small man, and neither was Daniel, which meant the farmer's idea of 'a bit of a squeeze' was looking a lot more like a game of sardines.

"Ah, no. That's fine," she breezed, but was still chewing on her bottom lip when they parked in front of the farmhouse. Scooting into the centre seat, she fastened the lap belt as Clem hopped out.

Nerves ate at her. It had been fairly simple to keep out of Daniel's way since he'd kissed her on the lake-shore a couple of days ago, but it'd never crossed her mind he'd be involved in this island clean-up thing.

———

When Daniel threw his daypack into the back of the pickup, he spotted Kanako's distinctive lime-green one, settled next to Clem's canvas fishing satchel. Eyes skipping to the cab, he could just make out a human form through the thick layer of dirt obscuring the back window.

He'd been groggy this morning, having slept badly, but was suddenly wide-awake.

"Got company?"

Clem chuckled. "Of the best kind." He eyed Daniel knowingly across the deck of the truck. "You behave now," he warned in a low tone.

"Clementine, I *always* behave," Daniel lied.

"Yeah." Clem laughed outright. "You behave—like a man with his own best interests at heart."

"Is there any other way?" Daniel joked, before wrenching open the rusted passenger door.

"Yes, young man," Clem returned with great seriousness over the cab roof. "I think you'll discover there is."

Kanako sat upright and rigid in the very centre of the bench seat, looking straight ahead with her hands pressed between her knees. She turned with a quick glance and tight smile as Daniel squeezed in next to her, arm and thigh inescapably bumping up against hers in the limited space.

Wearing walking boots, and colourful polypropylene under denim shorts, Kanako looked like an advertisement for trail mix, or fruit-and-nut bars.

Fresh faced, and glowing with a faint blush, she could easily be mistaken for something edible. She smelt good too, lemony-clean and feminine. In the close confines of the cab, Daniel's groin reacted on autopilot, and he struggled to keep the corresponding groan internal.

The last thing he needed was a reminder of Kanako's potent effect on him. This short trip bore all the hallmarks of exquisite hell.

Daniel had laid his first card on the table down at the lake—the next move was up to Kanako. He was damned uneasy to realise he had no idea if she'd be interested enough to make one.

"Good morning." Starched politeness oozed out of Kanako's every pore.

"*Ohayo gozaimasu*," he returned the greeting in Japanese, and got another good look at Kanako's fascinating eyes for his trouble when she glanced up at him, startled.

"*Ohayo*," Kanako finally conceded, then turned back to speak to Clem as the older man climbed in.

Kanako refused to acknowledge Daniel's presence for the rest of the short trip, chatting to Clem instead. She asked questions about Ruby Island and its history—about Clem's farming property and family.

She seemed determined to bluff it out, pretending her thigh, hip, and elbow weren't pressing into Daniel's, and that she wasn't burning up from the heat of body against body. If her shallow breathing and peachy glow were anything to go by, she was feeling the physical side of it just as much as he was.

But in a good way, or a bad way?

As soon as Clem stopped the truck and got out, Kanako scooted across and escaped out the driver's side, her urgency almost comical.

Daniel wasn't remotely match-fit for romantic pursuit, and the realisation slammed him with self-deprecation. The potter hadn't exactly blown him off, but she wasn't beating down his door, either.

Refreshing, to say the least.

For what seemed like eternity, he'd been experiencing the polar opposite from the women he met. So much so, he'd almost forgotten the thrill of the chase. There was a huge element of uncertainty to it, the cliff-edge of potential failure counterbalanced by the possibility of sweet success.

Kanako wouldn't be easy to convince, and she sure as hell wasn't a sure bet, but Daniel found himself unfazed by those salient facts. There was just something about her. Something real. She lit a fire under him; shot him with a tangible surge of adrenaline, and he found he had both the time and the inclination to follow up on it.

If he could just remember how.

Kanako's lips were on his mind—soft and pliant when he'd kissed her by the lake, drawing him in. Undeniable chemistry had surged between them. A pure hit, followed by an incredible, searing heat. Like fearlessly grabbing an electric fence with both hands.

There'd been shocked disbelief in Kanako's eyes when she'd opened them to stare up at him for a moment afterwards, mirroring exactly what he'd felt himself. Instant addiction.

But he could so easily have read her wrong.

Daniel sat for a while longer, watching as the small gathering grew. Mostly middle-aged and older-generation residents, coming together to help with the working bee. On the whole, they were a decent bunch of people, and he considered himself lucky to have ended up in this particular community. Right now though, his eyes were seeking out another hit of chilli-chocolate braids, and the flash of a lime-green backpack.

Carissa and Marianne were unashamedly running the show. They organised and bossed, with bulldog-clipped notes, maps, tools, and job lists. They assigned volunteers under team leaders, and made sure everyone was kitted out with life jackets, sunscreen, bottled water, and food for the day.

Kana's nervousness evaporated, and excitement built as the group began loading the five motorboats they'd be taking across the lake. She hadn't seen Daniel since their arrival in Clem's truck, and was now looking forward to the trip across the crystal water almost as much as setting foot on the island.

"Tie these to your backpack." Carissa handed her three plastic bags, each one tied in a knot. "Collect any rubbish you find as you go, and there'll be bigger rubbish bags to empty it into at lunchtime."

"People leave rubbish?"

Carissa nodded. "I'm afraid so. Here's your map. I've put you in Daniel's boat." She placed a concise tick next to Kana's name and pointed to the sleek white speedboat at the end of the dock.

"Of course you have," Kana muttered under her breath as Carissa moved off, officiating as she went.

Kana waited until the last minute, helping pack the other boats and handing people on before walking the length of the dock. She was supremely relieved to see Clem was once again with them, and she wouldn't be alone with Daniel.

Clem passed Kana and her backpack down before clambering in himself, a cheeky grin showing hints of what his broad face would've looked like in younger years. With his fisherman's hat pushed far back on his head, he claimed his half of the back seat with his battered satchel.

"Don't you have a boat, Clem?" Kana dumped her bag beside his, thinking of the salmon he'd brought to pizza night.

"Yes, I do." Clem scratched at his jaw. "More of a dinghy, really. Nothing as flash as this one. I'm hoping to get my hands on *Yen* in a poker game." He chuckled.

"*Yen*?" Kana was momentarily confused. Clem and Daniel played cards with Japanese currency?

"*Yen*'s the boat's name." Daniel unfolded from stashing some tools and supplies in the front of the hull, looking Kana up and down.

Her temperature rose.

"Come here," he growled.

Mr Demanding, upping her heart rate.

When she ignored him, Daniel tugged on her life-jacket strap, and she took a stumbled step forward. He seemed so *big* all of a sudden, his feet spread wide to counteract the unpredictable movement of the boat. His expression, as always, bordered on unfriendly before it softened. It took her a moment to realise what his hands were up to, pulling the bright yellow floatation device lower, so it sat more firmly on her shoulders. He tightened the waist strap, then moved to work on her chest buckle.

Acutely aware of Clem watching, a knowing smirk on his face, Kana slapped Daniel's hands away. "I can do it," she insisted, securing the chest strap herself.

"It needs to be snug to do its job." Again Daniel spoke gruffly, staring down at her for a long moment before turning to start up the engine.

"I'm not a child." She eyed the breadth of his back mulishly.

"Then don't act like one." Daniel may've muttered the words, but Kana heard them, loud and clear.

Clem cast off the ropes and settled back into the plush white seating with Kanako, as Daniel drove. The older man appeared to be thoroughly enjoying himself in the potter's company, brimming with sociality as they sped across the lake, following the other boats. The sheep farmer usually came across as shy in company, letting Daniel's mother do all the talking when they were out and about together.

Daniel frowned, realising how unusual it'd become to see the two of them apart. Clem and Poppy. Poppy and Clem. If Clem's jovial, self-depreciatory conversation with Kanako was to be believed, he proposed to Daniel's mother on a regular basis, and she refused him just as frequently.

Huh. That was news to Daniel.

No one but Poppy could answer why she would consistently refuse someone she didn't seem to be able to get enough of. She was her own person—a highly independent woman.

Daniel's father, Gray, had been dead for almost twenty years, but his presence still loomed large. Maybe that had something to do with it?

Daniels's agitation about the life-jacket situation eased as they got further out onto the lake. Very little wind meant very little swell, though he couldn't help glancing back at the occupants of the bench-seat every now and again.

Purely for safety reasons, he told himself. Nothing to do with the strange warming in his chest to see these two, relaxed and clearly enjoying each other's company.

Giving up on trying to catch the spray with her hand over the side, Kanako had turned her face up to the sun and now basked in the autumn glow, her two side-braids whipping back in the wind.

Daniel thought about the potter's solid progress with Halfback. He also mulled over her connection with Adele and Saffy—the school trouble his cousin had informed him of, and Kanako's positive input.

She had a real spark, this woman. Feisty, but kind. Definitely able to stand firmly on her own two feet, which was attractive as all hell. No glitz, no glamour, but a serenity transcending both.

Kanako definitely wasn't one to fawn over celebrity... Though maybe she wouldn't be all that keen to be seen with it, either?

"You like speed?" Clem raised his voice to be heard over the drone of the engine.

"*Love* it!" Kanako laughed.

"Ever been at the controls before?"

"No."

"Ah. *Shame*! That's the best bit!" Clem rose, keeping his centre low and his feet widespread, angling forward to grip the back of Daniel's seat.

"Hey, Dan! How about giving the little lady a go at the helm?"

Daniel moved the throttle back slowly until they were all but idling. He turned and narrowed his eyes at Clem's wicked grin, before switching focus back to Kanako.

The only sound was the slap of water on the side of the hull, and the rasp if bristle on skin as Daniel ran a hand over his jaw.

"You want a turn?"

"*Can* I?" Kanako looked like she was about to clap her hands and stamp her feet in excitement, golden eyes shining.

Clem half-smothered a chuckle, the cheeky bastard, knowing full well no one was ever invited to handle Daniel's boat other than himself. The farmer didn't bother feigning apology, either, instead adding under his breath, "Resist *that,* you big brute."

Daniel couldn't, of course.

Clearly satisfied with his shit-stirring, Clem re-settled himself on the comfy squabs and relaxed, as Kanako scrambled into Daniel's place to take her first boat-driving lesson. She looked small and potentially breakable gracing the drivers seat, and it took Daniel a while to unclench. It wasn't like anything tragic was going to happen on his watch.

Yen responded well to the turns and paces Daniel set for Kanako, giving her a feel for the controls while drilling safety measures in at every opportunity.

Kanako's gleeful whoops and Clem's low laughter were the soundtrack for the rest of the short trip, and by the time they reached the dock, Daniel had forgotten his earlier tension altogether.

Ruby Island was larger than Kana had first thought. The little dock nestled at the low lying waist of land, but hillocks rose on either side, with groves of trees, rocky outcrops, and patches of grassland.

They were the last boat to arrive, and as Kana thanked Daniel for the lesson, she regretfully relinquished the controls so he could ease them into the crowded dock.

Clem and Daniel had been assigned to jetty maintenance in the morning, while Kana assisted Marianne on a section of shore clean-up. Other groups took weed-whackers and loppers towards the picnic tables on higher ground, and still more carried spades for path clearing.

Marianne, like her sister, was a talker. She chatted away as they worked, beginning at the small beach and moving their way around the rocks, wearing gardening gloves for protection. Kana learned more about the history of Wānaka in one morning than she would've thought possible.

They found beer and cola cans, random bits of plastic, fishing equipment, picnic paraphernalia, and the odd piece of clothing.

"If you find any broken glass, I have some newspaper in my backpack to wrap it in," Marianne informed her.

The morning sped by, Kana thankful for the sunhat she'd

brought to protect her face, although her scalp grew clammy with the sun beating down.

"Lunchtime!" Marianne called chirpily when her cell phone sounded. She must've been in her seventies, but was unbelievably agile, scrambling over rough terrain like a rock crab.

The volunteers met under the willows on the saddle, and though they'd all packed lunches, a few had also brought containers of home-baking to share. It was a convivial group, discussing the work they'd completed, and what was still to do.

Kana noticed Daniel and Clem had settled themselves on a log a little separate from the group, with a first-aid kit open beside them. Clem was hunched over Daniel's hand, concentrating hard, while the younger man sat, stony faced.

"What happened?"

Daniel glanced up through obscenely lush eyelashes, his dark hair damp, and holding more curl than usual. Vividly and viscerally reminded of the view of him opening his door to her on pizza night, shirtless and wet, Kana swallowed.

Dishevelled suited this man altogether too well.

The afternoon had just taken on a different calibre of sultry, and Kana resisted the urge to fan herself.

"Splinter," Clem answered distractedly. "Can't move the bugger. Have you got good eyes?"

"Twenty-twenty. Want me to have a look?" Pretending the proximity changed nothing—the heat radiating off the big man's skin meant zip—Kana took Clem's place along with the tweezers and held Daniel's large hand in hers. Bringing it close to her nose for inspection, she muttered, "Wowza, that's not a splinter, it's a log."

Clem chuckled.

A solid chunk of the wood from the docking planks was embedded into the fleshy part at the base of Daniel's thumb, already swollen and irritated by the intrusion.

It must've been incredibly painful.

Glancing up, Kana met amused eyes.

The deep-green of Daniel's T-shirt commandeered his irises to match, and today they were almost jade. Kana had first noticed it in the confines of Clem's truck, and she noticed it all over again as she held his hand.

She was loath to admit it, but the temperature between the two of them had skyrocketed since that kiss. She cleared her throat, suddenly parched.

"*Itai desu ka?*" She gave the surrounding skin a light press, offering Daniel the privacy of the second language in case he didn't want Clem to overhear him talking about pain.

"*Ma ma… Chotto itai, dake,*" Daniel negated, his voice all low and rumbly.

The sensuality of Daniel speaking Japanese to her added a whole other level of intimacy.

How did he manage to make the moment seem so incredibly secluded, despite the hodgepodge group of people all around them, and Clem sitting at her back? It was the way he looked at her as if she was the only other person on the island.

He probably makes everyone feel that way, Kana scolded herself, pressing her knees tightly together in an effort to ignore the little electric zing.

Trust a man to pretend it didn't hurt much. But the splinter would be easy to remove if Daniel kept up the pretence, and remained still.

With a combination of tweezing and applying pressure, Kana was able to dig deep enough to grab hold of the end of the wood. Sliding it clear in one piece, she held it up in elation.

"I believe you enjoyed that." Daniel caught her eye again, making heat prickle on the back of her neck.

"Not as much as I'll enjoy this part." Kana flashed him an apologetic smile as she got out Dettol and a swab, liberally washing the wound.

Daniel didn't even flinch.

"Tough guy, eh?" She couldn't help teasing him, giving the wound a decent blob of antiseptic cream before covering it up with two large Band-Aids in an x-marks-the-spot. "That'll sting for a bit."

"I think I'll live." Daniel grabbed her fingers with his undamaged hand as she made to move away. Turning her palm upward facing, he placed a firm, hot kiss there before folding her fingers shut over it. "Thank you."

"*Sheesh!*" Clem stirred behind Kana. "I'm glad I couldn't get the bugger out, if that's what was on offer as payment."

Kana turned to him, opening her mouth to speak.

"Oh, glory-be!" Clem exclaimed, eyes focussed the rest of the clean-up crew, a weirdly plastic smile on his face. "Here comes Talulah with an offering of rock-hard savoury scones." He semi-covered his mouth with his fingers, but kept talking urgently in an undertone. "Kana, listen to me. You're to take one of those, polite as anything, then slip it into your pocket when no one's looking. Dry-as-a-bone and hard enough to break teeth," he finished in a hoarse whisper as Talulah, the school's part-time librarian and art teacher, neared with a shy smile.

"Bacon and cheese scone, anyone?"

"Oh, that's very kind of you, Talulah." Kana took one tentatively, avoiding eye contact with the hulking men sitting either side of her.

"They look great." Daniel followed suit, offering Talulah a slow, lazy grin. The librarian blushed to the roots of her hair, one hand pressed to her chest.

Kana knew *exactly* how the woman felt.

"Thank you, don't mind if I do." Clem removed the last scone from the Tupperware container, turning Talulah's faltering smile into a beaming one.

"Hide these!" Daniel shoved two more savoury scones into the top of Kana's backpack just as she was zipping it closed, lunch break over.

"Where did you get those?"

"Marianne." Daniel looked around furtively. "My pockets are already full."

"So *everyone* does it?" Kana huffed, indignant. "Why doesn't someone just tell her?"

"And ruin that smile?" Daniel shrugged. "No one has the heart."

"Pussies," Kana scoffed, but she was semi-joking. Hadn't she just played along with it herself?

"Okay. Coast is clear. Come with me." Daniel grabbed her hand and took off with a momentum that had Kana stumbling after him.

"Wait! Where are we going?"

"We're on feeding detail."

Feeding detail? Like that made any sense.

The path Daniel took wound through scrubby bush, eventually leading to the vineyard-facing side of the island… And a sheer drop.

Kana's heart shuddered, the familiar buzz of warning beginning in her toes, and shooting up from there. Very little ground lay between the two of them and a whole lot of nothing.

The large hand holding hers tightened once as they neared the edge, then let go. "I came here once with Nana Nona when I was a kid, and she showed me this very spot." Daniel's voice was low and soothing as he knelt on the flat rock, so maybe he could sense Kana's nerves jangling.

He began emptying his pockets of rock hard scones—five in all.

Kana hung back, sliding off her backpack to take out Marianne's two scones, plus the one she'd ferreted away in her pocket.

Sitting on his heels, Daniel crumbled the baking. Picking out pieces of bacon and saving them, he threw the crumbs further away, where sparrows and finches were already gathering to squabble over the spoils. Then, sliding his legs back into plank position, he lay flat on his chest, peering over the precipice as he drip-fed bacon pieces over the side.

"What are you feeding down there?" Not sure why she felt the need to whisper, Kana was positive Daniel was laughing at her when he turned around to grin.

"Come and see."

She looked at the scones in her hand, then at Daniel, sprawled on the rock. She looked at the cliff edge, and the deep water beyond.

What the hell, you only live once… Or twice.

Kana took her time getting down, easing herself forward on her hands and knees.

Daniel ignored her slow progress and continued slipping bacon over the edge until she was lying fully beside him.

"Afraid of dogs *and* heights?" he teased.

"Yes, but not for the usual reason."

Daniel turned to her, his tanned face very close and eyes unbelievably green. "What's the usual reason?"

"Afraid you'll fall, or slip. I'm the opposite. I look at the edge and I'm afraid I'm going to jump. It makes me want to jump," she clarified, a little wary admitting the weird neurosis to Daniel, of all people. "It's ridiculous."

"Is it, though?"

"I don't know. Most people think so. It used to freak the hell out of my mother when I was little."

Daniel laughed, deep in his belly. It wasn't the first time Kana had watched his face do that—lose all the strain and really relax into mirth. It was so attractive she forgot to breathe for a minute, and by the time she did the air burnt her lungs.

"I should take you up skydiving sometime. Jumping's encouraged."

"I've always wanted to try that, is there a jump site near here?" Kana could just as easily go on her own. Much less latent danger.

"Yeah. The view's outstanding. I'm addicted, to tell the truth." Daniel cleared his throat, and a shadow passed over his features. "I'm glad you didn't jump here though, Kanako. There's a shelf down there." He nodded over the edge, and Kana edged forward to get a better look, unreservedly enjoying the way he said her name with all the syllables evenly spaced.

Less than a metre under the water was a naturally occurring stone shelf running about thirty centimetres wide, with globs of scone-covered bacon resting on it. Kana started when she felt the weight of Daniel's hand on the back of her denim shorts, his thumb sliding through the belt loop.

"That's far enough, kiddo," Daniel cautioned gruffly, and it was her turn to laugh.

"It's alright, I'm not planning on taking a dip," she promised, but Daniel's hand remained where it was. "What are we feeding, then?"

"Patience. Wait and see. Here they come."

There was a shadow of movement lower in the depths, and Kana watched, fascinated, as first one, and then two dark bodies emerged to slither over the water-covered shelf. Emulating snakes with their movement and death with their eyes, the eels followed the scent of food.

"They're *huge*!"

"Yeah, those ones are pretty big. Here comes a juvenile." Daniel slid the remaining handful of bacon towards Kana. "They can smell the meat."

Kana shuddered.

After a few minutes, there were multiple writhing bodies below, making it difficult to see where one eel ended and another began.

"It looks like an orgy down there." As soon as the words were out of her mouth, Kana wished them unsaid, and she chewed on her lower lip.

Daniel looked at her sideways, and seemed to hesitate for a long moment, their faces so close it was difficult to remember what they'd been talking about.

"I'll take your word for it," he finally replied, pushing back to sit on his heels and brushing off his T-shirt. "I'm out of scones."

The small of Kana's back felt bereft, it had gotten so used to the weight of Daniel's hand on it. She'd been wondering if he'd try to kiss her again, and was now left pondering why he hadn't.

That would've been the perfect moment, right?

Maybe a single taste had been enough for Daniel Dante? Exactly as the rugby star had said at the time, he'd just wanted to try it out.

Like fishing with the intent to catch-and-release.

Kana was no expert on kissing strangers, but perhaps it was an arrogance she should've expected from such a well-known player. Reel her in just to show he could, then toss her back out.

She touched one finger briefly to her top lip, remembering the delicious heat, while wishing it away in the same instance. Pasting a small, polite smile on her face before getting up, Kana joined the tall, dark, and unfortunately sexy man who was waiting for her by the path.

11

HAPPINESS

"There is no path to happiness:
happiness is the path."
- Buddha

Daniel knocked on the door of the barn and waited. He'd tried the annex already with no luck, but assumed Kanako was somewhere around as her SUV was parked out front, and he could see her backpack hanging on the hook inside the door.

Unless she was up on the property somewhere.

Yoga in the orchard?

He squinted uphill. Realising he had no idea what else Kanako liked to do with her time, he knocked again, looking around himself.

There was a large pot of mixed herbs that hadn't been there when the last tenant was in residence, thyme and rosemary growing in profusion next to the annex step, and some kind of bowl on the other side. He frowned and moved over to it, giving it a tap with his boot.

A stainless steel dog's bowl, filled with fresh water.

Kanako poked her head out of the barn at that moment. Her hair lay in one thick braid over the shoulder of her fleeced cotton shirt, and she had two elbow-length kiln mitts tucked under one arm.

"Sorry. I was in the middle of unloading the kiln," Kanako burbled, obviously excited. Her cheeks were pink and there was a barely contained energy buzzing about her.

Daniel remembered the sun dance he'd interrupted once before, and wondered if Kanako would've been doing another one right now if her landlord wasn't standing on her doorstep.

"Bisque or glaze?" he asked, subtly angling for an invitation into the barn to see the work she'd been producing.

"Oh!" Kanako blinked across at him, clearly surprised. "Bisque. I forgot you have potters at the annex all the time, and of course your grandmother…" she trailed off, looking slightly nonplussed.

Her confusion made Daniel wonder if he'd come across as an uncultured rugby-head. Brawn without brains? It wouldn't be the first time.

"You're welcome to have a look if you like. Anytime." She pushed the barn door further open with a hard shove.

"If that door's giving you trouble, I can re-oil it for you." Daniel followed her into the darker space and moved towards the workbenches, lit naturally by the large bank of windows on the far wall.

"No. It's fine. I can hear people coming, which is a good thing. How's the palm?" She looked pointedly at the hand she'd pulled the splinter out of, so he held it out for inspection.

"No worse for wear." He wiggled his fingers to prove it, realising as he did so the potbelly wasn't lit.

Although the open kilns warmed the air on one side, the exhaust vents pulled the majority of the energy from the barn. Kanako's workspace was practically arctic.

"You haven't got the stove on. Have you got enough fuel?" He strode over to the other side of the barn where the small fire stood, angry with himself for not giving Kanako's needs enough thought. He'd largely avoided being down here at all with this particular tenant, and as a consequence, had potentially reneged on his landlord duties.

"No. And yes. There's plenty of wood, but I'm on the kilns today, so I don't need it. Also…" Kanako nodded towards some large, covered pieces on one of the workbenches. "I'm putting the last touches on one of these and don't want it to dry out too fast."

Daniel glanced towards the shapes. The two shrouded in cotton sheeting sat at less than half a metre in height. The third was twice as large and narrower at the top, completely swathed in plastic.

"Urns?"

"No." Kana turned to smile at him, and her golden eyes caught the light from the window, shining with a secret light. "Something else entirely."

She motioned towards the kilns. Two large pieces radiated freshly bisqued warmth from the loading bench, the paleness of the clay almost luminescent, and Daniel was hit by a wave of disbelief as he strode forward to get a closer look.

"Careful, they're still hot," Kana warned.

No wonder she'd been so excited. Her artwork was incredible.

Saffy and Adele, in stylised form, had been crafted with superb attention to detail. Saffy's likeness was built a little shorter, her hair in the cornrows she often wore, while Adele's curls had escaped her hair-tie to frame her face.

"God." Daniel flicked a stunned glance back towards the artist, before staring again at her work. The trapped warmth radiated off the stoneware, and onto his face.

He hadn't given Kanako enough due credit as a creative; had never taken the time to wonder what kind of work she was producing down here until recently. Poppy always chose skilled artists, but the pure beauty of these portraits simply blew him away...

The stylised features, the human need.

"They're amazing. I want them."

Kanako laughed in delight, clapping her hands together.

"Great response! Okay, watch this." Sliding her mitts back on, Kanako edged the two large pieces together, inch by bench-scraping inch, until the busts were touching.

Daniel could suddenly see what Kanako had done—why the faces, angled softly to either side, had such content smiles. They were leaning on each other, hugging. Somehow Kanako had conveyed the love between mother and daughter, and the necessity of one to the other.

"This series is called Two Halves. Two halves of a unit making a whole," Kanako elaborated.

"I'm not kidding. I really want them. Name your price." He turned back to her, trying to convey how serious he was, but Kanako merely laughed again.

"They're not glazed, and not for sale… Yet. These are for my first-term exhibition at the gallery." Kanako studied him, and he felt her intensity burn. "But I *will* note your expression of interest to the gallery before we show, if you like. You'll have the option to buy beforehand, and they'll put a 'sold' sticker on it for the show."

"Yes." Both visceral and spoken response was immediate. "Do that." He moved to the huge shelving units where more large pieces sat—wrapped and unwrapped, glazed and unglazed—hungry to see more. A serious faced man in formal kimono stared back, oozing authority. "Who is this?"

"That's Tanaka-sensei. My tutor. More than that really, my mentor, and his wife." Kanako carefully unwrapped the second glazed bust from bubble wrap. "Yukiko-san."

Glazed clear, the white clay shone through in all its minutely worked detail, the woman's soft, Mona Lisa smile overwhelmingly magnetic.

"How do these two fit together?"

"They're a little more formal, more Japanese. I'm calling this one Marriage. She's in front, with her back to him, and the birds reach beaks towards each other. Opposites attract. It's a bit old-time-romantic, really," Kanako shrugged, suddenly appearing shy, and not so sure of herself.

"I think they're exceptional," Daniel confirmed, in case she'd misread his overall impression. "Will the Tanakas be at your exhibition in person?"

"Oh, no. Only in spirit." Kanako stroked the cheek of the serene pottery woman once, before re-wrapping her. "They've both passed away." She moved away from Daniel, but not before he caught the flash of sadness overlaying her features.

"I'm sorry to hear that. You worked these from memory then, or photos?"

"From memory."

"And Adele and Saffy?"

"From memory, mostly. But I couldn't get Saffy's chin right, so she came in to sit for me for that bit."

"She has her father's chin," Daniel muttered absently.

"Did you know Moses well?" Kanako queried, and he turned to her on a knife-edge of shock.

"Adele talked to you about Moses?"

"Just in passing." Kanako shrugged one shoulder up towards her ear.

"Just in passing," Daniel repeated in disbelief, watching Kanako's efficient, no-nonsense movements—putting her mitts away, hanging up her heat resistant apron, and switching off the fans.

Poppy was right, Adele had found someone to talk to.

The sudden silence in the studio was louder than the continuous noise the extractor fans had made.

Moses had come and gone like a whirlwind, and Adele, straight out of high school, had fallen hard. Daniel held no malice towards the man, though he'd left carnage in his wake. He liked to believe Moses had felt the same for Adele at the time. But their circumstances... They'd had no choice but to be apart.

"What are you working on now?" Changing the subject with purpose, Daniel moved back towards the workbench with the greenware.

Kanako seemed to pick up some nervous energy as he got closer, and though she fussed with the thin plastic on the largest one, she didn't move to unwrap it. Turning to look at him, her fidgety fingers were compounded by the cornered look she threw his way.

"More busts."

"Of...?"

She hesitated, then lifted the cotton off the smallest of the three.

It was Halfback, the dog's soulful expression and long snout unmistakable, one ear cocked in query as he looked up.

"*Jeee*-sus." Daniel hunkered down low to examine the details.

Kanako had even gotten his old collar right, the splitting leather at the buckle, and bent tags.

How the hell did you even begin to make something like this out of clay?

"You recognise him, then?"

"Absolutely."

"Oh, good." Kanako seemed to relax a little. "This is the second attempt. The first one didn't have the right… um, atmosphere."

"You've obviously studied him in some detail. How did you get close enough?" Daniel unfolded to his full height again. "You two didn't exactly hit it off, originally."

"Oh." Kanako's cheeks flushed and one hand came up to her ear, fingertips playing with the soft lobe. "Clem helped me a little there, and I've put a water bowl out, so Halfback comes by sometimes after he's been…" She shifted her weight from one foot to the other. "You know, chasing stuff."

Clem. That figured.

"So what's the pair to the dog?" Daniel indicated towards the other two pieces, still wrapped on the workbench.

He got the distinct impression Kanako was stalling.

"Actually, you could possibly help me with that." She fidgeted with her plait, then flicked it over her shoulder so it lay in a thick auburn cord down her spine. "I got a bit stuck on that one, too." Stepping forward, she surprised him into silence by placing two fingers briefly on the bridge of his nose. "I have the nose now, I think. But Clem's right, your eyebrows are a little less foreboding than I first imagined."

Daniel held his breath as Kanako's fingers moved to follow the line of his brow.

"And I wasn't sure…" She eased to one side and tucked his hair gently behind his ear. He felt the shock of it tingle all the way down his spine. "Oh! You have very nice ears, for a rugby player."

"Thank you," Daniel choked out. "First-five doesn't usually get caught in rucks, and I was never in the scrum, so…" He shrugged.

"Is that right?" Kanako wrinkled up her nose. "I don't know much about it, but better out than in, I'd assume."

"Mmm," he answered noncommittally. The fact Kanako was standing so close, studying him, had him buzzing with awareness. Her soft touch moved to his cheekbone, then skittered along the line of his unshaven jaw. She wasn't flirting, exactly, but it was the closest Kanako had ever come to it, and definitely the first time she'd ever voluntarily touched him with anything other than politeness.

"I take it Halfback and I are a pair?" he mused in a low voice, not wanting to scare her off.

"Yes."

"Will you show me?"

"No." Kanako's eyes flickered as they met his, her hand immediately dropping back to her side. "Not yet."

"When?"

Kanako laughed suddenly, her face shining up at him. "When I say so."

"And when do I get to kiss you again?" Daniel slid the request in silkily.

"Um…" Kanako looked at his lips, then back into his eyes.

She didn't move any closer, but she wasn't moving away either, and Daniel's blood immediately felt thicker in his veins.

"When I say so," Kanako repeated in a whisper.

"*Say* so, Kanako. You're killing me, here."

Kana laughed again to cover her nerves, moving to re-cover the bust of Halfback. She wasn't used to this game, and found her fingers were shaking.

She'd wanted to kiss Daniel since she'd found him at the barn door in his black hoodie this morning. Since he'd given her an impromptu boat-driving lesson on the way to Ruby Island. Since he'd been squished up against her, playing sardines in Clem's truck.

This gnawing curiosity had been irritating Kana on and off since he'd kissed her on the lakeshore, if she was being honest. Though she'd been desperately trying to hold the compulsion at bay.

It was difficult to think of anything else now he'd mentioned it.

Daniel seemed to be the type of man who took whatever he wanted, so until he'd made that comment about kissing, she'd just assumed he *hadn't* wanted it.

Not like she did.

Daniel was her landlord. Some crazy kind of auto-rebound thing her body had decided on without her say-so. A cocky, arrogant, sexy distraction to her work… That was all.

A distraction who happened to be standing too close for comfort.

Kana took a deep, steadying breath, and a small step sideways.

"I wanted to thank you for your generosity with the artist in residence opportunity," she began formally. "I'm very grateful for the chance to work in such a fantastic studio."

Daniel sighed, pushing his fists into his front pockets and eyeing her across the space she'd just manoeuvred between them.

"Thanks aren't necessary. Mum runs it. She chose you."

"I tried to thank her, but she says it's your funds that cover everything. You're financially supporting the artists that come here —supporting me with my pottery—and that *does* deserve my thanks. I really needed it. I had to... " Best not to get into the details, and come across as desperate. "Well, suffice to say, it meant a great deal to me."

Daniel blinked at her for several seconds. "Glad to be of service." He finally turned away. "Thank you for showing me your work, Kanako. It's phenomenal." He glanced back at the shelving unit along the barn wall, well stocked with pottery in all stages of creation. "I'll let you get back to it." The words were wooden, and spoken as he made his way toward the light spilling from the open barn door.

He was about to step outside when she spoke from behind him, having tailed him there. "My castle is your castle, Dante D. Literally. You're welcome anytime, of course."

Daniel shook his head. "Don't call me that." Though his voice was little more than a groan, his brows when he turned were almost as heavy as she'd originally portrayed on his clay likeness.

"Why not? Everyone else does," Kana returned, surprised when Daniel's expression showed a fleeting glimpse of something much more vulnerable.

"Because..." Daniel started, then trailed off. "It doesn't matter." Shaking his head again, he seemed to change his mind. "That's not who I am to you, though... Or is it?" Again, there was a degree of uncertainty in his voice, in his stance, in the set of his shoulders.

"No," she whispered, reaching out to touch Daniel's arm.

She knew all too well how it felt to be called something that didn't sit right, and for a moment it was like glimpsing inside Daniel's soft, warm, and surprisingly vulnerable centre. Looking down at her hand, she wondered at the molten heat and latent power of the man under her fingertips.

Who was he to her, really?

Generous benefactor, sexy neighbour, and the grouchy instigator of many of her confused emotive states.

A kiss stealer, with the warmest, gentlest lips.

"Daniel." Unable to help herself, Kana slid her fingers from his forearm to bicep, then up to touch the side of his face. "You're Daniel to me."

She sunk into his questioning eyes for a moment before lifting on tiptoe to lay her lips softly on his.

There was no responding pressure from Daniel. He let her kiss him, ever so lightly, for two heartbeats… Three…

Then he let her pull away.

"Sorry, I thought—" Kana stepped back, disorientated by Daniel's marked lack of input.

"*You* might be sorry, but I can tell you now, I'm not going to be." Daniel moved into the space Kanako had just separated them with. "I'm going to take that kiss as your 'say so,' okay? So if that's not how you meant it, you'd better run now," he warned her, only half joking.

Kanako stood her ground, those almond eyes lifted to challenge, a slight smile playing on her lips.

God, one more touch of those lips and he was gone. She tasted like mānuka honey, smelt of clay and lemons, and made little moans in the back of her throat that drove him near insane.

Soft, soft, then firm.

Daniel's want, and heat, compounded under Kanako's willing mouth. She slid both hands around his neck without any shyness as he held the curve of her waist, his fingers inadvertently discovering bare flesh between her jeans and shirt. Sliding up and up on the smooth skin of her back, he reached her shoulders without meeting a barrier.

No bra.

Shit. He lost it for a second, his brain clipping into overdrive and speeding ahead as Kanako touched her tongue to his in a silky tango.

He was ready to take Kanako here against the barn door, her sweet body pressed against him.

Yes?

Her body seemed to be saying 'yes,' arching into him, stroking up against him…

No, no, no. Not a good move.

He managed to gain some control of himself, easing back to a calmer state only when he broke away from her delectable lips. Pressing his mouth to her pulse, he tasted the pale skin a few centimetres below her ear.

"Wow. How do you *do* that?" Kanako murmured, pulling away to stare at him.

Her eyes were still dark, filled with lusty velvet, and the sight sent an extra pulse down to his cock.

"Do what?"

"Make me forget everything."

"Oh, that wasn't me. That was *us*." He laughed. "The forgetting part was entirely mutual."

"Well," Kanako smiled up at him dreamily, squeezing on his heart muscle just a smidgen with her softened expression. "We're *very* good at it. I'm no expert, but that was kind of… exceptional."

Daniel chuckled in agreement, lowering his head to kiss her a third time, but Kana wiggled out of his arms guiltily as the crunch of tyres on gravel denoted a car turning onto the annex driveway.

He watched, equal parts amused and thwarted, as she tucked in her shirt with hurried swipes, smoothing her hair back with fingers that shook.

If Adele could feel the tension between Kana and Daniel, she didn't mention it.

Saffy bowled into the studio alongside her mum with one thing on her mind. Glazing fruit.

"We missed you on pizza night." Adele lamented as she helped Saffy into her apron, looking with some curiosity from Kana to Daniel.

"Thank you for the invite," Kana side-lined the topic,

embarrassed to be discussing pizza night with Daniel within earshot.

It would've been held at his home, again.

Slapped with a cold dose of reality, Kana suddenly remembered how Daniel had spoken about her last time she'd been in his house.

'I don't trust her. She's a liar.'

At least she'd known to refuse to attend this time, telling Adele 'family nights' should be just that.

"Oh. My. God!" Adele caught sight of the two white clay busts cooling next to the kilns, still pushed together in an embrace. "Are they done? They're *done*!"

"Careful, they're still hot!" Kana and Daniel spoke at exactly the same time when Adele reached out, repeating the warning in stereo.

They locked eyes, and the corner of Daniel's mouth tweaked up in a minute show of humour.

"Just bisqued. I haven't glazed them yet," Kana added a little more softly.

"Look at you Saffy, my beautiful baby." Adele got her face close to Saffy's clay likeness and gazed at it, looking a little moist-eyed.

"I am *not* a baby." Saffy spoke with absolutism.

Kana felt another wave of cool reason hit home when she remembered Daniel's reaction to Adele and Saffy's likenesses.

'I'm not kidding. I really want them. Name your price.'

What *had* she been thinking? Adele and Daniel.

Kana didn't want to look at Daniel, and had the urge to go and scrub her hands and face in the sink, though there was nothing tangible to wash away.

"Have you seen your one, D?" Adele chattered on, too excited to catch Kana's warning glance. "So serious. So furious," she teased.

"Jet-lagged Uncle D," Saffy chimed in.

Kana turned guiltily to Daniel, watching as his expression changed from surprised to suspicious. He raised one eyebrow.

"Is that so?" he queried, his eyes moving to the plastic-covered greenware on her workbench.

"It's a work in progress," Kana flustered, sliding surreptitiously in front of her work so her body was between Daniel and his grumpy clay bust.

12

THE PRESENT MOMENT

*"Do not dwell in the past,
do not dream of the future,
concentrate the mind on the present moment."*
- Buddha

Kenneth had the most annoying habit of popping up when Kana was right, smack-bang in the middle of something else. He'd done it right at the beginning, when they'd originally met, bowling into the wrong seminar room looking for a city planning meeting when she'd been half way through a salt-firing lecture. He'd held her up for a full ten minutes, but she hadn't minded at the time. He'd come across as so charming.

She minded now. Not just for the intrusion of the phone call, but for every bloody time he'd interrupted her life-in-progress from the minute she'd met him.

"What is it now, Ken?"

"There is no need to take that tone. This is the contact phone number I was given, and I needed to speak to you. End of story."

End of story was almost prophetic. *From Ken's mouth to Buddha's ears*, she prayed.

"Then let's get this over with, shall we? Is it done?"

"By 'done,' I'm assuming you mean, have I signed the divorce papers?" Ken countered pompously.

"Kenneth, have you signed the divorce papers?" Kana gritted her teeth, laying it out in black and white.

"As you will come to realise, Kana. Some things take time and due diligence."

She wanted to scream.

"My lawyer and I have been deliberating a counter proposal, and it's not a matter to speed through," Ken continued.

"What's the counter proposal?"

"The details are not something I intend to discuss with you over the phone."

"Then why are you *calling* me?" Her voice went shrill without her meaning it to. His superior tone got her every time. "I'm in the middle of loading a kiln."

"Kana, pottery shouldn't take precedence over the important things in your life. I'm talking about your house and contents here." Ken sounded truly shocked.

"Pottery *is* one of the most important things in my life. Above house and contents, mortgage payments, insurance, and divorce details. I know that's tantamount to sacrilegious to you, but it won't change. We're both aware that's one of the reasons we have divorce papers on the table in the first place."

"About that. I'd be happier if we could meet face to face. It's best I deliver these in person."

"No, thanks." She had absolutely no desire to see him. Eight years, the last four of them entrenched in bone-grinding debate, had been long enough. "If you send them to the Dunedin gallery, they'll forward them. Better still, attach it as a document to an email, and I can get it printed here."

"Where *is* 'here,' exactly?"

"The boondocks," she evaded. "Let's get on with this, Ken. Neither one of us needs this dragging on."

After Ken's surprise phone call, ricocheting nervous energy kept getting the better of Kana.

She'd been working solidly all week, but was still tiptoeing through the unfamiliar territory of running behind on her glaze plan, and hated the sensation. At the risk of being late to teach her yoga lesson, she had to get the kiln loaded beforehand. It was imperative she got her schedule back on track.

Trust Ken to call the morning before her birthday, and carefully forget to mention anything about it.

Kana managed to load her final busts into two separate kilns for glaze firing without mishap, but kept second-guessing herself. Did the low shelf have enough kiln-wash? Was the glaze wiped back enough from the bases? Should she have done a final glaze test with the new batch of clear on a less important piece, before firing these two?

Not that she had enough time for any of that. Kana sighed.

Her self-esteem and psyche always took a kick whenever she had dealings with Kenneth. With distance, it became easier to see how destructive their relationship had been for her. They hadn't shouted, or thrown things, but his increasing habit of debating even the smallest of her decisions had worn her down to the nub.

The final straw had been over toothpaste. Ridiculous, but true. She'd bought a new tri-colour toothpaste that promised the three-in-one deal of cleaning, whitening and freshening breath. A good gimmick, but wholly untrue, Ken had insisted. If Kana had bothered to check the ingredients listings, she would've seen they were practically identical to the pure whitening toothpaste, which Ken himself preferred. She was gullible to false advertising, he'd decided aloud.

Kana had stared at Kenneth over the toothpaste and finally stated, her voice full of conviction, "I want a divorce."

Ken had been self-important enough to think she was wrong about that, too.

Even if she eventually lost her half-share in the house in Christchurch and had to live out of her SUV, she owed Poppy a solid for the pure escapism and clarity this artist in residence position had afforded her.

Scrambling her yoga gear together, Kana shoved everything in the SUV, dislodging gravel as she sped down the driveway towards the community centre.

When Kana turned her phone back on after her yoga lesson at the Community Centre, there was a text from Ken waiting for her.

Document to be sent via email tomorrow. Confirm receipt. Ken.

He even texted like an asshole.

She sighed, re-locking the SUV instead of getting into it. She needed a Creme Egg before she dealt with any more of Kenneth's bullshit.

He hadn't always been an ass, she reminded herself as she walked the two blocks to her favourite dairy. The whole thing was less abrasive on her ego if she remembered it'd been good once, and therefore hadn't been a massive mistake on her part from the get go.

"Hi, Andy."

"Oh, hey, Kana."

She stood in front of the familiar purple and gold box of chocolate eggs and almost burst into tears.

None left. Not a single one.

Andy, the dairy owner, took stock of her face before disappearing under the counter for a second, his circle of male pattern baldness on show as he rummaged around. When he popped back up again, he was beaming through his rimless glasses, holding two shiny eggs aloft.

"Saw that we were getting low, and thought maybe it'd be a good idea to save these for you."

"Oh Andy. I could *kiss* you!"

Andy blushed furiously. "Can't be doing that when I'm working," he muttered. "Not professional."

"No, of course not." Kana laughed. "But, thank you!"

As she paid, Andy unwound enough to shoot the breeze.

"So, will you be at the rippa-rugby fundraiser tomorrow night?"

"Yes, Adele's taking me." She looked around herself to check no one else was within earshot. "Um, Andy, what *is* rippa-rugby, exactly?"

Andy laughed. "It's rugby for the little 'ns, before they learn the tackling side of things. Instead of grabbing each other, they rip a Velcro ribbon off the back of their opponent's vest."

"Oh. So we're fundraising for kids' sport?"

"Yep."

"Cool." She could deal with that.

Ken labelled the email 'FYI', and didn't send it through until the following *afternoon*, probably just to keep Kana on tenterhooks.

The counter divorce papers were complete and utter bollocks.

Ken wanted two thirds of the Christchurch house '... *as the principal breadwinner throughout the marriage.*' He also wanted her SUV in exchange for his much older work sedan, knowing damn well the larger vehicle had been gifted by Obāchan. She'd given it expressly to Kana so she could have her own transportation for pottery.

Ken must know no judge would award that. *Surely* they wouldn't award that?

Kana hoped like hell this was just another one of Ken's stalling games. Underneath it all, she knew Kenneth still believed she was going to change her mind, when nothing could be further from the truth.

When Adele came by to pick Kana up on her birthday, the potter prayed her new friend wouldn't notice anything amiss. She fixed a bright smile on her face, but knew there were two high points of colour on her cheeks, and a glitter in her eyes that had nothing to do with her evening makeup.

"Wow, you look nice," Adele complimented her with a nod. "I hardly recognised you."

"Thank you." Kana smoothed her hands over her figure-hugging dress. She'd made an effort tonight for her own benefit, proving she could be whoever she felt like being—not beholden to anyone else.

"I don't think I've ever seen you in a dress. Green totally suits you," Adele continued.

Kana laughed, already feeling a little more at ease. "I don't own many, but sometimes you feel the need to *look* like a female, right?"

"Amen to that!"

"Is this new?" She reached over to touch the sleeve of Adele's rose-gold bomber jacket.

"No, it's pre-Wānaka. James-era." Adele sighed. "Everything

vaguely hip I own is pre-Wānaka, or James-era. Now I just shop in the second-hand mummy aisles."

"You're a *yummy*-mummy, though."

"You think?"

"Are you kidding me? You're like a warrior goddess. I've never seen anyone rock a cleaner's uniform like you do."

Both women laughed.

It was fun to be dressed up and heading out, even if they were just going to a local fundraising event. Kana would have a good time on this milestone birthday, or die trying. She was sure as hell going to forget all about Killjoy-Ken.

On arrival at the school hall, Adele collected their complimentary glasses of wine from the crowded trestle-bar. Then steered Kana through to their table to meet up with the rest of their all-female team.

Adele introduced the women, all mums from Saffy's school, and Kana memorised their names by word association. Pamela-pants-on-her, Carly-rides-a-Harley, and Linley-shows-her-boob-valley.

It was fun. They lost by a huge margin, but the women were out for a good time, not to prove their trivia knowledge. By the end of the last round, Kana knew all four of her teammates a lot better than if they'd just had a drink together.

Bubbly and vivacious Linley had answered the movie and celebrity questions with both speed and accuracy, whereas everyone had turned to Kana for the art-history ones. Pamela and Carly had quite a bit of sporting history tucked away in their blonde heads, and Adele knew a lot about politics, law, and world events.

None of them had any idea about music.

The price of the trivia table wasn't the only fundraising that went on during the night. There was an auction of goods and services donated by local retailers and artisans, sold to the highest bidder.

Pamela won a Kanako Janssen original cup and teapot set in celadon-green, and Kana narrowly missed out on a voucher for a kayak lesson and guided lake tour. She was still accepting condolences from Adele when Daniel Dante was called up on stage, so focussed on her conversation she missed his introduction.

The crescendo of applause following the ex-rugby player up the steps was amazing.

"Is he presenting something?" Kana turned to Carly, who sat next to her on the other side.

Daniel was dressed more formally than she'd ever seen him, in a black suit and tie. It exemplified his height and the breadth of his shoulders. He was clean cut, with no sign of the enticingly raspy stubble she'd brushed up against a week ago by the barn door.

Not that she'd been counting the days.

Not at all.

A tingle began in the depths of her belly.

Linley brought her fingers to her mouth and emitted a long, shrill wolf-whistle, and Kana blushed at the coarse sign of appreciation. It exactly matched what *she'd* been thinking.

Hot damn, her landlord looked good.

Daniel turned towards the distinctive high-pitched sound, and catching Kana's eye, gave her a long stare before turning his attention back to the sea of other faces in the hall.

The now familiar prickle of awareness blossomed and grew.

"He's presenting something alright." Carly laughed. "Himself!"

"Himself? What do you mean?"

"Bachelor Auction." Carly rubbed her hands together in glee. "Highest bidder gets dinner with Dante D. Let the catfight begin!"

It wasn't so much of a catfight, more like a freeze-out.

Women bid against each other with cold stares and serious game faces. Then, as the bidding crept up into the hundreds, the crowd took on a more jovial team-against-team approach. It soon became clear who the serious contenders were, and groups of women took sides.

There were shouts of "Go, Sharon!" and "You get him, girl!"

It was absolutely fascinating.

Kana cheered and clapped along with everyone else when Carissa stood to give her bid of five hundred and fifty dollars. The retired widow stayed in the game until eight hundred. Blowing a coquettish kiss to Daniel as she gracefully bowed out. Dante D pretended to catch it and plant it over his own heart, but he didn't smile at all after that.

The bidding teetered near a thousand, with only the woman

called Sharon left. The blonde deserved the win, having coolly outbid everyone who'd stepped in from the seven-hundred-dollar mark. But she looked hard, and a little scary, and Kana glanced across at Adele with a growing distaste for the process, imagining how revolting the spectacle would be if the sexes were reversed.

"This doesn't feel right. He doesn't get a say?" she asked in a small voice.

"Nope. Highest bidder. He'll be polite as all hell, but I don't think he'll have such a good night tonight. She's a bit of a pushy one." Adele appeared to be choosing her words carefully, and kept her voice down.

They both turned back to look at Daniel, and Kana tried to read his expression from his profile.

Politely resigned?

As if sensing her regard, Daniel turned and caught her eye for the second time in the evening, just as the auctioneer was finishing his closing spiel.

"... Dinner with one of Wānaka's most eligible bachelors. Going *once...*"

Yes, Daniel was clearly resigned to his fate, but there was a questioning quality about him, too. Or was it a silent plea? Daniel raised one eyebrow, almost imperceptibly.

"Going *twice...*"

Daniel continued to hold her gaze as Kana stood, her chair scraping loudly on the wooden floor behind her. Those nearby turned to see who'd made the disruptive sound, perhaps keen for a dramatic end to the bidding.

She raised her hand to confirm she wasn't just on a badly timed trip to the ladies.

"One thousand, five hundred and fifty two dollars." Kana called out the exact balance of her savings account.

There was a moment of monumental silence, before the room erupted with exclamations both in support of, and against the bid.

Kana caught Daniel's small twitch of a smile before he schooled his features back into neutral, and looked away.

What had she just done?

Blinking, Kana looked across at the woman she'd outbid.

Sharon wasn't so particular about hiding her emotions. 'Bitch!'

The sharp-faced blonde mouthed silently to her, clearly fuming. Sitting back down in her chair, she shook her head at the auctioneer and folded her arms, effectively removing herself from the bidding.

Adele jumped up and gave Kana a quick squeeze. "Oh, you're a dark horse. Love it! Did you see her face? Ha!"

"Can anyone top the new bid of one thousand, five hundred and fifty... Ahh..." The auctioneer looked to Kana in askance as he aimed his gavel at her.

"Two," she supplied.

"...Two," he continued. Going once, going twice... *Sold* to the pretty young lady in the green dress."

Although Kanako was standing across from him, she was having real trouble looking at him, Daniel noted with some interest.

"Regretting your bid?" he drawled.

"What? No. Not at all," Kanako negated hastily as she signed for her donation, then stood and adjusted her bag strap with a nervous tweak.

She looked stunning in green, the dress hugging her waist and dipping tantalisingly low into the v of her breasts. Daniel had never seen her in anything other than jeans, pants, or sports gear, so he took his time checking her out.

Killer heels on those black boots, too. You could stop a man's heart if you weren't careful, or at least drain all the blood-flow elsewhere.

"Thank you for your very generous donation." Vie, one of the little-rippa-rugby mums on the payment table spoke to Kanako, then turned to him with much less formality. "You'd better show her one hell of a good time for that price, Dante D."

"I intend to, Vie. Are we all done here?"

Kanako let him help her with her coat, and standing behind her he could smell the faint traces of her scent—a freshness that cleansed his palette and started a low growling hunger deep within.

As they walked out together, across the asphalt of the netball courts towards his car, he heard Kanako take a deep breath and release it slowly.

"You okay?"

"Yes, thank you." Kanako turned to look at him for the first time since the auction, and he could see her jittery tension had eased somewhat. "Let me just…" Her lips twitched as she wiped at one of her shoulders, then the other. "Brush these daggers off my back."

"Oh, right." He laughed. "Allow me." He swept both hands down her back, shoulder to waist, smoothing the black wool of her coat into the shape of her spine. "There, all gone."

Kanako took the familiarity of his touch in the joking manner he'd aimed for, but that didn't mean his body was unaware of the contact.

"*Phew*. Thank you. Wouldn't want to cark it from severe blood loss before the date had even started."

"A *date* now, is it?"

"A dinner date was implied in the advertising," Kanako replied smoothly.

"Well, then. I'd better step it up a bit." Daniel held out his palm in invitation, and Kanako only hesitated for a moment before putting her hand in his and letting him kiss her knuckles. The zip of awareness from the touch, and the way she looked up at him challengingly, upped the temperature.

Bring it on. He was more than ready.

"Where would my lovely date like to eat? I've been presumptuous and made two tentative reservations, but I can highly recommend both restaurants. Would you prefer Italian, or French?"

Kanako shrugged as they reached the car. "Whichever. You choose." She reached to open the passenger door when he unlocked the sedan with the remote.

"*Nooo*." Daniel was quick to slide his hand over hers. "We're on a *date*. Remember? *I* open your door, and *you* choose where we eat."

Kanako let him open her door and hand her into the low seat, swinging her legs neatly in. He got a fleeting view of smooth thighs, along with those heavenly, calf-hugging boots.

Daniel leaned his arm on the roof of the car and regarded her from above. He'd never seen her wear much makeup before, and the stuff made her eyes even more striking. She'd left her lips nude, and glossy. Any colour would be sacrilegious on that peachy fullness, and if tonight went the way he was hoping, he'd be kissing it off later, anyway.

"Not sold on Italian or French? Anything else tickles your fancy?"

He watched Kanako deliberate, thinking she was going to bite her nail when she brought her thumb to her mouth. He forgot to breathe for a few moments, fascinated, as she nibbled on the fleshy pad instead.

Straight white teeth—maybe she'd had braces as a kid? The thought was closely followed by the vivid image of those teeth sinking into his skin, and he deliberately loitered, daydreaming about how how that could feel.

"Actually, the first day I was in Wānaka, I saw a family down by the lake with fish and chips, and it's *such* a lovely evening, I—"

"You paid *fifteen hundred* for fish and chips by the lake?" Daniel interrupted, incredulous.

There was a weighted pause.

"It was just a thought. No, you're right, of course." Kanako appeared to whiten under the light of the street lamp, and withdraw into herself. Speaking with quiet coolness she turned away from him, looking straight ahead through the windscreen. "Whichever you prefer is fine with me."

Shit.

Daniel closed her door carefully and walked around the car, jangling his keys.

Kanako was an enigma. He'd trodden on her toes just then, but couldn't for the life of him figure how. He'd never been out with a woman who would actively choose to turn down five-star *anything*.

———

Kana was used to a partner pretending you had a choice, then taking it away. Kenneth used to do that all the time. Offer you both, or ask for your opinion, then debate or bully you out of your decision. It was a game; a competition with a clear winner, and it was mentally exhausting.

She chose not to play.

Daniel pulled in at the liquor-store, and Kana assumed the restaurant he'd chosen must be BYO.

"What kind of wine do you like? or would you prefer to come in and choose?"

"Oh, I'm not a big drinker, so maybe just get whatever you'd like."

Daniel stared at her.

"You're happy for me to choose the restaurant *and* the alcohol?"

"Yes," she answered simply, wondering what his problem was. Wasn't this exactly what he was after?

Daniel strode toward the store, and Kana eyed his movement. There was never any obvious sign of the old knee injury, but if she watched carefully, every now and again he faintly favoured his left leg.

Daniel didn't make it inside the front doors. There was a group of young people hanging by the entrance who rallied around him wanting to talk, excited to shoot the breeze with Dante D.

Kana opened her door a fraction to try and catch the conversation, but only managed to pick up snippets of relaxed banter.

One of the girls pulled up her top seductively, and Daniel hesitated before taking the offered pen, signing the teen's arm, rather than her offered navel.

13

BEING SHARED

"Happiness never decreases by being shared."
- Buddha

Daniel chose a six-pack of light beer for himself, and chilled Champagne for Kanako. Up at the counter, a bag of pineapple lumps called to him, so he grabbed those as well.

"The good stuff." The liquor-store owner, Perry, checked over the wine approvingly before bagging it. "You on a date, D?"

"Rippa-rugby fundraiser tonight."

"Oh, yeah! The auction. Who'd ya end up with, then?"

There was no point hiding it from Perry. The whole town would know by tomorrow, anyway.

"The latest ceramic artist from the annex." Daniel kept his voice neutral.

"Well! You lucky young bugger. She's a honey, that one. No mistake!"

Daniel shrugged noncommittally. He couldn't agree more, but wasn't about to tell Perry that.

"My Sally's been going to the yoga lessons she runs, and it seems to help the RSI in her wrists."

About to leave, Daniel hesitated. "Yoga lessons?"

"At the Community Centre," Perry reiterated, as if that explained it.

"Oh, right." Kanako really had been getting around.

"You taking her up to the French place?"

"Ah… I've given her the option to choose." Daniel settled on a nice, vague answer.

"Good idea." Perry winked conspiratorially. "Well, you go on and have a great night."

Relieved the kids had moved from outside the store, Daniel waited until the door slid closed on Perry before ringing in an order to King's Catch, adding to the classic F&Cs with oysters, mussels, and squid rings to cover his bases.

"Can you add some tartare and tomato sauce to that order, and cut me up a lemon, too?"

"Sure, I can do that for you Dante D."

"Are you busy tonight?"

"Flat out."

"How would you feel about delivering to the backdoor?"

"You trying to keep a low profile?"

Daniel laughed. "You got it. Couple of Mac's light in it for you if you keep it on the quiet."

"No worries, ready in ten."

When Daniel walked back towards the car, Kana could see he was grinning. He opened the boot and rummaged around before folding himself back in the driver's seat next to her.

As soon as he sat down his presence took up far more than his half-share of the front seating, and Kana wondered idly why that was. Maybe it was the breadth of his shoulders, or his aftershave? It could also be the latent energy she could sense in him; the strength of his hands on the steering wheel as he drove.

"We're still ten minutes early for our booking. Are you happy if we get some gas on the way?"

"Of course." She glanced over at him. "So, ah, do you do this Bachelor Auction thing every year, then?"

He smiled, eyes on the road. "It's for a good cause. Sometimes

I'm not available, but I'm not the only candidate. If we'd stayed longer, you would've had to sit through a couple more."

"It's a bit cruel though, isn't it?" She clenched her hands together in her lap. "You didn't get any say."

Daniel looked directly at her as he parked at the pumps. "I wouldn't have chosen any differently this evening," he said simply, making her pheromones prickle with his level gaze.

"Oh, that's very polite of you to say," she mumbled, getting a light laugh out of him.

"I don't think Sharon would agree. I owe you one for that save, though it's probably very ungentlemanly of me to mention it. And you sure made me sweat it with that last minute reprieve."

The corners of her mouth twitched.

"You know the daggers you helped remove from my back earlier?"

"Yeah?"

"Sharon's was the size of a *samurai* sword."

Daniel laughed outright, and her body did that now familiar *skip* and *ping* in response.

When Daniel came back from paying for the gas he had another package to put in the boot, but it wasn't until they pulled into a dark service lane behind a strip of shops Kana began to get suspicious.

"What are we doing down here?"

Daniel left the engine idling.

"Waiting."

"Waiting for what?"

But he was already out of the car, opening his wallet, counting cash, then sliding behind the car to get something out of the boot. There was an exchange of male voices and some kind of transaction going down.

Something illicit?

No.

Fish and chips!

A large bundle of hot, paper-wrapped take-outs arrived on Kana's lap without any fanfare.

"The lady wants fish and chips?" Daniel grinned at her. "The lady gets fish and chips."

"How did you manage that?"

"Magic." Daniel slipped his phone out of his pocket and flicked it into the centre console.

He *was* just a touch magic when he turned on the charm, and Kana wondered if she should be fretting about how easily and deeply she was entangling herself in trouble as he drove her down to the lake.

Daniel chose the spot, and Kana hadn't realised the little bay was even there, further along from the main lay-bys and off the beaten track.

He'd bought some other supplies too; wine, beer, insect repellent, a picnic rug, and a couple of car blankets. It was perfect— just like she'd imagined. Only better, due to Daniel being surprisingly good company.

They talked about Japan, travel, food, and the glories of natural *onsen*. He seemed more relaxed, like he'd shaken off the residual distrust, and they laughed about language *faux pas* in general.

"What's your biggest mistake in Japanese?" she wondered aloud.

"Who, *me*? Make mistakes?" Daniel pretended to have trouble thinking of any, before chuckling. "Pick a genre. And I mean *any* genre."

"Food."

"Food." He dipped the last squid ring into tartare sauce and popped it whole into his mouth, mulling it over as he chewed and swallowed. "Okay. Here's one. I once ordered *neko* instead of *niku* in a well-to-do restaurant, quite insistently, with fairly offensive connotations to the chef about the cat on the menu."

Kana snorted a laugh, choking as the bubbles in the sparkling wine tickled the back of her nose. Daniel had apologised about the paper cups, but she found it kind of charming he'd thought to get any at all.

"I don't usually drink. This is going to my head." She tapped the sparkling wine bottle and squinted at the label. "It's very sparkly."

"They should put that on the label. Very French, and very sparkly. Here…" Daniel handed her half a piece of crispy battered fish. "Soak it up with this."

"No, thank you. I'm full." She lay back and patted her stomach. "But I have a new favourite."

"The mussels?"

"Yes. Who knew? Such an unassuming little shellfish. But battered and deep-fried? Food for the gods. Especially with the lemon drizzled over." Kana wasn't surprised Daniel had noticed her hogging the mussels, she must've eaten at least four of the six.

Bad luck if they were his favourite as well.

"I guess you would've grown up with a lot of kaimoana. You said your mother's Japanese?"

Kana laughed. "Put it this way, I had *sushi* and *surimi* in my lunchbox way before it was cool."

The trees rustled softly above, still holding a faint glow though the sun had long since gone down. The golden yellow leaves shone faintly iridescent in the low light.

"These Poplars are beautiful. So pretty." She sighed as Daniel wrapped the remaining fish and chip scraps up in the paper.

"*Kirei desu ne*," Daniel agreed, but when she turned her head lazily to look at him, he was staring at her, not the trees. He cleared his throat. "Speaking of food for the gods." He dug into another plastic bag. "Are you too full for dessert?"

Daniel lobbed a pineapple lump, landing it neatly on her stomach.

"I'm never too full for chocolate, though my true weakness lies with Cadbury Creme Eggs. I have to buy them one, or two at a time, or they call to me from the cupboard and I can't get any work done," Kana confessed, popping the rectangle into her mouth to suck the chocolate off the candy. "I get sugar withdrawal headaches like a junkie." She laughed at her own lack of self-control.

Early thirties, Daniel guessed, though Kanako appeared to have done a lot of travelling within those years. Multiple trips to Japan, Europe, Asia, and back again.

The potter was well spoken, and intelligent. Sophisticated in a way that kept rounding him back for more. She had an interesting take on society, and Daniel discovered a lot of her theories were a quirky mix of cultures.

He was also enjoying Kanako's somewhat kooky sense of humour. She had a knack of surprising him into laughter.

Kanako described her 'no English' gag as a defence mechanism when she insisted on apologising about it again, and Daniel, of all people, understood. He had plenty of defence mechanisms of his own.

She'd been married once already, which was intriguing, though she spoke very little of her ex-husband. That could mean something, or nothing at all.

Kanako wore no rings and kept her nails short, without polish. When she played with the gold locket around her neck, Daniel couldn't take his eyes off her long elegant fingers, or the smooth neck they danced near.

When she asked about his grandmother, Nona, he didn't feel the least bit uncomfortable telling her what he knew. It was no secret Nona's life had been an uphill battle.

"It was my grandfather's gambling that compounded it all. A couple of hard winters and stock numbers were down, but Gramps got it into his head he could gamble his way back into the black, and ended up losing the farm instead. I'm not sure Nana Nona ever forgave him for that. The homestead had been in her family for a long time.

Nona had to take the five girls—my mother and her sisters—to live with family in Dunedin."

Kanako shivered.

"Are you cold?" Daniel sat up from where he'd been lounging, unfolded a rug, and held it up.

Kanako misunderstood the action.

He had his arms wide with the woven wool, but instead of just taking the offered rug, she climbed over the small litter of take-out rubbish between them and settled into his arms.

He blinked, as Kanako turned her back into him and snuggled close.

It was a much cosier option, with her cocooned in wool under his arm, and her head nestled neatly against his shoulder, but it showed a level of trust from Kanako that both surprised and humbled him. His intentions had not been *entirely* trustworthy, especially when he'd caught a glimpse down the cleavage of her low V-neck from his higher vantage point.

Daniel tucked the rug lightly around Kanako's torso, covering the tempting view before lying back with his hands behind his head and continuing with the story.

"So, in a strange and roundabout way, when Clem asked me if I wanted first option on the farmhouse, I did it for Gramps' sake as well as my own."

"The farm had gone to Clem?" Kanako's words vibrated lightly against his chest.

"His father bought it when the bank foreclosed on Gramps, then left it to Clem when he died. They rented it out for a long time, and I now lease the working land back to him for his sheep. We've been discussing switching it over to grapes, but that'll be a few years down the track. Mum wasn't impressed, not with Clem offering it to me, and not with me buying it. But she came around."

"She did it for Nona," Kana murmured. "The artist in residence program, I mean."

"Yeah, she did." Daniel smiled to himself, watching as a flurry of leaves were blown from the slowly emptying branches above, and steered out over the lake by the wind. "So now both grandparents can rest easy. It's been cathartic for Mum. You're the fifth potter in the annex, and each time, she seems a bit more comfortable with it."

"I saw the other potters blurbs on the entry form. What were they like?"

Daniel squinted a look at the top of Kanako's head on his shoulder, very aware of the length of her, pressed warmly against his side. "Compared to you? I'd say, on the whole, extremely unattractive."

Kanako laughed, elbowing him lightly in the ribs.

"You're just saying that because I saved you from Scary Sharon."

"No. I'm saying that because you're incredibly hot," he murmured.

And that was putting it mildly.

"Mmm? Well, you're not so bad yourself, I guess. Once you get around the gruff exterior. And you *smell* really nice," Kanako returned somewhat sleepily, turning sideways into him. "I think I could curl right up here and have a wee snooze under the stars."

Daniel laughed.

Gruff? Like a Billy-goat?

He had a sudden image of sliding Kana up to lie on top of him and roving his hands under her blanket…

"I think that's the first time I've been told my armpit smells nice. Are you sure you're not drunk?"

"Tiddly, maybe."

"Tiddly. Right." Daniel gave himself a mental shake. Not his style to get a woman drunk and take advantage. "Want to get going?" he asked suddenly, pushing back up on his elbows.

"No. Not yet. Show me which stars you can name."

―――――――

They lay beside the lake for another half-hour, until the air was crisply cold off the water and the hard shore began to bite into Kana's hipbones.

Daniel must've felt her trying to get comfortable.

"How about a take-out coffee?"

"Ohh…" She scrambled up to kneeling, turning to look down on him. "Have you tried a turmeric latte? They're *so* delicious."

Daniel made a noncommittal sound in his throat. "I was thinking more along the lines of a decaf." He checked his watch. "Late night at Wanderer's Cafe. Ten minutes till closing."

Kana helped him swiftly pack up their take-out picnic, but by the time they'd parked a little down from the café, they only had five minutes to spare.

"If I go on my own, I might be less, um… conspicuous," she decided.

Daniel's eyebrows snapped together, so she indicated towards his black suit and overcoat. He looked down at it with some surprise, as if he'd forgotten he was wearing it. As if he'd forgotten he turned heads no matter *what* he was wearing.

Pulling her own coat closed over her low-cut dress, Kana buttoned up, while Daniel tugged his wallet out of his back pocket and handed her a twenty-dollar note.

"I can pay." Kana met Daniel's hard stare, blinking back at him.

"Fifteen. Hundred. Dollars." Daniel reminded her, each word succinctly defined.

"All right. *Your* date, *you* pay," she backtracked, plucking the note from between his fingertips.

They sat in the car, sipping from take-out cups and watching the final customers trickle out of the coffee shop, as Maddie and the other barista closed up.

"I think Maddie is secretly in love with the owner of the coffee shop, and that's why she goes that extra mile with the smiles and the dimples and all that," Kana decided aloud.

"Is that so?" Daniel, obviously amused, played along. "Well, I think the two women putting their coats on have been plotting how to best kill the taller one's husband. Getting away with murder."

"Gruesome." Kana looked across at him with growing interest and just a touch of awe, nodding. "They've decided on a shed fire, because she hates the fact he secretly smokes cigars out there, and tries to deny it."

Daniel laughed, "But she'll make doubly sure the cat isn't in there first. She likes the cat."

"A tabby, with one eye missing."

"And the man sitting on his own...?" Daniel turned to look at her expectantly, his eyes still glinting with humour.

"Was a circus performer in his youth, before safety nets became commonplace. His sister fell from a great height. He was supposed to catch her, but he'd been drinking that night..."

"And so has never performed, or touched alcohol, since," Daniel finished for her.

"Do you actually know any of these people?" Kana suddenly wondered, swivelling towards him.

It was a small town, and someone like Daniel had probably met the majority of permanent residents.

He laughed, "Just Maddie and Todd, the baristas. Though the trapeze artist looks vaguely familiar."

"That's probably just from the old posters advertising his death-defying high-wire act," Kana noted with mock seriousness.

"Probably," Daniel agreed, still smiling. The spice of his aftershave was more tangible in the car than it had been beside the lake, mixed now with the heady fragrances of coffee and turmeric.

"Would you like to go halves?" Pulling the unable-to-resist yoyo from the take-out bag on her lap and twisting it apart, Kana gave Daniel first choice, as he had for her.

The centre icing was softer than it had been down at the lake, and it slid apart evenly.

Craving the sweetness, Kana licked the passionfruit icing off her half reverently, before biting into the crumbly biscuit, eyes closed with the pure indulgence of it. She was embarrassed beyond words when she looked up and realised Daniel had been watching her actions with avid curiosity.

"Sugar hit?"

She cleared her throat before returning a little testily, "I've already admitted I'm addicted. Don't you have any vices?"

"Ah, yes." Daniel's demeanour changed to watchful. "Well documented ones."

"Really?" Realising she'd hit a nerve, Kana trod carefully, not sure what he was referring to. Women? Gambling? Collecting expensive boats? "I'm afraid this is the part where I have to inform you, I've never followed rugby."

"You don't say," Daniel quipped, his tone wry. "And here was I thinking I had a fanatic on my hands."

Kana remained silent, eyeing Daniel across the car as she slowly finished her half of the biscuit, mulling on his serious profile. The contours had changed from softly amused to closed in a very short space of time.

He was like three or four characters all rolled into one, and she was never sure which mask was going to show up next.

When Daniel finally spoke, his voice was low and even, and she wondered how much it cost him each time he pretended he was made of stone. "I've come to realise everyone has their own little addictions, be it three sugars in their coffee, or cocaine for breakfast." He shrugged, then took the last swig of his coffee, exposing the freshly shaved cords on his neck. "Though most are relatively private, mine were splashed across headlines. There are worse things in life than being well known, but when it starts crushing the people you care about, that's something else."

"Yes. That must be awful," Kana returned with honest feeling. "I don't envy you the fame or the publicity. I'd much prefer to lie low and skim under the radar." Scrunching the empty biscuit bag into her take out cup, she hesitated before taking Daniel's cup out of his unresponsive hand and sliding it under the stack. "What about the older couple?"

"What?"

"The older couple, just getting out of their seats now. What's their story?" She watched Daniel mentally shake off their previous conversation to glance at the pair.

"Oh, I think there's a bitter feud building there. She's just been handed photographic proof he had an illicit affair when they were young lovers," Daniel decided.

Kana looked at the angry lines etched onto the woman's face. "With her much younger, far more beautiful sister," she added cheerfully.

Daniel grunted, with what she had to assume was humour.

"But although they've been married for thirty years, they're childless, and she blames him for that..." he began.

Kana hadn't expected Daniel to turn and look at her right then, and her face must've shown something by mistake.

She tried to school her features back to nonchalant and non-affected, but it was too late. His hand shot out to grab her arm and she chose to look down at it. It was less confronting than having to look into his eyes.

"Sorry, I didn't think. You were married, and you don't have children, do you?" Daniel apologised.

"No. It's okay." Kana looked back towards the café window. "Forget it." Watching Maddie lock and bolt the front door, she purposefully changed conversational tack again. "Maybe the barista —did you say his name was Todd?"

Out of the corner of her eye, she caught Daniel's nod.

"Maybe he'll give Maddie flowers tonight, and tell her he's had a crush on her since he was twelve years old."

"Maybe he will." She could feel Daniel's eyes boring into her. "Kanako? It wasn't my intention to hurt you. It was just a bad call."

"No. I know." She finally looked across at Daniel and smiled a little ruefully at his concern. There was just enough alcohol still floating in her system to push her to elaborate. "It doesn't matter. I assumed we'd have children eventually, my ex-husband and I. But after eight years of marriage, it was pretty clear I couldn't. I guess that was the beginning of the end, really. The blame eats at you."

She turned to look back at the older couple, who were now getting into their car.

"But I'm glad I didn't find out he'd had an affair with my much younger, far more beautiful sister. Look how that information's ravaged her face." Kana tried to make light of the situation.

"Do you have a sister?"

"Luckily, no." Though Kana's tone was flippant, her heart had shifted back to melancholy, thinking of her lone half-brother, Finn. They were far from close. Practically strangers. "I was always a bit sad about that, but now see it was for the best," she finished a little flatly.

14

FIRE LIKE PASSION

"There is no fire like passion,
there is no shark like hatred,
there is no snare like folly,
there is no torrent like greed."
- Buddha

Daniel was still kicking himself about the 'childless' call when he turned into the annex driveway, tires crunching on the deep new shingle.

"Home." He turned to Kanako as he pulled up next to her SUV.

"For now," she corrected, looking a little jumpy in the dash light.

He could guess where her nerves were rooted. Kanako would be worrying about expectations, unsure of what came next.

"Goodnight, Kanako." Picking up her hand, he kissed her knuckles once more, meeting her eyes. "Thank you. I had a wonderful evening, and I hope you did as well." Then he returned her hand gently to her lap.

"Oh," Kanako blinked across at him like a little golden ruru, seeming to shrink back into her seat. "Is that the end?"

He shrugged, "If you want it to be, then it is."

"What if I chose something more? Something else?" Kanako

fidgeted with her locket again, and not for the first time, Daniel wondered what she kept in there.

"What did you have in mind?" He held her gaze.

"I was thinking." Kanako cleared her throat and looked down at the hand in her lap. "You might kiss me again. Kiss me goodnight."

"Would you like me to?"

Kanako surprised him by laughing. "Hell, yeah."

"Okay, then. Where?"

"Ah, well, I was thinking on the lips." Kanako's eyes jumped to his mouth, and lingered there, making his blood throb heavy in his veins. "Then, if we enjoyed that, maybe a bit of necking?"

Daniel began to chuckle. "No. I meant *where* would you like me to kiss you? Here in the car, or I walk you to your door…?"

"Oh!" The blush crept quickly up Kanako's cheeks, but her hand left her locket to slide across the top of his thigh, making him suddenly intensely aware, and fully alert. "Here."

"On your *thigh*?" He deliberately misunderstood her meaning. "My pleasure. Outer? Inner?"

"God!" Kana laughed openly again, and he relished the purity of the sound. "You're a cocky bastard, aren't you Mr Dante?"

"I told you if you ever called me Mr Dante again, I wouldn't be held responsible," Daniel growled.

Kanako took the length of his tie in her hand and tugged, pulling him closer. "Be *irresponsible*, then," she whispered.

In the snug confines of the car, all sound was magnified; Kanako's unintelligible murmur as their lips brushed, feather light. The swish of her satin coat-lining against her dress as she shifted, squirmed sideways, and made room for his bulk.

Sighs, soft moans, and the wind in the trees.

Their combined breathing became louder as heat quickened between them—hands roaming. Daniel heard his own groan escape, low and wanting, when Kanako's knee brushed lightly across his hard-on.

The sound of the car horn splitting the inky darkness made them both jump. Kanako jerked upwards in surprise, smacking the back of her head on the low roof.

"Shit!" There was a shocked silence, then giggling. "Sorry, that was my butt on the steering wheel."

Kanako was straddled across Daniel's thighs in the driver's seat, and he couldn't exactly remember how, or when she'd gotten there. His hands cupped the back of her legs, and her hair brushed his cheek as she slowly lowered her head and touched her forehead to his.

Bloody smooth. He was making out in the front seat of his car like a randy teenager.

"Do you want to get out of here?" he mumbled, his voice not entirely his own.

"Only if you're coming too," Kanako quipped, manoeuvring awkwardly to open his door and slide out. She stood on the shingle looking deliciously rumpled, tugging on his hand. "Come inside."

Kana was nervous. Her hands shook, making the keys jangle tellingly as she tried to slot them into the front door of the annex. Daniel was behind her, his hand on the small of her back, and that was enough to give her goosebumps.

The man was hotness personified.

She'd decided not to think about the consequences, just run with it and forget everything else. That's what kissing Daniel did—made her forget everything but the pleasure of the moment. But it was harder to do when faced with the mundane actions of unzipping her boots and taking off her coat.

Real life flooded back in.

He was her landlord, a big shot rugby star, and at the moment, her benefactor.

Kana found she couldn't actually look Daniel in the eye when she took his jacket from him, hanging it over the kitchen chair next to her own coat.

"Kanako?" Daniel waited until her gaze met his. "You could just offer me another coffee, and we sit here at the kitchen table and talk."

"Ah..." She blinked, somewhat surprised at the underlying kindness she could see in his deep hazel eyes—in his darkly handsome face. She cleared her throat. "That wasn't exactly what I had in mind, actually."

Taking hold of her nerves and self-doubt, she squashed them firmly underfoot as she stepped towards Daniel.

Standing on tiptoe, she leaned into him.

"Kiss me again, Daniel," she whispered.

———

Thank Christ for that. Daniel was aching for more of her.

Kanako had a softness he could sink into, a sweetness a man could drown in if he wasn't careful, and Daniel was vaguely aware as he plundered her mouth he was being anything but careful right now.

There was a trusting openness in the way Kanako gave to him; her mouth, her hands, and even the soft sighs escaping as she curved against him.

They moved as one, from kitchen to lounge, as he drank in the citrus freshness on Kanako's skin and hair. He trailed a line of kisses from her jaw to her collarbone—hungry for the taste, smell, and feel of her.

"Mmm, I like that." She groaned the words, and his body pulsed in response.

"What else do you like, Kanako?"

"Ah…" she sighed into his ear, "I like how you say my name."

Kanako arched her head back as he began his foray again, murmuring as he went.

"Kanako…" He moved a little lower. "Kanako…" Nudging aside her locket with his chin, he skimmed the deep V-neck of her dress. "Kanako…"

"Mmm." She tugged on his shirt. "I think you should take this off."

"Do you, now?" Daniel reigned it in long enough to get a good look at her.

Kanako's eyes were dark and dilated in the low light seeping through from the kitchen.

"*Hai.*" She smiled at him, and any resolve he'd had to step this down a notch left him on her soft, mussed expression. Not waiting for him to comply, her fingers got busy on his tie.

"What do *you* take off, then?" he asked as Kanako threw his tie in the vague direction of the sofa and began on his shirt buttons.

Kanako hesitated only a second before stepping back, her hands going to the back of her neck to unclasp her locket, before placing it gently on the coffee table. Then she turned and levelled a look at him.

"*Anata no ban.*"

There was something very sexy about Kanako speaking to him in Japanese.

"My turn?" He laughed. "Okay, you're on." He tugged the dress shirt from his pants and undid the remaining buttons without ceremony. Bunching the white cotton, he aimed it in the same direction as his tie.

Daniel was all male, muscly, and *beautiful*.

The contours of his broad chest pulled a visceral response from Kanako, one she couldn't recall feeling with any other partner before. It throbbed deep and low in her core.

She stepped forward, dreamlike, to trace her fingertips over Daniel's stomach, and he grabbed at her hand, laughing.

"That tickles."

"You have a very nice chest," she said, a little breathless.

"Thank you. I'd like to return the compliment," Daniel teased, his tone light, but his eyes serious. "*Tsugi.* Your turn."

"Oh." She smiled up at him a little shyly. "So it is."

Taking her hands behind her back, she went to unzip her dress, then changed her mind, moving instead to unhook her gold hoop earrings and place them alongside her locket.

Daniel stood with his hands on his hips and his head tilted slightly to one side, considering her.

"Really? That's how you're going to play it?" There was a small, sardonic twist to his mouth.

"*Hai. Tsugi.*"

Daniel waited another beat, then Kana felt the buzz begin to build as his hands moved to his belt buckle, undoing both that, and the catch on his dress pants. She waited for him to unzip, nibbling at her bottom lip. But Daniel was hesitating—waiting until he caught her eye.

She began to laugh when Daniel pointedly slid his belt from its loops, and threw it carelessly towards his shirt.

"Touché," she conceded, still smiling.

"*Anata no ban desu.*" Daniel didn't miss a beat, switching back into Japanese with great seriousness and formality.

It's your turn.

Kana unzipped herself without ceremony this time, and sent up a silent prayer to the gods.

Please—let the big, beautiful rugby guy like what he saw.

Then she slid her shoulders out of her dress, one by one.

She needn't have worried. He was a man, after all, and boobs were boobs, no matter how daintily proportioned.

Kanako wasn't wearing a bra. She wasn't wearing *anything* under her dress other than a triangular scrap of fabric that hardly passed as underwear. Daniel sucked in air that suddenly seemed lacking in the room.

Like the wolf at an extremely tasty Red-Riding-Hood's table, he ached to devour her whole.

Kanako's skin had a satin sheen, and dark nipples sat high on her perfectly rounded breasts. There was a small horizontal scar to the right, just to the side of her navel, and a petite swallow tattoo on the opposite hipbone.

"*Kirei desu yo, Kanako-sensei,*" he complimented her, reaching for the cool smoothness of her hips and drawing her closer—needing more than anything to feel her bare skin against his.

"You can't call me *sensei*." Kanako laughed, putting her hands on either side of his face and standing on tiptoe. "I'm not your teacher."

He just smiled as he lowered his mouth to meet hers in a slow and torturous dance. "Yes. You are. I want you to teach me," he growled, low and quiet. "Teach me what your body likes."

"Oh!" Kanako grinned impishly. "That, I can do." She grazed her pert nipples across his chest, and her breathing became shallower than before.

Daniel watched in fascination as Kanako's eyes lusted to dark amber.

"Mmm, but first, it's your turn, again." Kanako tugged on one of his belt loops to illustrate her point, before kissing him once more. This time she slid her arms around his neck and brought her tongue into play, so he was groaning by the time he stepped out of the remainder of his clothing.

Lifting Kanako by the waist, he boosted her up to his height, gathering her close to his chest and revelling in the cool length of her pressing against him. Drunk on the kiss, he almost lost the plot when she bore down on his shoulders and brought her slim thighs up around his hips, locking her ankles behind his back.

Snug and tight, the wet heat of her brushed against the tip of his eager cock. His hands slid under her thighs to help take the weight, and he held back the instinct to drive into her with a growl.

"Lesson number one," Kanako began, pulling back from his lips and breaking him out of his visualisation. "I really like feeling your strength, but I don't like it if it makes me feel weak. Okay?" Kanako was looking down at him quite seriously, and considering her position, more than a little shyly. "If I say stop, I'm not playing games."

"Understood."

"I like your mouth." Kanako kissed it again for good measure.

"I got that."

She laughed, "No, I mean I like it *everywhere*. Tongue, but no teeth."

Daniel gulped, his cock giving an extra pulse. "Okay, good to know."

"I like it on top." Kanako squirmed her hips from side to side and grinned at his rolling moan.

"Me too," he admitted hoarsely, walking her towards the sofa.

"Awww, okay. You can have a turn on top, too."

"Kanako."

"Mmm?"

"Enough talking, now."

"Mmm, good point." She brought her lips back to his.

Daniel's body was made for sex, Kana decided, watching him concentrate intently on rolling on the condom he'd slid from his wallet. She'd never really gone for brawn before, but she could see right off the bat she'd been missing out.

All that rugby training meant he was built for lifting, holding, and endurance. His hands were almost large enough to circumnavigate her waist, which made her feel incredibly feminine, and his shoulders gave her stomach butterflies in the best possible way. The muscles on his chest were to die for, and her fingers were drawn to touch and explore every centimetre.

Daniel wasn't, however, built for the rather small couch.

They slid as one to the floor, laughing.

Kana pushed him back to lie flat on the rug, kneeling astride his midriff. "My turn first," she decided, gliding her wet self along him a few times for her own gratification before angling her hips to take him in. Daniel moaned her name, his hands coming to her waist as she inched her body downwards, naturally bucking up to meet her.

"*Stop.*"

Daniel's eyes flew to Kana's, fingertips biting into her hips. "Stop *now*?" he choked out.

"Don't worry, *I'm* not going to stop." She frowned in concentration, manoeuvring them both until the head of his warm circumference was snug in her own wetness, getting the angle just right. "Give me a moment to get used to the size of you." She hoped like hell they'd fit, Daniel was big all over.

She saw the flicker of comprehension in Daniel's eyes, followed by a look of intense focus. As she edged him slowly inside, taking in more of his length, she could feel the hot, thick pulse of Daniel's want deep in her core. The tight strain of every other muscle in his body was like a spring, wound up tight as he lay stock-still beneath her.

Kana exhaled when she reached his full length, her pubic bone meeting the warm pressure of his body. The combined power of being in charge, and filling herself to the hilt coursed through her veins.

Daniel's arms snapped back into action, and he began to lift her off. "Did that hurt? Are you...?"

She smiled in answer, bearing down on him again—a little

smoother this time—and Daniel's head rolled back on a moan. Her own breath was coming in gasps. He *was* big, but hell, it felt good to be full, and she was so wet for him.

Once more, faster. Then faster again.

Kana felt the hum begin with the rhythm, like a sugar rush building to hit. Smooth as silk, and sly as liquid.

"Daniel?"

"Ah…"

"Help me. Touch me," she whispered, taking his hands and showing him where, showing him how, as she slid up and down his shaft. "Help me come."

"Holy… *fuck*." Daniel was about as coherent as she felt.

Time warped into infinitesimal portions. Every slide of Daniel's clever fingers on her clitoris, every rasp of his palm on her nipples sent her closer to the edge of that high cliff. His hips were thrusting up to meet hers and she wanted to jump into the void.

God, she was *dying* to leap.

Her back curved into the pure release of it, as her mouth formed one word.

"*Motto…*" More.

Daniel gave her everything, and when she careened over the edge of the precipice, he fell too.

———

When Daniel became aware of his raging thirst, and the TV remote digging into his back, he found Kanako was lying spread-eagled across his chest like a cat on a beanbag.

Her breath was deep and smooth, and she didn't stir, even when he brought his hand up to take the weight of her hair and bring it up to his nose.

Maybe it was more grapefruit than lemon. Sweet and tangy.

He was loath to disentangle himself. It was warm under Kanako, and she seemed sublimely content snuggled into his chest. He tried to edge them both sideways off the obstacle, accidentally switching the TV on with his shoulder instead.

The late night infomercial brought Kanako's head up, and she blinked first at the screen, then at him.

A slow, self-satisfied smile tugged on the corners of her mouth. "Hi."

"Hi, yourself." He laughed, re-adjusting his body under her.

"Am I squishing you?" Kanako rolled off to the side and knelt, stretching both arms above her head.

"No, but…" He reached behind himself and pulled out the offending remote, switching the TV to mute. The blue light from the screen glowed across Kanako's naked body.

"Oh! How uncomfortable." Kanako stood without any self-consciousness, feline-like, and held one hand outstretched towards him. "Would you like a shower?"

His body gave another solid kick of awareness.

"Maybe a cold one," he muttered, following two steps behind her, and very much enjoying the rear view.

———

"How are you feeling?" Daniel asked Kana as they both flopped on her bed, still wrapped in towels.

"Very clean," she stated, after a little thought.

"Clean, as in I'm just so clean-tired, I could sleep for a week?" Daniel paused, "Or clean as in clean enough to eat?"

Kana rolled over to face him with some surprise, pulling up on one elbow.

He wasn't done?

"Are you making me an offer I can't refuse?"

Eyes twinkling with humour, Daniel grinned as he looked her up and down overtly.

"I bloody hope so." He ran one finger lightly from her collarbone, all the way down her arm to the tip of her middle finger, leaving goose bumps in his wake. "Tongue, but no teeth," he promised.

Kana shuddered, the sensual tone of Daniel's voice and the fact he'd actually listened to her wants doing crazy things to her.

"*Waaait* a minute… are you just angling for a turn on top?" She narrowed her eyes.

"Oh, that too." Daniel laughed. When he did, his face relaxed into full humour, and Kana leant over and kissed him hard on the lips without thinking twice.

"That's your most attractive feature," she murmured against his ear a moment later.

"What, my mouth?"

"No. Your laugh."

When Daniel woke the second time, it was in the annex bed with Kana's body curled into a ball next to him, her forehead resting against the side of his ribs.

It was so quiet, he could hear the faint hum of the extractor fans in the barn, pulling the glaze-tainted air out of Kanako's workspace. She'd told him she was firing some exhibit pieces, and he knew she'd be unloading sometime in the morning. Better if he wasn't underfoot at that stage.

He tried to gauge the time by the moonlight, and brightness of the stars. The curtains were open, the night view blanketing him with the memory of his father's old stories. Possibly because he'd relayed some of them to Kanako earlier in the night, when she'd asked him to name the stars.

Te ao Marama. A world of mythology shone from the beautiful moon. Full, round and heavy, she ruled the night sky, throwing silver light across the room. The sky god, Ranginui, slept deeply under his cloak of jewel-like stars, dreaming of his lost lover, Papatūānuku. But although his earthly woman lay lush below him, seemingly close in the shrouded darkness, she was forever out of his reach.

Daniel blinked. He should leave now.

They hadn't discussed this part, but Kanako hadn't invited him to stay overnight, and what with the landlord thing...

He should go while Marama still shone.

15

DOUBT

"Doubt separates people.
It is a poison that disintegrates friendships
and breaks up pleasant relations.
It is a thorn that irritates and hurts:
it is a sword that kills."
- Buddha

Kana stretched her body out in starfish-mode, spreading herself across the cotton sheets. Her bed smelt delicious. It smelt of Daniel.

Her head snapped up.

Daniel.

She held her breath, but couldn't hear any movement in the annex. All was still, except for the faint hum from the barn.

The sun shone through onto the duvet, denoting another pretty, blue-skied day. Stretching again, she took a moment to register how her body was feeling. Muscles she hadn't used for a while let themselves be known, but underlying that she was experiencing a deep-seated contentment.

If she were a cat, she'd purr.

Kana padded silently to the bathroom to brush her teeth, then went in search of Daniel.

The only thing she could find in the annex that proved he'd been there at all was his evening jacket hanging over one of her kitchen chairs. She sat down heavily on one of the neighbouring chairs, staring at it.

That was it? No message? No *nothing*?

The contented buzz she'd been experiencing shifted to a slightly cheapened form, making her realise she'd been a bit of a dork not to factor this into her expectations. Just because the earth had moved for *her*, didn't necessarily mean the feeling was mutual.

A piece of paper poking out of the dark jacket pocket caught her eye, and she pounced on it.

Kana realised the instant she unfolded the note and glimpsed the lipstick transfer that it wasn't meant for her eyes, but she went ahead and studied it anyway. Under the kiss mark was a name and phone number.

Charlotte.

Whoever that might be.

"Well, happy birthday, Kanako. You prize idiot," she muttered to herself.

So far, so good.

The bust of Halfback sat on the fibreglass matting on the kiln bench, the clear glaze showing every tiny detail worked into the white clay. Like a laughing white wolf, he smiled back at Kana, and elation lifted her.

He was better than good. He was *perfect*.

With her protective mitts covering her right up to her elbows, she moved to the second kiln and eased the heavily insulated lid further open. Closing her eyes for a moment, she sent up a mute prayer to calm herself, as she always did before taking a peek into the depths of the large, cooling oven. Her eyes took a second to register what she was seeing before she had to back away from the intense heat.

Oh, *God*, no.

No!

What could've possibly gone wrong? This couldn't be happening.

The single most important thing Kana had to remember when loading the kiln was the slim-fingered ceramic heat gauge—*and there it was*—lying redundantly on the shelf beside the second appliance.

She'd never placed it in?

That messed up by Ken's phone call the day before yesterday, she'd totally forgotten to put the bloody *temperature* probe in.

"Oh, shit… *shit!*" Kana moaned, backing away from the mess.

The extractor fans in the wall and ceiling continued to chug away, pumping and filtering warm air out, and in that moment she fervently wished she could fly off with it.

Without any means of registering heat levels, the kiln would've heated to maximum temperature and stayed there, rather than following the carefully programmed series of steps she'd planned on the timer.

Such a rookie mistake.

She was lucky she hadn't burnt the whole damn barn down, while she and Daniel fooled around on the lounge floor.

When the kiln was finally cool enough to unpack, it was even worse than Kana had imagined. She'd not only totally destroyed a piece of work that'd taken her weeks to complete, but fried the expensive elements in Daniel's appliance as well. The interior shelf was also ruined, the run-off from the over-cooked glaze morphing it into an unsightly, bubbly grey.

Her final piece. Daniel's bust.

Ugly as all sin.

Time and energy was one thing, but it paled in comparison to her reputation as a serious potter if this piece ever saw the light of day.

The first sob rose from deep within her as she sank to her knees on the concrete floor, then she put her head in her grubby old kiln mitts, and howled.

There was no answer at the barn door.

Daniel was sure Kanako was supposed to be unloading the kiln this morning. Maybe she'd finished already and gone out to celebrate? Gone for an early lunch in town with Adele?

He walked around Kanako's SUV to the annex door, giving that a knock too.

Where was she? Still sleeping?

He looked down at the offering in his hand. Wildflowers from the embankment above the orchard, where he'd been working since early this morning.

Sleep had come easily after he'd crept home to his own bed, ridiculously late last night, but he'd woken again at six a.m. with a longing that wouldn't budge. He'd been imagining Kanako curled naked under the bedspread in the annex, her rich sheen of hair kinked from the braid she usually wore, spreading in invitation across the pillow.

Daniel groaned, imagining snuggling her sweet body close to him and waking her with kisses in her hair, kisses on her neck, kisses all over.

'I like your mouth,' Kanako had said, and he'd listened. Thank God he'd listened, because she hadn't been kidding.

Kanako's little moans and writhing hips had been the best form of encouragement a hot-blooded male could have, and Daniel had taken his time discovering exactly which areas of her silky anatomy liked to be kissed, and how. Her body had arced into a taut bow as she'd come, pulsing against his fingers and mouth, and the insistent tugging on his hair had brought him back to gaze down on her satiated, lazy grin.

"Holy *hell...* you're a quick study," Kanako had murmured, stroking her fingers down the side of his face. Her cheeks were peachy with post coital warmth, and the delicate skin on her neck still bore the faint rash from his kisses.

He didn't say it aloud, but holy *hell*, Kanako had given him an incredibly responsive body to commit to memory.

Kanako had brought her hips up in invitation, brushing her sex against his stomach. "Correct me if I'm wrong, but while you're up there... *tsugi.*"

It was no use to get all cranked up about it again, so Daniel tried to mentally push the arousal from the memory aside. To stop himself from barging back into the annex at dawn, he'd dragged his bones up to the orchard instead, with a bucket-load of tools in one hand, and a spade over his shoulder.

He'd been meaning to prune the grape vine since the arborist had given him concrete instructions, and he needed to clear the ground for the new flower garden.

His surge of morning energy had been put to good use, after all.

The dawn light had been beautiful, soft dew on the grass under the freshly pruned apples, and the final tatty leaves of the grapevine glowing golden. He'd whistled as he'd worked, and Halfback had kept him company, racing off at every new sound, and returning with a stupid grin on his face.

Content, just like his master.

Feeling slightly sheepish about the romantic sentiment, Daniel had taken the time to pick Kanako a bunch of lupins. It was probably okay to let himself into the annex and leave the flowers on the table for her. He had some lemons in his pocket, too.

He checked his watch before knocking once more and letting himself in through the unlocked door.

Just gone eleven.

Taking his workbooks off in the mudroom to the right, he then headed into the kitchen in his thick farm socks, calling out as he went. He was slightly unsure what their footing would be, now.

"Kanako? I've let myself in. Are you home? "

"Go away." Kanako's voice was rough and flat—completely devoid of any warmth.

Daniel felt the cool cut of it somewhere around mid-section.

He could see her now, as he reached the door jam to the kitchen. She was sitting at the scrubbed pine table, or more precisely, was half sprawled across it. Wearing the old fisherman's cable knit that was far too big for her, she was gazing out the latticed window with her head down, left cheek resting on her forearm.

She didn't raise her head to look at him.

"I mean it. Leave me alone." Kanako may've been cruising up towards anger, but Daniel could hear she was reining in some other emotions, too.

Tears? Was she crying? He hesitated.

"What's up, sweetheart?" The endearment slipped out of his mouth without him meaning it to.

Moving further into the room, he padded silently on socked feet, squatting next to the table so they were eye level.

Kanako ignored him, continuing to stare out the window.

She'd definitely been crying, but was dry eyed now. Still, she was beginning to worry him. His hand reached out to stroke an errant strand of hair off her forehead.

"Kanako? Tell me what I can do to help."

"Help? You can't help me," she ground out. "I'm a mess. This is all such a big *mess*." Her voice was tired, and more than a little slurred.

Still no eye contact.

Daniel looked furtively around the room, spotting the long oven mitts thrown down on the other end of the table. So Kanako *had* unloaded the kiln. He also noted the empty wine bottle next to the sink, and the fact Kanako's right hand was curled around the neck of another one, open on her lap.

"Ahh, you're pissed." He was somewhat relieved. Something he knew how to deal with.

Weird time of the day to be sloshed, but drunk as a whaler all the same.

"Yes, I'm bloody pissed!" Kanako raised her voice and head at the same time. Thumping the second, partially drunk bottle down on the table—hard enough to slop some of the contents from the narrow opening.

She looked straight at him for the first time since he'd come in.

"Pissed off, used up, and fucked over." Her anger flared brightly for a moment before moving on to desperation. "You're so beautiful, Mr D, and I'm just *sooo* toast."

Kanako slurred the word 'beautiful,' to the point Daniel wasn't exactly sure that's what he'd heard. She looked completely spent.

"Kanako… What?"

"I mean it, Rugby. Could you just…? I can't do this right now." Her speech was muffled as her head slunk back to its former position, and again, she looked out the window.

Had she just called him Rugby?

"Sure…" Daniel placated quietly, his optimism from the orchard sinking slowly into his socks. "Sure, okay." He rose up to his full height. "I'm just going to put these flowers in water, then I'll get out of your way."

Daniel found a jar big enough to house the bunch of

wildflowers, moving quietly around the kitchen, putting the empty Riesling bottle in the recycling and the lemons in the fruit-bowl on the counter. Kanako's eyes were closed when he knelt back down next to her and eased her fingers from around the second wine bottle.

Merlot on top of Riesling? Man, she was going to feel this later.

Looking into her half-hidden face, tenderness gripped Daniel's guts at the faint blue shadows under her closed lashes, and the little indented frown between her brows. There was a small nick out of one cheek, along with a smear of blood.

What brought Kanako to this? She said she didn't usually drink.

Her lips parted slightly in her sleep, giving her the aura of childlike vulnerability, and a cold finger that felt a lot like doubt settled between Daniel's ribs.

Was she regretting last night? That must be it. Well, shit. Maybe he'd misread…?

No. It'd felt right, then.

This was the part that felt all wrong.

Daniel knew Kanako had enjoyed being with him—*more* than enjoyed. She hadn't tried to stage it, or hide anything from him, and there'd been an honest rawness in the way they'd made love. Being with Kanako had felt good like he'd thought it never could again. Immersed, free, fun, and insanely hot. He'd been forced by the ceramicist to actually be himself, not some trumped up media-friendly version of Dante D.

After tipping the red wine dregs down the sink, he ran a fresh glass of water and placed it on the table, deciding against laying Kanako down on the sofa in case she threw up. He eased into the lounge, taking the sofa rug to throw across her shoulders and a small cushion to slide under her head.

Checking she was still breathing fine, Daniel stopped to gaze at her again.

Ever since she'd turned up on pizza night, with mānuka flowers in her hair. Since he'd first kissed her on the shore, tasting of turmeric and cinnamon. Hell, ever since he'd first spoken to Kanako at the lake, her soft smile had taken away his capacity to breathe, and there didn't seem to be any turning back.

It was inconvenient, but highly likely, he was falling for his mother's artist in residence.

Kanako's hair had loosely flopped across one eye, and Daniel manoeuvred it back behind her ear, careful not to wake her. Her skin was as smooth as fine porcelain, and that went for very bloody millimetre of her.

He frowned again at the blood. What had scratched her face?

"Stop it," Kanako muttered in her sleep, swatting at his hand as if it was an annoying blowfly. She scrunched the cushion between both hands and plopped her head back onto it, facing the other way this time.

Sassy wee madam.

Daniel was grinning when he lifted the kiln mitts off the end of the table, intending to slip them inside the barn door on his way out. He stood stock-still, staring down at the hammer that had lain hidden underneath.

What the hell?

His smile faded and he was filled with a wave of unease. Picking up the hammer he tested the weight of it, and as he turned it over in his hand, the sinking feeling deepened.

Letting himself quietly out of the annex, Daniel walked around to the barn door, which was also unbolted. Mitts and hammer in hand, he pushed it open with a creak, waiting for his eyes to adjust to the softer light, and the carnage.

"Holy *crap*," Daniel let out the expletive in a soft puff. "Jesus, Kanako, what've you done?" He walked further into the interior, wincing as shards of pottery crunched under his work boots, and turned a slow three-sixty.

Pulling his phone out from his back pocket, Daniel drew up the number he needed—speed dialled.

"Hi, Adele. Look, I think I need some backup of the female variety... Yes, it's Kanako. She's okay, but... How soon can you get here?"

16

WHO GETS BURNED

"Holding on to anger is like grasping a hot coal
with the intent of throwing it at someone else;
you are the one who gets burned."
- Buddha

"Oh my god, I want to die," Kana moaned.

Adele held her hair as she retched into the bowl again, but her stomach was finally empty.

"Two bottles of wine will do that." Adele handed her a wet flannel. "What was your reasoning, hair of the dog?"

"No." Kana rolled onto her back with great care, willing the world to *please* stop spinning. "I screwed up."

"I'm well aware, having just flushed the evidence down the loo," Adele wisecracked.

"Not just with the alcohol. I screwed up a glaze-load, and fried one of your cousin's kilns. Ruined some work."

Adele didn't say anything, just kept on looking at her with intent focus.

Kana dug her fingertips into the pressure points on her clammy forehead, easing the throbbing tempo. "My ex, Kenneth, wants two thirds of the house in Christchurch, and he's hell bent on getting my car, too."

"I don't think he can do that. Unless it's all in his name?"

"No." Kana tried to open her eyes again, but the overhead light was too bright. "The car and half the house are mine."

"Right. So it's possibly just bluff and bluster on his part. You need a lawyer."

"I can't afford one right now."

"I bet that's what Ken's banking on, and I happen to know a very good divorce attorney who'll take payment after the papers are finalised."

"I forgot you were married." It was easier if Kana took shallow breaths through the mouth, giving her stomach less to complain about.

"I've known this woman much longer than that. I was working for her part-time when I met James, and she now has clients nationwide. She took me on as a student when no one else would… Not with a toddler in tow." Adele sighed as she stood, moving just out of Kana's line of sight. "Are you feeling any better?"

"As long as I don't move a muscle," Kana lamented. "What was I thinking?"

"Escape." Adele re-emerged from the ensuite bathroom with a fresh cloth, and aspirin. "We all seek it in our own way, for our own reasons. Me? I read romance. Guaranteed happy ending, no matter how crappy my day's been." She sat gingerly on the edge of the bed again. "Kana, do you mind if I ask what happened in the studio?"

"*Ugh*," Kana groaned, squeezing her eyes shut and conjuring the image of the hammer in her hand. "I took my frustration out on some stuff."

"Did you break *everything*?" Adele's voice was a little *too* soft.

"What? No." Kana cracked one eye open.

Adele was worrying at her thumbnail, gnawing at it with her teeth. She dropped her hand hastily when she realised she had an audience.

"It's just, Daniel said you'd smashed up something *big*, and I didn't want to go in there and look." Those glacier eyes were blinking rapidly. "Is the portrait of Saffy still…?"

"Oh, Yeah. *That's* fine. I was angry, but I'm not completely bonkers."

Adele leaned over and squeezed her hand in unmistakable relief.

"I smashed up Daniel's one, instead," Kana confessed.

Adele sucked in a quick breath, fingers flying to cover the O-shape her mouth had just formed.

"You didn't!" She studied Kana for a moment longer. "You *did*?"

"It was ruined, anyway. I couldn't look at it like that." She gave Adele a wry sort of half-smile.

"Still. Extreme measures."

"Trust me, it deserved them."

Adele checked her phone. "I have to go pick Saff up from her playdate now. Are you going to be alright on your own?"

"Yeah. Thanks for coming and looking after my sorry ass. A sleep and a good slap upside the head should take care of the rest."

"Should I check there's no more alcohol on the premises, or can I trust you?" Adele teased.

"I'll never touch another drop as long as I live."

"That's what they all say." Adele moved towards the door.

"Adele? I think I might've been horribly rude to your cousin." Kana felt the acute embarrassment all over again, aware the only reason Adele could've known to come and check on her was through Daniel.

Adele shrugged. "He'll live. Are we still okay for one-on-one yoga tomorrow afternoon?"

"To be honest? The thought of downward facing dog makes me want to hurl right now, but I'll go with a 'yes' at this stage."

When Kana crawled out of bed late the next morning, it wasn't with her usual verve. She managed a shower, but took her car to town rather than walking. Her legs were still a bit on the shaky side, and the sun a tad too bright. She bypassed the sushi shop and went directly for greasy hot chips instead, her body craving the fatty carbohydrate hit to soak up the remainder of her hangover.

It was standing room only at the King's Catch. She must've inadvertently hit peak time.

"How did your date go?" The stranger in front of Kana in the pickup queue received her order, and lowered her sunglasses to consider Kana over the top.

"Pardon?" She looked behind her to see if the woman was actually talking to someone else, and the simple twist of her neck made her head mutiny all over again.

"You won Dante D, didn't you? Paid for his *attention*."

"Oh. The fundraising thing? Yes." Kana rubbed at her temple, remembering with a thud she'd have to take it even easier on her spending, now. Her savings account was empty, and the kiln repair wouldn't be cheap.

The woman leaned forward conspiratorially. "Is he as good as they say?"

Kana stared at her, heat rising.

Of all the *crass…*

Hang on a minute. Was she implying Daniel slept with *all* the women who won him at auction?

Kana looked around herself again, this time noting the nods and glances her way, the whispers-behind-hands. It was worse than bloody high school.

She hated the attention, it made her want to shrink down into her jacket collar. Squaring her shoulders and lifting her chin instead, she met the other woman's eyes with a direct lack of apology.

Sure, she preferred to stay below radar, but once her invisibility cloak had been compromised, there was no point assuming the position of doormat.

"Actually, he was the perfect gentleman," she said, loud enough for more than one set of ears to pick up. "I can't have been his type." She shrugged.

"I'd say *not*." The woman looked Kana up and down, perhaps pissy about not getting any fresh gossip. "Blonde, high-society type you definitely *aren't*."

"It was worth a crack," Kana croaked, taking her own order from the server and trying to hide the shake in her hands by gripping the package tightly. "And all for a good cause."

She exited the shop seething.

―――――

"I'm so pleased you won D's bachelor auction." Adele was inverted in a downward facing dog, looking backwards at Kana through her ankles. Bits of her mind-of-its-own hair were springing out of her severe bun, surrounding her pink-cheeked face. "It was touch and go there for a while with gnarly Sharon."

Kana's own face was reddening, and she moved out of view to put her hands gently on Adele's shoulders, getting her to release tension there.

She remembered Sharon distinctly, and how her own protective streak had kicked in when the blonde had smugly upped her bid to a cool thousand—false eyelashes batting.

Or had it been Kana's dormant competitive side, finally kicking in?

Daniel had turned to look at her for one measured second before she'd stood, and something about the way his eyes had sought hers…

"Turn the eyes of your elbows to face each other, and ease your shoulders away from your ears," Kana tutored Adele, trying to retain an outward sense of calm.

No wonder Sharon was so pissed off. The newest addition to Wānaka's female population had gone ahead and wrenched the woman's scratching post right out from under her.

"It keeps your back more supported, and strengthens your arms."

Kana had opted out of attempting the positions herself today, her head still delicate, and was merely putting Adele through her paces.

"It's a bit of a gamble who he gets, poor baby." Adele laughed.

"You weren't tempted to bail him out yourself?" Kana prodded, the devil in her still a touch uncertain on the cousins' relationship status.

Adele had displayed a total hands-off approach at the fundraiser. Surely if the other woman had any romantic interest in Daniel, she would've put forward a bid?

Instead, she'd supported Kana's win.

"*Pay* for a date with my *cousin*?" Adele enunciated each word incredulously, as if the very idea left a bad taste in her mouth. "No, thank you. And fifteen *hundred*? Jeez, I hope he treated you to crayfish and candlelight for that price!"

Kana bit her lip. "I'm more of a cheap date, actually." Adele's arms began to shake. "Ease back down onto your hands and knees. Elbow eyes," she repeated as the redhead's elbows crept towards hyperextension again. "Buttocks to your heels, and reach out with your arms. Further if you can." She pressed gently on Adele's hips. "This is extended child pose. You should feel the release down here in your lower lumbar."

"Ahh…" It came out muffled by the mat. "That feels good. Where did D take you then?"

Heaven.

Daniel had taken Kana to heaven, twice, then walked out while she slept.

She cleared her throat, not willing to divulge any more than she had to. "I don't even know the name of the place."

Adele continued to shoot the breeze about her cousin, not picking up on Kana's increasing discomfort with the subject matter.

"It's great he got a real date, with a real person. Women tend to see him as muscle, money, and sex appeal, and ignore the brains and heart behind the operation. He gets propositioned all the time, like he's some sort of gigolo offering a public service. They think if they can get him alone, he'll be only too happy to sleep with them.

One bat-shit crazy woman even claimed to be having his baby, and he got slapped with a court order to take a paternity test. He'd never even *been* with her. He was so polite to her about the whole damn thing, but he must've been livid on the inside."

Adele moved back into cat pose.

"Knees hip-width apart," Kana reminded her, amazed her voice came out even when her mind was in turmoil, and her stomach was threatening to mutiny again.

She'd gravely miscalculated Adele's agenda with the cousin-on-cousin thing, and it appeared she'd also misused Daniel in the worst possible way.

His behaviour wasn't reprehensible, *her own* was.

"Then there was Cam's fiancée. She went after Dan too," Adele added with a disquieting show of nonchalance.

"Shal?" The name squeaked out of Kana, an image of the dark-haired beauty popping into her head, complete with designer everything.

"No!" Adele laughed, twisting to look back at her properly.

"Before Shal. A woman called Jody. She pulled a real number on Cam."

Kana was so embarrassed, she was amazed she could even meet her own eyes in the annex mirror. She'd bought Daniel's time, then used him—exactly like the gnarly blonde would've done. No wonder he'd disappeared by the time she woke up in the morning.

She applied some mascara, but decided against blusher. Best not, under the circumstances.

It'd be okay. She'd walk up to the main house and apologise until she was red-faced, and Daniel could revert to his usual cold and gritty.

When Kana knocked on the farmhouse door, her hands a tad shaky, she gripped Daniel's dinner jacket even tighter. Returning the single item of clothing was a reasonable excuse to turn up uninvited, though he might not even be home.

He'd gone out. Thank Buddha.

She released the breath she'd been holding and turned with some relief to leave, just as the front door swung open behind her.

"Kana! Lovely to see you!"

"Poppy, I didn't know you were… Are you, um… Hi." Kana stumbled over her surprise, awkwardly returning the hug Poppy offered with one arm. "I'm surprised to see you. Has Daniel gone?"

"Gone where?" Poppy cocked her head to one side and considered Kana with those all-seeing eyes, making her nerves jangle.

"I don't know. Japan? He's usually in Japan, right? When you're here."

"Not always." The voice from behind Poppy was sardonic. "Sometimes she just turns up for the hell of it," Daniel teased his mother.

"Come on in." Poppy threw the door wide, and for a split second, Kana considered bolting in the other direction. She was still holding Daniel's dinner jacket in one hand, trying to hide it behind her back without appearing shady.

"Thank you." Her smile felt twitchy and unnatural on her face, as she looked from mother to son.

"I've just boiled the kettle. Cup of tea?" Poppy offered, moving towards the kitchen.

As soon as the older woman's back was turned, Kana shoved the jacket at Daniel.

"You left this," she hissed.

He didn't immediately take it, so she pushed it against his chest again, a little more urgently.

"Thanks." Daniel finally took his jacket and threw it with careless, but accurate aim onto the hall chair. "You look a lot better than the last time I saw you."

"Still green, Kana?" Poppy asked from the kitchen doorway.

Kana scowled at Daniel. Had he told every damn person in Wānaka she'd drunk herself sick as a dog?

Unnecessarily thorough of him.

"Green tea for you?" Poppy re-issued the invitation when she didn't initially get a response.

"Oh!" Green *tea*. "Yes. Yes, thank you."

When Daniel's mother disappeared, Kana took stock of her options. She could get this over with now, or come back another time.

"I'm sorry," she blurted. "I've come to apologise. My behaviour was just awful. I don't usually drink. At all. I don't remember much, frankly, but I remember you being there, and think I was possibly quite rude."

"You don't remember our date?" Daniel sounded quite taken aback.

"No. I remember *that*!" She punched his arm. "I mean the morning *after*."

Poppy chose that moment to stick her head back into the hall, and Kana slid away from Daniel with a guilty sidestep.

"D, don't make Kana stand in the doorway for pity's sake. Take her into the lounge."

"Right." Daniel turned, closing the door behind Kana with a definitive click.

Kana watched mutely as her number-one escape route went up in smoke.

Daniel's hand slid to the small of her back, making her jump. His touch brought back distinct memories of the annex, and what they'd gotten up to there.

"I know where it is," she muttered, scuttling ahead of him, out of his solicitous range.

The lounge, like the bedrooms they'd just passed, faced the view of the lake and the Canadian maples lining the driveway. Kana loved this room; its furniture reminiscent of a gentleman's library, with deep browns and greens complimenting the dark oak panelling... Though right now she'd rather be anywhere else.

When they sat, Daniel on the square-armed sofa and Kana on a leather armchair, she leant forward conspiratorially, knowing her cheeks were already flaming.

"I had no intention of using you," she started, the words painful to come by. "I paid for your time, and..." She was scrambling around for the right thing to say, and Daniel wasn't making things any easier. With his elbows on his knees, he was craning forward and frowning at her. "I'm sorry if you felt obligated."

"Are we still talking about the morning after?" he clarified evenly.

"No," Kana squeaked, trying to talk in a whisper, but finding her throat had all but closed up. "Our one night stand."

Daniel raised his eyebrows and opened his mouth to speak, but Poppy was already breezing in with a tray.

Kana hoped like hell that Daniel's mother was extremely hard of hearing. It would be nice, around about now, if the earth could just open up and swallow her whole.

"You take honey and lemon in yours, don't you Kana?"

She nodded mutely, her tongue stuck to the roof of her mouth with pure embarrassment.

"Bittersweet." Poppy smiled softly, moving the teapot to the forefront of the tray.

Kana stared at the crockery. "Oh!" Her hand went out to touch the familiar lid of the little two-toned teapot, snuggled into its cup. "You bought one of my teapots!"

"Yes." Poppy beamed. "I found it in the Dunedin gallery, and it was love at first sight. Don't you just adore it when that happens? Serendipity."

Perhaps immune to the undercurrent in the room—but going by the smirk on her face, fully aware—Poppy continued with the centuries-old ceremony of pouring tea. After chattering for a few minutes about the Dunedin gallery and its owner, she rose again.

"Oops, forgot the biscuits." Poppy sauntered out.

"Let me get this straight," Daniel began the instant the door shut behind his mother, his voice icy. "You've come to apologise for using me as a one night stand."

"Yes," Kana answered miserably, unable to meet his eyes and staring instead at the teapot, still nestled into its cup.

Yin and Yang. A perfect pair.

"I had no intention of making you feel cheap. It's not something I make a habit of, it just happened. You're very attractive, and it all just kind of clicked for me. I haven't been single in such a long time, and you…" He'd gone and blown everything out of the water. "I wanted you to know I wasn't expecting that. I didn't plan *any* of that when I bid on you."

Daniel made a growling sound, deep in his throat. "Come over here."

Squirming, Kana looked up at him. His brows were drawn in a hard line.

"Ah, no. I don't think so," she decided solemnly.

"Chocolate-chippie," Poppy announced, walking in and placing a plate of biscuits on the coffee table.

Daniel turned to glare at his mother, but Poppy just smiled serenely back.

It was the most awkward afternoon tea Kana had ever sat through, and she'd experienced a fair few on her trips to Japan as a child. As soon as she gauged it polite to do so, she stood, brushing her hands on her jeans.

"Well, I'd better be off. Thank you so much for the tea, Poppy. Lovely to see you back." She scooted out of there as fast as she could without actually breaking into a run.

———

"I wouldn't think any less of you if you went after her, Datsun," Poppy poked at Daniel.

"Stay out of it, Mum," he ground out, but he was rising even as he spoke, already moving towards the door. "I mean it. If you pop your head out to offer us fudge slice, I could be forgiven for snapping it clean off."

He could hear Poppy chuckling behind him as he stormed down the hall and out the front door after Kanako.

She'd just made it to the verandah steps, and he swung down one below her, blocking her exit.

Kanako blinked at him, but didn't say a word.

They were eye to eye, and Daniel found the change in height strangely unsettling. It no longer felt like he was even *remotely* in charge. Rectifying that, he slid one hand to the back of Kanako's neck, and the other to her waist, pulling her in for a long, hard kiss.

She tasted sharply of citrus, mellowing into honey and smooth green tea. Coolly aloof eased into softly pliant in his arms, and Daniel forgot everything around him but the heady infusion of Kanako's mouth.

He'd been bemused by her intentions when she'd turned up at his door today. As far as he was concerned, their tryst at the annex had been as much his idea as it had been Kanako's.

He'd also been incensed by her use of the term 'one night stand.' That's not how it'd felt at the time, and wasn't how he viewed it now.

Kanako seemed confused about where he stood, and what he wanted from this. Hopefully kissing her senseless would clear that up. Perhaps she'd assumed because they hadn't actually dated, as such…

"Kanako?"

"Mmm?" Her eyes were darkly golden and incredibly close.

"Come skydiving with me today."

17

WE OURSELVES

"No one saves us but ourselves.
No one can and no one may.
We ourselves must walk the path."
- Buddha

"You never asked me what my vices were," Daniel's voice rumbled behind Kana.

It was the strangest of sensations to be strapped to him without being able to see his face, the small aircraft shaking and rattling as it took off. He felt solid and dependable, but although the Jump Master had confirmed Daniel's assertions he was qualified to jump tandem with her, Kana's belly had begun to quake with her split-decision to say 'yes' to this madness.

The afternoon training session was now just a blur in her head, and she remembered precisely diddlysquat from the intensive lesson.

"That's your business, you're not obligated to tell me."

Daniel remained silent, but perhaps sensing her nerves, found one of her hands and laced his fingers into it.

"Unless you want to confess your sins before we plummet towards certain death?" she ventured, practically shouting above the strain of the engines.

"Don't even joke about it," Daniel negated near her ear, though he was laughing himself. "Safety's paramount. I packed our chutes myself."

"Holy Buddha, I hope you know what you're doing," Kana muttered under her breath, catching another glimpse of the incredible landscape below as the plane banked around, forever climbing. "Alright, you'd better tell me, then. What's your vice?" she raised her voice to the level she knew he'd be able to hear.

"Painkillers," Daniel stated clearly. "Codeine. Demerol. Methadone. Whatever I could get my hands on. Took me years to get off, but I've been clean for a long time now."

Kana tried straining around to see Daniel's face, but the harness prevented it.

"Well, that beats Creme Eggs, hands down," she finally called over her shoulder.

Daniel's returning laughter rumbled against her shoulder blade.

"They were prescription drugs, at first. I finished playing rugby on a fairly substantial injury."

"Adele told me."

"I'm not trying to justify it, but that's when it started, and my life spiralled down around it. I guess I was mourning my career, but I hurt a lot of people on the way. It's one of the reasons I jump. Skydiving's the best high I've found to replace it, though I've been dabbling with some other possibilities…" Daniel drew Kana's hand back above her head, his fingers still threaded through hers, and surprised a squeak out of her when he licked the sensitive flesh of her inner wrist.

His mouth was warm and wet, and she felt the answering tug deep within her core, making her want a lot more of that. Much, much more.

The pilot called out something unintelligible.

"We're up," Daniel interpreted.

Kanako hadn't been kidding that day on Ruby Island. Faced with the open door of the plane and the view from fifteen thousand feet, Daniel could feel her body itching to jump. No shrinking back into

166

him or changing her mind at the last minute. Instead, he was holding her back as she strained towards the roar of the wind.

"Waiting for my signal," he reminded her, eyes on the pilot. "Hold on to your straps. Head back on me." When she didn't follow the final instruction, he cradled the front of Kanako's helmet, easing her head back against his shoulder as he counted aloud, "In three, two, one—"

They were out into the great abyss.

Gravity pulled and snatched, sucking them down toward the earth, while the air pressure seemingly held them up. There was an unbelievable thrill in handing yourself to the fates, velocity fierce against face and body as you hurtled towards the dirt.

Daniel tapped Kanako's shoulder; the signal to let her know she could wing her arms out now, and fly.

A hit like no other—a place where loss and disappointment had no hold. The pure joy of living became the only choice, and the only way forward.

Through the adrenaline, Daniel counted out the timing, pulling the chute before his watch set off its altitude warning. He felt the distinctive, solid tug of it deploying, but counted out again before looking up to check their rig, watching the final corner of yellow silk unfurl and fill out on catching the updraft.

Sublime, this calm after the storm, the quiet of the bird's eye view and jaw dropping scenery. But the woman harnessed in front of him was shaking.

"Okay?" he called forward, before realising Kanako was laughing—hard out laughing with the thrill of it. "You liked that, then?" He laughed himself. Her effervescence was contagious.

"It felt like we were everywhere and nowhere all at once! Like we were jumping into a wormhole, or a vortex through to another dimension…" Kanako's shouted words were whipped away by the wind and she spoke fast, her language tripping all over itself. "I knew it would feel good, but that was beyond my expectations. That was amazing! Look at this place, just look at it. You *live* here, you lucky bugger!"

Daniel did look at it, really taking it in this time; the lake, the crests and cavities of the mountains, the untamed rawness, offset by the welcoming settlements below.

Not to mention the woman he was sharing it with.

"Yeah. I'm a lucky bugger," he agreed.

When they touched down and unharnessed, Kanako bounced around him like a puppy, her eyes shining with excitement.

"Let's do it again, can we do it again?"

Daniel took Kanako's face in his hands and kissed her, not caring that their helmets clonked together, and loving the way her energy transferred to her mouth. Their combined adrenaline highs built immediate heat, and when they broke apart, both were breathless.

"I'd have to say, that's a better response than Adele," he quipped. "She screamed from the moment we jumped, until the moment her feet touched Papatūānuku."

Kana became very still.

Of course, Daniel would've brought Adele here. Probably multiple women. She'd been so eager to think of it as a special connection, because it'd felt like Daniel had shared an inner part of himself.

But that was just plain ridiculous.

He'd just meant it as a way to spend time—have some company on his high. He'd been coming here anyway, and it'd proved to be a convenient, all-in-one way to show her the sights.

She was merely the annex tenant, his mother's little art project.

Kana reined herself in.

What was she expecting from this man? She'd told him she wasn't looking for anything complicated, and that was still true, right?

"Adele didn't enjoy it, then?" Kana asked in a carefully even tone.

Daniel grinned. "That's an understatement. She definitely prefers her feet on the ground."

"But it rings your bell. Along with rugby, and your boat. This is what you like best," she surmised, throwing her arm wide to encompass the sky, the airfield, and the little plane coming in to land.

"Yeah, I guess you could say that." Daniel had bundled the

chute, and looked down at her as they walked side-by-side back to the clubhouse. "I also like to keep fit and play in the odd charity match. I've been getting more involved in kids' sport, and motivational speaking, too. The grassroots—that's rewarding."

"Like rippa-rugby?"

"Yeah. That's one of them. Special training days, ball-skills and activities for when the grounds are closed, that sort of thing."

"You should teach them yoga. Not just for stretches, but relaxation techniques. Adele said something about Saffy last week that made me think children should be learning breath regulation. Meditation." She turned to Daniel as the idea took hold. "Wouldn't it be a great way to release nervous tension before a game?"

Daniel stared at her. "Are you offering?"

"What? No," she backtracked. "I don't know anything about rugby."

"And I don't know anything about yoga," Daniel countered. "But together we could come up with something."

"Maybe," she hedged, about to step back into the hangar. "Where do we pay?"

Daniel blinked almost comically. "It's taken care of."

"I can pay my own way," she argued.

"I invited you," Daniel insisted. "And I have a long ways to go before I come anywhere near covering what you paid for fish and chips," he muttered.

Daniel dropped Kanako back at the annex.

He'd offered another jump, so sure she would say yes he'd already started checking out their gear, but she'd inexplicably changed her mind somewhere between the jump and the clubhouse. He'd been surprised into silence when she'd thanked him politely, then firmly turned him down.

"You enjoyed it, though?" he'd finally asked.

"Absolutely!" Kanako had grabbed his forearm and smiled right up into his face, eyes sparkling, and the light from the dive shining through. "I can honestly say that was one of the coolest things I've ever done." Then she'd looked down at her hand on his arm and quickly removed it. "But I should come back down to earth now."

Stupidly, within the superhuman brain-space of the free-fall, Daniel had forgotten to compensate for his stuffed knee, and landed heavily on landfall. He rubbed at the ache absently as he pulled into the annex driveway.

"Sore?" Kanako nodded towards the offending knee.

He moved his hand back to the steering wheel and parked.

"Coming right." He used the fallback response he'd used for years, whenever anyone asked after his bloody knee.

"Is it?"

Daniel could tell by the tone in Kanako's voice she knew damn well he'd just brushed her off with a half-truth.

"Sore," he conceded, perhaps a little on the gruff side.

"Would you trust me to try something?" Kanako asked quietly, turning towards him, not showing any signs of moving off the subject.

"Do I have a choice?"

"Of course." Kanako pulled back. "I'd never do anything to you without your say-so."

Feeling like an ass, Daniel shot his hand across to block Kanako's door-handle when he realised she was aiming to leave the car.

"Sorry. It's a touchy subject for me."

"I see. No problem. I'll mind my own business." Kanako went to move again, but he kept his hand where it was. She tapped on his knuckles pointedly. "Let me *out*, Daniel."

The silence stretched as he breathed in the citrus-blossom scent of her, curiosity eventually getting the better of him. "Purely out of interest. What did you have in mind?"

"You'll never know now, will you?" Kanako answered with false sweetness.

Unable to help smiling at her prim comeback, Daniel gave in. "All right. Show me, then."

Kanako's answering grin was slow, wide, and definitely self-satisfied.

"This feels vaguely familiar," Daniel teased, as Kana instructed him to lie on the living room rug of the annex. "Shall I get my kit off?"

"Not if you want me to get anything constructive done," Kana muttered, hearing the tension underlying Daniel's joking tone, loud and clear. The view of him lying there had her mind flipping back a couple of days, too.

She was probably pushing the rugby side of him a little outside his regular comfort zones, so would have to tread carefully. Tone down anything that might come across as mumbo-jumbo, and get the job done.

All achievable aims, though Kana's own comfort zones were feeling a bit squished. She tried to come across as fitting into the realms of 'normal' with people she didn't know well, not keen on attracting undue attention to herself with her eastern ideas.

Daniel belonged in the strange no-man's-land of not being a trusted friend yet, but neither was he a mere acquaintance. In fact, specific parts of them had gotten very well acquainted on this rug, not that long ago.

"My Obāchan used to do this for me when I was little. Then, when I was older, she taught me what she knew. It's very gentle. Non-intrusive," Kana explained, not really sure how else to introduce the practice. "I'd usually use a massage table, but I don't have one here. Are you comfortable enough?" It was disconcerting how directly Daniel looked into her eyes when she slid a cushion under his head, and she got caught staring at the decadent length of his eyelashes again. "It's, ah… It's a way of balancing your energy," she stammered, glancing at his lips.

The fullness of the bottom one looked both sensual and inviting from this angle.

"Reiki?"

"Oh! You know it? Of course you would, from when you played in Japan." Relief eased through her like a sigh, as she settled on her knees behind Daniel's head.

Previous knowledge took some of the stress out of it, making her look less like a nut job.

"May I touch you?" she asked formally.

Daniel's laughter rumbled deep in his belly.

"Yes, Kanako. You *may*."

She began by holding her hands, palm down, about a hand span above Daniel's temple, then cheeks, then shoulders, then neck. She hovered, trying to concentrate on the energy, but found it hard to relax with hazel-green eyes watching her every move.

"You can close your eyes."

"You can touch me," Daniel countered.

It was her turn to laugh. "I will, later. I'm just feeling what's there first."

"What do you mean?"

"Shhh… Close your eyes. I won't hurt you."

It was the strangest sensation. Though Kanako didn't lay a hand on him, even with his eyes closed Daniel knew exactly where her hands were hovering from the radiating heat and sense of pressure.

Kanako moved to kneel at his side, working over his torso, then downward, over his legs.

The team doctor in Osaka used to have a Reiki specialist come in occasionally, promoting healing and a good sleep before a big game, but it hadn't felt quite like this. The sensation of heat from Kanako's hands increased over his hips, knees and ankles, then she was back, kneeling behind his head and actually laying her palms on him for the first time. She placed them on his head with a feather light touch.

"Your hands are so warm," he murmured, half to himself.

"Mm… Shhh… Relax."

Kanako's hands moved in the same slow sequence; from his cheeks, to his neck, to his shoulders, and he began to float on a peaceful sense of calm. Diaphragm, solar plexus, hips…

By the time Kanako got to his knees, Daniel was cocooned in a sense of wellbeing. His ankles were next, then some kind of sweeping motion, over and over.

He became alert again when he realised that Kanako's hands had ceased. From the residual warmth on his chest and forehead, he imagined that's where they'd been resting until recently.

"I think I fell asleep for a minute," Daniel blinked up at Kana, and she smiled at his vaguely confused expression. She'd been sitting in a lotus position behind his head for the last five minutes, just watching his face in rest. The vulnerability and trust he'd shown her by fully relaxing into the Reiki session was a little humbling.

Daniel may not have actually fallen asleep, but he'd definitely settled into deep resting mode after she'd cleansed the energy above his body, and laid her hands on his heart and head.

"You rested. That's healing. Take your time sitting up." She unfolded herself to stand, and moved towards the kitchen. "I'm just going to get you a glass of water."

Cutting a slice of lemon into it, Kana got herself a glass, too, giving Daniel some time alone before she re-entered the lounge.

"How do you feel?" She handed him his water, and sat on the rug a little further off with her own.

"Ah, balanced," Daniel quirked one eyebrow upward.

"Now you're just being a smartass. I mean really. How do you feel?"

"Calm. Rested," he answered after some thought.

"Good. It's not a cure-all, but kind of overviews what's going on. The theory being it reminds the body to act holistically, sending energy where it's needed."

"Thank you."

The appreciation appeared heartfelt, and Kana relaxed a little more.

Ken had distrusted the idea of Reiki and healing energies intensely, and Kana had taken to keeping her massage table at Sam's house to silence the fractious arguments.

"Can I see you again tomorrow?" Daniel asked.

Kana laughed, "You want another session? You should probably give yourself a day off in between. You'll sleep like a log tonight."

"No, I'm meaning do you want to come out with me again tomorrow? I have something in mind I think you'll like."

"Oh." Kana mulled the invitation over for a moment. Was Daniel meaning like a date, or a thank you in exchange for the Reiki? Maybe another host-the-artist sort of thing. Or did he really feel he had to pay her back in full for her Bachelor Auction donation, out of some misguided sense of fairness? "What kind of something?"

"Say yes, and I'll show you tomorrow."

"I have to pack up a Dunedin order in the morning," she hedged.

She also had an appointment to see a lawyer.

"Then let's make it the afternoon," Daniel decided with a nod.

18

TRUE LOVE

"True love is born from understanding."
- Buddha

Daniel *did* sleep well—solidly—unable to remember any of his dreams.

He took his morning run down to the lake, taking the path to the left, away from the township. It was the less travelled of the two, invariably making it more relaxing for both the dog and himself.

It was on the return leg he noticed the figure on the shore, just before the turnoff to the access road leading home. He probably wouldn't have looked twice, except Halfback's ears perked up before he barked an excited greeting.

On closer inspection, the woman sitting on the twisted log had a distinctive lime-green backpack settled at her feet.

Kanako certainly wasn't packing up her Dunedin order right at this particular moment. Going by the sketchpad, it looked like she was in the process of drawing Ruby Island.

"Got a crush on her, haven't you, boy?" Daniel stopped, put his hands on his hips and contemplated the dog. "Is it because she won't give you the time of day?"

Had Kanako actually needed this morning to work, like she'd said, or had it been a line to fob Daniel off with?

He considered continuing on his way and leaving her to her solitude, but Kanako had turned, no doubt alerted by the barking. She spotted him and rose to her feet, her sketchbook falling unheeded to the ground. He saw the moment she recognised Halfback, and himself, because she surreptitiously dropped the long stick she'd been gripping.

Leading Halfback off the path and onto the shore, Daniel made the dog stay under the willows, ten metres from Kanako, and approached alone.

"You run," Kanako stated unnecessarily. Standing a little awkwardly, she slid her fingers into her front pockets. "I wondered how you kept fit. But you run."

He shrugged. "Yeah, I run, and have some gym equipment in one of the outbuildings at the farm."

"You have a *gym*?"

"I wouldn't go so far as to call it that." He laughed. "An old bench press, some hand weights, and a pull-up bar."

"Oh, right. I prefer walking."

Kanako looked down at her boots, and he noticed they were street shoes, not her usual walking sneakers or the chucks she wore when she was working in the barn.

"I know. I've seen you down here, but you usually go the other way." He pointed vaguely in the direction of the township.

Kanako bent to put away the drawing pad, and he caught a glimpse of the island's outline, drawn in pencil.

"Can I see?" He pointed to the picture.

Kanako hesitated for so long, he thought she was going to refuse.

On passing the drawing to him, Kanako kept her hand on the side of the pad, clamping the other pages together and effectively ensuring he only saw the top sketch.

"You're very good," Daniel decided aloud, looking up from the page and squinting at Ruby Island's actual outline.

Kanako made a non-committal sound in her throat.

He pushed his luck for more, lifting the corner of the page to see what Kanako was trying to hide from him, but she snatched the pad back and ferreted it away in her backpack. "Oh, no you don't."

"What else do you draw?"

Kanako shrugged. "Whatever takes my fancy." Then her eyes widened slightly, and he watched in fascination as a blush settled on the apples of her cheeks.

"People?"

"Oh, yes. Especially if I'm working on them." Kana's eyes flew back to his. "In clay, I mean."

"You'll have to show me sometime," he returned, amused.

Kanako fussed with the backpack zipper and took a water bottle from beside where she'd been sitting, offering it up a little shyly.

"Thanks."

Reminded of the state he was in, Daniel was glad he hadn't tried to kiss Kanako hello. He'd considered it, but it was early days yet, and coated in sweat and fine dust, he was far from savoury.

"You've never said hi." Kanako watched him closely as he took the lid off the drink bottle and drank deeply. "When I'm out walking."

"No." He wiped the back of his hand across his mouth and handed the water back.

Rather than say hi, he'd turned and run the other way.

"Why not?" Kanako dropped the bottle back onto the sand without looking at it.

Daniel shrugged. "We weren't on the best of terms." Slightly embarrassed about that, he bent to readjust the support sleeve around his right knee with some agitation.

Wearing the damn thing made him look like damaged goods, but not wearing it allowed the stress on his knee to build, forcing him to *walk* like damaged goods. Giving up running simply wasn't an option, he needed the daily blowout, so he continued putting up with option-A.

He'd seen Kanako around the lake and downtown on occasion, and in those early days, had actively avoided her. Looking back now, he kicked himself for wasting time.

She'd twisted the hem of her white T-shirt to tuck it into the waistband of her jeans, and he needed no imagination to see her outlined shape, as the sun beaming from behind her did a fine job.

A solid pulse began to throb in his groin, nothing to do with his half-hour jog.

"And people often come down to the lake for the pleasure of

their own company. I wasn't so sure you'd appreciate the interruption," he added.

Kanako pursed her lips and considered him. "Next time, feel free to say hi," she said quietly. "Presuming you're not down here looking for solitude yourself."

"Okay." He smiled at her, flicking his chin towards the large stick she'd dropped beside her on the pebble-strewn sand as he'd approached. "Unless you have a solid rākau in your hand and look like you mean business. Do you always carry a weapon with you?" he teased her lightly. "Is it for protection against dogs, or guys like me?"

Kanako's eyes skipped quickly over to Halfback, lounging comfortably under the tree, before meeting his again.

"Handy for both," she replied dryly, then surprised him by bringing two forefingers to her lips. She whistled for his dog like an old pro, and as if he'd been waiting for her signal, Halfback bounded over instantly. "Sit!" She commanded, pointing to the ground, and Halfback did exactly as he was told, tail thumping.

Daniel raised an eyebrow, "I see you two've gotten to know each other a little better."

Kanako shrugged in an attempt at nonchalance, but her eyes were full of mischief.

The dog behaved himself, but whimpered when they parted without him getting any other sign of affection or acknowledgement from Kanako. Daniel ruffled Halfback's coat as they re-emerged on the path, giving him a quick finger-comb.

"Hang in there, boy." He laughed. "She's still a bit skittish. Give her time."

As Daniel picked back up to an easy jog, he wondered if he was playing this right by taking it slow. Was it shyness he was coming up against in Kanako, or disinterest? The dating thing had been his way of showing her he was serious about moving forward and getting to know her, but maybe Kanako wasn't interested in anything more than one night?

That would bite.

Daniel wasn't used to women backing off. Being the one doing the chasing made him feel like he was back in high school, all gangly and unsure of himself.

He'd never been one to give up easily, though, and spending time with Kanako was proving to be both a gratifying, and highly compelling tug of war.

———

Daniel had told Kanako he'd pick her up that afternoon at one, explaining sports clothes would be best, and to bring swimwear. He turned up at the annex a little before time, keen to get another look at Kanako's work, but she was already waiting on the front step, lime-green backpack at her feet.

"Are you always early?" he called out the ute window.

"*Hai, so desu.*" Kanako smiled, picking up her bag and walking over. "Obāchan calls me *jikan ni seikaku na hito.*" No doubt noting Daniel's blank expression, she translated, "The always-on-time person. I'm a time pessimist, constantly assuming things'll take longer than they actually do."

Halfback chose that moment to yip a greeting from the back of the ute.

Kanako slowed her approach, and her nonchalant stroll took on a more watchful step.

"Is Halfback coming, too?"

"No. I have to pick up something from Clem on the way, so I'll drop the dog with him for the afternoon. I thought you two had reached some kind of truce?"

"Yes. I guess we have. Sort of." Kanako climbed in the passenger seat and pressed her palm up behind her on the rear window.

Daniel had never seen the idiot dog act so soppy. Halfback was fawning over Kanako's arrival by wagging his whole body and licking at the glass.

"It's not his fault, it's dogs in general."

"Halfback wouldn't hurt you."

"Clem says the same thing." Kanako shrugged, lips twitching into a sad little half-smile. "I'm working on it. You've got your demons, and I've got mine."

———

At the neighbouring farm, Clem was ready with a two-man kayak.

"Adele mentioned you made a bid on a kayak lesson at the fundraiser, but missed out." Daniel turned to face Kana, and she could see he was trying to gauge her reaction.

She blushed, because a kayak trip wasn't the only thing she'd bid on that night.

"Yes. I really wanted to go to… Um, kayaking. That was very thoughtful of you." She'd been really disappointed at the time.

"Ruby Island?" Daniel guessed.

"Yes, please." She breathed the words out reverently, and Daniel laughed.

"It's cast its spell on you—The island's Saffy's favourite destination, too."

As Daniel strapped the narrow boat onto the back of the ute, Clem fitted Kana with a life jacket.

"This is Adele's. Daniel will insist you wear one," Clem muttered. "Can you swim?"

"Yes, of course."

"Good. That's good," Clem looked her in the eye, as if deciding whether or not to tell her something.

"Too big." Daniel strode up behind Kana and yanked upwards on the scruff of the neck, until her arms came up and she almost slid out of it. "Put her in Saffy's one." Then he ferried the paddles to the ute.

"Why does he have to be such an ass about it?" Kana complained under her breath, suddenly hypersensitive about her small chestedness and juvenile shape. She undid the straps and tried on the next one Clem handed her.

"Well, there are more polite ways to go about it, that's for damn sure," Clem agreed, worrying at the stubble on his jaw with fidgety fingers.

It was clear he had more to say, but perhaps didn't quite know how to spit it out. Kana was good at waiting, silently watching the older man struggle to divulge as she tightened her straps.

Clem finally cleared his throat. "Um, you know Daniel's father drowned in a fishing accident?"

Every hair follicle on Kana's arms rose up in goosebumps, and she shuddered.

"No. I didn't."

"Gray got washed off the rocks, and they couldn't get to him."

"In the lake?" she whispered.

"No, no. Out on the coast—in the ocean." Clem looked behind himself, checking on Daniel's whereabouts. He was still well out of earshot. "The boys were just teenagers. That's one of the reasons Dan's so anal about life jackets. Gray wasn't wearing one." He cracked a half-smile. "The other reason, of course, is that the boy enjoys coming across as a complete ass."

Kana smiled back, despite Clem's earlier disclosure. "I'm glad it's not just me who thinks so."

Clem laughed. "Oh, don't get me wrong. You seem to bring out the worst in him. But that's a guy thing."

"What's a guy thing?"

"Acting like a noodle around the woman you're fielding feelings for." Clem chuckled.

Kana pulled back in some confusion. "I'm pretty sure you're barking up the wrong tree there, Clem. Daniel's just playing host, and, um… Helping me settle in."

"Is that what they're calling it, nowadays?" Clem gave her a broad wink as Daniel strode back over. "Settling in."

Kana thought it over on the short trip to the lakeshore. Why was Daniel taking her kayaking? She'd thought at first he'd meant skydiving as a date, but then he'd alluded to the fact he'd taken other women, and felt some kind of obligation to pay Kana back the amount she'd spent on the bachelor auction. Although they'd shared a heated kiss on the airfield under the influence of their combined adrenaline, there'd been nothing else to gauge what kind of territory they were heading into with this next… excursion.

Trip? Outing.

How the hell was she supposed to classify these things?

Daniel had left the annex yesterday after their Reiki session on purely friendly footing, and though she found him fairly hard to read, he'd played it the same again this morning, when they'd bumped into each other on the lakeshore.

Chatty, with a bit of light teasing thrown in.

Neighbourly. She sighed.

Out on the water, Daniel took the back position and Kana the seat in front. She was happy with that arrangement, as it seemed to mean he did the lion's share of the paddling, and she didn't want to miss a single minute of the changing view as they angled out towards Ruby Island, then circumnavigated it.

Daniel pointed out the kāmana as they cruised past. The crested birds were unperturbed by the gentle movement of the kayak, not bothering to look up from their ritual grooming. Their rust-brown head-feathers set them apart from the more familiar coastal cormorants.

The day was calm, light glinting off the water in long, lazy starbursts. It was a great relief to be free from the studio, making Kana realise the past week had been pretty stressful. Getting ready for the gallery showing, she'd been drowning under the unwelcome sensation of time running out.

The slick swish of the paddles dipping, over and over, was soothingly regular—almost trance inducing. Without thinking, Kana laid her double-paddle across the hull and began releasing the straps of the too-tight life jacket.

"What are you doing?" Daniel growled from behind her, his own paddle suddenly coming to rest with a solid 'clunk' on the sides of the kayak.

Kana's hands automatically stopped moving at the tone in his voice, but she willed them back to slowly undoing.

Daniel wasn't her boss.

Nor was he Ken.

She was never going to go back to the person she'd been when she was married, pussyfooting around to avoid confrontation. It was about time she took some responsibility for the fact she'd *allowed* herself to change; meld into a shape that didn't suit her, just to keep the fragile peace.

"This is a bit tight," she explained. "I'm a very good swimmer and won't take it completely off." Hopefully that'd be enough to placate Daniel, because she wasn't going to change her mind, or exchange her comfort for his.

The silence stretched, and she could feel Daniel's eyes boring holes into her back before his double-paddle eventually began to work again.

"We'll have to get you one that fits you properly," Daniel finally stated, his voice a little softer. "The water's deep, and cold. It brings on cramp, so promise me you won't ever go out on the lake without a lifejacket."

Despite the warmth of the day, a chill crept down Kana's spine.

"I promise," she murmured.

Though Kana could see two speedboats with water skiers in the general vicinity, Ruby Island's jetty was empty. It appeared they had the place to themselves, at least for the time being.

Daniel dragged their kayak up onto the beach and tied it to one of the lower willow branches, tossing their life jackets inside.

"You've got a wet bum." Kana laughed, patting her own to check it was dry.

"The kayak sits lower at the back." Daniel had a definite glint in his eye. "But if you think you're missing out on the authentic experience, I can make sure you get wet on the trip back."

"No, thank you." Kana primly raised her chin. "I like my bum just the way it is."

Daniel laughed as he pulled her in towards him by the hand. "I like your bum just the way it is, too." He slid both hands down her back, then over her butt. "It's perfect."

Daniel's light, playful tone did nothing to dispel the sexual tension, which built immediately with his touch.

"Are we on a date?" Kana spluttered. Feeling ridiculously uneven in her footing, and under-prepared without the clear classification.

Daniel froze, then pulled back enough to get a good look at her face, his expression quizzical. "I thought so. Were you aiming for something else?"

"No." She flushed, disconcerted to be under his scrutiny. "I wasn't sure if you were being neighbourly, showing me around—"

Daniel laughed, and Kana was a little freaked out by the magnitude of the quake it produced on her personal Richter scale.

She'd told him it was his most attractive feature, and she hadn't been joking. The man was unbelievably magnetic when he was having fun.

"Do you see me complimenting Clem's ass, or kissing the old bugger on the lips?"

"No," she admitted, adding with a smile, "Not in public, anyway."

Daniel's comment about kissing had her glancing at his lips, then away again.

He lifted her chin in his hand, making her look directly at him.

"Do you like kissing me, Kanako?" Daniel's voice was low, and she couldn't gauge which emotion moved across his face as he waited for her to answer.

"Yeah," she admitted in a sigh. "I *really* do."

Daniel grinned, lowering his head to bring his lips to hers. The world before and after them ceased to matter as they kissed under the willows, with the sun dappling through golden leaves. Daniel's hands were on her hips, and her fingers found their way into the thick, dark hair at the back of his head.

The groan from Daniel when they broke apart ran another fissure of pleasure through Kana, and she shivered.

"Cold?" Daniel asked, rubbing her arms.

"After that kiss? Not even remotely."

Daniel laughed, bending to pick up her backpack and hand it to her.

"Did you bring togs?"

"Yes."

He nodded towards the lake. "Come swimming with me."

Kana felt ridiculous, because although Daniel had seen her without a stitch of clothing on before, she felt the need to find a private space to get changed. By the time she came back to the cove, he was already in the water.

She got up to her thighs before the cold really soaked in, and she wrapped her arms around herself, hopping from foot to foot. Deciding she wasn't willing to let the water to reach any higher up her body after all, she turned and waded back towards the little beach.

When Daniel called out her name, she was barely knee-deep.

"Scared of dogs, heights, *and* cold water?" he teased from out near the end of the jetty, where he was treading water.

"I'm not scared," she called back. "It's bloody freezing!"

"Prove it!" Daniel yelled. "Come and jump off the end of the jetty like a *big* girl."

"How old are you, ten?" she shouted back, and Daniel barked a laugh.

"Chicken!" was his juvenile response.

"I'm not chicken," Kana muttered to herself, back on the shore now, but feeling a little cheated out of the swim. She'd *wanted* to go in.

Oh, what the hell.

Stepping up on the jetty, she edged her way gingerly down to the end, wary of splinters.

"I'm not ch-chicken," Kana repeated for Daniel's benefit, but violent shivers made her stutter, ruining the effect.

He laughed up at her from the water, eyes glinting in fun. His body was no less appetising than Kana remembered, with broad shoulders and muscular arms working to keep him afloat.

"*Jump, jump, jump,*" Daniel taunted.

"God. You must've driven your brother insane when you were kids," she grumbled.

"I'm pretty sure I still do. It's a sibling's prerogative, isn't it?" Daniel asked rhetorically.

Again, Kana thought of Finn with some regret.

They'd never been afforded enough time to reach anything like that kind of connection.

"How deep is it?"

In answer, Daniel took a breath and porpoise-dove down, his shape distorted by the water. He resurfaced some time later and shook his head, dark hair separating into loose, wet tendrils.

"Deep and wet." He laughed. "You're procrastinating. Get in."

Kanako bounced off her toes and dove, her body sleekly following her hands in a crisp, straight cut. The elegance of her dive was thwarted only by her spluttered expletives when she resurfaced.

"Keep moving," Daniel advised, grinning. It *was* bloody cold, making the only way in straight off the jetty.

No pain, no gain.

He took the few strokes separating them, pulling Kanako closer. She was still trying to catch her breath, so he took each of her thighs and wrapped them around his waist as he trod water for both of them.

"You… should… play… water polo," Kanako managed between blue lips.

"Hmm, I prefer *other* games."

Even in the cold, his body was beginning to respond to hers. Kanako's form was slick in the dark one piece, her legs smooth around his back, and her eyes close enough for him to see himself in her pupils. She slid her arms around his neck, and he smiled at her before dipping in to taste her cool mouth.

Like kissing an ethereal mermaid, without the tail.

"I get hungry for you." Kanako's murmured words against his lips gave his body another solid thud.

Daniel knew exactly what she meant, but until this moment hadn't realised she felt the same way.

"But now you've made me go and break my promise," she finished, pulling back.

"What promise?" He frowned.

"I'm on the lake without a life jacket." Kanako smiled at him as he chuckled.

"Swimming's different. We could get back to the jetty, and I'm with you."

"I see, and you're immune to the cold, are you?" Kanako eyed him with some measure of calculation.

"No, but I have a damn sight more body mass than you, and I'm used to it."

Kanako nodded, seemingly digesting that.

"Did you touch the bottom before?"

"Yeah."

"Mmm, that's impressive. But then, you could be just *saying* that. Bet you can't prove it," Kanako challenged slyly.

Daniel could see by the glint in Kanako's eye she was up to

something, but he took the bait and dove down anyway, searching for suitable proof along the lakebed.

Daniel clearly couldn't leave a challenge unanswered. The man had to be seriously competitive by nature; unable to help himself.

The instant he went under, Kana kicked off as hard as she could back to the shore. She was a strong swimmer, but Daniel was faster. When he resurfaced, she could hear him take off after her, and feel him gaining.

She was nearly there, fingertips scraping the bottom where the shore rose, when Daniel grabbed her foot. Though she'd been expecting it, an involuntary squeal sneaked out, along with her laughter.

She was still laughing when Daniel dunked her, and she came up spluttering. Trying without much success to dunk him as well, their limbs tangled together in the shallow water.

"That was an underhanded move." Daniel tugged on her wet plait in light reprimand. "Did you think you could beat me with a head start?"

"I *did* beat you with a head start." She grinned, kneeling on the granular sand. "I hit bottom first."

Smiling slowly, Daniel took her hand as he stood, drawing her up with him. He opened her fingers with the slide of his own. "No, *I* did."

He placed a perfectly rounded grey stone in her palm, the size of a bantam egg.

Daniel laid the picnic rug out in a sheltered, sunny spot, and Kanako took her hair out of its plait to dry as she sat, a colourful beach towel wrapped around her shoulders.

Her tresses mesmerised him; darker when wet, but still richly vibrant in colour, the sun catching auburn highlights. He'd only seen her hair loose a handful of times before, once at the pizza night she'd come to, that first kiss by the lake, and the night of the rippa-rugby fundraiser.

Kanako had worn a green dress that evening, but Daniel's memory was more caught up on how she'd looked when she'd stepped out of it.

Reaching a hand out, he twirled a ribbon of her long, damp hair around his index finger. He'd thought at first she must colour it, but unless she dyed it all over to match, this was her natural shade. When they'd made love…

He let the hair unravel off his finger and laid it back where he'd found it.

"You have beautiful hair. You don't often wear it out." He consciously moved his mind off more sexual parts of Kanako's body, trying to keep his tone light.

"It's a pain in the ass," Kanako returned in a vaguely dreamy tone. "Much more practical tied back, or short, but I can't bring myself to cut it."

"No. Don't cut it." Daniel remembered it splayed over him in a citrus blanket as she'd snoozed on his chest, naked.

He lay back on the picnic rug and closed his eyes, tucking his hands under his head and trying to concentrate on his objective. He had to keep his brain out of his shorts, for chrissakes. Wasn't he supposed to be showing Kanako he had more depth than a one-night stand?

"*Ahem…*" Kanako cleared her throat and he opened one eye to squint up at her. With the light behind her head, it was hard to read her expression. "What are you doing?"

"Getting dry," Daniel returned lazily, the sun working its lethargic magic. He closed his eyes again.

"Don't you want a towel?"

"No."

There was a long pause.

"A shirt?"

"No." He sighed, pushing up on his elbows so he could study her. "What's up?"

Kanako fidgeted, but the eyes that met his were steady.

"I can't relax around you when your chest is naked."

"Really?" He raised an eyebrow at her vaguely prudish

statement.

"Really. It makes my heart bang."

He laughed outright. Kanako's way of putting things was incredibly refreshing.

"Kanako, your chest makes my whole *body* bang, so I'd say we're more than even."

She scoffed at that, but looked quite pleased with herself at the same time, cheeks pinking prettily.

"But, I don't have mine out on display."

Daniel looked around himself pointedly. They were completely alone.

"Be my guest," he teased. "You'll get no complaints from me. Though I might have trouble keeping my hands to myself."

Along with some apples and chocolate muffins, Daniel had made Kana a thermos of green tea, complete with a slice of lemon and a decent shot of honey. The simple, thoughtful gesture made her insides go slightly gooey.

Not that she was comparing Daniel to her ex, but Kana would be highly surprised if Ken remembered she no longer drank coffee, let alone had any idea how she took her tea.

She was trying to retain the view her connection with Daniel was a light one, but was finding it increasingly difficult to wade through her deepening feelings. It was no use trying to pigeonhole the man as her supercharged, good-in-bed landlord. He was proving himself to be a pretty thoughtful and attentive human as well, which was the confusing bit.

If he wanted to get between the sheets again, the guy only had to take his shirt off and look at her sideways, and she turned into a puddle of mush.

Kana stole another surreptitious glance at Daniel over her thermos-cup. He was still shirtless, and obviously spent quite a bit of time that way—his chest lightly bronzed all over.

She'd told Daniel, completely honestly and quite early on, that she wasn't in a position to get into anything complicated. And though he'd seemed to be totally on the same page, it felt like they were sliding towards something different now, something *else*.

Or was that just her interpretation of it?

Kana mulled over whether she even wanted to clarify what was going on between them. Did she need to? It would probably come across as uptight and inexperienced to the world-savvy rugby star. It wasn't as though there hadn't been men before Ken, but that was a lifetime ago, and Daniel was from another planet entirely. Maybe for once in her life, she would simply take what was on offer, and enjoy it. Play it by ear.

Daniel seemed happy enough with that, so she would be too.

Kana put her tea down and lay on her side next to Daniel, unable to help herself from sliding one hand across his taut, muscular stomach. He turned his head towards her and smiled, and her heart was warmed by the natural welcome in his eyes, the soothing sun, and the perfect day.

"Thank you for bringing me here," she whispered.

19

WATER WILL FLOW

"When you dig a well,
there's no sign of water until you reach it,
only rocks and dirt to move out of the way.
You have removed enough;
soon the pure water will flow."
- Buddha

"The problem is, I've named the exhibition Two Halves. And the Gallery Manager, Annabelle, loved the bust of Halfback so much, she insisted he go on the front cover of the advertising brochure." Kana replayed her stressful day down the phone to Sam, as she gazed out the bank of studio windows and pondered her upcoming exhibition. "The whole premise is it takes two halves make a whole, and Halfback's other half's missing-in-action." She shifted the phone to her other ear.

"Missing, or smashed to smithereens?" Sam insisted on clarification from the other end of the line.

Kana had the grace to laugh. Her old friend and neighbour knew her too well, and had seen first-hand what happened to artwork she considered under par. Yes, she was a perfectionist when it came to ceramics, but there was no point being anything else.

If she did something, she did it right.

Kana had mentioned her glazing disaster, but she hadn't told Sam about her resulting temper tantrum, or the fact it had taken the best part of the next day to clean up the resulting mess.

"You've got me there." She glanced behind her at the cavernous studio, but there was no longer any trace of disarray. Everything was right where it should be, except Daniel's likeness. "Daniel ended up shattered on the floor."

"The sculpture, or the man?" Sam chuckled. "Did you wrestle that hunk to ground again, yesterday?"

"No." Kana sighed. "Not again. Just the once, so far. Well, you know, *twice*, but that one night." The bachelor auction.

"What the hell is this guy's game plan?" Sam spluttered. "He's not pulling his weight on team Single-Kana-Gets-Some. I thought you two went on a date yesterday?"

"We did. He took me kayaking." Kana sat at the wheel, though she had no intention to pot, and ran one finger lightly around the circular gouges in the steel. "He even *called* it a date. Then he dropped me home."

"No kiss?" Sam sounded dissatisfied with that ending. "No hanky-panky?"

Kana would've been highly dissatisfied, too, if it'd been the case.

"Plenty of kissing, and I'm talking sear-your-pants-off stuff." She laughed, making light, though still feeling a little wounded.

"*You* called it off?"

"No. I most certainly did not." Why on earth would she? Kana was still stumped as to why Daniel hadn't come in when she'd invited him. Getting hot and heavy in the car was becoming a habit. His excuse about having a flight in the morning hadn't exactly been a strong one. She hadn't been pushing him to stay over or anything. Just... *stay*. "Now he's away on business," she mused.

Daniel hadn't come to say goodbye before he'd left this morning, either, and the omission added an extra tug of disappointment. He'd be absent for her first gallery opening in three days' time, though he'd initially shown such interest in her work.

Obāchan had tied the date into her annual trip. Her grandmother and parents would be travelling down from Christchurch together, and somewhere in the back of Kana's mind, she'd imagined her grandmother and Daniel meeting.

"I should veto the dog, and just show the other pairs," Kana muttered, purposefully moving off the topic of her unpredictable sex-life. "Everyone will assume he was from another show. There's nowhere near enough time to build, bisque, and glaze another bust."

"What about the other dog? You said you'd made two."

"No. He's completely different. Fierce," Kana replied, still thinking of Daniel, despite having planned not to.

"Like Jekyll and Hyde?" Sam prompted.

"What?" Brought back from her reverie with a start, Kana's hand froze mid wheel-circuit, her heart rate jumping with the half-formed idea.

"Jekyll and—" Sam began again.

"Yes!" Kana interrupted. "Yes, of course! You're a *genius*, Sam. Have I ever told you that? Gotta go!" She unceremoniously hung up on her friend, lobbed her phone onto the workbench, and hurried towards the bisque shelf.

Right at the back, still in bubble wrap, was the bisque-fired bust of her first attempt at Halfback, lips curled back in a snarl. Alongside the friendly-faced version, the sculpture would be the perfect Yin to Halfback's Yang.

She just needed to get the bloody thing glazed.

Calling off all of her usual appointments, Kana turned down each invitation that came her way, no matter how small. No yoga, no drinks-at-the-bar, and no lakeside walks. She had half a kiln-load of her new dinnerware design, plus a fierce dog bust, to glaze, load, fire, and unload, all before the Friday night gallery opening. It would take some careful manoeuvring to get it all into the single working kiln, but that was her only option. The other one still stood forlornly by the barn door, awaiting pickup to replace its fried elements.

Kana crated and carefully packed her other finished busts and tableware late into the night, getting them ready to transfer, and the resulting morning-fatigue proved incredibly counterproductive.

Even more frustrating, she found herself having to obsessively double, triple, and *quadruple* check her temperature probe in the kiln over the space of the two day glaze firing—unable to trust it was right where it should be.

Friday dawned cool and wet—thankfully not torrential enough to interfere with the transportation of all Kana's pieces to the gallery. The usually friendly gallery manager, Annabelle, was obviously stressed about the show opening, and snapped more than once at Kana when she was asking for guidance with the display plinths.

By lunchtime, all exhibits—bar the select few now cooling in the kiln—were unpacked, labelled, priced, and artfully set around the large exhibit room.

The two side-rooms were also undergoing changeover. A stone jeweller, and an oils landscape artist were both sharing Kana's opening. Rather than taking the limelight off her work, the varied art added to the atmosphere, with incredibly detailed workmanship from one, and opulent colour from the other.

"Your jewellery's beautiful." Kana turned a carved river stone over and over in her hand with some reverence. This particular one had been fashioned as a large pendant and carved with an intricate raranga design. "Can you carve *any* kind of stone?" she wondered aloud.

The artist, Aden, smiled. "Some are more difficult than others, it's all dependent on density and strength."

"Greywacke?" Kana thought of the small grey stone she'd been given on Ruby Island, now residing on the kitchen windowsill of the annex.

"Not a problem."

She smiled, thinking it would make a great gift for Daniel.

Pointedly taking one of Aden's business cards from the display unit, she winked at him before slipping it into her jeans pocket.

"Would you like to join me for lunch, Kana?" As Annabelle beelined towards her, Kana was again struck by the unusual tension in the tall, whippet-like blonde.

"Absolutely." Still at a loss to fathom where Annabelle's strain was coming from, Kana's welcoming smile wavered in the face of such seriousness.

The gallery set-up appeared to be running smoothly, why so uptight?

When the two women sat at the café, Annabelle with a green

salad and Kana with a generously proportioned sausage roll, the gallery manager seemed to loosen up a bit.

"Two Halves is a superb collection of work." Annabelle complimented Kana on how her pieces had come together. "You know we pre-sold the duo 'Hug,' sight unseen?"

"To Daniel Dante?" Kana hoped he'd secured the portraits of Adele and Saffy, as he'd clearly wanted them.

"Yes." Annabelle's lips pursed again. "And I hope you don't think I'm presumptuous for asking, but what are your intentions, there?"

"My *intentions*?" Kana stopped mid-chew, very aware she had flaky pastry down her shirt and was gaping with her mouth full.

"D's very welcoming to the artists his mother brings through. Generous to a fault with the potters in residence; showing them around, etcetera." Annabelle paused, pointedly perusing Kana from the top of her scruffy plait, right down to her clay-smeared chucks.

Annabelle's own business suit and pumps were immaculate, even after a morning of moving stock around, and there wasn't a hair out of place on her sleek golden bob.

"I'd hate to see you get hurt. It would be easy to—shall we say— misconstrue D's meaning? He's very easy with his affections."

If Annabelle weren't so serious-faced, Kana would've laughed out loud.

Easy with his *affections*?

"Mr Dante hasn't sugar-coated anything, Annabelle. Don't worry, I think we understand each other just fine."

"Yes, well." Annabelle's tight little mouth gave the slightest pretence of a smile. "I'm well aware of his past reputation, but I had no small role in getting Dante D to settle down. I was out of town last week, but if I'd been here, I would've talked D out of the rippa-rugby bachelor auction. Such a tacky little event. I understand you won the bid?" Annabelle's eyebrows rose like elegant little bridges, but her eyes were as hard as bitumen beneath, and Kana's ire rose at the thinly veiled insult.

"Just a bit of fun." She narrowed her eyes. "And *such* a good cause." The cause in question being her own sexual gratification, as it turned out.

"Dante D does love his causes."

"Indeed. He goes all out, with bells on." Kana knew she was smirking, which was unattractive in any way, shape, or form. But she'd enjoyed getting one up on Annabelle after that little put down, whether the thoroughbred snob knew it or not.

"Well, I'm glad we cleared the air. I wouldn't want any bad feelings harboured between us."

Cleared the air? They'd hardly cracked open a window! Annabelle had flashed an ownership badge, and expected Kana to swallow it.

Daniel would hate the gallery owner calling him 'Dante D'—like he was a piece of prime meat she wore on her arm.

"As in, you're seeing Daniel, so back off?"

Annabelle's laugh came out as a nervy splutter. "You have a very direct way with words, Kana."

"So I've been told," she muttered, flicking at the front of her shirt as she stood to leave, sending pastry flakes flying. "I'll be gone in a few months, Annabelle. I really don't think I'm much of a threat to your, ah… your long term goals, do you?"

Annabelle looked Kana up and down again, her chin tipping slightly upward.

"No." Annabelle stated firmly, and the smile on her glossy red lips looked more like a sneer than anything friendly.

Did the gallery owner look down her nose at Kana because the potter refused to fork out a hundred bucks for a designer haircut? Because she wore clay on her jeans, and abstained from makeup most days?

Annabelle's personal opinion didn't matter. Best to let it go.

"Good. Well, great chat," Kana lied breezily, before picking up her wallet and heading towards the door. "I'm aiming to be at the gallery an hour before kick-off with my final pieces tonight," she called over her shoulder as she exited.

Kana went back to the annex to unpack warm pieces from the kiln, and sent a heartfelt *arigatou* to Buddha and any Shinto gods who may've been listening. The glaze on the second dog bust had cooled with a perfect, unmarred sheen.

She spent more time on her makeup for the gallery showing than she had in months, pulling out every trick she knew to make the absolute most of what she had. The styling of her hair took forever —there was so much of it—but confidence was imperative tonight.

War paint on, she slid into the long, red satin number with the Chinese collar. It fitted like a glove, and she was glad she'd thought to pack it. Her legs looked killer with the slits running thigh high in the embroidered satin, especially when teamed with the peep toe stilettos her mother had insisted she buy as an 'up yours' to Ken.

Kana had always been super careful to keep her height below his, which seemed ridiculous in retrospect. Just one more way she'd catered to his ego.

Kana couldn't be assed going through all this rigmarole on a daily basis, but was pretty pleased with the results in the full-length mirror when she'd finished.

She was philosophical about her conversation with Annabelle, though the blonde's assertions had got her thinking.

Kana would've known if Daniel was seeing someone seriously, wouldn't she? Surely Daniel would've told her…

Straight-shooting Clem would've told her if she was treading on toes, rather than encouraging 'settling in,' right?

Had Annabelle meant Daniel was 'easy,' as in he wasn't picky? Or was he in the habit of sharing himself around? More than one on the go at a time? Maybe that was it.

Kana tried to put Daniel out of her head, instead concentrating on the fact Obāchan and her mum and dad were at the hotel already, freshening up from their long drive and getting ready to meet her at the opening.

She'd maintained it was no problem if they couldn't make it, but the fact they were all here was a huge show of support. She was proud of what she'd achieved in two months—more than happy to parade it off. She was also incredibly humbled to have her family's unquestioning backing in everything she'd chosen to do. Especially over the past year, during the disintegration of her marriage.

Sam called as Kana was shrugging her coat on, and she could immediately tell something was wrong.

"I rang to say break a leg." The words were light, but Sam's voice sounded strained.

"Thank you. That's sweet of you. I might just do that if I don't watch it in these heels."

"Right." Instead of laughing with her, Sam was silent for a minute, before switching tack completely. "How did the fierce dog pan out?"

"*So* good. Better than I could've hoped, given the timeframe." Her old neighbour was clearly hedging, skirting around whatever was bothering her, but Kana went along with the flow before asking quietly, "Is something the matter, Sam? You don't sound like yourself."

"Ah, I was wondering if you'd had anyone calling, or snooping around. Like asking questions for publicity and the like?"

"You mean for the exhibition?" Kana clarified, a little confused.

"No. I mean on a personal level."

"Um, no? What's this about, Sam?"

"So, you know when you get stuck waiting in the aisle at the supermarket, and you're so bored standing around you pick up a woman's magazine and flick through it to pass the time?"

"*Yeees*." Kana drew the word out, checking the time on the microwave absently and wondering if this was going to be a long story.

"But deep in your heart, you *know* the real gossip and pictures of celebs in their bikinis will be in the back, so you delve straight in there."

"Uh-huh," Kana agreed, pouring herself a glass of water and taking a sip. Sam's pause was huge, and she began to wonder...? "Sam? Are you still there?"

"Yeah. Just lost my nerve for a second there. I was hoping you'd already seen it."

"Seen what?"

"The pictures of you and hunky Mr Dante in the latest My Woman magazine, frolicking in the water like seal pups."

"*What?*" Kana smacked her glass back on the bench.

"It calls you *Dante D's mystery woman*."

"No. It does not." Sam must be joking, she was extremely good at pulling the wool. Comedy was her usual go-to. "*Really?*"

"It'd be a great gag, wouldn't it? Especially for a media-wary person like yourself. Only, I'm not kidding, I'm afraid." Sam sounded truly sorry. "It really *is* you, and you really *are* in the back of a rag mag."

"Read it!" Kana demanded, suddenly unsteady enough to need a dining chair to plonk herself down on.

"Okay, so it's mostly pictures."

Kana groaned, putting her elbows on the table and resting her forehead in one palm.

"Only three of you guys together. The other ones are old shots of Daniel with birds he's dated in the past."

Kana gave up on her hand, and just laid her forehead straight on the table with another knee-jerk moan.

"It's not all bad, your ass looks damn good in that one piece, Kana, and you weren't kidding about Daniel's pecs. Superb definition. You should wear your hair out more often. It's absolutely gorgeous. You can't see much of your face in the one when you're both in the water, because you're sucking face. Looks like some sizzle in that kiss, missy. I'm surprised you didn't both drown."

"*Read* it," Kana repeated in a reedy voice.

"Right, so after the headline, 'Dante D's Mystery Woman,' it goes on to say: 'Ex-rugby royalty and bad boy, Daniel Dante, thirty-four, was caught on Lake Wānaka with a mystery brunette, looking loved-up and relaxed. A far cry from his usual extravagant dating style.' " Sam put on a snarky voice when she read it out, and Kana loved her for it.

Her neighbour was trying to make light of a potentially crappy situation.

"I didn't realise he was only thirty-four," Sam added. "That makes you a bit of a cradle snatcher, doesn't it?"

"Really, Sam? That's what's important here?" But Kana laughed, despite herself.

Kana hurried into the dairy with a supermarket bag, thankful the corner store was devoid of customers. She scooped up the last two copies of the latest My Woman, and slid them over the counter towards Andy.

"What, no Creme Eggs?"

"Oh, go on, then." She picked a single egg from the box, plonking it atop the magazines.

"Egg's on the house, today." Andy couldn't quite meet her eyes.

"You've read it?"

Andy hesitated only a moment before conceding, "Yes." He finally looked at her. "It came in today, and I have a lot of free time on my hands. It's not right, them delving into your private lives like that." He pulled a third copy of the magazine out from under the counter, handing it over with two bright pops of colour on his usually pallid cheeks.

"I don't know what to do," Kana wailed, opening her bag and showing him the ten copies she'd already picked up at various stores around town.

"Well…" Andy considered her with serious brows. "That's a good start. Might give you a few days grace. Though some people get theirs delivered by mail."

Kana's shoulders slumped in dejection.

"Tell you what." Andy ripped off a bit of scrap receipt paper from the till, flipped it facedown, and grabbed a pen. "Write down where you've already been, and I can ring around the rest. I've got the magazine distributor's number here too, so we'll see what we can do."

"Oh, thank you, Andy. You're a lifesaver!"

Andy beamed. "Least I can do."

Sam hadn't mentioned it, but in the other three pictures connected to the article—if you could even call it that—Daniel's dates were stunning blondes. One in a skimpy summer dress, walking hand in hand with him through a tropical marketplace, and two in red-carpet style evening dresses. The one dripping jewellery was called Tilly, and the woman in the more recent photo was Annabelle.

No wonder the gallery owner had been so riled today. She'd obviously seen the magazine layout, and felt the need to warn Kana off.

Kana remembered the stranger's snarky comment in the fish and chip shop when she'd been hung-over. '*Blonde, high society type, you definitely aren't.*'

No. She wasn't, and had never aspired to be.

Sam was right, though. Her ass did look good in that one piece, and she should wear her hair out more often.

A little stressed about getting the last pieces into the gallery from the SUV, in heels no less, Kana was more than happy to accept Aden's help when he turned up at the same time. After the stone carver held the back door of the gallery for her to carry in the dogs head, she loaded him up with a crate of tableware, and went to carry the final one herself.

"No, leave it here. I'll do a second trip," Aden said somewhat shyly.

Huh. Put on a pair of heels and some mascara, and suddenly guys thought to open doors and help carry stuff? Maybe Annabelle was onto something.

Kana slid off her shoes the instant she was inside, working around the catering staff to get her final pieces on display. Annabelle was nowhere to be seen, which was a mild relief. The other gallery assistant was efficient, and anything but confrontational.

As she leaned against the wall, sliding one stiletto back on at a time, Kana became aware Aden was watching her from across the room. His work dungarees from earlier in the day had been replaced by a jacket and collared shirt, and his scrappy shoulder length hair had been pulled back into a neat man-bun.

"You scrub up well." Kana smiled.

"Funny, I was thinking the exact same thing about you. Only mine was more along the lines of *holy shit*, are you even the same chick I was talking to earlier today?" Aden grinned back. "Fifteen minutes until opening. Can I offer you a boost of Dutch courage?" He nodded to the catering table, already set up with glasses of red and white wine.

"Only if you're buying," she joked. "I'm an artist on the breadline, here."

"Join the club. Not much money in it, but you'd be lost not doing what you love, right?"

"Guilty as charged. Totally addicted." Kana turned, laughing, and caught a familiar profile in the front window.

Realising the front door of the gallery would still be locked to the public; she excused herself from Aden and hurried out the back entrance, then around to the front.

"Papa!"

Her father was a tall, lean, wolf of a man, enfolding her in a tight hug before placing her back on the footpath and kissing both cheeks soundly. His once pale-blonde hair had moved to pewter, and white gold.

"Beautiful Kana. I love you in red. Your women insisted on walking, but I couldn't wait, so bought the car and bet them here." Papa looked a little sheepish.

"*My* women?"

Papa laughed. "*Our* women."

"They drove you crazy on the trip down, then?"

"Absolutely. Have me committed. They squabbled the entire way. Thankfully, mostly in Japanese." He placed a hand on each of her shoulders and really considered her. "It looks like Wānaka agrees with you." He smiled.

Kana was taken back to the last time she'd seen him, when he'd helped her pack the SUV with the few belongings she was taking with her. Her father had calmly wiped the tears off her face for her before she'd driven away from her home of eight years, her life, and her marriage.

"I missed you, Papa."

"I missed you too, my sweet-and-sour thing."

She wrinkled up her nose at his pseudo-endearment. Her father came up with weird little ones all the time, it was a game he liked to play.

"D'ya wanna come around through the back, or shall we wait until the doors open?"

"Let's wait." Papa squeezed her hand. "And get the full experience. Tell me about the exhibition."

Kana told her father about Saffy, and how she'd inspired the 'two halves of a whole' concept. She told him about the Yin and Yang dogs, the Tanaka's Marriage busts and the Hug duo.

With their hands blinkering the sides of their eyes against the gallery window, she pointed out the plinth with the busts of Poppy and Clem engaged in a hongi, and the new glaze design on the platter displayed on the back wall above the dinnerware.

She said nothing of Daniel to Papa. What was there to say? Yet his name kept popping up in her head throughout her explanation. Somehow the man had managed to tie himself into everything.

20

IN CONTROVERSY

"In controversy the instant we feel anger
we have already ceased striving for the truth,
and have begun striving for ourselves."
- Buddha

Going by the mile-wide grin Obāchan was wearing, she was having a whale of a time, and Kana breathed a sigh of relief. The octogenarian had travelled thousands of kilometres over the past week, but didn't look any worse for wear, sipping water from a wine glass and introducing herself to random strangers at the show opening. She was wearing a full, formal kimono, and looked as fresh as a tropical flower in the peach and orange silk.

Kana saw Annabelle stride past out of the corner of her eye, and turned to touch her arm on the way.

Annabelle smiled politely, before doing a double take. "Kana!" She squeaked, not fully in control of her usual facade. "Ah, I didn't recognise you there for a moment with your, um... your hair out."

Mission accomplished, though the result felt strangely hollow.

Kana mentally put aside their conversation from earlier in the day. There was no reason to continue carrying around the scratchy distemper she'd been feeling for the woman. Annabelle was a colleague, after all. Much better kept as an ally than an enemy.

"You've done an amazing job on the opening. Thank you. I know it took a lot of organising," Kana was able to say with full honesty.

"Oh, no problem. Just doing my job." But Annabelle's shoulders seemed to square off a little. "Actually, the sales from your Two Halves busts have been exceptional this evening. I've just secured the Yin and Yang pair for Clementine Jamison.

"Oh! That's perfect," Kana exclaimed, truly happy with the news. "He loves dogs."

"Yes." Annabelle studied her as if trying to gauge exactly what planet she was from. "You know he breeds prize-winning border collies... Farm dogs?"

"No. I didn't." No wonder Clem had such an easy affinity with Halfback; he must've bred him. Hadn't the farmer said something to her about both training and breeding contributing to the dog's good behaviour?

Feeling obtuse, Kana turned to try and spot Clem in the crowd, but he was nowhere to be seen. There was a lot she didn't know about this little community of people—their connections and alliances, their past and present passions.

"I'm surprised he didn't go for 'Hongi,' " she murmured, half to herself.

Annabelle raised her manicured eyebrows. "He expressed serious interest, but the pair had already sold."

"Really? You've sold three out of four pairs?" Kana exclaimed. "We're only half an hour into it!"

"*Four* out of four pairs. Marriage is going to be winging its way to Japan, from what I gather."

Obāchan? Well, of course.

"The dinnerware's moving well too, particularly the lotus and swallow motif," Annabelle continued.

"Annabelle, I'm impressed," Kana conceded with open honesty.

The woman might be a bit tightly wound, but she was clearly a good saleswoman.

"Truthfully? The artwork sells itself when it's this calibre."

When their eyes met, some form of truce travelled between them before Annabelle smiled twitchily, then moved away.

Kana turned back to the catering table, focussed on getting

another glass of water. She was totally unprepared to find Kenneth standing there, watching her.

Buddha's belly! Who'd invited her ex?

"Kana. Lovely to see you." There was a level of predation in his gaze.

"Ken!" *Not* so lovely, actually. "What the hell are you *doing* here?"

"Now, that's no way to welcome someone who's brought you a gift." Ken tapped the folder under his arm.

"You signed?" Kana couldn't keep the eagerness out of her voice, and saw the responding coldness wash over his features.

"A private space would be more appropriate to discuss this."

"Ken, you've purposefully ambushed me at a gallery opening. Of *course* I'm going to be surrounded by people." The man was totally frustrating in his capacity to insist the world revolved around him.

"There must be a private office?" Ken looked around himself vaguely, as if one might magically materialise before him.

Kana stared at him for a moment, before sighing and moving towards the back room.

"Follow me," she intoned, annoyed he felt the need to take her arm as if to steer her, even though she was the one showing the way.

———

Daniel watched Kana's exchange with the unknown man from the door. He'd spotted her as soon as he'd entered, because she was absolutely unmissable. In a scarlet, form-fitting dress, she outshone the room. Her hair was shiny waves, deep brown through to auburn as it cascaded over her shoulders, and down her back.

Goddamn beautiful, as always. And he'd missed her, like nothing else.

As she moved, her dress revealed toned legs, calves to mid-thigh, and the heels accentuated the slender turn of her ankles. His body responded with a deep-seated longing, like a growl from a hollow stomach on recognising its favourite food.

This was a different level of desire. One he hadn't felt before.

He frowned, watching as the couple separated themselves from the crowd and moved to the back of the gallery, towards the office. The man had his hand on Kana's arm, then slid it to the small of her back, his touch either familiar, or far too bold.

"Dante D."

He turned with a start to find Annabelle at his elbow, but was unable to return her bright smile.

"Great show, Annabelle," Daniel conceded instead, nodding to the room at large. Running a hand over his face, he realised although he'd managed a clean shirt, he'd forgotten to shave in his haste to get here.

He was desperately tired, having squeezed four days worth of meetings into two. Leaving directly after kayaking to catch an earlier flight to Osaka had bought him a day, and he'd managed to push the less urgent set of negotiations back to next month. The jet-lag had played havoc with his sleep patterns though, and he hadn't been able to get much shut-eye over the past few days—not even in the plane this evening on the domestic flight back to Wānaka.

There was only one person he really wanted to speak to tonight, and it wasn't the cool, blonde businesswoman standing beside him. They'd gone out a few times, but as a pairing they'd lacked any sort of spark. Annabelle had played the game when there'd been necessity for a plus-one, as was their arrangement, and she'd made the most of rubbing shoulders with the *crème de la crème* of the sporting world with her polished sales pitches.

Their parting had been a mutual shift sideways, without animosity.

"Come through to the oils." Annabelle manoeuvred him with well-versed skill, and he stepped with her, though he was about as interested in buying a garish landscapes as he was in jumping onto another international flight.

Annabelle began to explain the artist's take on the Lake District, but the two Japanese women talking animatedly in front of a mountain scene caught Daniel's attention, and held it.

Feeling he'd somehow become caught between two worlds in a haze of jet-lag, Daniel lost all focus on what Annabelle was saying, listening instead to the women. The two were obviously related, most likely mother and daughter, arguing with some heat about which area the painting was reminiscent of.

He caught the words 'Hokkaido' and 'Nagano,' and understood.

The artist had portrayed the New Zealand mountains and bush in such a way, the tree species were undefinable. The scene could easily be the peaks of the Japanese archipelago.

The older of the two women was intriguing. Daniel had never seen a full kimono worn outside of Japan before. Though her clothing was completely foreign in the Kiwi time-space continuum, the woman somehow made it appear understated, her backchat, easy smile, and bubbly laughter belying her snow-white hair.

She turned to catch Daniel staring, so he nodded respectfully, a little surprised by her giggled response. She behaved as a young woman would, and if she'd had a fan, he was almost sure she'd have hidden coquettishly behind it.

"Daniel-kun, *desu ka*?" she asked suddenly, stepping out of her argument mid-sentence to move towards him. The other woman rolled her eyes at her elder's perceived rudeness, and stalked away.

"*Hai*. Daniel *desu*." He agreed. Though, how the old woman knew his name was beyond him. A rugby fan? Not completely inconceivable…

More likely this was one of Kanako's relatives, in Wānaka for her show opening.

"*Tomomi Yamada desu*." She introduced herself with a mixture of both east and west—bowing first, then offering her hand to shake.

"*Hajimemashite, dozo yoroshiku, Tomomi-san*." He greeted Tomomi formally, wondering if that was the correct move, since she'd just given him the informal suffix of 'kun.'

White-haired Tomomi laughed. "You can call me Obāchan."

"You speak English!" He hadn't meant to sound so astounded, but her look was so completely old-style Japanese it'd taken him by surprise.

Realising he'd rudely ignored Annabelle, he looked around to introduce her, but she'd melted back into the crowd at some stage and was now nowhere to be seen.

"*Tokidoki*." Obāchan grinned impishly, and Daniel recognised a likeness to Kana's mouth in humour, when the older woman quipped, 'sometimes.'

"You came over from Hiroshima for Kanako's opening," he realised aloud.

Obāchan broke into a stream of Japanese, the gist of which was fairly easy to follow. He had the distinct impression she was going easy on him and didn't mind one bit, considering the state his head was in.

Kanako's grandmother and parents were planning to stay a week in Wānaka, before heading back to Christchurch. It would be another month before Obāchan travelled back to Japan, where she lived alone. She usually came once a year, though flying was becoming more tiring now she was older.

Daniel could totally relate.

She switched back to English. "One day I'd like to settle here, and be done with it. We just have to see if your immigration likes the idea."

"Your English is very good." It was fairly unusual in the older generation he'd met. "When did you start learning?"

Obāchan eyed him with great interest, seemingly searching deeper than his skin. "This is a *long* story, Daniel-kun."

He looked around himself and shrugged. "I have time, Obāchan."

There were other similarities between the two women. Kanako's grandmother laughed just like she did, with a child-like burble that ended in a real belly laugh.

"I was born in Hiroshima prefecture in 1936." Daniel's brain automatically did the math. That would make Obāchan eighty-one. "Japan was very different then..." she paused, and he looked at her expectantly. A shadow crossed over her features, and he suddenly realised what she meant—what she must've lived through as a child.

"Before the war."

"Yes," Obāchan nodded in agreement. "Before the bomb took my sister and father."

He put his hand on her arm. "I'm so sorry."

"It was a long time ago." Obāchan looked at the painting she'd been arguing with her daughter about. "English was banned in my household after that." She turned back to him, and smiled with quiet steadiness. "Contraband is incredibly enticing, isn't it? More addictive than it should be."

Daniel grimaced, wondering how much this close relative of

Kanako's knew of his history. It was all there on the Internet for anyone who cared to look.

"I began learning when I was nine," Obāchan continued. "In secret. I've never stopped. My mother died in her eighty-eighth year. If she knew what I was doing, she never let on, though I worked for a large corporation as an interpreter for years before I had children."

The older woman switched focus and languages, like a butterfly alighting on flowers. She asked him a lot of questions about his work and lifestyle, before surprising him again. Clip clopping very close to him in her *zouri*, she measured her height against his with a hand held flat atop her head, then left it on him as a marker when she stepped back.

Daintily proportioned, Obāchan only came up to mid-chest.

"Mmm, you're big." She spoke in English again, looking up at him seriously for a few seconds before jabbing his arm and pointing to the archway through into the other room.

Her granddaughter was beautifully framed there, like an artwork in her own right.

Kanako stared at Daniel for a shocked moment, before sashaying towards him in her red dress, concern obvious.

"Kanako-chan wa, totemo yasashii ko desu. Korekara mo yoroshiku." Obāchan hastily tried to finish their conversation before Kanako arrived, insisting her granddaughter was a kind person, and asking for Daniel's assurance that he would take care of her in the future.

Kanako's grandmother spoke again, even more rapidly, and her *Hiroshima-ben* kicked in. It was tricky to follow the slang, but she seemed to be saying something about it being lucky...

Lucky Kanako had inherited Japanese breasts and Dutch hips, and not the other way around?

"Obāchan. *Stop* that!" Kanako now stood in front of them with her hands on those very hips, as if berating a wayward child. She looked purely magnificent with her eyes glittering and colour on her cheeks.

Daniel longed to pull her into his arms and kiss her senseless, but considering the presence of her grandmother, shoved his hands into his pockets instead.

"I apologise for my grandmother, Daniel. She forgets her

manners." Kanako fixed Obāchan with a hard stare, but the old woman merely smiled serenely back. "Aren't you supposed to be in Osaka? Is everything alright?" Kanako turned from the older woman and pinned him with a worried look, fidgeting with her high collar.

No. Something was very clearly *wrong*.

Daniel had miscalculated Kanako's reaction to him being here. Completely. Hell and high water had been waded through to get him back in time for Kanako's opening. But rather than surprised and pleased, she looked nervous, highly-strung, and somewhat cornered. The opposite of happy to see him.

"Finished earlier than expected." He shrugged, more than a little uncomfortable with the situation, and Kanako's tension. "I thought it'd be good to support the Artist in Residence's first showing," he continued with some formality, measuring his words carefully.

"Oh. Thank you. Yes." Kanako, still distracted, glanced back over her shoulder before continuing. "And, ah… Thank you for purchasing 'The Hug.' That was very nice of you."

Nice of him? What was Kanako going on about?

"I wanted it," he growled.

"Yes, of course. Testosterone gets what it wants," Kanako bit back, before touching her fingertips to her mouth, eyes widening.

Her hand was shaking.

"Sorry, that was uncalled for," Kanako apologised quickly. "Would you excuse us? Obāchan, I need to speak with you." She turned to her grandmother a little desperately, but the older woman was now fixated on the man talking to Annabelle—the same man Kanako had walked away with earlier.

"What's *Baka-Ken* doing here?" Obāchan hissed.

"That's what I need to *speak* to you about," Kanako returned, grabbing her grandmother's arm and hustling her back through the archway.

Their hasty departure left Daniel to mull on the strange exchange.

He watched Annabelle flirt lightly with 'Baka-Ken,' while she tried to engage him in the artwork. She was good at her job, and always sold well above her commission quota. When the couple moved back through to the larger room holding Kanako's ceramics, Daniel followed them.

Both Kanako and her grandmother had disappeared.

Obāchan clearly had no time for this well-dressed man, who was still speaking with Annabelle. Adding *baka* to his name was tantamount to calling him the village idiot.

Annabelle turned and caught Daniel's eye, motioning him over. Rather than clearly snub her for the second time in the evening, he moved to join them, standing in front of a pair of Kanako's ceramic busts he hadn't seen before.

He glanced at the name of the piece. 'Hongi.'

That figured.

The clay man was stooped slightly in greeting, about to touch his forehead and nose gently together with that of a much shorter woman. The proportions of the woman's face and her wild hair reminded him of…

"D, I'd like to introduce you to Kana's *husband*, Kenneth."

Daniel wasn't sure if Annabelle had stressed the word 'husband,' or if his fuzzy brain had done that all by itself, but the status reverberated around in his head like a Buddhist gong.

He put his hand out on automatic pilot and tried to school his features into some semblance of welcome, suddenly hating the rituals of polite western society, stipulating he touch the man.

"Ken travelled down from Christchurch to surprise Kana," Annabelle continued, all bubble and fizz. "You must've missed each other so much. Two months is a *long* time to be apart." She turned back to Daniel with a bright smile and touched his arm. "Dante D is Kana's landlord."

Daniel looked into the hard grey eyes of the man who shook his hand.

Absolutely no love lost there, and the feeling was completely mutual. They sized each other up like opponents in the ring.

Ken was possibly in his fifties, and shorter, but appeared to look after himself.

"If you'll excuse me." Like one of the girls holding the round number aloft, Annabelle smiled prettily and sauntered off with her head held high, probably fully aware someone's blood would be left on the floor before the end-of-round bell.

21

CONQUER ONESELF

*"To conquer oneself is a greater task
than conquering others."*
- Buddha

Obāchan was yabbering so fast, Kana had to ask her to slow down.

"I can't understand all of the insults. Take it down a notch." She breathed in and out to calm herself, and held Obāchan by both shoulders. "I know you're pissed off. I am too. But if I sign over the car to him, I get half of what the house sells for, no more stalling."

While Kana detached the sat nav, then cleared the glove box and backseat contents into the box her grandmother held for her, Obāchan continued in Japanese. This time at a speed Kana could follow.

'Why does Baka-Ken need the new SUV? He's only doing this out of spite! Spiteful man! The car was a gift from me to you, not him. And not even one year ago! Son of a hairy fish! It's incredibly small of him to palm the much older sedan off onto you, and keep the new vehicle for his business. He's an idiot, a super big idiot, a stinky idiot!'

"Obāchan, what's a few thousand dollars in the scheme of things? We do this, and I'll be free of him *now*," Kana wheedled, shoving the plastic bag full of My Woman magazines out of view under the thick map book. She'd deal with them later—in private.

"You know I love this car, and I'll be forever grateful to you for giving it to me, but it has to go."

"It's the *principle*." Obāchan argued stubbornly.

Kana thought for a moment, sorting and discarding Buddhist quotes in her head until finally finding one she thought might sway her grandmother. " '*To conquer oneself is a greater task than conquering others.*' " One of Tanaka-sensei's favourites.

They didn't need to conquer Ken—they needed to let this fight go.

Obāchan muttered to herself, but Kana knew she'd won the battle when her grandmother put down the full box, and picked up an empty one, ready for the contents of the boot. Jumper cables and a full bottle of engine oil preceded a stash of jute supermarket bags.

Let it go, and start new.

With Daniel?

Kana would be smart to remember the quote when she was able to talk to Daniel again. She had no idea if he'd seen the photos of them together in the rag mag, and didn't know how he'd feel about them. She *did* know the publicity had been the catalyst that had brought Ken out of the woodwork, and subsequently pushed her into signing over her precious SUV.

If she'd waited for her lawyer to deal with it, the split would've been kept fair, but Kana was no longer willing to draw this out.

Daniel had looked dead tired, like a giant with a sore head, standing there next to her tiny, fast-talking grandmother. It'd been so unexpected to see him, she'd longed to walk straight up to him and hold on—bury her face in his neck and forget about everything else.

She had one more job to do before she spoke to Daniel, though.

Back in the main gallery, she approached Ken when she saw he was on his own. Slipping the SUV keys into his pocket, she stepped a little away from him, rubbing her bare arms. She'd forgotten to wear her coat in her haste to clear out the car, and the autumn evening had soaked in and chilled her bones.

"It's done. The papers are all signed and on the front seat."

Ken put his hand over the bulging pocket and looked at her with an uncharacteristic hangdog expression. "I was almost expecting you to change your mind," he murmured.

"I know," she hesitated. "That's why you asked for the car, isn't it? You thought I wouldn't part with it."

Ken shrugged.

"There was really no point coming all the way down here. I would've sent it up," she added.

Ken angled his head to the side. "I had to come and see for myself."

"See what you were saying goodbye to?"

"No." Ken twisted his lips, but there was no humour there, only defeat. "See if you meant it."

"I mean it." Kana reached out to touch his arm. "We were good once though, weren't we?" She urged him to remember.

"Yeah, we were." Ken smiled. He really did have a handsome face, though the frown he wore all too often had created fissures between his brows, making him look older than his years. "We were better than good. We were great." He sighed. "The house goes on the market next weekend."

She nodded in mute response.

When he pulled her into his arms, she let him, but drew the line at a kiss, turning instead to present him with her cheek.

"Goodbye, Ken."

"*Sayonara*, Kana." He smiled down at her, and she found herself smiling back. Despite all of his faults, she'd loved him once.

Kana couldn't find Daniel when she went looking for him, but she did find Adele in the throng, slightly inebriated and very smiley.

They shared a hug before Adele complimented her on the show.

"It's amazing Kana. They're *so* beautiful." Adele was swaying a little, so Kana slid an arm around her waist to keep her steady. "D bought the 'Hug' busts. I'm so happy."

Adele *did* look happy… and actually pretty drunk.

"How many wines have you had?" Kana murmured under her breath, very aware they were still within earshot of the group Adele had been talking to.

"Three." Adele held up three fingers to reiterate her point. "But I'm stopping now, honest." She attempted to smile cheekily before her face actually crumpled, clearly downcast underneath. "Tomorrow is Saffy's birthday, so I needed a bit of a pick-me-up."

"You're sad she's getting older?"

"No." Adele levelled Kana a gaze, then whispered with a catch in her voice, "I'm sad Moses doesn't get to see how wonderful she is. And James. I'm sad about James."

Tears were glittering in Adele's eyes, but before Kana could ask more about Saffy's two fathers, the mother of one was pinning a bright smile back on her face, and turning back to the group. "This is Kanako Janssen," she announced loudly. "The ceramic artist whose work you've all been admiring."

Kana recognised a few people in the circle—the auctioneer from the trivia night, and an older couple from the Ruby Island working bee.

The group was welcoming and friendly on the face of it, but when the Ruby Island couple turned to each other to converse in Dutch a short time later, the woman's words smacked Kana squarely in the face.

"Bloody Asians, taking over the country."

So used to being surrounded by those who spoke the language, Kana automatically looked around the group to meet the eyes of anyone else who'd understood the bladed comment. No one batted an eyelid, and the woman who'd spoken still wore a light, somewhat Plasticine smile on her face.

Thank Buddha Papa hadn't overheard that little titbit of casual racism, or he'd be throwing someone through the front window round about now.

Kana had a bit of her father running through her veins though, and for the third time that day her own fury rose up, and snarled.

She turned pointedly to the couple, and replied in clearly enunciated Dutch. "Actually, I'm a Kiwi. What's your excuse?" The man spluttered on his wine, but the woman merely stared at Kana in open-mouthed shock as she reverted to English and quoted Buddha. "To conquer oneself is a greater task than conquering others."

Kana reminded herself the teaching was meant for her as well, before she took it any further. It was turning out to be the mantra of the evening. Her hand was itching to upend the woman's wine all over her lemon suit, but she managed to control herself.

She smiled at the rest of the group—catching their eyes one by one, with careful deliberation—before excusing herself from the people and the situation. Walking quickly away, she was surprised when Adele trotted after her.

"Was that German?" Adele asked, clearly confused.

"Dutch."

"You speak Dutch as *well*?"

"My father's originally from the Netherlands." Spotting the man in question in the crowd, Kana bee-lined towards him, suddenly needing to be near someone stoically familiar, and undeniably on her team.

"Kana-Berry." Ruben Janssen, perhaps gauging her mood correctly and looking to make her smile, gave her a new nickname on the spot before opening his arms wide. She strode into them to hug him fiercely, before breaking away to the side.

"This is Adele, Papa," she introduced them. "My father, Ruben."

"Oh! Lovely to meet you. Kana says you're originally from Holland?"

Once the two were engaged in animated conversation, Kana slipped silently away to look for Daniel again. He hadn't sought her out, but she knew he was here somewhere, and she needed to talk to him. She was scoping the three gallery rooms for the second time when she came across Carissa and Marianne.

"You're such a clever thing!" Marianne gushed, grasping her hand. "I've just bought one of your lovely pestle and mortars for grinding my pepper."

"And I just about came to blows with Daniel Dante over a swallow and lotus platter," Carissa chimed in.

"Oh, did you see where he went? I was looking for him…" Kana trailed off, noting the twin's exchanged looks and matching grins. She lifted her chin automatically.

She'd never been one to shirk ridicule, and it looked like there was a pinch more of it coming her way.

"I think he's left, love." Marianne explained, her voice gentle, and Kana was relieved to find she'd misjudged these particular women.

"Right, of course. Thank you," she murmured, deflated. Why would he leave without saying goodbye? Without even properly saying hello?

It was becoming pretty obvious 'fly in, fly out' was exactly Daniel Dante's style.

"I think he needed to lie down and get some shut-eye," Carissa answered Kana's unasked question. "He looked like hell."

"Very handsome hell," Marianne amended with cheerful certainty. "It's all that long distance travel he does."

"What he needs is a wife and family to ground him in Wānaka. That'd soon clip the boy's wings," Carissa decided. The sisters exchanged another loaded look, nodding.

Kana snorted at Daniel being referred to as a 'boy,' and the idea he'd allow himself to be shackled by anyone.

"That'll be the day," she muttered under her breath.

The sleep that should've claimed Daniel refused to come, and he took it out on the pillow that wouldn't mould to the correct shape. What the hell was wrong with him? He was tired enough to sleep for days on end, but his brain was going a million miles a minute.

He got back up to run himself a bath.

Easing his body into it, he let the hot water take care of his cramped muscles and joints. Maybe he was getting too damn old for this amount of flying in a year—it was clearly doing his head and body in.

Maybe something to take the edge off…? The thought came slyly, like a thief in the night.

Screw that. What he needed was to burn off the need for it.

Daniel got dressed again, flicking an uninterested look at his alarm clock. Two a.m.—perfect time for a jog. Letting himself out the back door, he was greeted by Halfback's welcoming yip.

"You should be asleep too, dog. Wanna run?"

There was no traffic to speak of, so Daniel headed away from his usual lakeside beat and towards the township on the lit roads instead, Halfback loping beside him. Attacking the streets as a grid,

218

they'd been out for about an hour and a half before his knee started to give him serious grief.

At least the niggling pain was something to take his mind off Kanako, where it had been securely latched since he'd met her, all of two months ago.

Daniel headed back to the farm, easing himself down to a walk on the gravel, and stopping short when he spotted an unfamiliar car parked at the annex.

His first thought was for Kanako's safety, and he moved forward in stealth-mode, listening for anything out of the ordinary. The only sounds were the wind rustling the toetoe, Halfback lapping at the water bowl Kanako had left out, and his own curses as he got close enough to read the logo on the sedan door.

'Kenneth O'Connor, Civil Engineering.'

So Baka-Ken had been telling the truth—he was still with Kanako. Daniel guessed that meant all the other shit the smarmy suit had told him was true as well, and his chest constricted painfully.

They'd never properly split, though Kanako had needed a break after their first round of IVF failed, and had taken this position in the 'boondocks' while she 'got over it.'

Ken and Kanako were scheduled for their second round of IVF soon, and Ken maintained Kanako wouldn't be working anymore, she'd be shutting down her 'ceramics hobby' when they got back to Christchurch.

Most of that was hard to swallow, but it was Kanako's deception that hit Daniel the hardest. She'd had nothing to gain by her dishonesty, other than playing him—baiting him into getting involved. No wonder she'd been so apologetic after their 'one-night-stand.' She'd been on a short break from her husband at the time, and had effectively cheated—Daniel fitting squarely into the role of asshole.

The asshole who'd fallen for her, hook, line and sinker.

Just like the first time they'd met, Kanako Janssen had managed to pull the wool over Daniel's eyes, absolutely and completely.

The thought of Kenneth O'Connor in Kanako's bed right now made Daniel feel a sick rage that was anything but healthy. Ken had come across as a conceited prick, and if Daniel ever saw the man again, he'd be hard pressed not to break the man's nose.

Daniel half contemplated waking the two of them up and having it out with Kanako right then and there, but there was little merit in the plan. He'd only come across as a poor loser, and he didn't need to be told twice Baka-Ken held the belt for this particular title.

22

ANGER

"You will not be punished for your anger;
you will be punished by your anger."
- Buddha

"Kana, can you help me with this?" Adele was trying to get the plastic tablecloth onto the patio table at the farmhouse, but wasn't having much luck fighting the breeze with the corner clips.

"Sure." Kana climbed down from the stepladder, careful not to let go of the handful of helium balloons she was holding—the purple ones announcing the number 9, and the blue, 35.

Kana was helping Adele set up for Saffy and Daniel's combined birthday party, and though she was trying not to panic about it, they were fast running out of time. Apparently it was a family tradition to celebrate the two birthdays together, as they were only a week apart, and extended family would be arriving anytime now.

Daniel was with Saffy at her rugby game, and by Kana's calculations, would be heading back to the farmhouse in about ten minutes. She was keen to make herself scarce before then, due to the fact Daniel and herself were barely speaking.

Communication had plummeted since the gallery show opened a week ago, and Kana had to assume that meant it was over between them. She hadn't had the chance to discuss the magazine article with him, as Daniel never stuck around long enough to exchange more than a nod. She had to conclude the leaked photos were the reason behind his latest black mood.

It wasn't like she'd orchestrated the exposé, and the invasion of privacy had affected her too, but if he wanted to act like she was to blame, so be it. If he was going to behave like a child about an event *his* lifestyle had brought about, then she was better off out of this… this… Whatever this was.

Maybe Daniel had been forced to realise just how different Kana was, compared to his usual women. Or maybe Annabelle had cried foul?

Rather than hang around and rub her own nose in Daniel's obvious change of heart, Kana had chosen to spend as little time in his company as possible. He was clearly not man enough to talk to her about it, and she was certainly woman enough to completely ignore his rude-assed-self.

It wasn't like she hadn't been busy throughout the week, putting a bright face on every morning for Obāchan and her parents, and showing them around the area. She'd also had to find the time to trade in Ken's sedan for a god-awful, kaka coloured station wagon, which would at least be capable of transporting some of her stock.

Kana was a touch guilty about the relief she'd felt in seeing her family off yesterday. She needed thinking space, and working space, and although this birthday party wasn't helping either of those aspects, at least she didn't have her mother and Obāchan bickering in her ear at the same time.

When Adele had asked her to attend, Kana had been completely open about her concerns.

"That's not a good idea, Adele. Daniel and I aren't on the best of terms right now. I think it'd be wise if I just stayed out of it."

"Nonsense!" Adele had negated, more hopeful than forceful. "Saffy would be *so* disappointed if you weren't there. Mum and Dad are coming, and you said you'd like to meet my sister, Katie, and her husband," she wheedled. "Their little boy, Tobias, will be there. And Levi, Shal and Cam's wee one."

All of that was sway-the-resolve material—along with the classic 'I need your help' line. So here Kana was at the farmhouse, hanging decorations and listening out for two things: the oven timer, and Daniel's truck.

Climbing the ladder again, Kana squealed and rocked precariously when Halfback rounded the corner at speed, jumping up to snatch a couple of solid licks at her bare toes. One of the '35' balloons sailed up and away, escaping only to tangle itself in one of the Canadian maples.

"Halfback! Down! Find *Daniel*," Kana commanded with a snap, pointing in a random direction and clutching the remaining balloons even tighter.

"I'm right here," Daniel drawled from behind her, his boot on the bottom rung of the ladder to steady it.

If Kana hadn't known better, she would've sworn there was amusement in his voice.

"Oh, right." She swiped stray hair away from her forehead and cleared her throat before lowering her eyes to meet his gaze.

Realising she would be rubbing up against Daniel if she climbed down now, Kana perched awkwardly on the top rung, instead.

"Happy birthday," she offered a little awkwardly when he didn't say anything. "Where's Saffy?"

"Having a shower. Two tries today, and she's got a decent coating of mud." Daniel didn't bother keeping the pride out of his voice, and Kana studied him from her high vantage point as he turned to leave.

"I'm glad I saw you before the party started." It wasn't entirely true, but she did have something on her mind that'd been worrying her.

Daniel halted his retreat, turning back to her ever-so-slowly.

"Ahh," Kana hesitated, aware this wasn't anywhere near her jurisdiction. "I noticed some blood in a paw print on the annex doorstep yesterday, and I thought I should let you know in case Halfback has hurt himself. Maybe the tar-seal…?" She knew Daniel no longer ran the lake tracks in the morning, had instead taken to pounding the pavement late in the evening.

"Right." Daniel narrowed his eyes a smidgen. "I'll look him over."

This was the longest conversation they'd had in a week, and Kana couldn't help being drawn to the tiredness in his face.

"Daniel, you look… Are you sleeping okay?"

"Don't *you* start." He spun from her and stormed into the farmhouse through the backdoor.

It was the first time Kana had ever seen him move with a clear limp.

"Great work, Kanako," she muttered to herself, tying the last balloon to the string-line above the table, and dangling the ribbon down artfully.

The timer began to bleat from the oven as she was stowing the ladder back in the back shed, indicating Daniel's birthday cake was ready.

Kana breathed a sigh of relief Adele was the only occupant in the kitchen, and Daniel was nowhere in sight. The strawberry-blonde was putting finishing touches to a plate of fruit-skewers before tucking it under the net covering with the rest of the food.

Kana pulled on an oven mitt and took out the chocolate cake, pleased with its spring-back.

"Smells good!" Adele leant over to take a deep sniff. "That's it, I think." She picked up her list and went through it again. "Just the savouries to go in the oven now the cake's out, and these little cocktail sausages to be heated up."

"I can do that, you go." Kana was aware Adele wanted to get changed before the others came. "I'll put them both on low, so they won't overcook."

"Thank you." Adele was already halfway to the door and pulling her apron off.

"Where are the big plates? A platter for the cake?"

"Top right-hand cupboard, above the knife block." Adele smiled before disappearing.

Dragging a chair over, Kana climbed up. Choosing a large, hand-thrown platter from the bottom of the pile, she hefted it down, feeling the prickle of recognition well before she got a good look at the design.

It was one of hers.

The red glaze was a tricky one to master in a high firing, but she'd been really pleased with this one—fired in the annex kiln only a week ago. The ruby-red stylised lotus in the centre was the focal point, but the swallow flying away from it set this platter apart from the others in series. The black glaze had pooled on the bird's tail and chest, giving it a midnight sheen. She placed it carefully on the bench, ready for the cake, and put the chair away before starting to set savouries out on the pre-heated tray.

Hearing the door swing back open behind her, Kana laughed. "Don't you trust me? I told you, I've got this."

When Adele didn't immediately answer, Kana turned to look over her shoulder, directly into Daniel's forest-green eyes.

"No. I don't trust you, since you ask," Daniel murmured darkly, and she pulled back from the clear distaste in his tone, and expression. "You lie, and you cheat."

"I *beg* your pardon?" Kana's hackles rose at the insult, and she lost awareness of what she was in the middle of doing—grasping the hot tray with the hand that *wasn't* wearing the oven mitt. "Ow!" she squawked, dropping it with a clatter, scattering savouries everywhere. "Fūjin *damn* you, Daniel."

"No. Fūjin damn *you*, Kanako." Daniel snapped. "What the fuck do you think you're doing, making yourself at home in my kitchen?" He thrust out his hand. "Show me."

"Get stuffed." Kana pulled the throbbing fingers to her chest, balling them into a fist and turning her back on him. "Leave me alone. I'm helping Adele."

Stubborn little…

Daniel stood behind Kanako and willed himself to calm down, but it wasn't everyday he wandered into his own kitchen to find a laughing, barefoot Kanako-witch—baking cakes and savouries, and generally looking like she belonged there in the centre of his life.

What was she trying to do, wrench his bruised heart out and stomp all over it?

She'd taken him by surprise; he'd assumed she'd still be outside.

Kanako wore an old-style dress with flowers on it. A fitted top with a pleated skirt, skimming the top of her knees like some '60's poster-girl for cocoa-powder. The style made her look unbelievably feminine, and incredibly appealing. She'd been wearing a cardigan when he'd seen her teetering at the top of the ladder earlier, legs all bare and pretty with the dog licking at her toes.

His hands still itched to slide around her waist and pull her back against him. She'd left her hair loose, and he knew exactly how it would smell if he buried his face in it.

Daniel grabbed Kanako's arm instead, propelling her towards the sink while ignoring her expletives. Running the cold tap, he held her burnt hand by the wrist and forced it under the flow.

"I'm not a *child*," Kanako fumed, trying to tug her hand free.

"Then stop *acting* like one," he returned gruffly.

Kanako turned slowly to stare at him, and remembering they'd had the exact same back-and-forth on the boat over a lifejacket, Daniel found himself giving her a wry smile.

She stopped fighting him then, and her look softened a little.

"Buddha's wonders never cease. I think you might've just cracked a smile," Kanako murmured, but rather than smiling herself, her mouth downturned, and her eyes sparkled with something other than happiness.

Daniel's lips found hers without him consciously meaning them to, and possessed more roughly than he ever would've consciously liked to. But rather than pull away, as he'd half expected, Kanako pushed up against him and gave as good as she got.

It was fierce, and it was hot. His body immediately wanted more, and by the way Kanako was moving against him, so did hers.

He pulled back only when Kanako bit his lower lip, hard.

"What happened to no teeth?" he muttered.

Kanako's breathing was shallow, and her eyes narrowed as she watched him automatically run his fingers over his lip, checking for blood. The water gushed from the faucet, ignored and forgotten, and he still had Kanako pinned against the edge of the sink with his own body.

Ever so slowly, Daniel took Kanako's hand from his chest and brought it up for inspection. Her forefinger and middle finger had a little pink welt running horizontally across the pads at the tip. Catching her eye, Daniel drew the fingers deliberately towards his mouth, amused when he saw her realise the implications of the movement.

She licked her lips, nervousness palpable.

Kanako whimpered when he slid her fingers into his mouth, but didn't pull away. Clearly expecting a retaliation bite, she seemed to be allowing him the rite, as she'd bitten him first.

Daniel gently sucked her fingers instead, the act more sensuous than he'd expected, and after a moment Kanako's eyes clouded. She melted into him, laying her forehead on his shoulder.

"You're so different, Daniel. *We're* so different." Kanako whispered. "Are you…" she hesitated, and he felt the shock of her warm lips on his neck as she turned into him and murmured against his skin, "Are you using?"

No, he wasn't using!

In reprimand, Daniel let the base of her fingers feel his teeth in a light graze, before shaking his head.

"So it was the pictures?"

He didn't know what she meant by that, so shook his head again.

"But, you and I… We're finished, right?" Kanako whispered.

Daniel hesitated before nodding reluctantly, glad he couldn't speak, and that Kanako couldn't see his face. The burn in his throat was suddenly excruciating.

Finished before it'd really started, cemented by Kanako's half-truths, blatant lies, and withholding. But that didn't mean Daniel didn't ache for it to have ended differently.

Could he still twist this around, and *make* it end differently? If there was honesty between them they had the potential to start fresh, with a clean slate.

Sliding Kanako's fingers from his mouth, he turned her by the shoulders and put her burnt hand back under the running water.

This time, she didn't fight him, leaving her fingers in the cool flow. When she lay her head back against him it felt like the most natural thing in the world, like they were meant to fit together like this.

Maybe Baka-Ken thought the exact same thing?

Daniel put his hands on Kanako's hips, lowered his mouth to her ear, and asked a question he already knew the answer to.

"Kanako, are you with Ken?"

"What? No, of course I'm not with *Ken*."

Kanako tried to turn bodily towards him, but Daniel kept his hands firm on her hips, not allowing her to. She was a damn good liar; it just rolled off her tongue easy as pie, without hesitation.

He had a sudden memory of Tilly, eyes wide and falsely innocent as she told him she had nothing to do with the leaked story, the missing money, the drugs. She'd had *no idea* what he was talking about, eyelashes batting like crazy. And against his better judgement, he'd chosen to believe her.

Daniel had no inclination to watch Kanako's golden eyes lie as effortlessly as her mouth did.

Taking a deep breath in through his nose, smelling her skin, her hair, along with the warm overtones of chocolate, Daniel released it in a sigh before turning his mouth to her ear once again.

"There's a card game called Bullshit we used to play when we were kids. You have to lie about what's in your hand. I think you'd play an excellent game, Kanako. I think you'd beat the crap out of me."

Then he turned and left the room before he did anything stupid, like kiss his mother's married ceramicist again, or put another part of her anatomy in his mouth.

Cam and Shal's child, Levi, had his mother's blue-green eyes, and the most outrageously lush eyelashes. The one-year-old's dark ringlets begged to be touched, and Kana found herself doing so on more than one occasion as he waddled past.

Adele's nephew, three-year-old Tobias, was obviously well trained in the game of fetch, following Levi around and getting the toddler whatever he squealed for.

Tobias' mother, Katie, was two years older than Adele, and heavily pregnant with her second. She reclined on a deck chair, laughing at her son's dedication. "Tobias has no idea how to play hard to get. He's completely under the thumb of Mr Bossy-Boots."

"I'm just happy Levi has someone else to order around right now, I'm totally bushed." Shal smiled indulgently, also stretching her legs out.

The women sat in the courtyard out the back, with the debris from the party littering the table in front of them. The rest of the extended family, along with assorted aunts and uncles, were all inside.

"This is pretty." Shal leaned forward to touch a finger to Kana's gold locket. "I've seen you wear it before."

"Yes." Kana smiled. "It was my grandmother's, and her mother's before her."

The chain had been replaced by a sturdier, longer version, but the engraved locket was otherwise exactly as Obāchan had worn it.

Kana opened the dainty catch with her thumbnail, holding it up for Katie and Shal to see. The women pushed their faces together to peer at the tiny sepia photo of Kana's great grandfather, and she was struck by how different the close friends were. Where Shal was dark and exotic, Katie looked as wholesome as apple pie.

Catching a movement out of the corner of her eye, Kana jumped up with a squeak, clutching her open locket. "The dog!"

Halfback had been lying in the far-off shade, minding his own business, but the small children had spotted him, and were now bee-lining it towards him.

"Gentle with him!" Katie called.

Kana realised with shocked surprise Katie was instructing the *children*, not the dog. Looking from face to face, she also realised the women had no intention of moving.

"You trust him with the little ones?" Kana was moving towards the children as she spoke, manoeuvring into a more protective position.

"If they bug him, he'll move." Katie decided aloud, and though watching the interaction, stayed seated.

Levi was standing back, pointing at Halfback with chortles and squeals, but Tobias was a lot more gung-ho. Kneeling, he threw his arms around the dog's neck in one swift movement.

Kana squatted down next to Levi, feeling semi-confident she could intervene if either child got in trouble. "Dog," she explained.

"Duh, duh, duh," Levi agreed excitedly, still pointing.

"*Hasst*-bat," Tobias lisped. Scrambling back up to stand, he poked a chubby finger clean into the dog's eye.

Halfback pulled away, giving Kana a look of entreaty.

"Be gentle." She moved forward, took the offending hand and brought it back to Halfback's white ruff, hesitating just a moment before encouraging the little boy to stroke the fur in the right direction.

The dog was surprisingly soft, with fine fur that was obviously well groomed. His pelt was thicker around the neck, then changed to a sleek, glossy black on his back. When she gained confidence, burying her fingers deeper into the fur, Kana could feel the insulated warmth of his skin underneath.

When her hand moved slowly to Halfback's flank, the dog turned his head and began licking her fingers gently.

Kana watched with a mixture of fascination and trepidation, as his soft, manoeuvrable tongue worked between her digits. Breathing in for four, and out for five, she allowed a trancelike calm to wash over her.

The children had lost interest and were wandering off towards Clem, who'd arrived with a large box.

But still, Kana stayed.

Just Halfback and herself under the tree.

Their eyes met, and the collie seemed to smile at her. "You're a good dog," she whispered, suddenly close to tears. "Thank you for being such a good dog."

"I thought you didn't like dogs." Saffy's voice was petulant behind her, and Kana turned with some surprise. She'd been too absorbed to hear anyone approach.

"I thought so too," she smiled, blinking rapidly as she got up to stand next to the birthday girl. "But Halfback's different."

23

A SINGLE FLOWER

"If we could see the miracle
of a single flower clearly,
our whole life would change."
- Buddha

Daniel tore his eyes from Kana and Saffy under the tree, both patting the damn dog.

What the hell had brought that on?

Clem slid his hefty birthday gift to Saffy under the outdoor table. "Time for cake." He nudged Daniel's shoulder and rubbed his hands together.

Daniel found a smile for the older man. "Always thinking with your stomach, Clementine."

Clem patted the belly in question. "Yep. *Almost* always, though sometimes I hear from other parts of my anatomy." He winked broadly at Poppy, who was walking past with a pile of serviettes and a large knife.

"You watch your step *and* your anatomy there, farm-boy." Poppy warned with a tight smile. "I'm wielding a rather sharp weapon here."

Clem grinned in response.

"Did you orchestrate that?" Daniel murmured for Clem's ears alone, nodding back towards the quiet trio under the tree.

"No." Clem scratched his chin with a small, secretive smile. "I reckon they orchestrated it themselves. Good timing, though." He tapped the side of his boot gently against the large box at his feet, and the cardboard appeared to move a little in answer.

Daniel's eyes widened when he realised the implications.

"Does Adele know?" He turned to look across at his cousin, who was pushing candles into Saffy's unicorn cake.

Clem turned to stare at him. "You think I'd put the responsibility of a pup on someone without their say so? She's the one who talked me into it. Came and chose the pick of the litter herself."

Shal came up behind Daniel and propelled him to the head of the table by the shoulders. "Sit," she commanded.

"Saffy!" Katie yelled. "Cake!"

After the candles were blown out on Saffy's trussed up cake, all eyes turned to Daniel. Poppy placed a chocolate cake in front of him with aplomb, and he stared at it in surprise.

Sometime since he'd seen it last, it had been plastered with icing stencils, and there were now little hearts all over it. His eyes caught Kanako's, and he glared.

Was this some kind of sick joke?

Kanako took a step backwards and brought her fingertips up to her locket. "Ah… Saffy made it pretty for you," she murmured by way of explanation, eyes distressed.

Right. Of course. Saffy.

Daniel rubbed a hand over his own eyes, suddenly tired beyond belief.

"Do you like it?" Saffy brought her face in close, eagerly watching for his reaction, and he dragged up a smile for her.

"Thanks Sass-a-frass. It looks great." Turning back to offer some semblance of apology, he found Kanako had slipped aside, out of view.

Daniel's family sang for him, first in English, then in Te Reo Māori, in the tradition of his father. As he cut and handed out pieces of cake, the platter underneath became more and more exposed; the dark swallow and the red blush of the lotus flower. It reminded him of Kanako's gallery showing, and how shocked she'd been to see him. It reminded him of Kanako in her red dress, embracing her husband and smiling up into his face.

It reminded him of the sting.

Growing up as Poppy's son, and Nona's grandson, Daniel had seen his fair share of art, and met his fair share of artists. He'd also seen first-hand the calibre of the work Kanako was producing.

Ken had called Kanako's ceramics her 'little hobby.'

Daniel ran his finger over the delicate line of the swallow's tail, just visible under the icing.

Ken was an uncultured asshole.

The puppy was a good distraction. Daniel had forgotten just how sharp their little teeth could be, like a mouthful of bloody needles. Saffy wanted to name the pup 'Winger,' which was only fitting really, as she'd scored two tries from that position earlier today. To everyone's surprise, the nine-year old handled herself without too much fear around the puppy, only pulling back when the teeth got too actively involved.

"Look at Halfback," Adele chuckled. "He's not impressed!"

The older dog had reprimanded the pup for biting his tail with a sharp bark, and stalked away with that particular appendage held high in the air.

Kana felt a little sorry for him.

Clem explained the pup would be going back to its mother tonight, but Saffy could come and visit it anytime over the next two weeks, so they could get used to each other before Winger was ready to go to her new home.

"And, when she's growing up, you can bring her back to the farm whenever you like for a run around." Clem smiled. "That's the life, eh? Mucking around on the farm, chasing rabbits." He stalled, turning towards Kana to nudge her shoulder with his big fist. "No offence?"

She smiled, reassuring him. "None taken."

"They serve rabbit in some of the fancy restaurants in town, you know," Clem continued, obviously feeling comfortable enough to tease. "Can't stomach it myself. Stringy animal. You'll be going out for dinner tonight with the others?"

"Oh—" Kana started.

"No." Daniel stated firmly. "That's just for family." Then he turned and stalked towards the table, every inch of him cold-shoulder.

Clem grunted in surprise.

Though Kana had no knowledge of dinner plans, and no intention of going, she still felt the slap of Daniel's words.

Adele, standing on the periphery, was obviously close enough to have heard. She stepped forward to grasp Kana's arm. "I'm so sorry, I don't know what's gotten into him. Of *course* you're invited."

"Thank you, but I'd really better not. I have a lot of work to catch up on," Kana declined as politely as she could.

Looking around herself, she realised she was the only non-family member at the party. Clem was with Poppy, whereas Daniel had just made it perfectly clear she was in the way.

It was well past time for her to leave.

She should've made herself scarce ages ago, but she'd actually been enjoying herself with the children, with the dogs, and with Daniel's family.

Shame about the moody man himself.

Remembering their confrontation in the kitchen, warmth crept back into her belly. So much fire in that kiss, and she'd all but melted with her fingers in his bloody sensuous mouth.

Damn him.

Kana removed her cardigan from the back of Saffy's chair, and ignoring the collection of adults laughing and talking, squatted down to say goodbye to the child.

"Thank you so much for inviting me to your party, Saffy. I had a wonderful time."

Saffy turned and squeezed her around the neck. "Thank you for coming, and for my present," she returned politely, referring to the little ceramic jewellery box with an oak-leaf and acorn lid. "Will you invite me to your birthday this year?"

"Saffy!" Adele admonished, overhearing.

Kana laughed. "I would, but I'm afraid I've already had it. I'm an April baby too, but mine was at the very beginning of the month."

"How old are you?" Saffy continued matter-of-factly, and Kana caught Adele rolling her eyes.

"A woman never tells the truth about her age, Saff." Daniel directed the words towards Saffy, across the table from him, but his focus was deliberately on Kana. He seemed to pause and reload with her clearly in his sights, and she stared at him like a deer caught within rifle range. "Some women have trouble telling the truth about anything," he muttered.

Though softly spoken, Daniel's words were shot with precision.

Way to kill a connection. *Bang*. Dead.

Kana found herself gaping at Daniel, and she wasn't the only adult at the table doing it. All conversation had come to a standstill.

Finally blinking, she turned back to Saffy, and painted on a bright smile. "I think Daniel's still a bit jet-lagged, don't you? Or maybe he's just grouchy because I bet him. He's just a *baby* at thirty-five," she put a minute stress on the word. "And I turned forty this year."

"Bull!" Shal leaned forward in her chair to get a better view. "Are you really? I assumed you were around the same age as me."

"No." She smiled back at the dark-haired woman, grateful for the intercept. "People often assume I'm younger, especially if the lighting's dodgy. I can thank my mother for her inherited skin, but I really did hit the big four-oh this year."

"But you came to Wānaka at the start of *March*," Adele wailed. "You mean you had your fortieth here?" Again, her friend looked distressed. "Please tell me you didn't stay home on your birthday."

"Oh, no, actually. I did go out. On a sort of date." Kana couldn't help but look back across at Daniel challengingly as she said it.

Irrespective of his rude behaviour and obvious dislike for her lately, the rippa-rugby fundraiser had been really fun.

On their subsequent 'date' by the lake, they'd gotten on so well. Daniel had played his role incredibly solicitously. He'd humoured her with fish and chips, laughed at her jokes, and given her every pretence of romance.

Attentive. Sweet. Then later in the evening…

Kana had a sudden flashback to their naked bodies, tangled

together on the living room floor. The feel of Daniel's large hands encircling her waist as he'd groaned her name and thrust into her.

She couldn't help it if that still fizzled her blood.

Feeling her blush kick back in with full-force, Kana stood to put on her cardigan. Hiding her glow from the table-full of people, who all suddenly seemed intensely interested, she took longer than necessary to right her clothing.

She snuck Daniel another look. He caught her doing it and held her gaze, full comprehension written on his face, and something else she couldn't quite place.

"That was your birthday? You never said." Daniel all but growled the words.

"No. I didn't mention it at the time," Kana replied, as flippantly as she could manage.

"A woman's due her own little secrets." Poppy smiled as she walked over to Kana and patted her arm, filling the awkward silence with her own input. "Not to be confused with lies." Turning, she raised an eyebrow at her eldest son.

Kana sunk her hands in her pockets, bumping into the gift she'd had carved for Daniel's birthday, but now knew she would never give him.

She held the perfect stone in her fist and breathed in for four, out for five.

Daniel was outside, tearing down decorations on the back patio, alone. That's just how he wanted it, so when he heard the back door swing closed, he turned towards it, glowering.

Poppy continued on approach, unperturbed by her son's distinct lack of invitation, her own face set like an anvil.

"I don't want to hear it," Daniel growled.

"You *will* hear it though, and what's more, you'll listen." Poppy sat off to the side, out of Daniel's direct line of sight as he worked.

Smart.

That way she could time her assaults like stealth missiles.

"When I saw you and Kana on my last visit, you could've cut the sexual tension with a knife. But now you're all fractured and icy, sliding into downright nasty. What happened?"

Fuck. He didn't have to answer that.

Daniel ignored his mother and started shafting the odd balloon with the knife he'd used to cut up the cake. Collecting scraps of blue and purple latex, he stuffed them into the burgeoning rubbish bag along with everything else.

"Now she isn't worth your time-of-day? Worse than that, in fact. Not even worth the courtesy you'd afford a stranger." Poppy targeted Daniel's weak-spot, going with the guilt-bomb. "I happen to know Kana's no stranger to you, and just because you're finished with her does *not* mean you can cast her off like yesterday's socks. I raised you better than that, Daniel Tāroaroa Dante. Graham and I raised you much better than that."

Yes, his behaviour this afternoon had been abysmal. He'd slipped back into ass-mode.

"She's married, Mum." Daniel spoke quietly, continuing to crush streamers and pull down balloons—putting a touch of savagery into it. "After this gig, Kana's heading back to her husband."

Just saying the words aloud was enough to rile Daniel well beyond his recent, seemingly constant level of pissed-off-ness.

"I highly doubt she'll spend a moment more of her time with that particular man." Poppy spoke with calm authority.

Getting up to remove two cake platters, a chip bowl, and the cake knife from the table, she stacked them in a pile on a random chair and eyed him down.

Possibly for the best.

Nothing on the outdoor table was going to survive at this rate. Daniel was now shoving whatever he could get his hands onto in the bin-liner.

"Stop." His mother grabbed his hand, and held on. "Just listen. Whether Kana is in the process of divorce, or actually divorced is a moot point. She took on the artist in residence position to remove herself from her marriage. I know that to be true. Maybe you should try *talking* to her, as she obviously means a great deal to you, and find out the truth of the matter."

Daniel barked a laugh without mirth. "The *truth?* I don't think

Kanako would know the truth if it jumped up and bit her on the ass."

Her perfectly delectable ass.

"You're wrong." Poppy released his hand to smooth her skirt into submission, before stalking around the table to save a couple of balloons, tying them to her wrist. "Your judgement's been skewed by your own emotions, and your own history. Kana is not Tilly," she added in a softer tone, unable to bring Daniel's ex's name to her lips without a small curl of her lip.

Daniel pointed a warning finger her way. "Don't even go there."

Though he had himself. He'd been likening this whole thing with Kanako to his gullibility with Tilly.

Yes, Tilly had played him, but he'd strolled right into that relationship a lot younger, with a fully fledged addiction up his sleeve, and party-till-you-drop attitude. What the hell had he been expecting to go down?

With Kanako it'd felt different. Seriously real. Something with actual longevity. Somehow, though they'd only known each other for a couple of months, her betrayal of trust felt a thousand times worse.

"You care for this woman, quite a bit by the looks of it, but you hold yourself back from being the partner I know you could be. When something comes between you, you're helping no one by shutting down. Your anger is so raw, D. I could slap a marinade on you and barbecue your hide. You can't treat people that way. You need to give her the opportunity to at least *talk*, for heaven's sake."

"I'm telling you, she's back with this Ken asshole," Daniel grumbled, pissed off his mother was right about his tendency to forestall important conversations for fear of what they might disclose.

In truth, Daniel didn't really want to know why Kanako had chosen to get back with her husband after what she and himself had shared, but he owed it to her to listen.

Poppy frowned, shaking her head. "I don't believe that. Not for a second. You're obviously not sleeping well, and if the shadows under your eyes aren't evidence enough, the hall pacing and three a.m. jogs cement it. If I didn't know better, I'd worry you were on some kind of substance, or coming off one."

"For the last time, I'm not using!"

"I didn't say you were. I said if I didn't *know* better. I'm warning you, if you don't get out of your own way and repair what you've broken, you'll lose this girl through your own stubbornness. Then you'll have something to be angry about. She won't put up with another alpha-hole speaking to her like she's not worth diddlysquat, and she shouldn't have to." Picking up her stack of table-saves and stalking towards the house, Poppy stopped before she entered, turning back for one last observation. "Kana's begun to mean a great deal to Adele and Saffy. A great deal to me." Balancing the platter on one hand, she brought the back of the other up to her nose and sniffed, setting the tied balloons dancing.

"*Mum*," Daniel groaned.

"I suggest you try to get some sleep this afternoon if you don't want Adele to boycott your birthday dinner tonight. No one wants to be around a bear with a sore head, or a jet-lagged Datsun." His mother's voice thinned to nothing more than a whisper. "Go to bed, son."

24

INCOMPLETE

"If your compassion does not include yourself,
it is incomplete."
- Buddha

"Oh! There's Kana!" Adele called out after they'd parked outside the restaurant.

Daniel's head snapped up from locking the car, and he surveyed the street quickly.

"Just gone into the dairy." Adele looked him over sullenly, not bothering to be surreptitious about how pissed off she was with him. She lifted her chin. "I'm going to see if I can change her mind, and convince her to join us."

"I'm not sure if that's…" Daniel started, but Adele was already half-way across the street before he could give his opinion, curls flicking in the wind that'd picked up off the lake.

What if Kanako was in there with her husband?

Daniel didn't know what to do with his body while he waited, unsure if he was gunning for Adele to return empty handed, or with Kanako in tow. He thrust his fists deep into his pockets, leaning against his car as he stared down the sloping length of Main Street.

White caps ruffled the surface of the lake, like a flock of woolly sheep.

He'd tried to smooth it over with his cousin in the car, but they were far from convivial. With a couple of solid hours of sleep under his belt, Daniel could see where Poppy was coming from, and where Adele was fast headed. He hadn't exactly been the best version of himself today, nor the past week for that matter.

Kanako had begun to mean far too much in a very short space of time, that was the problem. But he'd have to learn to deal with seeing her and Baka-Ken around, and keep a civil tongue in his head.

Relief—that's what flowed through him when Adele exited the small corner store with Kanako.

Just Kanako.

Svelte in slim-fitting jeans, Kanako's hair was once more swept away from her face in her usual braid, Ugg-boots her only concession to the coolness of evening.

"I've bullied Kana into joining us." Adele breezed, willing him with her eyes to dare challenge her call.

"Great," he replied, realising only after he'd said it the word could easily be misconstrued as sarcastic.

"I never gave you a birthday present." Kanako moved forward, holding a closed fist towards him. Something round and shiny peeped from between her slim fingers.

He automatically reached out to receive the gift, and a single Cadbury's Creme Egg landed neatly in his palm.

By the uncertainty lurking in Kanako's eyes, the chocolate was very much in the form of a peace offering. One *he* should've been offering *her*.

Daniel couldn't help the corners of his mouth pulling up into a slight smile. "Thank you, but I wouldn't want to deprive you of your favourite."

"That's okay." Kanako shrugged, returning his smile tentatively before moving away from him, around the other side of Adele. "Andy has a steady supply," she named the dairy owner. "And if it gets low, he holds emergency rations for me under the counter."

Daniel didn't know if that was the truth or just a line, but it was enough to make him laugh. He slid the chocolate egg into his jacket pocket, aware Adele was watching him like a hawk, and Kanako was avoiding looking at him altogether.

Kana felt acutely awkward, using Adele as a physical buffer. She was also relieved. True to Adele's word—Daniel's mood seemed to have finally flipped.

In a black jacket and dark jeans, Daniel looked good.

Better than good.

He'd obviously showered and shaved, and appeared more approachable. She caught her bottom lip between her teeth and gnawed at it. A woman would be smart to remember looks could be extremely deceiving, and only idiots trusted a wolf in sheep's clothing a second time around.

We're done, she reminded herself. *Done, done, done.*

She was just along for Adele's benefit, though giving in to her friend's pleas was already proving torturous.

Shal and Cam arrived in a late model sedan, making their way across the street to join the trio, and Kana was once again struck by the similarity of the two brothers, and their differences. Where the younger of the two had a ready smile and a relaxed way about him, setting her instantly at ease, Daniel looked more like he was deciding whether or not to bare his fangs.

Shal also gave Kana a broad, welcoming smile, gaze flicking from Daniel, back to the potter. "Kana! I'm so glad you decided to come."

Kana had less 'decided' and more been 'coerced,' but she kept that knowledge to herself. If she just had a single drink with them, then scooted off, it might be enough to appease Adele's sense of decorum; her desperate need to 'make everything right.'

Daniel and Kana weren't necessarily ever going to be 'right,' but they could be civil, and that was the next best thing.

They turned as a group to enter the family owned tapas restaurant, Adele first, and the others arm in arm. Kana was left pointedly with Daniel. He held the door for her, and she felt the simple courtesy keenly in contrast to his clear dismissal earlier in the day.

It'd be fine once they were with everyone else, Kana reasoned as she slid through the door, avoiding eye contact and holding her breath. Sniffing him right now would be a mistake.

She'd be able to find a spot next to Poppy and Clem and keep out of the way.

Katie and Rue arrived directly after them, without little Tobias, but it still took Kana another five minutes to realise the others weren't actually coming. To her infinite discomfort, when they were shown from the bar to their table, a hasty seventh setting was being placed next to Daniel.

The poor man had been actively paired off with her again; coerced into sitting next to her despite having shown everyone at the party today it was well and truly over.

"Look, I'm sorry, I assumed there'd be more people and I would just, you know, blend into the background," Kana whispered to Daniel as they sat down together along the length of the table.

Daniel seemed to have re-mastered his manners, which would no doubt enforce he stayed put, whether he wanted to or not.

"Blend?"

Kana took the tone for sardonic, and looked quickly across the table at Shal, who was laughing at something Cam had said. The woman's eyes matched her expensively cut suede-look jacket in deep teal. Seated alongside Shal, Katie was the picture of health, her pregnancy proudly shown off in a clingy gold tunic. Adele, all curves and confidence, returned from the bar with a trio of beers in tall glasses. Floating in a riot of strawberry-blonde hair, she looked like a Celtic queen.

Kana's mind skipped to Daniel's immaculately dressed blondes in the magazines, and realised how incredibly underdressed she must look in her work jeans.

'Inherently scruffy—all the time,' was Ken's favourite line to describe Kana's style. He'd always disliked the sheer filthiness of her work.

After Saffy and Daniel's birthday lunch, Kana had needed both yoga and clay to calm herself down, and had immersed herself in the studio. She would've still been there, if it hadn't been for the call of chocolate.

Looking down at the hands in her lap, she realised there was still clay wedged in around some of her cuticles, and smears of the same earth marked her thighs where the apron hadn't quite reached.

Ken would be disgusted.

Kana didn't want to think about her ex-husband right now, she wanted to bolt—curl up in her own little cave back at the annex. Making up her mind to do just that, she pushed her chair a little further back.

She'd paid her dues with one drink, and mended the bridge.

"No. I don't tend to blend in, do I? I think I'll head off."

Daniel looked confused at first, but his hand snaked out to grip her wrist as she went to stand, surprising her.

"Don't." Daniel's single word request held a world of meaning, and Kana hesitated.

"Look, I know you're on your best manners this evening, and that's all very nice, considering the alternative." She eyed him pointedly. "But you shouldn't have to sit here next to me when you've got family around you for your birthday." Waving her free hand around expressively, she alluded to everyone else at the table. "Adele obviously doesn't need me here. She made out like…" She cleared her throat. "It doesn't matter. Whatever was between you and me is over, and this is clearly uncomfortable for both of us. I'll just make up some excuse and get going."

Again she moved to rise, but Daniel's grip remained the same.

Kana tapped on his knuckles, reminded of when they'd been in his car, and he wouldn't let her out.

"Let me go, Daniel," she advised him with as much calm as she could muster.

"I apologise for how I spoke to you today. I was rude." Daniel spoke with an urgency that had her blinking. "I always come across as raw with you, and that's not my intention. It's never my intention. What if I asked you to stay?" He met her surprised stare, and held it. "Please, stay." The second time Daniel said the word, it was with more entreaty, and therefore harder to ignore.

"That's, ah, kind of you, really. But not necessary. You're not on the clock now." If Daniel's eyebrows were anything to go by, Kana had confused him again. "I mean I haven't…" She didn't quite know how to say it politely. "Bought your time."

"*Bought* my *time?*" The hushed conversation they'd been conducting was blown wide open when Daniel repeated what she'd said in a thunderous growl, much louder than 'private' volume.

It sounded a lot uglier when he said it.

"Ahh…" Kana looked from Shal to Katie, who were now ogling Daniel and herself unashamedly. She leant a little closer to Daniel so she could whisper again, the scent of his soap and aftershave starkly familiar.

It aimed a small, fierce punch at her gut.

This whole thing would be easier if Daniel wasn't so damned attractive. Much easier if she didn't know how his mouth would taste if she leaned across to kiss him now, and *immeasurably* easier if she didn't know how it felt to lie naked with him.

"Look, I know I'm underdressed, and not your usual, kind of, well… *date*." Kana laughed a little to cover her unease as Daniel continued to stare at her. "I don't fit in." She shrugged.

"You think you're underdressed?" Thankfully working with her on the privacy issue, Daniel kept his voice down.

"Yes." Grateful Daniel appeared to understand her on this point, Kana eased her chair back again. "I hope you have a lovely evening."

"I will, if you stay," Daniel maintained, watching Kanako's free hand move in a jittery motion to the base of her unadorned throat, searching for the locket that no longer appeared to be there. "I had no right to speak to you that way this afternoon. *No one* has any right…" Trailing off before bringing Baka-Ken into the conversation again, he grappled with his multitude of reasons. "I haven't been sleeping… The jet-lag…"

Excuses, now? Was he willing to slink back to being *that* guy? He hadn't been *that* guy since he'd kicked his addiction.

Daniel ran a hand over his face. "There's no excuse," he amended, hoping his honesty would mean something to her, and wishing it could change something. "I'm just sorry."

Kanako had never said she was available. She'd never said she was free. She'd told him the opposite, in fact, right before he'd kissed her that first time.

She'd never wanted anything complicated.

With Kanako's hair pulled back, Daniel could see the little pulse below her ear beat its nervy tattoo. *Ba-boom, ba-boom, ba-boom.*

"You know it doesn't matter what you're wearing, Kanako. You'll always be the most beautiful woman in the room," he added softly, wishing it weren't so.

"Oh!" Kanako had been staring at Daniel's fingers, still locked around her wrist, but now those honey-gold beauties flew to meet his. "You're making fun of me," she decided aloud, her twitchy smile unable to diffuse the underlying sadness in her eyes.

"No. It's Buddha's honest truth." Daniel smiled back with his own regret, and something in his expression must have registered, because Kanako blinked furiously in response.

Everything in him had hoped for something serious with this woman, but if she'd chosen someone else over him, he had to concede. Free will was everything.

That left him with friendship. A friendly basis.

A landlord and tenant relationship? God help him.

Daniel struggled to pull himself up from the despair of it. He needed to say something to replace this awful tension, something to keep Kanako here by his side, knowing he meant her no harm—no malice.

"I would even pay for the privilege of dining with the best looking female in town." He banked on the other thing Kanako and himself had shared; their sense of humour.

"Pay?"

"Buy your time," he teased lightly.

"*Oh*!" Kanako was obviously surprised to have her own words thrown back at her, and chewed on her lower lip before admitting, "I'm sorry to've used that term. It's awful."

"You'd prefer to work for free?" He grinned—actually having fun for the first time in days.

"*Shhh*. Stop it!" Pushing at his shoulder, Kanako relaxed enough to allow a bubble of laughter to break through.

———

Perhaps unwisely, Adele began a discussion about the sticky ins and outs of love. *Definitely* unwisely, Kana allowed herself to get drawn into it, laughing with Katie about the piece the skincare developer had chosen to leave out of her wedding vows. *'In sickness and in health.'*

"I swear, if I'd seen how Rue handled man flu before we married, it would've been serious grounds for an end to our engagement," Katie maintained.

"God, yes," Adele agreed wholeheartedly. "And I'd like to add that although love's supposed to conquer all, it rudely forgets to pick up its dirty socks, or pay the tax bill."

"Jaded, much?" Shal laughed. "No one ever said love was a smooth ride. Feeling loved at the beginning and the end is totally up to fate—the luck of the draw. But the middle bit of finding a mate and making it work? That's in our own hands." She slid her hand across the back of Cam's chair, clearly happy with the choices she'd made for herself.

"You've been married, Kana. What do you think?" Adele turned to ask quietly.

Kana took her time to mull it over before sharing a Buddhist quote that resonated with her own personal experience. "My Obāchan likes to say, *'Pain is certain, suffering is optional.'* That's how I'd sum it up."

Realising all eyes were suddenly on the pair of them, Kana automatically glanced at Daniel.

All the lightness from earlier had gone from his face. "God. That's bleak," he muttered.

The tapas were simple and delicious, and with the glaring exception of the awkward 'love' topic, talk and laughter flowed freely throughout the meal.

Daniel stood at one point to steal a plate from the other end of the table, returning to place it in front of Kana. "I think you'll enjoy these."

"What are they?" She eyed the little circular stacks suspiciously.

"Lemon mussels on whitebait fritters."

At the mention of the shellfish, her eyes jumped to meet Daniel's.

"I would've made it more special if I'd known it was your birthday," he murmured, telling her with both his words and eyes he was thinking about the same night she was.

"It was special to me," she returned with simple honesty.

Ridiculously special.

When Kana returned from the bathroom, Katie's husband, Rue, had taken her seat and was in the midst of a heated discussion about the English football team with Daniel. Cam was also leaning across the table joining in, so she moved around to the corner, where Katie and Shal sat sipping from tall glasses. Adele was again up at the bar, talking to one of the staff she clearly knew quite well.

"Kana." Shal pulled a chair out for her. "Come and join us." She gestured towards the brothers. "The guys are trying to live up to the Kiwi male stereotype. The only way they could get any more boring is to begin discussing the heavyweight championships, or formula one." She laughed, tossing her mane of dark hair back over her shoulder.

"You're not into sports?" Kana queried, surprised.

"I like surfing, and I watch a bit of tennis. That's my limit."

"Oh, I guess I just assumed..." She turned her gaze to Katie.

"Don't look at me. I'd rather surf too. I do love watching New Zealand play rugby though. Don't miss a game. But to be honest, it's the haka I'm interested in. It's all downhill from there." Katie got a pained expression and began to push at the side of her basketball-sized belly. "Hell. Just the mention of sport and this little guy's getting a boot in."

Amazingly, *miraculously*, Katie's hard, round tummy began to manoeuvre and shift. Acting on instinct, Kana reached a hand out to feel the movement.

"Hey, Dante D." Katie called across the table to her cousin. "If this kicking's anything to go by, this one could give you a run for your money as first-five!"

Kana looked up at Katie in wonderment, the baby twisting under her palm.

"It's moving so much!" Tears came, unasked for and unheeded, due to the little miracle happening right in front of her. "Doesn't it hurt?" she murmured.

"No, it just sort of..." Katie smiled at her a little wistfully. "Takes your breath away sometimes."

"Takes your breath away," Kana repeated as if in a dream, her hand still on the kicking baby, amazed by the sheer tenacity of it.

"Did you plan on children?" Katie wondered aloud.

"Oh, no. My husband and I… We… we decided not to."

Kana caught the sound and movement vaguely out of her peripheral senses, as Daniel grabbed his cell phone from the pile and pushed back his chair to stand.

Turning to smile up at him, she encountered the bitterly cold expression from earlier in the day, firmly back in place.

"*Excuse* me," he grated out before leaving the table.

Kana came down to earth with a thump, instantly reminded not only was she an outsider in this group, she'd once again overstepped the mark.

She hadn't even asked to touch, sitting there with her hand on another woman's stomach, someone she'd only just met today for Buddha's sake. No doubt with a cuckoo expression on her face, she'd been patting Katie's flank like she was a heifer carrying a prize calf.

Kana removed her hand hurriedly and stuttered an apology. "I'm so sorry. That was extremely rude of me. I just went ahead and grabbed you. I've never seen..." She pushed to stand and wiped the palms of her hands down the front of her work-worn pants, glancing sideways at an open mouthed Shal, a fish out of water beside this tightly connected pair of women. "Please, excuse me."

Taking liberties. Forgetting herself. Acting weird.

Katie stood too. "You don't have to apologise. It's fine. You're fine. Daniel's a dork. Don't let him shake you up. Here." And before Kana could move, she'd been folded into a tight hug. "Now I've grabbed you without asking too, so we're even." Katie laughed, her eyes kind. "Come, sit." She gestured to the chair beside her.

"Oh, thank you, but, no." Kana tried to smile, but it felt more like a nervous twitch. "I really should go. I wasn't intending to stay for dinner, and it's getting late."

She resolutely bowed out, refusing coffee and dessert, thanking the group at large for inviting her, and asking them to pass on her best wishes to Daniel. Slinging her backpack over one shoulder and pointedly paying her own way at the door, she couldn't get out of there fast enough.

Social glitching was not a new phenomenon. She should stick to clay, she related to it better. Kana berated herself on the way back to the butt-ugly station wagon, but she was fighting a battle within herself as she went. The others had tried to be friendly and welcoming, but Daniel had been rude up at the farmhouse. Abrupt, and unkind. His distaste for her company had been so palpable it wasn't just her that'd noticed.

Then this evening, he'd rolled over and been so attentive again, though admittedly pushed into the situation by Adele's insistence. Kana had given him a clear out, and he'd *still* talked her into staying; complimenting her, and purposefully making her feel special.

Was it a charm thing Daniel could just switch on and off at will?

She couldn't fathom his moodiness—Jekyll and Hyde, just like the dog busts. Maybe he was always like this? A spoilt child, used to getting his own way, ignoring other people's emotions altogether. Or maybe Daniel had been putting on a front, a charming public personality? Was the phenomenal kissing and mind-blowing sex all part of the charity package? Dinner, conversation, and earth shattering orgasms, at your service.

'Clean as in clean enough to eat?'

Kana shrugged off the tingle of want sneaking in with that particular memory.

Where was the guy she'd gone on dates with? The laughing skydiver, the one who'd given her a boat driving lesson, and passed up a five star meal for fish and chips at the lake. Did he even exist? Where was the man who'd fed bacon scraps to the eels, and taunted her into the frigid lake with *'Jump, jump, jump?'*

Where was the guy she'd fallen for?

Oh, *shit.*

Was that what'd happened? Had she gone ahead and fallen in love with Daniel Dante?

Of course she bloody had—of all the unbelievably stupid things to do.

"Where's Kanako?" Daniel asked without preamble when he returned.

"You used your phone. Drinks are on you and I'm ordering another mocktail as we speak." Katie had implemented the 'no phones' policy at the beginning of the evening, piling various cell phones face down in the centre of the table. If anyone dared break protocol by picking up their device, the drinks bill was on them.

It was a family ritual.

"An *expensive* one," Katie reiterated, sharing a conspiratorial smile with the waitress. "Kana left."

"She *left*? Why?" His glare was accusatory and aimed directly at his cousin. "What did you say to her?"

"*Me*? What did *I* say to her? Oh, you piss me off Datsun, you *obtuse* man. We were having a moment, Kana and I, and you scared her off with your bloody grumpiness. Shame on you." Katie huffed and pouted, reminding Daniel acutely of Adele, and the conversation they'd had in the car on the way here. "It's like watching a bull ransack a china shop."

"I wasn't grumpy," he grouched.

"I practically forced Kana to come." Adele put her two cents worth in, hackles clearly back up. "Assured her that you wanted to apologise. I *insisted*. Then you choose to go with: *Excuuuuse me!*" Adele purposefully made her voice gruff when she mimicked him, and Daniel shifted on his feet uncomfortably.

"I don't sound like that."

"You *do*," Shal added unhelpfully. "Especially around Kana. Right Cam?"

"Oh, *Hell*, no. Don't bring me into this. Bait Dan if you enjoy the sport, but keep me out of it."

"Honest opinion?" Daniel turned to pin his younger brother with a stare.

"Ah… My honest opinion?" Cam looked around for support, and Daniel saw the shadow of a go-ahead nod from both Adele, and Katie. "You seem to be shovelling a lot more nasty than nice in the Kana arena, don't you think?" Cam began. "If I didn't know you better, I'd think you were trying to warn her off the property, so to speak. Or is it a 'treat her mean, keep her keen' kind of thing?"

Cam held his hands up in mock surrender as Daniel's stare turned into a glare.

"You asked for honesty," Cam muttered.

"Kana's a sweetheart," Adele continued stoically. "I love her to bits and so does Saffy. She's clearly still raw from her marriage break-up—maybe a bit rusty. If you're no longer interested I wish you'd back the hell off, D." She eyed him coldly. "Don't string her along then get all sharp. It's completely beneath you. She's had enough wanker-age in her life. Her ex-husband's a real ass. Did you meet him at the gallery? So up himself."

Yes, Daniel had met Kanako's bloody husband at the gallery, and she was planning on going back to him in four short months. What *had* he been hoping to achieve, sitting here with Kanako at his side, pretending she could be his?

"They're still married." Daniel tried to make the comment expressionless.

"What? No. That can't be right. She came here to get away from all that. She filed for divorce and walked," Adele debated.

"That's not what I heard."

"Is that what's got you riled up? Jealous of an ex in the mix? Used to it all being all about *you*, Dante D? Because you were nasty, back at the house. That 'just family' crap was purposefully hurtful, then the pointed dig about women telling the truth? In front of Saffy, no less, who in case you hadn't noticed, is growing *into* one." Adele waved her hand at him in a 'go away' gesture. "I'm not surprised Kana walked."

"Leave it, Dell." Katie ruffled the back of her sister's hair. "Let him stew on it."

Daniel did stew on it.

Adele chose to catch a ride home with Katie and Rue, so after dinner, he drove to the lay-by where he'd first met Kanako. Pulling into a park facing the dark water, he killed the engine.

Kanako's face when she'd felt the baby move, her rapture in it, golden eyes swimming with deep emotion—he just couldn't get it out of his head. The urge to hold her had been so strong, he'd had to get out of there before he'd dragged her bodily to him.

It wasn't his place to show Kanako comfort and love, and it wasn't his place to stroke her back and tell her everything would be okay.

Daniel knew too much about her, that was the problem. Kanako had revealed too much, and Baka-Ken had filled in the gaps.

He worked his way back over their whispered conversation when they'd sat down for dinner. Kanako had wanted to leave, then. Her eyes had been wide and dark when he'd held her captive by her wrist, and the sexual tension had blasted apart every resolve to remain unmoved. Especially on top of their physical contact in the kitchen earlier in the day.

He hadn't felt completely at ease the whole evening, knowing the arm brushing his was Kanako's. He'd been obsessively drawn to watch her smooth golden fingers move, ring-less, as she held her wine glass and played with her napkin.

Yes, he'd been the one who'd insisted Kanako stayed for dinner. And she had, possibly through resolute politeness because it was his birthday?

Daniel was even less comfortable when she'd left. Disappeared.

Had he been abrupt? Also, yes.

That Buddhist quote about pain had got to him. What was it? 'Pain is certain, suffering is optional.' In his world, that was pure shite. Suffering came with pain. It was a two edged sword. But to see her marriage that way? That *was* bleak.

And Kanako lied. He knew she'd lied about kids, because her story was constantly changing. There was a great injustice in Kanako feeling Katie's baby move if it was true she couldn't have one of her own. According to Baka-Ken, Kanako had opted for another round of IVF, yet she'd just told his cousin she'd chosen not to have children.

Kanako had lied about being divorced, too—about it being finished with Baka-Ken. Along with the whole non-English speaker stuff she'd pulled when he'd first met her, and petty crap like fibbing about his newspaper… None of it boded well.

Daniel had no love for dishonesty, even less after Tilly's constant lies, so why did he keep finding his time consumed by thoughts of his mother's unbelievably magnetic ceramist in residence?

He should've gone after Kanako when she'd left.

And said what?

'I apologise for being such an 'obtuse man,' as my cousin succinctly puts it, but although you're married—are back with your estranged

husband, and seem to have trouble telling me one iota of truth, I want you with a crazy need that freaks me out. You've completely flipped the axis on what I value.

Honesty. Loyalty. Fidelity... '

Daniel needed another addiction like a hole in the head, yet here he was, totally hooked on this woman.

No. Even if she were standing right here in front of him, he wouldn't say any of that. He had his pride.

He couldn't trust Kanako, and she wasn't his to ask for. Worse than that, he didn't seem to care, on either point. He wanted to be with her anyway, and that wasn't smart.

Daniel had tried to date Kanako with a hands-off approach. Like an idiot, he'd wanted to 'woo' her, for want of a better word. He'd held back on the physical side to show her he was interested in so much more than what she'd assumed was a one-night-stand. But instead, he'd managed to ensure it'd been just that.

Once.

Why couldn't he have just read it like an affair in the first place, and played it casually from there?

Because Kanako was different, and he genuinely felt something for her. Because that something was beginning to consume both his waking hours, and his sleep.

Daniel was glad his final public speaking gig for the season was coming up. It would get him out of Wānaka for a spell, and give him time to think.

25

A GOOD MAN

"A dog is not considered a good dog
because he is a good barker.
A man is not considered a good man
because he is a good talker."
- Buddha

Kana packed a light bag for her trip to Queenstown. Rather than crate the stock and send it off to the gallery, she'd decided to drive it over herself and stay for a couple of nights. The first payment for the Wānaka gallery showing had come through, and she felt like treating herself.

A change of scene wouldn't go amiss, either.

She was halfway through packing a boxful of dinnerware when she stopped, and looked slowly around herself to take stock of the place that had become so incredibly special to her. The studio was deathly quiet, with no fans or kilns running, and a shiver ran clear up her spine.

She'd had a major clean-up, wiping down all of the wooden workbenches so it smelt of wet dust; of concrete after rain. One of her favourite smells, now following at a close second behind the scent of Daniel Dante.

His clothes, his neck, the rasp of his unshaven face.

Buddha knew, she had it bad.

What the hell was she doing here, waiting for Daniel to come back and have another change of heart? Why was she waiting for scraps from someone's table who'd shown, time and time again, he was just plain over it?

It was pure insanity to stay here in Wānaka, chugging along with her work whilst craving Daniel. Her grouchy, rude, devil-take-you, incredibly delicious landlord.

This self-destructive behaviour had to stop.

Poppy would release her from her contract, Kana was sure of it. Maybe she could send Annabelle down pieces for the second gallery showing from her studio space in Christchurch, or organise another potter to take over the residency for the last four months?

Either way, she couldn't stay here.

Needing to talk to Samantha, Kana picked up the phone, then placed it down again without dialling, putting her head in her hands instead. It didn't matter what Sam said, where Kana would stay, or how she'd make ends meet. She simply had to leave.

Kana took one more look around the studio.

Leave it all.

Now.

When the butt-ugly station wagon was loaded with all the stuff she could feasibly fit in it, Kana walked up to the farmhouse with a tiny package, hoping Poppy was in. She'd had the gift made for Daniel, originally, and had planned to give it to him on his birthday.

Aden had done a beautiful job of carving a double-headed koru into the greywacke stone, but the little treasure had remained a heavy weight in her cardigan pocket since the party. There'd been absolutely no point in giving it to Daniel. It would've meant nothing to the person he'd become.

Clem's farm truck was parked on the gravel, Halfback spread across the front step like a pelt, so it looked like Kana was in luck. The dog barked twice in welcome, flipping up into a sitting position and thumping his tail.

"Stay," she told him, still very much preferring to approach at her own speed and not to be run at.

Halfback did as he was told, waiting with a soft whine.

"I've come to say goodbye." She offered her palm, thinking she saw the curtain to Poppy's room twitch out of the corner of her eye as the dog licked her hand.

"Shake," Kana commanded, and Halfback gave her his paw. She twisted it lightly to the side. The pads did seem worn, and a little split, but there was no blood. Going by the vague smell of sheep, and some greasy ointment between his toes, someone had applied a lanolin-based product.

Satisfied, Kana placed his paw back down, just as Poppy opened the front door, looking decidedly mussed-up, and rosy-cheeked.

"Hi, Poppy." Kana looked from the older woman to the cheeky grin on Clem, who was standing behind her, and came to the realisation she'd just interrupted. "Excuse me for just turning up."

"Nonsense!" Poppy fussed, but Clem chuckled.

"Come on in," he invited, pulling the door open wider. "We've finished settling-in." His wink was broad and friendly, even though his ribs were on the receiving end of Poppy's sharp elbow.

"No, I won't today. Thank you, Clementine." Kana took a solid breath and let it out slowly.

This was even harder than she'd imagined.

"I've come to say thank you ever so much, and I'm so very sorry... And goodbye."

Daniel was halfway through the Q & A segment of his motivational speech to a hall full of high school students, when he slipped his hand in his jacket pocket and found the Creme Egg Kanako had given him a couple of days before. He smiled to himself, before nodding to the next raised hand.

"Yes?"

"Is it hard, not doing the thing you love most?"

Was rugby still the thing he loved most? That inquiry opened one hell of a large can of worms.

"Yes, sometimes it is," Daniel agreed without pause. Kids asked questions like this all the time, as recently as at another school yesterday, in fact, but he'd never given the answer as much thought as he had on this particular tour. "But some people are never fortunate enough to be given the chance to do the thing they love. I was incredibly lucky to play rugby professionally, and for New Zealand. I'm not able to do that now, but I've found other things I'm passionate about. I don't take them for granted anymore." His hand closed around the foil wrapping, the chocolate egg fitting perfectly into his palm, as the jolt as his own words hit home. "Some things are with you for the long haul, and some things are fleeting. Enjoy them to the fullest while they're in your life."

He remembered Kanako's words on the airfield. *'This is what rings your bell…'*

"My advice is to find what rings your bell, and follow that. I really enjoy talking to you guys, and I'm happy to be here." He smiled at the spotty teen who'd asked the question, for once knowing his answer to be the honest truth.

In the cab on the way back to his Wellington hotel, he pulled out the Creme Egg, intrigued Kanako was so addicted to them and intending to try it. A piece of paper came out of his pocket with it, and he turned it over and glanced at it, thinking it had to be a receipt.

It wasn't.

Someone called Charlotte had kindly left him her number and a lipstick imprint, which wasn't entirely unheard of, but it was the second neatly written name at the bottom of the small note that grabbed him.

Kanako.

Daniel's breath stuck in his throat.

When…?

She'd left the annex phone number, and a little heart—coloured in with red biro.

God, that just wasn't right, even if she'd meant it as a joke. Kanako had put herself in the same category as some faceless fan Daniel couldn't even remember meeting. Had she found this note when he'd left his jacket at the annex? He hadn't had it dry cleaned since the little-rippa fundraiser…

How insulting would that've been for her? It certainly shed a bit more light on their one-night-stand conversation.

Daniel pulled out his phone and dialled before figuring out what he was going to say.

"Kia ora, Poppy Dante."

"Oh, hi, Mum." Daniel was unable to mask his surprise. "Sorry, I thought I'd called the annex."

"You have. I'm here with Adele." Her voice was a little wooden. "Cleaning."

"Right." The silence stretched. "Ah, I was hoping to speak to Kanako."

"She's gone, Daniel."

"No worries. I'll call back later, then." He went to disconnect, but Poppy interrupted the action.

"D?"

"Yep?" He drew the phone back to his ear.

"I meant, she's *gone*, love."

"Gone?" Gone *where*?

It took just three weeks for Kana and Ken's house to sell, and the agent handled all the gory details. It gave Kana plenty of time to sort through the leftover belongings from eight years of marriage.

The only thing she cried over was the wedding photo Ken had left on the shelf of his home office. She broke down after stroking the glass to remove the dust off their smiling faces.

Maybe if she'd learned to stand up to him, spar with him, it wouldn't have come to this. Maybe if Ken hadn't ever gotten his promotion, working long hours and learning how to bark orders.

Maybe, and maybe not. All water under the bridge, now.

Samantha had been incredibly welcoming, flexible about the timeframe, and supportive of Kana's seismic emotional state. It was a relief to finally have every last vestige of Ken removed from her life, and a huge bonus to be living with a close friend she could talk openly with.

Kana didn't know exactly what she'd expected from Daniel when she left Wānaka, but complete and utter radio silence wasn't it. She'd read way too much into their connection, clearly, believing there was at least some deeper feeling on his part. Even during the rocky end, there'd been *some*thing…

Daniel had never asked for her number, or given out his own.

Kana had assumed at the time it was because they hadn't needed to. After all, she'd virtually lived on his doorstep.

In retrospect, it was more likely a privacy thing.

Cling-ons were no doubt worse when you were well known, and he would've been protecting himself in case she was a nutter.

The jury was still out on whether she'd actually reached 'unhinged' status in Daniel's mind. Their whole relationship was possibly a bit of a game to the ex-player. He was no doubt used to taking his pick of women, and she'd been a much more reluctant pull. Had he charmed, romanced, and wooed her merely for kicks?

The time and energy expenditure didn't make any sense.

It'd been a lovely daydream while it lasted, but Daniel had never been seriously interested in her. She was a complete sidestep from his regular style—an unusual flavour on his plate.

Daniel had certainly been a sublime shock to *her* taste buds, and it was proving difficult to get him out of her head. He resided there, thoughts of him popping up when Kana least expected them to. Daniel Dante had been so much larger than life, all other men seemed to be vaguely lacking something in comparison.

Kana had no illusions about it. She'd need some serious time to get over him.

"That's a little bit disgusting." Sam wrinkled up her nose at Kana's choice of breakfast—a thick slice of cheese, slathered in raspberry jam.

The little platinum blonde had entered the kitchen with her cropped pixie-cut all awry, the imprint of the book she'd fallen asleep on still creased firmly across one cheek.

Sam was a dynamo—a pocket rocket, but at seven in the morning before she'd downed her first coffee, she was downright slouchy. All five-foot-four inches of her.

"You'd think so, right? But it's actually the perfect combination of sweet and fatty." Kana held the slice up and contemplated it. "I think I could eat the whole Kg." She motioned to the large block of Edam she'd left out on the bench as Sam settled down next to her at the breakfast bar.

"That's plain weird. Are you getting your period, or something?"

"Maybe," Kana shrugged. "It's been a bit up and down with the stress. Do you want to try it?" She offered the smeared cheese.

"Not on your nelly." Sam pulled back in distaste before flouncing off her stool to pour herself a hot coffee. "Your usual?" She tapped the green tea box in invitation.

"No, thanks."

Sam raised her eyebrows and waited. Kana saying no to green tea was *very* strange.

"I think that box of tea might be a bit off." Kana tried to explain. "It tastes kind of wrong."

"Wrong?" Sam brought the tea in question up to her nose and sniffed. "Green tea *always* tastes kind of wrong. Have some coffee, instead." She poured a second cup and slid it across the bench.

Kana stared at the swirling dark liquid, the smell of rich, musky caffeine overwhelming her senses.

Her stomach lurched.

"Oh, shit." Sam grabbed her arm in concern. "Are you going to faint?"

"No," Kana managed through clenched teeth, easing herself off the stool and making her way to the loo as quickly as possible. "But I think I might hurl."

She'd been experimenting with some strange foods recently, and the cheese and jam combo for breakfast had obviously been a step too far.

Kana made it to the bathroom, her nausea fading almost as quickly as it'd begun. As she cleaned herself up in the sink, she found Sam silently studying her in the wall mirror, her head to one side.

"What?"

"When did you say your period was due?" Sam inquired quietly.

Oh, *shit.*

Kana had never been pregnant before in her life. She didn't know how long she stared at the little blue cross before she stepped out of the bathroom and held it up for an unsurprised Sam to inspect.

Looking back, the signs were all there; the constant fatigue, the weird food cravings, the emotional outbursts and unexpected tears. Her boobs had seemed a little bigger, her chucks a tad pinchy, and her jeans a smidgen tighter. She hadn't been alerted to it, because it wasn't unusual for her periods to be screwy, or even completely absent when she was stressed.

She hadn't been *expecting* it because A) she couldn't *get* pregnant as a rule, and B) they'd used *protection.*

And it was just the once… Well, twice.

"I know condoms aren't a hundred percent, and I fell asleep after that first time on the floor. Maybe we both did? I should remember him taking that condom off… But I don't."

"Shh, babe. It'll be okay. It'll all be okay." Sam held her, soothing as best she could.

Kana sat heavily on the side of her bed and put her head in her hands.

"Sam. Where's the iPad?"

Sam had a medical background, but obstetrics wasn't her field of expertise, so what she didn't know they looked up. Some of it was scary as hell, especially foetal alcohol exposure.

Kana had drunk champagne that night, and two bottles of wine the next morning. She'd also been having half a glass of wine with her meals, having gotten back the taste for it.

She also happened to be forty. Frickin. Years. Old.

That placed her squarely as a 'geriatric pregnancy,' according to the search engine, which was in no way flattering *or* comforting.

"Let's take all of this with a grain of salt." Sam closed the page with the graph relating the upward age of the mother directly to chromosomal abnormalities. "It'd be better to talk to someone who knows what they're on about."

Sam typed in 'midwives, Christchurch,' and began filling out the contact form for the first one they both liked the look of.

"It's asking for the date of your last period, or a conception date."

"April seventh."

"What? No, not *your* birthday, the conception… Oh right, of course." Sam two-finger typed, jabbing at the touch screen with efficient speed. "Next of kin details?"

When Kana remained silent, Sam looked up from the screen, her fingers poised.

Kana stared at her friend for a full minute, suddenly comprehending what this could come to mean for life as she knew it. It rendered her completely speechless.

For years she'd longed to be pregnant, ached for it. And now she was.

The difference being she'd never imagined being *alone* in this scenario.

Change gears. For God's sake, get with the programme. She could do this. Girls could do *anything*.

"I'll put mine," Sam breezed, filling the silence.

26

IN THE HEART

"The way is not in the sky.
The way is in the heart."
- Buddha

"Kana! Come quick. Dante D's on the telly!" Samantha shouted.

Kana dropped her tea towel in Sam's kitchen sink, and hightailed it to the lounge.

"It's play-on-demand." Sam assured her, when the camera flicked away from Daniel's face and back to the presenter, before cutting to ads. "Something about water safety." She murmured, face still glued to the screen.

"Life jackets?"

"Yes! Is it a rerun?" Sam finally turned to Kana, seeming disappointed. "Have you seen it already?"

"No. It just figures. Daniel has a thing about them."

"Right." Sam looked unconvinced. "I missed the first bit. Let me rewind to the start." She tracked backwards, until Daniel's face filled the screen.

Kana sat very slowly on the edge of the sofa, heart in throat.

There he was, larger than life.

His hair was shorter, and his face a little slimmer, but it looked good on him.

Anything would look good on him.

He had a light in his eyes as he spoke, and it was obvious he was deeply enthused with the topic.

Daniel talked about raising money for life jackets in schools. He'd pledged a percentage of his income to the cause, and he was asking school boards to match him. "We're encouraging schools to loan out their water safety gear to families during the summer break, like a library borrowing system. The Dante Foundation is offering free annual gear-checks to optimise the safety of the equipment, if the school books an approved water safety program into their curriculum."

"This must be a cause close to your heart, as your father tragically drowned in a preventable accident." The presenter casually opened a new line of conversation.

"*Ouch*." Sam blinked.

"You asshole, don't make him talk about that," Kana hissed at the T.V. as the camera angle switched back to a close up of Daniel's face. His eyes had narrowed slightly, but he gave little else away.

"Of course." Daniel nodded once, then waited for the next question.

"Cool customer," Sam muttered approvingly. "Don't let him rile you, Dante D."

Kana chewed on the flesh of her thumb.

"We have footage of the search and rescue, and eventual recovery operation in 1999, when your father and uncle were washed off the rocks while fishing off the Otago Peninsula." The presenter looked appropriately sombre before the screen cut to a stormy coastal scene. A female journalist, buffeted by the wind, was explaining how two brothers in their forties had been surprised by a rogue wave, and dragged into the water. The two teenage boys with them had sounded the alarm, and were being praised for their quick thinking. They'd formed a human chain to drag their uncle to safety, then hailed others to their aid. The chopper and inflatables were combing the area for the second man; missing husband, and father of two.

When the camera moved sideways to take in the ambulance and the group gathered beside it, Kana clutched one of the sofa pillows to her chest to buffer her from the excruciating intensity of her own emotion.

A slim, gangly Daniel, not yet filling out his shoulders or his features, stood next to a shorter, narrower, and very young Cameron —grey blankets wrapped around both of their shoulders.

Vacant, lost, and soaked through to the bone. Two teenage boys who'd just watched their father get swallowed by the sea.

"Fishing accidents are a major cause of drowning in New Zealand, and Daniel Dante, who is here with me today, is looking to change that, starting with water safety in schools." The presenter turned back to Daniel, as did the camera.

Two fat tears oozed out, creeping down Kana's cheeks, as the big, stoic rugby guy held it together and even smiled politely for the asshole presenter.

"That's right."

The piece cut to a pre-filmed clip about the foundation and how schools could apply for funding, then was over.

"Shitsticks," muttered Sam, who'd been standing throughout. She switched the T.V. off, moving to sit next to Kana on the sofa. "Did you know all that?"

"Yes, and no." She sniffed, not yet completely in control of herself. "I knew his father drowned. I didn't realise Daniel and his brother were actually *there*." She shuddered, turning to look at Sam. "I need to know more. I want to know everything."

Sam gave a single nod. "Lets ask the iPad."

Trawling the Internet, they found a mine of information. Daniel's rise to fame, his sporting prowess, his fan base, his family, his relationships, and his drug scandal. The video hits were mostly rugby games, or highlights, but there were a couple of interviews.

It was so strange to watch Daniel grow up backwards, as the videos got older.

In one of the short clips, not long after his knee injury, Daniel was clearly high. His pupils were so dilated his eyes appeared black. Using Tilly, the fashion model next to him, as a crutch, his answers to the questions about his recovery were vague and unrelated.

"I think this is the game where he got injured." Sam touched one of the listings down the menu. "Against South Africa."

Conversely, Kana leaned forward to press pause.

Sam sighed, putting down the iPad altogether and looking at her levelly.

"I just need a minute," Kana flustered, blinking at her friend and realising there was no point waiting.

She'd never be ready.

"No. On second thoughts, just play it."

Sam fast-forwarded. "It wasn't far into the game. Right near the beginning," she murmured, scanning. "There!" Rewinding the previous play, she explained a little as it ran, knowing Kana wasn't remotely rugby savvy. "They can't throw it forward, and you can only tackle someone if they've got the ball. *Look*! See that run? *God*, he was sneaky, you could never tell which way he was headed. Dante D's passed it back now, but he's still in support. See?" Sam paused the clip again and turned to Kana, checking she was keeping up.

"Okay."

"Before I play this next bit, there was a lot of contention about the tackle. Dante D didn't have the ball, but he'd just passed it, so it could've been a genuine late tackle, or a deliberate foul. He was a game changer—so accurate with his passing, it's feasible the opposition wanted him out of the tri-nations."

"Isn't that…?"

"Against the rules? Cheating? Yes."

"Okay,' Kana replied again, trying to keep up. "One more question. What's a tri-nations?"

"Are you *shitting* me?" Sam lost her cool for a second. "It's only the fiercest Rugby tournament in the known galaxy! Australia, South Africa, and New Zealand…?"

Sam's pause was telling. Apparently even Kana should've heard of this event.

She shrugged.

"Forget about that, it's not important at the moment," Sam muttered and again pressed play. "So we're looking at a really classy little one-two with the centre, then wham…"

Oh. My. God.

'*Wham*' didn't even come close to describing the way Daniel went down.

The tackle was at knee height, and vaguely side on, and the full

267

weight of both players rammed down onto Daniel's right knee at a sickeningly awkward angle.

The replay was far worse, because it was in slow motion.

Kana pulled her knees up to her chest and moaned.

"Brutal," Sam agreed soberly.

With his mouth guard knocked out, it was suddenly Daniel writhing on the ground—not some unknown athlete—his face contorted in pain.

"Turn it off." Kana got up to stand, her hands under her opposing armpits to give herself some semblance of comfort. "That's enough." Her cheeks were wet, which was becoming an all too familiar experience, emotions all skewed with her fluctuating hormones.

"He was a jerk to you—" Sam started.

"Not all the time! Sometimes he was purely lovely," Kana defended fiercely.

"Are you for real? You *can't* still be in love with this guy, Kana. He's totally ignored you since you left Wānaka."

Kana knew that. She knew it all too well, and was unable to stop the raking sob that came from low in her frame.

"Sorry, sorry. I shouldn't have said that." Sam came to stand next to her, her voice softening as she put her arms around her friend. "But you've got to try and get over him, Poppet."

***

Kana didn't do any more searches regarding Dante D when Sam was present, but when her flatmate was at the hospital on kooky shifts, it was another story. She'd pull out her sketchpad to leaf through her quick studies of him, or hook into his online story.

When interviewed for a fitness magazine, Daniel spoke pretty openly about how rugby had brought him closer to his father.

Other articles were more like sordid exposés. Girlfriends tell all. Drugs, and endless partying...

Sensationalism ran the media, and they often used the same portion of game footage when they interviewed Daniel. The tackle that wrecked his knee. The surgery had been extensive, recovery even more so, and though he'd played in the top league in Japan, he never wore a New Zealand or Otago strip again.

Kana's favourite video clip was from much earlier—before the injury, and before the drugs. It was easier to watch than more recent ones, which were too close for comfort; her memories still too fresh.

"And where did the name come from, Dante D?" The interviewer had been young and pretty, leaning forward for Daniel's answer. He'd smiled rakishly, his youthfully handsome face alight with underlying laughter.

"You'd have to ask the Otago fans."

"Apparently it was to distinguish you from your Uncle Brett, who was known as 'Dante' for the length of his rugby career."

Daniel shrugged, then smiled at the interviewer again. She fawned a little in response, re-crossing her legs and angling towards him.

"I don't think Uncle would like hearing his career referred to in the past tense," Daniel corrected lightly. "He's still a formidable presence in local rugby." He winked at the interviewer, eyes shining with humour.

"Oh, of course." Though obviously caught out, the woman battered her eyelashes, recovering easily.

"Come on, lady," Kana heckled, years later, tucked snugly into bed in Sam's spare room. "Call yourself a sports journalist? Do your flippin' homework. Even *I* know that, and I know *diddlysquat* about rugby."

"*Goddamn* it, Daniel!" Poppy Dante stormed into Daniel's bedroom like a platoon of angry killer bees, slapping a couple of magazines down on his chest before tearing open the curtains.

Too late, he threw an arm over his eyes to block the white-hot light.

"*Crap*. Mum." Grabbing a pillow, he stuck his head under it and rolled onto his side.

"Oh no you don't." She tore the pillow off and leaned close to his face. "I want to talk to you, now!"

"Calm down," he muttered.

His father had cautioned him once that telling an irate woman to calm down was like throwing petrol on an already cranking fire. Daniel now knew this to be true, but had just been woken from a deep, deep sleep, and couldn't be held fully responsible for his actions.

Poppy hit the roof.

"Okay, okay," He placated when he could get a word in edgeways. "I'm awake now, just let me get some pants on."

His mother glared at him. "You have precisely *one* minute," she decreed, snatching up her magazines, and turning on her heel.

Daniel took twice that to pull on a pair of jeans and sluice water over his face in the ensuite. It'd been a late night going over the books and answering emails, and he'd slept in well past his usual seven a.m. rise.

He found Poppy at the kitchen table, and wandered over to get a glass of water before joining her there.

"I thought you were staying at Clem's?"

"I am." His mother looked at him long and cool, making it clear he was dead in the dog box.

"What's up?"

Poppy took one of the magazines lying in front of her, folding it deliberately to the back page before sliding it across the table.

It took him a moment to recognise himself and Kanako at the lake.

A buzz started up in his head, blocking out everything else, and he drew the pictures closer, frowning.

"Is this why Kana left?" Poppy demanded.

"What?" He looked up, feeling woozy. "No, she went back to Christchurch to be with her husband."

It wasn't something he really wanted to chat about, especially with photos of Kanako laid out in front of him. One with her hair loose, smiling lazily into the sun.

There were older pictures of him and Tilly, too, one in Fiji and one at a movie premiere. Strange how that relationship seemed so far away now, so shallow.

"Bullshit!" Poppy slapped the table, and Daniel pulled back from the volume. "I've told you before, Kana wouldn't touch that man again if he was the last cockroach on earth. This!" Poppy pointed fiercely at the picture of them in the lake, kissing. "*This* is why she left."

On autopilot, Daniel reached for the second mag. Only one shot this time—himself and Kanako at the restaurant on his birthday. The piece was entitled '*Wedding bells for Dante D?*'

It looked like they were holding hands and cosying up, heads close together in private discussion, but Daniel remembered it being distinctly less romantic.

A wrist grab. Awkward apologies.

"Mum, I get that you're upset." He reached out to touch her hand, but she pulled it away. "You didn't like the way things worked out." And neither did he. "But I had nothing to do with Kanako leaving. I came home, and she was gone. End of story."

"Are you telling me you never even asked her to come back? Have you even called her? Look at those pictures, Daniel. *Look* at them. That's a couple with something special between them. Any idiot can see that!" Her voice raised a notch. "Why wasn't Kanako good enough for you? Not enough silicone? Not addicted to posting pictures of herself? Not blonde enough?"

"Stop, Mum!" He couldn't stand it. "Kanako was more than special to me, okay? But she was *never free* for this." He flicked at the pictures with the back of his hand.

"I saw how 'special' you thought she was on your birthday," Poppy dug. "We all did."

Daniel hesitated, remembering the hurt in Kanako's eyes. "I admit, I wasn't at my best that day. We'd had a disagreement."

"About what?"

He ran a hand over his face. "The fact she was *married*, Mum. Her husband came to her gallery showing, and they were making another go of it, trying again for a kid. He stayed with her for a few days. I saw them together and they seemed, you know, close."

"What? Kana verified this?" Poppy's brows were drawn together and she leaned forward across the table.

Daniel looked back to the photos of Kanako by the lake. The one on the picnic rug had captured a moment when they were both laughing, and he remembered what that day had felt like—the promise of it.

"No, she denied it. But Kanako had issues telling the truth."

"*Goddamn* it, Daniel!" Poppy repeated the line she'd woken him up with, at the same decibel. "Maybe you *deserve* to be sleeping in that big old bed all alone, then. When are you going to get it through your thick skull, *she's nothing like Tilly!*"

Poppy got up to leave and took a swipe at the magazines, clearly intending to take them with her.

Daniel had other ideas.

Further infuriating his mother, he scraped his chair back and stood, holding the magazines out of her reach above his head.

Other than a profile picture from her website, they were the only photos of Kanako he had.

Kana was finding it difficult to sleep.

The midwife had come around and checked her spot bleeding, telling her she was supposed to spend less time on her feet, and take on less stress. That meant less time walking, and less time in the studio, both practices Kana considered imperative for her mental health. She *was* still allowed to run the pregnancy yoga classes at the local women's gym, although she now had to drive there, not bike.

Her bedside table held an array of supplements, though she was fully aware some of the most important milestones of development had happened before she'd known this baby even existed.

She hadn't been taking supplements then. She'd breathed in silica dust, had her hands in and out of chemicals, and hefted twenty Kg bags of clay on a daily basis. She'd drunk wine, forgotten to eat on occasion, and worked from dawn till dusk without breaks.

Obāchan had extended her stay in Christchurch, which bolstered Kana's emotional status no end… But she still turned onto her side and curled into the foetal position, tears sliding to her pillow.

She'd received an email from Poppy today, lying hidden in her inbox like a sniper among the orders and invoices. Ignoring everything else, Kana had pounced on it.

Newsy and bubbly, Poppy had avoided all mention of Daniel, writing instead about Winger, Saffy's puppy, and the obedience class they were planning to attend together. Adele had been offered another job, one day a week working as a legal secretary for a local solicitor. It was right up her alley and could lead to full-time work. Poppy and Clem had set their wedding date in February at a local winery, and they'd love it if Kana could keep the date free.

That was the most upsetting bit, because Kana knew she'd eventually have to tell them no. If she managed to carry this baby to full term, it'd be born in early December, and there was no way she could turn up with a two-month-old. It would be like saying 'you do the maths' to the entire population of Wānaka—to every single person who'd seen that magazine.

Kana was very aware Daniel had been manoeuvred into this form of trap before, and she had no intention of doing that to him, or the child. Her best form of defence was to slowly sever ties, giving Daniel full freedom. He hadn't asked for any of this.

It hurt though. It hurt terribly.

She felt disloyal sending a short, clipped reply to Poppy, who'd given her the artist in residence position in the first place. Poppy Dante had believed in Kana's worth, and if everything turned out, she'd be the paternal grandmother to this child. Poppy had every right…

And Daniel.

Kana curled herself a little tighter.

Adele had come to the annex to try and talk Kana out of leaving that day. Daniel's cousin had cajoled and manoeuvred and wheedled, to no avail. Finally she'd just sat at the kitchen table and put her chin in her hands, watching Kana clean down the bench tops and wipe out the fridge.

"Leave that." Adele's voice had been devoid of emotion. "I'll do it when you're gone."

Kana had read through Adele's flatness, to the sadness below. "I have to go, Adele. I've made up my mind."

"You went and fell for Daniel, didn't you?"

Turning slowly, she'd looked her new friend in the eye. "Yeah. I guess I did." She hung the cloth over the faucet and gazed back out of the lattice window to the roof of the farmhouse, just visible through the Canadian maples. "I'm sure I'm not the first, and probably won't be the last."

"But he…?"

"I'm afraid not. He told me he wants this to be over, now."

"But, I thought... I was so *sure* about you two."

Kana had wiped her hands dry on the seat of her jeans and turned with the best smile she could muster. "You win some, you lose some, right?"

Kana knew she'd been a fool, giving her heart to someone who'd just been playing a game, and was desperately trying to convince herself she no longer cared. None of it mattered if she could just do right by this child. She'd wanted to be a mother for the longest time, and didn't mean to be ungrateful for the precious little miracle growing inside her.

Sam sneaked her head into Kana's bedroom on arriving home from her shift. "You awake?" she whispered.

Kana sighed and nodded.

"Bad day?"

She nodded again, and without needing to ask for details, Sam came in, kicked off her soft-soled shoes and climbed onto the bed beside her.

"Shh, don't cry, Poppet. Your Obāchan's coming over tomorrow, and together we'll figure it out," Sam murmured, reaching over to grasp Kana's hand.

Sam didn't make it out of her uniform or into her own bed, and listening to the even, childlike sound of her friend slowly succumbing to a light snore, Kana was finally able to fall asleep herself.

Maybe she dreamed of Daniel every night because she held his child warm in her belly, or perhaps it was because the most vulnerable part of her was allowed to wander freely in her dreams, and would always care.

At least she'd be able to tell this child honestly, 'I loved your father.'

He was moody, wildly unpredictable, and didn't feel the same way, but he was stunning in every way, and Kana had fallen—like a skydiver without a parachute.

27

THE DARKEST NIGHT

"The darkest night is ignorance."
- Buddha

"Hi, Papa." Kana looked beyond him, but neither her mother nor Obāchan were anywhere in sight. "You're not working today?" She leaned in for a one armed hug, a little confused to find her father on Sam's doorstep on a Monday morning.

"Taking the day off—practicing for when I retire." He grinned, pulling a tiny posy of violets and a Cadbury Creme Egg from behind his back. "Flowers from your mother, sugar from me."

Tears welled in Kana's eyes for no reason other than her parents loved her, and she loved them right back.

"Thank you." Kana scanned the lines of Ruben's face as she sniffed the dainty purple blooms, finding a decent amount of worry behind his smile. "Sam called you," she realised aloud.

Her father hesitated. "We have an understanding, Samantha and I, with the same goal in mind."

"Kana's ultimate happiness?" she asked a little caustically, leading him into the house.

"Not exactly—though that'd be an added bonus. At the moment it's more like a support club."

"The Kanako Janssen and Child in Utero Support Group?" She managed some semblance of a smile. "You could sell T-shirts."

Her father had to duck his head slightly to make it under the lintel into the kitchen.

"Not a bad idea. Maybe coffee mugs with your sweet wee mush on them." Ruben chose a breakfast barstool and settled his long legs under it.

"What's the order of the day for my uplifting therapy session?"

"So you're admitting you're on a low?"

"Papa…" She sighed.

"Okay." Her father held up one hand in resignation. "I was thinking of taking my favourite daughter out for lunch."

Kana glanced at the large clock behind her father's head. "Your *only* daughter, and it's just gone ten o'clock."

Her father grinned again, this time seeming to relax fully into it.

"Time for you to make me a coffee before we go then, and talk to your old man."

She fidgeted with her braid, feeling the pressure before it'd even started. "Talk about what?"

"When are you going to move back home?"

"Never. We've been over this. I'm forty years old for Buddha's sake, and Mum and I would throttle each other within a week. If Obāchan doesn't get to her first," she added in a mutter.

"Closer than this, though. Within walking distance would work for everyone," he pressed.

"But the studio—"

"We could look for a property that has a garage or outbuildings to convert. If it's more than the collateral you got out of the other house, your mother and I will help until you're back on your feet."

"There's plenty of commission work coming in. I won't let you—"

"What, love you? Support you? What *will* you let us do? We're not allowed to speak to the father of your child, and we're not allowed to wrap you in wool and carry you home. I'd do anything for you, my little pumpernickel, and you've upped the ante here." Her father pointed to her midriff.

When Kana's face crumpled, her father stood, rounded the kitchen island, and enfolded her in a long-limbed hug. She leaned her cheek on his chest and looked out the window, feeling the latent energy in Ruben's wiry frame and mulling over what he'd just said.

"You did *promise*... No going behind my back and contacting Daniel," she murmured.

Her father shifted a little uncomfortably, hesitating before answering quietly, "He has a right to know."

She pulled back as if he'd yanked on her braid. "You *swore*!" she reminded him vehemently.

"That was *weeks* ago, Kana-banana. Don't you think this has gone on long enough? You know how I feel about it. Just because Finn's mother and I weren't together anymore, she had no right to keep her pregnancy from me. As a consequence, I missed out on him as a little one. More to the point, *he* missed out on *me*. It wasn't fair then, and this isn't fair now."

Finn, Kana's half-brother, was three years older than herself, but she'd only met him a handful of times. The chef was somewhat reclusive, still bitter about his biological father's absence in his early years, and unwilling to absolve Ruben of his desertion.

"*The darkest night is ignorance,*" Kana's father quoted softly.

"Don't you start going Buddhist on me, too," she muttered.

The fact history was doing a little repeat wasn't lost on her, but this was different. She *would* tell Daniel.

Somehow. Eventually. After the birth.

Daniel took the pizza dough out of the bread maker, cutting six segments before balling them, and leaving them to rise. Eight for dinner tonight, but Clem and himself were the only two who could wolf down a whole pizza each. Except perhaps uncle Amos? Adele and Katie's parents were coming across from Dunedin for the weekend, so maybe a loaf or two of garlic bread wouldn't go amiss.

He hadn't spoken to his mother for two days, but knew whatever beef she had with him, it wouldn't interfere with pizza night. Poppy Dante believed in family first, and fighting later.

Daniel hadn't felt any need to patch things up with his mother, but *had* experienced an underlying pull to apologise to Kanako, due to the invasion of her privacy. The fact they'd been followed and photographed was entirely due to his career, and he should've thought to warn her whatever he did publicly was fair game.

Someone had taken great pains to stay out of sight. At the time, he could've sworn they'd been the only living souls on Ruby Island.

The later photo could've been taken by any number of people, as the restaurant had been pumping that night.

The last time he'd seen Kanako. The last time he'd touched her.

The photos probably hadn't been easy for Kanako to explain to her husband. There was no mistaking the heat or connection between the Daniel and herself in the images, and anyone, including Baka-Ken, would have to know they'd had something going on.

Daniel assumed Kanako had seen them. It actually made some sense of their conversation in the kitchen on his birthday. He hadn't known what she'd meant about 'pictures' at the time, though why they were just surfacing now was a mystery to him.

The first magazine was dated early May, and it was now June. Usually, his mother and Adele would've been all over this at the time of publication... But Daniel hadn't seen as much of Adele this past month. His cousin had felt the need to distance herself from the farm after Kanako's sudden departure.

Daniel didn't blame her. He was still pretty raw himself.

Kanako had made a clear choice, and they were all getting used to it in their own way. The fact Daniel's mother blamed him for the loss of her latest artist in residence wasn't exactly news—she'd alluded to it several times before. Usually presented in a 'look what you did' kind of way, she'd only recently begun to add the 'look what you failed to do' tone.

He was content to shake off both. It was just Poppy's opinion.

Yes, he'd failed, but he hadn't *made* it happen.

The ceramicist had changed something in him though, and he couldn't go back to how he'd been before. His life was lacking something tangible in a way it hadn't in the past, and the gap was growing; discontent widening.

He'd assumed Kanako was younger than himself. But then maybe the 'big four-oh' call had been a line, too? Who knew? He wished he was able to trust Kanako's words as honest, for even one of their conversations, then he'd have more grounds to figure out what their connection had meant.

At first, he'd waited for Kanako to return after her IVF treatment, to see out the final four months of her stay. But the herbs in the pot by the annex door slowly curled up and died, and Halfback's water bowl by the step remained resolutely empty.

Daniel began to get the full picture as autumn turned to winter.

She wasn't coming back.

Was it supposed to be easier this way? Because it felt anything but easy. It felt like shite.

Daniel's sideways shift in work, with more interest in New Zealand youth and less international travel, meant he was spending a lot more time at home. Seeing Kanako on a daily basis would've cut, but surely not more than the absence of her did.

Daniel automatically patted his hand on his jeans pocket, feeling for the faint outline of the small circular object, and fielding the familiar surge of guilt. Two weeks ago, when the grapevine lost its final leaves, he'd put aside a couple of days to paint the arbour in the orchard. He'd also moved ahead with the half-moon garden bed, planting yellow daisies and white roses. As the weather warmed, the lilies, poppies, and irises would emerge, too.

A plot in memory of Nana Nona, with the flowers she'd chosen to name her five daughters after.

As a child, a cousin had asked Daniel if he thought Nana Nona was a witch. It wasn't a stretch of the imagination, by any means. Nona had always been a magical, creative, and mysterious creature, however unfounded the 'witch' claim turned out to be. His seven-year-old self had asked his Scottish Nana straight out.

Nona had guffawed with laughter, holding her hand up to her brow as a visor against the midsummer Otago sun, so she could look him clear in the eye. "Oh, I wish I were, Danny-boy. Wouldn't that be fun?"

They'd been in Nona's vegetable garden in Mosgiel, pulling carrots to scrub and dip in the hummus she'd made that morning. The earth was damp and fragrant from the light sun-shower earlier in the day, and wet carrot fronds left a tapestry of dark brush strokes on Nona's cotton dress.

"If I were a witch, I'd look into the future and see you standing next to your lovely wife. Maybe watch your children settle on the hills of Wānaka, and look down on Ruby Island like I did when I was little. It's a magical place, Danny. One day I'll take you there, and you'll never want to leave."

Up at the orchard, thinking about his Nana, Daniel had taken a break from painting the arbour's upper rungs. Sitting up against a strut, stripped bare of old paint, he'd sprawled his legs in front of him on the uneven flagstones and squinted up at the eggshell-blue sky above.

His eye had caught the glint of something shiny against one of the arbour supports, and standing slowly, he'd reached out in disbelief to unhook Kanako's gold locket off one of the gnarled vine spurs.

The exterior was etched with a faint lotus design on one side, worn by time and use, and the catch was tiny—tricky to open. The tight seal had protected the little sepia photo of a man in traditional Japanese dress, despite the fact the locket must've hung there a full, wintery month. There were two elaborate Kanji characters on the opposite interior wall—possibly the man's name? Daniel made out the symbol for mountain, but that was the extent of his Kanji expertise.

Daniel should've contacted Kanako and sent the locket to her immediately on finding it, he knew that. He'd fully intended to, had even gone online to look up Kanako's studio contact details that very day.

Her work was well photographed and presented, and seemed to sell almost as soon as it was listed, but the images didn't give the ceramics the same impact as seeing them in person. The same could be said for the portrait of the artist, with her shy smile and a backdrop of green foliage.

Even so, he'd taken a screenshot and kept it.

Kanako's current blurb stated she was back in Christchurch, in the same home studio she'd potted out of for ten years. That meant Daniel was right, and his mother was wrong, though for once he'd sincerely wished it'd been the other way around.

Kanako was back with her husband, so perversely, her locket had remained snug in Daniel's pocket.

There was only one light point in all that black news. Kanako still potted. Baka-Ken had been adamant, but Kanako must've stood firm, insisting her 'hobby' was so much more than that.

There were three distinct genres Kanako appeared to be working on. The lotus and swallow dinnerware she'd begun in Wānaka, a series of Gaia, earth-mother type pieces, and some sculptures she'd named 'Farcical Sport' which made him smile. The one titled 'Yoga' depicted a woman tied up in a pretzel by her own limbs. Going by the measurements, she'd be about the size and dimensions of a rugby ball. Her face was a study of immense surprise, as if she had no idea how she'd come to be so completely and utterly tied in knots.

'Rippa Rugby' also amused him. The runner had taken off so fast the tagger was flying airborne behind them, firmly latched to the rippa-ribbon that'd failed to disengage.

"Could you please pass me another slice of salmon pizza?" Saffy asked her Grandma Rosa politely.

Daniel was struck by how fast she was growing up. When she'd arrived back in New Zealand just over four years ago, Saffy had been sullen and controlling. Now she was bright, bubbly, social, fun-loving…

Saffy proceeded to pick off the capers and pile them in a little pyramid on her plate.

"Why don't you try them?" urged Adele. "Just one. Just a taste."

"I miss Kana," Saffy muttered glumly. "She ate my capers for me. When's she coming to see how big Winger's got?"

Okay, so still a little sullen on occasion.

"I miss her too," Adele commiserated, "And I don't know. She's stopped answering my texts."

Daniel attempted to distance himself from the group whenever Kanako came up in discussion, which was still relatively often. But as he pushed his chair back, Saffy turned to him and asked, "When's Kana coming back, Uncle D?"

"I don't know." Daniel, like a cornered animal, got ready to bolt. "Why are you asking me?"

Saffy wrinkled her nose and stared Daniel down as if he smelt a little off. "Because, she told mummy she loved you best."

"What?" Daniel shot Adele a black look, before clearing his

throat. "No, I'm pretty sure she liked Halfback best," he covered his dignity with a light reply for Saffy, hoping he'd managed to hide the lancing pain the child's simple sentence had just dealt him.

Clem leaned forward on his dining chair, elbow on the table. "That woman was something special, alright. The damn dog is still pining for her. Goes to scratch at the annex door most mornings and lament over his empty water bowl."

Daniel recognised the double meaning only when he intercepted Clem's knowing wink to Poppy.

So, the two of them were lumping him in with the dog, now? Rude.

He got up to leave the table, no longer hungry.

"It's past time I put another artist in the annex, I just didn't have the heart for it. There was a young guy from Westport that had a lot of promise. I might take another look at him. He applied the same time as Kana, but she really needed it more—what with the timing of her *divorce* and all." Poppy stressed the word ever so slightly.

Daniel whipped his head around and pinned his mother with a warning stare, but she continued on, relentless.

"What did Kana say about her marriage that first night, Adele, when we sat here eating stew?"

Adele tapped her front tooth. "Her husband didn't mistreat her, but she said living with him was like living under a blanket of grey, and she'd forgotten how to laugh. I remember, because I could completely relate, you know? With James…" Adele stopped, and touched Saffy's shoulder.

Saffy had lived with James too, and still called the man 'Dad,' so Adele was careful to never badmouth the guy.

In fact, she hardly spoke about him at all.

"Kana said her glazes and her car were the only colour in her day," Saffy stated matter-of-factly. "The big red one. It was a present from Obi…" she struggled with the name.

"Obāchan," Poppy supplied for her.

"Yes! Her Obāchan. The lady with the white hair. She was *so* funny." Saffy giggled. "Remember when she told the ducks off down at the lake for snatching food?"

"When did you meet Kanako's grandmother?" Daniel turned to Saffy, baffled.

"We all spent quite a bit of time with Kana's family when they came down for her gallery showing," Clem butted in with an uncharacteristically cool tone. "Her mother, father, and grandmother stayed for a week in one of the motels Adele cleans. She got them a good rate, remember? Or maybe you wouldn't remember, that being a jet-lag week for you. Or was it a jet-lag fortnight?"

Daniel scowled at Clem. What was this? Run down your host day?

"You only met Kana once, didn't you Mum?" Adele asked, turning to Rosa.

"Yes, at your birthday party, Saffy. She baked that delicious chocolate cake, and did some Japanese healing stuff on your father's hip. Didn't she love?" Rosa turned to Amos.

"*Reiki*." Daniel muttered darkly, shuffling his shoulders in discomfort.

"Not a fan?" Amos raised a gnarly white eyebrow. "Well, now, Dan, I was kind of sceptical too, until Kana moved her hands over me. Felt like she warmed the aches right off to Blazes. Can't tell you *how* exactly, but it seemed to do the trick for a couple of days."

"What does Blazes mean, Granddad?" Saffy sneaked in a vocabulary question.

"Blazes means Hell, sweetheart," Rosa answered serenely.

"Obāchan said Baka-Ken could go to Blazes for taking Kana's car," Saffy informed her Grandmother just as sweetly.

"Yes, I suspect he might," Adele confirmed. "You know, I've actually seen Baka-Ken's car around town. You can still make out the outline of the logo and lettering on the doors, even with the stickers removed."

"He's here in Wānaka?" Daniel all but barked the question at Adele.

What the hell was Kanako's husband doing, hanging around in Otago when his wife was back in Christchurch?

"No, D. Not the SUV," Adele explained patiently, as if to a child younger than Saffy. "I mean the sedan Kana traded in. The dealer just pulled off the stickers and put it straight on the lot when she switched to the station wagon."

Daniel rubbed at his temple. "What station wagon?"

"Kana's new car."

"What happened to the old one?" Daniel wondered, confused beyond belief.

"Well, *Baka-Ken* took it, of course! Where have you been living, under a rock?" Poppy exploded.

Daniel looked from one face to another around the table.

It was glaringly obvious everyone else was following easily, but this car switching stuff was foreign to him. Catching Saffy's intense stare, he chose the nine year old.

"Explain," he ordered.

Saffy sighed and rolled her eyes, evidently deciding he was an imbecile. "Kana had a nice red car. Baka-Ken liked it better than his, so he took it and gave her his stupid sedan that didn't fit any of her stuff. She gave it to the car place and they swapped it for a station wagon instead. It's ugly brown, but Kana said not to worry, it didn't matter, because it fitted her stuff. Then it was our birthday, and you were mean, so while you were away, she put all her stuff into her ugly brown car and drove away." She took a breath and looked at him with those big, baleful eyes. "And she never came back."

"Well put, Saff," Poppy congratulated her grandniece lightly. "That about covers it, now you can help me in the kitchen if you want to earn some brownie points. How many for coffee?" She got up to stand.

"Wait!" Daniel put his hand up to stop the outgoing traffic. "Not finished with her yet." He turned back to Saffy. "So, now Kana has her own car back in Christchurch?"

"The ugly brown one?" Saffy asked.

"No. The nice red one." He found himself using her primary school terminology for clarity.

"No, Uncle D." Saffy sighed. "You haven't been listening. Baka-Ken has that car. Kana has to wait for the house to sell and everything to get split in half, and then, if there's enough money, she'll get another one. Only this time, she'll choose a different colour, so it doesn't remind her of Baka-Ken."

Daniel scratched at his eyebrow. "Thanks Saff. That's, ah… clearer. You know what? I need to earn some brownie points with Mum myself. Okay if we switch places?"

"Sure." Saffy shrugged.

Adele and his mother exchanged a meaningful look before Poppy flounced towards the kitchen with a stack of plates, Daniel following hot on her heels.

"Why do I get the distinct impression you were the ringleader in there, and I just got ganged up on?" Daniel challenged his mother when they'd both reached the sink, out of earshot from the others.

"Beats me." They stared at each other for a loaded moment. "But I've been thinking about what you said the other day, about seeing Kana and her husband together. It just seemed so odd to me. Where did you say you saw them? Was that at the annex, or…?"

"In town, at the gallery. But he stayed with her for a few days here. His car…" Daniel came to a dead stop as the cogs finally dropped into place.

Ken's car had been parked at the annex for *days*. But they'd bloody *swapped vehicles*.

"When did Kana switch cars with her husband?" He asked with slow deliberation, quelling rising incredulity.

"*Ex*-husband," Poppy corrected smartly. "At the gallery opening." She narrowed her eyes at him before continuing, "Though how you haven't picked up on any of this is absolutely beyond me. Obāchan was *so* upset about it. She'd given Kana that car not six months before, and Baka-Ken was brazen enough to bring the change of ownership papers to her show opening. Demanded she sign them before he'd hand over the divorce papers.

I guess he'd found out where she was via the gallery publicity online, or maybe it was that magazine article with the two of you fooling around. Either way, he got the car he wanted, and she got the divorce she wanted. Everyone got what they wanted."

"Not me," Daniel murmured, looking away from his mother and through the window over her shoulder, up towards the mānuka scrub on the hill without actually seeing it. "I don't get why Kanako gave up on the ceramics grant, if it wasn't for Ken…"

"Oh, D," Poppy sighed. "Sometimes you really *do* remind me of your father. From where I'm standing it's as plain as the nose on your face." She touched one finger to the slightly crooked bridge of his nose. "Kanako Janssen left because she'd fallen for you, and you shoved her clean out the door."

28

CHANGE

*"One moment can change a day,
one day can change a life
and one life can change the world."*
- Buddha

When Daniel's family finally left his place, loaded up with leftover pizza, it was after nine. Too late to call Kanako? Too late in the evening, and too late in the proceedings...

He pulled Kanako's locket out of his pocket and stroked the engraved bloom with his thumb, coming to an easy decision. Trying to sleep after today's bombshell would be like trying to breathe underwater.

Pulling up the ceramicist's online contact details, Daniel input the number into his phone and dialled before he'd had time to form a strategy, or back out.

"*Moshi moshi*. This is Tomomi speaking."

"Obāchan?"

There was a pause on the line. "I am Kanako's Obāchan." Tomomi hesitated again. "Who is this?"

"Daniel Dante, from Wānaka, I was Kanako's landlord."

Obāchan cleared her throat. "I remember, Mr Dante. Are you

well?" She sounded a lot more guarded than she had when they'd met at Kanako's opening.

"Yes." If Daniel could call his shambolic state 'well.' "I'm surprised to hear your voice, though. You stayed in New Zealand," he stated needlessly.

"We think for the long term it's a good plan. I can help Kanako now, and in Japan I was alone."

"You were talking about immigrating when we met."

"That is true. We talked about many things."

Daniel scratched his jaw. Either Obāchan had a very polite phone manner, or she wasn't happy to be hearing from him.

"I was wondering if I could speak with Kanako?" He went for the direct approach.

There was another long pause.

"For her health, she must sleep now, and I won't wake her."

"Kanako's unwell?" Daniel kept his voice even, but that little titbit had sliced into his guts, and he felt a deep sense of foreboding when the old woman hesitated again.

"This trimester hasn't been easy for her, but I think the worst is over."

'The worst is over' sounded like something serious. 'Trimester' rang a bell, but Daniel couldn't place it.

Tri-nations. Trifecta. Trilingual. Trimester…

Pregnancy.

"Kanako went for IVF treatment?"

"Sorry, I don't know the word '*eye-bee-eff.*' "

Daniel could hear the sound of another person in the background, then a muffled argument, and assumed a hand had been placed over the mouthpiece. When Obāchan came back on the line, she cleared her throat again.

"Sam says I should tell you nothing, because you deserve nothing."

"Who the hell is *Sam*?" he barked.

"Kanako's chosen to live with Sam now. Sam is Kanako's new landlord."

Was that code for something?

Daniel could hear more muffled back-and-forth, then Obāchan's breathing was back on the line.

"Mr Dante? Do you know Buddha?"

"Not personally, no," he snapped, beyond frustrated.

"There is a quote Kanako's learning. Buddha says, *'Patience is key. Remember; a jug fills drop by drop.'* " Obāchan's voice became a little harder. "And there is another saying I think *you* should learn. *'Happiness will never come to those who fail to appreciate what they already have.'* "

Then came the deafening silence of the disconnect.

Fuck that. He'd go on up to Christchurch and hear it from the horse's mouth, like he should've done from the get go. Daniel stormed into the master bedroom and started throwing clothes into a bag before he came down to earth. He had a phone number, and knew Kanako was in Christchurch, but there was no address for the studio in the online information—just a blurb about it being her 'home studio' for ten years.

He sat on the side of the bed and put his head in his hands.

Poppy would have it, or Adele, but both those avenues would require a conversation he wasn't ready to have.

Daniel lifted his head with a jerk when he remembered his mother kept a meticulous file on each artist who applied for the artist in residence programme. He just had to find the bloody thing.

To his credit, Clem didn't bat an eyelid when Daniel turned up at the neighbouring farm at seven o'clock the next morning, dropping Halfback off on his way up to Christchurch. The farmer almost acted as if Daniel had been expected.

"I thought you might like this." Clem rummaged in his pocket and came out with a stone, placing it with some ceremony in the centre of Daniel's palm.

"A stone?" A bit on the eccentric side, old Clem.

"You don't recognise it?" Clem looked from the stone to Daniel's face, clearly disappointed. "Sorry, I thought it might be important. Kana gave it to Poppy when she left, and I had the distinct impression…" He reached over to take it back, but Daniel closed his fingers into a fist, effectively making the little orb irretrievable.

"Thanks."

"No worries." Clem grinned. "Might bring you luck."

Daniel grunted, and had already turned back to his car when Clem added, "New beginnings."

"What?"

"The koru. New beginnings."

Daniel opened his hand, again looking down at the river stone. Greywacke, round and smooth, like the one he'd found for Kanako on the bottom of the lake.

Exactly alike. It had to be the same actual stone.

Turning it over in his palm, Daniel discovered it'd been intricately carved with a double koru on the flip-side.

The trip was long, but Daniel didn't begrudge that—he had a lot to think about.

He'd finally found Poppy's files at twelve-forty-five last night, along with Kanako's address. The faint guilt of reading something Kanako had written as private correspondence to his mother had worn off as he'd gotten deeper into the guts of her application.

Kanako Nichole Janssen had turned forty on the night of the little-rippa fundraiser, just like she'd said. She'd grown up in Christchurch, had an estranged half-brother on her father's side, and had studied ceramics informally on annual trips to Japan from the age of twelve.

Twelve.

Daniel went back over that part, thinking he must've misread.

When filling in her marital status, Kanako had written 'divorce pending,' and underlined it. In the comments section, she'd elaborated, saying she'd filed for divorce and was looking for a respite to work on her craft, and refocus her ceramics career.

In the 'future goals' section, she'd listed a series of bullet points.

- *drink less coffee*
- *expand to larger studio*
- *increase amount of commission work*
- *find time for yoga everyday*
- *get my own place*

If Kanako hadn't been with Baka-Ken on the night of her gallery opening, then Daniel's radar, and his consequent reactions had been way off.

Jet-lag could only be blamed for so much—the rest was on him.

He'd assumed Kanako guilty, and sentenced her without a decent conversation to back it up. Only too happy to load all the miscommunications on her back, he'd turned away from her. Turned away from a potential life with the woman he'd fallen in love with, after labelling her with the same red marker as Tilly.

Daniel remembered standing outside the annex on the night of the gallery opening with a clear mind to wake Kanako up and demand answers. He wished to God he'd done just that. Perhaps he would've realised what a bloody jealous idiot he was being then, rather than weeks later.

Kanako had begun to mean too much; to burrow too deep under his skin. Fear was an excellent emotion blocker, and anger a very effective way of pushing those you cared about further away. It wasn't rocket science, and he'd been through all this before.

Kia ora, I'm Daniel, and I'm an addict.

Daniel remembered groaning in agony in hospital, years ago, his mother's face sheet-white as she'd hovered over him. The pain had hit him like a wave of heat, as if his entire leg had ignited.

He'd turned his head to the side and closed his eyes so he didn't have to see Poppy's face as he pushed the nurse-call button, urgent for another dose of morphine. He'd kept them closed until he'd heard his mother quietly leave, shutting the door behind her.

Daniel wanted to tackle meeting Kanako again with a clear head, and some semblance of manners, so he booked into a motel for the night on the outskirts of the city. Wired after a day of strategising, he lay on the bed counting the foamboard ceiling panels until sleep finally claimed him.

When morning broke, Daniel forced himself into a state of false calm, like he used to before a big game. He jogged through Hagley, the sprawling parklands on the edge of the city centre. Misty vapour rose off the calm sections of river, twisting and turning through the willows and harakeke, hazing the lines between dreamscape and reality.

Some of his father's people had originated from this land, but it'd been swamp and wetlands then, rich with wildlife and legends.

Daniel checked and re-checked his shave in the mirror. Changing his mind about wearing jeans, he pulled on chinos instead, procrastinating due to his nerves.

There was another guy on the scene now. Sam. How deep were Kanako's feelings for him?

Finally satisfied he was as presentable as he was ever going to be, Daniel drove the short distance to Kanako's address.

The woman at the door was friendly, but adamant no 'Kana' or 'Kanako' lived there. She thought that was the name of the previous owner, who'd moved out a month or so ago.

Daniel stared at her, refusing to believe this could be a dead end, after all.

"What about a ceramics studio?" he ventured, not holding out much hope.

"Oh, yes!" The woman gestured to the long driveway beside them. "I'm number twenty-one, and the studio is down at twenty-one-A."

Twenty-one-A was a back section, and Daniel swallowed his returned tension as he strode down the drive. The property was kept tidy with hedges and trimmed shrubs, the lemon tree against the side-deck boasting a mass of yellow fruit. There was a car parked along the side fence that exactly fitted Saffy's description; an ugly brown station wagon.

"What the hell do you think you're doing here?"

Daniel turned towards the voice emerging from the garage to his left, as a petite woman in a crisp medical uniform moved into the light.

"Kia ora, I'm Daniel—"

"I know exactly who you are," the little platinum blonde hissed coldly. "I asked you what you were *doing* here."

"I've come to talk to Kanako." Daniel eyed the inordinately shitty nurse with some wariness.

"Over my dead body," she growled. "At one time in my life I was a pretty big fan, *Dante D*." She placed both hands on her hips. "So, rather than kick your ass to the footpath, I'm going to ask you nicely to leave. I'm pretty sure you can find your own way out."

He blinked across the driveway at the woman who was approximately half his size. Hackles up and claws out, she resembled a street-wise kitten, snarling at a trespassing Rottweiler.

"I'm sure we can come to some sort of, ah… understanding." He scratched at his chin. Who was this woman, and where did she fit in? "You are…?" he queried, trying to factor her into the equation.

"I'm Sam," she stated firmly, chin raised.

"Ah, right." *The* Sam? Could it actually be that simple? Kanako had come back to live with her old neighbour?

"Do you own this place, then?" He waved a hand towards the updated bungalow.

"Not that it's any of your business, but yes. Most of it," she ended in a mutter.

Daniel found it impossible to hold back his corresponding grin.

"I see. And are you, um… straight?" He went ahead and asked the burning question, though he had no right to.

"*Also*, none of your goddamn business." Sam's eyes narrowed, and she enunciated each word succinctly.

Of course it wasn't, it absolutely wasn't. But he had to know. They stared at each other in a standoff, the silence as prickly as it was long.

Daniel cleared his throat. "I was just asking because I'm trying to establish whether you and Kanako are…" He paused.

Sam smirked. "Involved?" she supplied, seemingly amused.

"Involved. Yes."

"You don't know her very well, do you?"

Pretty sure there was no correct answer to that, Daniel remained silent.

"Kanako isn't bi," Sam stated it as a clear fact. "And I'm pretty sure the two of you have established she isn't gay." She looked him up and down again before glancing back at the car in the garage.

Daniel got the distinct impression he'd walked up just as she was planning to leave, and going by her clothing, guessed Sam was on her way to work.

"Don't let me hold you up."

Sam pursed her lips together, seemingly waging an internal struggle. Finally appearing to give in, she sighed, her face softening a little.

"Obāchan said you'd come," she stated fatalistically. "Then, after your phone call, she bet me twenty bucks you *definitely* would." Sam walked back over to the main door of the house and angled her key in the lock. "Personally, I had serious doubts you'd ever show your face," she muttered before slipping inside.

Not sure if he'd been invited in, Daniel stood in the open doorway and scoped the place out. The front door was more like a back door, opening into a light filled dining room with French doors to the verandah. Through an open archway at the side of the room, he watched Sam fill up the kettle and flick it on to boil.

There was zero sign of Kanako.

"I guess you'd better come in, then," Sam conceded. "But keep your voice down, Kana's still sleeping."

The nerves in Daniel's gut picked back up again.

Kanako *was* here. Close.

Sam took out the plunger and pre-ground beans, placing them on the small Formica bench and indicating he should sit at the breakfast-bar.

"Kana said you drink coffee?" she murmured, measuring the grounds.

"She's told you about me?"

Daniel caught Sam's eye across the bench, and the flash of hot anger.

"*Everything* about you." Her hands stopped their busy movements as she challenged him across the plunger, "I swear, if you hurt her again, I'll come after you and take out your good knee with a blunt axe."

Daniel raised his eyebrows at the gory threat from the little pipsqueak-nurse, but nodded in solemn agreement to the terms. "Understood."

Sam's eyes flicked to the retro clock on the wall, then back to the front door.

"Obāchan's at the consulate office with Kana's mother, trying to figure stuff out. They won't be back for a while." Sam hesitated, clearly unsure of what to do with him, and evidently needing to leave. She was saved the trouble of deciding when the door to the hall swung open, and Kanako stood framed in the rectangular space.

Beautiful, sleep-muzzy Kanako, who emitted a surprised squeak, followed by the quietly spoken, almost charming expletive, "Fuck-a-duck."

29

LAUGH AT THE SKY

*"When you realise how perfect everything is
you will tilt your head back
and laugh at the sky."*
- *Buddha*

Kana was still gripping the door handle, but it wasn't affording the full support she required to deal with the sudden view of Daniel bloody Dante in Sam's little retro kitchen.

Sam skipped around the bench and came to clutch Kana's other arm. "Sorry," she hissed. "He just turned up and I wasn't sure what to do with him. Shall I kick him back out?"

Kana blinked at Sam.

Her friend's spiked hair in no way masked her lack of height, and Kana wondered vaguely how Sam was planning to carry that threat out.

She swallowed the bubble of hysteria threatening to rise.

"No, that's fine." Her calm tone eased the frown on Sam's face, but did nothing to dispel her own angst.

Daniel. Here. In the house.

Her hand automatically moved to protect her baby bump, though she'd been told it was undetectable to anyone but herself, and Daniel's eyes followed the movement.

Comprehension? Shock? Surprise? He masked his feelings so well, she didn't know what Daniel experienced when he saw her hold her belly, but knew instinctively he'd grasped she was pregnant.

A lot more calmly than she felt, Kana latched the door carefully behind her. "You're going to be late for your shift, Sam," she prodded.

"I know." Sam glanced at the clock, then back to her. "It's just—"

"I'll be fine." She'd rather run with a calm line like that than break down in tears, which was what her body was constantly threatening to do to her these days.

"Okay. If you're sure." Sam looked uneasily from Daniel, to Kana.

"I'm sure."

Sam stalked back over to stand hipshot in front of Daniel. "Remember what I said," she ground out.

"I won't forget it," he replied, eyes never leaving Kana.

When Sam left, the gaping silence threatened to overwhelm the room.

Daniel stood, scraping the stool back on the floor, and Kana pressed herself hard against the door. She knew if Daniel touched her, even with something as inconsequential as a hug, it could be her total undoing.

"Did my father contact you?" She managed to find the words.

The kitchen door was actually quite helpful in keeping her upright.

"No?" Daniel looked confused. "I'm sorry if I've given you a shock, just turning up like this, but I found something." He patted his front pants pockets before diving in with one hand.

The man was so big, so all encompassing in the little kitchen. How humiliating would it be if Kana started hyperventilating?

When Daniel pulled her precious antique locket out of his pocket and held it up by its chain, Kana forgot everything but the pure joy of seeing it again. She surged forward and grasped the little keepsake in her fist, pulling it close to her heart.

"Oh, my locket! I thought I'd *lost* it! It was in Wānaka all this time? I'm so grateful." She looked up to thank Daniel, her eyes swimming. "Where did you find it?"

"Up at the orchard. On the grapevine." Daniel was watching her face intently, and realising how close she was standing to him, Kana took a quick step back. She could smell his freshly showered skin, and had to clear the frog lodged in her throat.

"I really appreciate you getting this back to me. It means a great deal. It's the only thing I have that belonged to my great-grandmother." Moving purposefully around the breakfast bar, she gained a little more control by placing a nice, solid barrier between herself and the man who made her heart thud painfully against her ribs.

It was easier to breathe when Daniel sat back down again, taking up less of the oxygen in the room.

Kana opened the locket with shaking fingers. Finding it exactly as she'd left it, she kissed her fingertip and touched it to the etched family names, before closing the tiny latch again.

Slipping the chain over her head, she sighed as the familiar weight and shape settled against her sternum, patting it absently as she filled the coffee plunger with boiling water.

"I hope you don't mind, but I opened it." Daniel sounded guilty as sin.

Kana shook her head. Why would she mind? "His name was Yamada Keisuke. My great grandfather. He died in the war."

"Keisuke," Daniel repeated, nodding. "There's something else I thought you might like." He seemed almost shy when he took a small, folded envelope out of his shirt pocket and slid it across the bench.

Kana opened it curiously, pulling out two daintily proportioned tail feathers, sleek and dark, with a midnight sheen.

"A pair of swallows have taken up residence under the eaves of the annex. They're way off season, but they're making a nest." Daniel readjusted himself to pull his phone out of his back pocket, flicking through until he came to a series of photos.

He handed his cell to Kana across the bench, his large, tanned hand dwarfing the small device.

Kana took the offered phone with polite caution, avoiding touching him.

"That's really cool." She flicked left to see the little mud-caked swallows nest a little closer up, stuck precariously to the topside of a crossbeam. "Will they survive the winter?"

Daniel shrugged. "It's not unheard of."

Swiping left again, there was a clear outline of a swallow's head emerging, and the fourth shot showed a delicately forked tail. Thinking there might be more images, Kana swiped again, but found herself looking at a snap of Saffy kneeling between Halfback and Winger, one hand on each dog.

"Oh! She's grown so much!" she exclaimed.

"Who, Saffy, or the dog?" Daniel laughed.

Kana's chest constricted at both the sound and view of Daniel's amusement.

"I meant the dog. 'Winger,' isn't it?" Kana slid the phone back towards him across the bench, then the envelope.

"Those are for you to keep." Daniel's fingers rested on hers for a moment over the swallow feathers. "In the form of an apology for the way things ended between us. For the way I ended it." He took ownership with the simple statement.

"Thank you." Kana pulled back and spoke with a brisk edge, not wanting to get into that when she felt so vulnerable at the mere sight of him. She changed the subject purposefully. "How are the rest of your family?"

"Good." Daniel shrugged. "Adele's waiting for you to text her back, and Saffy wants to know when you're next coming to visit Wānaka. I know it's pretty much the boondocks to you. You're probably glad to be shot of the place."

"No, I'm not," she replied, surprised. "I loved it there, I—"

"There's no need to sugar coat it, you're not going to offend me," Daniel interrupted. But by his tone, it appeared she already had somehow.

"I'm being completely honest," Kana retorted. "I miss it terribly."

Daniel reached out a hand and touched her once again, this time on her arm. She felt the contact as painfully as if he'd jabbed her with a hot poker, dropping her eyes to stare at the offending fingers, so warm and heavy on her skin.

"Sorry. I've had trouble believing you in the past. I wanted to apologise about that, too. I wonder if things could've been different if I'd just trusted you?" Daniel clenched his hand once, then mercifully removed it. "Did you ever actively try to deceive me?"

Deceive him? Daniel appeared to be deeply serious.

"If you mean the first time we met, I've already tried to explain. Multiple times," Kana huffed, pouring his plunged coffee with an angry flick, and consequently spilling some of the bitter liquid on the bench. She was over the gagging reflex, but her sense of smell was still super sensitive.

"No, I mean after that. Did you ever lie to me on purpose?" Daniel asked again, not dropping the subject.

Having fussed with the spilled coffee, Kana was glad to have an excuse to move away from Daniel. She ferried his drink, and her own teapot and cup, to the small dining table.

"Everyone tells little untruths, especially if you don't know a person very well," she finally answered, excusing herself lightly.

Pulling out his dining chair to indicate where he should sit, she chose to escape to the opposite side of the table.

Daniel followed with slow, deliberate movements, like a large cat stalking its prey, and Kana automatically gauged the movement in his knee.

It seemed unrestricted. No limp, and no favouritism.

"Yeah, I guess that's true." Daniel sat down and leaned back, his legs sprawled out before him. "Like when I told you that splinter on Ruby Island didn't hurt much, but it stung like crap." He surprised a laugh out of her, and grinned in answer, holding his palm up to indicate the spot.

"Oh, you were *very* brave," Kana commended his staunchness wryly, as if he were the same age as Tobias.

"*Anata no ban,*" Daniel informed her with considered softness, the use of the words 'your turn' dragging her right back to their night at the annex. "What were your 'little untruths?' "

Kana swallowed. "Is this important to you?"

"Yes, I think so." Daniel took his coffee but didn't attempt to drink it, allowing her time, but eyeballing her all the while over the rim of his cup.

Kana thought about it for a few moments, sifting through the things they'd experienced together. "I took your newspaper out of the toetoe and told you I didn't have it."

"I know that one already." Daniel cracked a small smile.

"Just being thorough," she flustered, pouring her tea. "I also told you I wasn't attracted to you when you kissed me at the lake, and I said I was happy to see you at Saffy's birthday." She eyed him with some wariness. "Neither of those were truthful."

"Understood. Anything else?"

"Um… I said it didn't matter you saying the woman at the café was unhappy because she didn't have children, but it did matter." She hesitated. "It hurt."

"I knew that one, too," Daniel muttered. "Again, I'm sorry."

"I also said I didn't want to skydive a second time, but I really would've liked to."

"I wondered about that." Daniel put his still-full cup back down and folded his arms across his chest. "Why?"

Kana looked down into her tea, ginger and lemon, the only flavour she could stomach the moment. "At the time, I was under the impression we had something going on. So I got a bit jealous when I realised you'd taken other women up. It made it seem like less, and made me realise I was letting myself get too invested."

Daniel frowned at her. "I've never taken anyone else up skydiving. Just family."

"I see. Though at the time, I found myself wondering if you and Adele…" Kana left the concept hanging, a little embarrassed.

"No shit?" Daniel appeared to mull on that for a moment. "I haven't ever thought of Dell in that way, though apparently there was quite a bit of gossip when she turned up from Australia to stay at my place. She didn't mind. It kept the single guys off her back. I didn't mind either, come to think of it." He continued to watch her. "Was there another reason you didn't want to get too 'invested,' Kanako?"

Kana made a non-committal sound in the back of her throat and lifted her hands in the form of a shrug. She was unwilling to discuss that, so they just sat in silence for a few moments.

She took a nervous glance at the clock. "Are you in Christchurch on business?"

"No. Personal stuff," Daniel answered vaguely, and seemed to re-gather himself before going off on another tangent. "I looked up the missing newspaper article in the library—the piece about the doctors failing."

"Yes?" Kana leaned forward expectantly, surprised Daniel had remembered their conversation, and suddenly keen to hear the end of the story.

"They failed to remove a clamp, and stitched a guy up with it still in his stomach cavity. Three years later, he went in with a burst appendix—totally unrelated—and they found it in an x-ray."

"Unbelievable! How big was it?"

"Big enough." Daniel gestured, holding his forefingers a decent width apart.

"Ouch." Kana grimaced, patting her own belly absently before realising Daniel was again studying her midriff. "I'm pregnant." She bit the bullet threw the combustible words out in the open.

"I gathered." Daniel cleared his throat. "Are you doing okay?"

Kana was both surprised, and dead pleased he hadn't asked the most common question, which was, 'When are you due?'

"Mostly good," she hedged.

Thinking Daniel would probably get going now he'd passed over the locket, attempted some form of apology, and rejected his coffee, Kana slid the cups together and gathered the handle of the teapot as well. Her fingers were a little jittery, making the ceramics chatter together.

She was conflicted, both looking forward to this hulking great man leaving Sam's kitchen, and wishing like hell he could stay as a permanent fixture forever.

"Kanako," Daniel leaned forward across the table with an intent expression before she could get up, and her breath locked in her airway. "Where is your red SUV?"

She blinked in surprise at the unexpected question.

"Kenneth wanted it," she whispered.

"So Baka-Ken gets what he wants?" Daniel leaned back on his uncomfortable chair and levelled Kanako a look across the poky little kitchen table. "Are you back with him?"

Kenneth O'Connor, the conceited prick of a man who thought of Kanako as something less than himself.

Kanako sighed, "I've told you before, Daniel. I'm not *with* Ken." She rubbed at her temple and turned away towards the window, looking tired. There were dark shadows under her eyes that wrenched at him. "I haven't been since well before you and I met. He dragged the divorce out for as long as he could, but we were never meant to be. I'm having this baby on my own." Kanako's voice was strong, but the words sounded forlorn.

"So, the baby isn't Ken's, then?" Daniel tried to keep his voice even, though his sense of relief was overpowering.

"No. After a while, I realised something was wrong—with Ken and me. I pushed for tests, IVF, anything. But he flat-out refused. There was no point continuing if we weren't both prepared to go down that long, winding path." She looked down and stroked her belly with a flat palm. "I assumed it was something to do with me and my random cycles, but clearly not."

"You've never tried IVF before?" Daniel attempted to get all the information crystal-clear in his head.

"No." Kanako hesitated, then turned in slow motion to stare back at him. "I've never tried it, full stop."

What?

The amber of Kanako's eyes was mesmerising, and she didn't blink or turn away. She seemed to come to a decision, taking a deep breath before continuing.

"This baby's yours, Daniel," she whispered.

He could read both sadness and joy in Kanako's face in that moment, and the truth of her statement shone out like the beam from a lighthouse.

It struck him square in the chest.

The emotions surging after hearing her clear admission were anything but mild.

Pure, hot anger was mixed with a pride so strong it rocked Daniel to his foundation. For a moment, he couldn't speak. It never struck him Kanako could've made this up, because for once he knew to his very core she was being completely honest.

How could he love something this much when it hadn't existed in his conscious world, mere moments before?

How could he want it, need it, with this level of intensity, to the point he'd move whatever mountains were placed before him?

———

"You weren't going to tell me." Daniel formed his reply as a statement, rather than a question, and Kana could see the furnace of fury inside him, aimed directly at her.

She gulped, but remained facing him, eyes meeting across the table.

"Daniel, I—" she began, jumping when he thumped a fist hard on the table, making the crockery jump and rattle.

"*Truth serum*!" Daniel demanded fiercely, emulating Fūjin, the Shinto god of the winds with all his pumped-up energy.

The devil god had every reason to be pissed off, but fronting up against him… Kana's father's words came back to haunt her, '*He has a right to know.*'

"Verbal conflict is a bit of a trigger for me. My ex…" Kana floundered. "I'll talk to you, but not if you bully me," she stipulated with as much calm as she could muster.

Daniel appeared even more pained. "Bully you? Please, do *not* lump me in with Baka-Ken." He slid back into his chair, further away from her. "I'll keep a lid on it," he added more contritely when she didn't immediately answer. "Promise." Folding his arms, he sat quietly and waited, though latent energy still eddied around him.

How should she approach this? Honestly, humbly… She'd made mistakes, and Daniel needed to know how sorry she was. Kana moved her right hand to her chest above her heart and solemnly mimed the 'truth serum' injection.

"I drank. During the pregnancy," she began. "Champagne the night we slept together, and wine the next day. I had two whole bottles, and more with meals later on. I was so sick, so exhausted. I've never been pregnant before, I didn't recognise what it was. And it was *completely* unexpected—I mean we used condoms, so I knew I wouldn't be, I thought I *couldn't* be—though they're not infallible. After the first time, I think I fell asleep on you," she confessed, pulling the empty teacup back towards her to play with its form. She encircled the lip, running a finger around it, anything to keep from looking at him. "I don't recall what happened to that condom. I don't know *how* it happened exactly, I wasn't paying attention to that part."

She was very aware of Daniel taking a long breath in, and finally out, while she sat quietly contemplating the many ways she may have screwed up. Not the least of which was failing to carry this child competently.

"I dealt with the condom, but you're right. It was after we woke up." Daniel frowned. "I thought it was a matter of minutes, but now I'm wondering how long we were out to it?"

Kana nodded. "Right." So that answered the 'how.'

"And it was one and a *half*."

"What?"

"You had one and a half bottles of wine the next morning," Daniel stated quietly. "I poured half a bottle of red down the sink when I came around."

Still too much. And the alcohol wasn't the only thing worrying her. Kana laid both hands on the table to steady herself before beginning to explain all of the other 'don'ts' she'd ignored, purely by not knowing.

Without being aware of when, she came to realise Daniel had been gripping one of her hands across the table, squeezing it as she talked, his face wreathed in concern. It all poured out, and she told him about her oversights, her missteps, her fears, and her early bleeding.

"I thought I could figure out a way to tell you after the birth, if I didn't miscarry. They need to get the nuchal fold measurement to work out the likelihood of chromosomal abnormalities. That's not till twenty weeks. Then I can give you a more definite long-term diagnosis."

Daniel's head pulled back as if she'd hit him. He blinked at her for an uncomfortably long time before stating with a deceptively calm voice, "You thought that would make a difference to me. You assumed I'd feel differently if our child had special needs."

Our child.

"I didn't know." Kana took back her hand with a jerky movement. "It's a big call, and I'm not qualified to make it for you. I knew you'd feel responsible, either way, and that's not necessary. You didn't choose this."

"Did *you*?"

"No, I didn't. But I've chosen to keep it, no matter what. Look, I know you don't like me much, and it might be hard to trust I'd do a good job… But I will. I swear to you."

"That's what you *know*, is it? That I don't *like* you much?" Daniel's voice was incredibly soft—much more dangerous than when he was being openly hostile.

Was it hate? Did Daniel Dante actually hate her?

Kana was exhausted, had a big day ahead, and that on top of the emotional upheaval of seeing Daniel out of the blue this morning made her want to curl up and have a really good cry.

How had she gotten herself into this mess? She'd fallen in love with this man and carried his child warm in her belly, but had somehow managed to twist a potentially sweet story into her own emotional nightmare by choosing someone who cared nothing for her in return. Hadn't it been clear from the very start she was nothing a man like Daniel would ever be looking for?

Kana gauged the distance from her chair to the door. In her current state and with Daniel's length of stride, there wasn't a hope in hell unless she took it slow. She rose to stand, gathering the crockery and moving calmly and deliberately towards escape. She still had some semblance of pride, and if she was going to bawl her eyes out, it was going to be in private.

"I'm so sorry, Daniel. Honestly I am. I never planned to trap you, no matter what anyone says. We don't have to have any contact, if you prefer it that way. I'd never—I mean, if your family would like access, of course…" her voice wavered, betraying her.

"You told Katie you'd chosen not to have children. I heard you. You told me you couldn't, but…" Daniel indicated towards her midriff.

So, he wanted to call her a liar one last time? Fair enough, and regrettably, true enough.

Kana placed the cups and teapot on the bench and edged around the breakfast bar. Looking back at Daniel's serious face, hopelessness crept up from her toes to wash over her entire body.

"Ken and I tried for eight years, and couldn't. But it's true I sometimes tell people we chose not to, when I think it would be easier for them to hear. I see how that makes me out to be dishonest. Katie's happily pregnant. The last thing I'd want her to feel is any guilt, or disappointment for me." Kana was nearly at the door. "If you want the truth though? It broke my heart a little, every month that went past. I don't care what challenges this little one faces, I'll be there for it, one hundred percent. I longed for a baby, and you gave me that, so I'll always be incredibly grateful. Thank you for returning my locket."

As Kana reached for the door handle, Daniel read the play and moved like lightning, wrapping his hand over hers before the door was even a few inches open. It slammed shut with momentum, and she leaned her forehead against it in defeat.

"Tell me again how I feel about you," Daniel whispered softly into the hair behind her ear.

"You hate me." It came out as a whimper, and wretched tears began to ooze out, one by one.

"No, Kanako. I don't. You confuse the hell out of me, drive me crazy, and sometimes make me want to throw myself out of a plane, but hate you? No, I don't."

Daniel carefully pried her fingers off the door handle and turned her to face him.

She kept her eyes down, not willing to look at him.

"Tell me something, is there any of that truth serum left in you?" he asked, his voice gentle as he moved first one thumb, then the other across each of her cheeks to remove the wet.

She nodded mutely.

"So, while you're under the influence, how do *you* feel about *me*?"

Looking at a central point on Daniel's chest Kana tried to gather herself, but surrounded by the warm smell of him, she lost all semblance of calm. "Don't make me do this!" she wailed. "It's hard enough… And I'm *so* bloody tired."

"What's hard enough?" Daniel pushed.

Finally, she looked up, and she could see the underlying nervousness there in Daniel's eyes. The anger had gone from him, and he was just a big rugby guy, cornered in the kitchen with a hormonal pregnant woman.

The poor, poor man.

"I didn't want to like you, or find you attractive even, but I did. You gave me butterflies, made me laugh, and you were interesting. Sexy. But *so* unpredictable. One minute acting like you really liked my company and my work, showing me the things you enjoyed doing, spending time with me... Kissing me." She glanced up at him, then away again. "And the rest of the time switching from rude to condescending. It was a bit of a roller coaster for me, never knowing if you'd call me the most beautiful woman in the room, or a barefaced liar. The sex was pretty mind bending, that was one of the best bits."

She noticed Daniel grinned at that. Bloody caveman, proud of his own sexual prowess.

"When we were together and it was good, I felt like you actually saw me."

"I *did* see you. You were all I could see."

"I felt like I didn't have to pretend to be anyone else to be good enough with you. By the time I realised I was in love with you, it was way too late," Kana finished, defeated.

"Wait. Repeat that last bit."

"Get stuffed, there's no need to rub it in."

"Truth serum," Daniel reminded her grimly.

"Oh for Buddha's sake. Is this for your ego? Isn't it big enough? Despite the fact you acted like a jerk, my feelings got tangled up in you, and I loved you. Happy?"

"Yes," Daniel nodded with a seriousness that would've been funny if it wasn't so damn sad.

"Well, I'm glad that rings your bell," she muttered, taking a deep stabilising breath.

"Thank you." Daniel pressed a warm kiss to her forehead, and it felt a lot like goodbye. "You said something earlier, about triggers. I have more trouble than most believing an honest truth, because I was in a relationship once where lies became the norm. Someone betrayed my trust, and sold me out to the press for a nice little deposit on a house."

Daniel had to be meaning the girlfriend tells-all exposé into his drug use.

Kana nodded mutely.

"What I'm trying to say is, I'm sorry. I should've known better than to take your silence as a guilty conscience."

Maybe not goodbye, then?

Daniels lips stayed close to Kana's hairline, his murmured words and warm breath caressing, melting away inhibitions. It would be all too easy to get used to this and sink back into him.

Kana pulled aside, scrubbing at her face with her hands. "We're a sorry pair, aren't we? I run from conflict like a greyhound out of the gates, and you suspect all women of espionage and corruption. The odds were stacked against us from the beginning. Now, I don't mean to be rude, but I have an appointment at the clinic and I should've left five minutes ago."

"What kind of appointment?" Daniel gripped her upper arms and searched her face.

"A scan. My check-in." She sighed as Daniel's obvious concern flickered, morphing into excitement, and he leaned over to grab his coat off a stool at the breakfast bar. "I'm guessing you want to come too?"

"Absolutely."

"In that case, you're driving." She slipped her car keys off the hook and handed them to Daniel. "I need a rest."

30

SALVATION

"Work out your own salvation.
Do not depend on others."
- Buddha

Kanako hadn't been kidding. Almost as soon as she was in the passenger seat, she was out like a light, her mouth slightly open and emitting soft breathing sounds. She had a glow about her with the pregnancy, her skin creamy and translucent at the same time. Daniel checked her out often during the twenty-minute trip to the clinic, eyes drawn less to her slim belly, and more to the hand resting protectively across it.

If Kanako hadn't switched on the satellite navigation system before she dropped off, Daniel would've been completely lost. It was in Japanese, but rather than fiddle with the controls and lose his destination, Daniel drove through Christchurch with the very polite intonations of *'Mamonaku migi houkou desu.'*

Loath to wake Kanako up when they arrived, Daniel scooted into the clinic first to check her booking.

The schedule was already running ten minutes behind, so he sweet-talked one of the staff into texting him when Kanako was needed, then returned to keep an eye on her while she slept.

Creeping back behind the wheel, he breathed in the warm scent of her, longing to bury his face into her soft neck and drown himself.

Saffy had alluded to it, and Kanako had said it herself... She'd loved him. What's more, Daniel believed her to be telling the whole truth.

That was good, right? Hell, that was great! It gave him something to work with.

Sam was a woman, Kanako was straight, and Kenneth wasn't on the scene. Baka-Ken had *never* been on the scene, despite the bastard's claims otherwise.

Poppy was dead right. Daniel had behaved like an asshole; rude, jealous, and cold. It wasn't unfathomable Kanako would assume he'd disliked her—hated her even—though hearing those damning words coming out of her mouth had ripped a hole in him.

He hadn't ever told her otherwise. Other than compliments on the way she looked, and feedback about her work, he'd purposefully kept his inner thoughts to himself.

Okay, so perhaps Katie and Adele were right too. He'd been obtuse. Boneheaded.

Daniel had to figure out a way to make it right.

He checked his phone. He had approximately five minutes to come up with a viable game plan to keep Kanako in his life.

Arching backwards, he managed to get the greywacke stone out of his front pocket, and worried at the koru with his thumb as he thought.

A new beginning. A fresh start. Growth. Life.

What had Obāchan said he needed to learn? Happiness didn't come to those who failed to appreciate what they already had. Did he already have Kanako? Is that what the old woman meant? He'd failed spectacularly in Wānaka, stepping back instead of fighting for her, unable to grasp the worth of the future he'd held in his very hand.

He wouldn't be caught dead doing that again.

Looking down, Daniel stared at the carved stone settled in his palm. Obāchan's quote for Kanako was about patience being key, and remembering a jug filled drop by drop. If he had the luxury of time, he could prove to Kanako he was worthy, capable and reliable, not a two-headed monster feeding on conflict.

Daniel respected her, and that respect had to come with inherent trust. She needed to know he was capable of that. If he could work on expressing his honest feelings, rather than locking them securely away, Kanako may even have the potential to love him again.

One day.

He would happily spend a lifetime filling the jug, drop by drop, if Kanako would only allow him to.

The move up to Christchurch was do-able. He was fonder of smaller towns, but he could make it work. Maybe a property a little further out? Somewhere with privacy, where the dog and kids could roam free.

A lifestyle block.

"Kia ora, I'm Daniel." He shook the female technician's hand and met her open stare with a smile, while 'Helen' fussed with the name-tag on her uniform. "I'm the father," he added, and it would've felt good coming out of his mouth, if Kanako hadn't spoken at the exact same moment.

"Daniel's my support person," she said.

He turned to stare at Kanako, but she wouldn't meet his gaze, looking in the general vicinity of his shirt buttons instead.

"Both." Daniel turned back to the technician with a polite, if somewhat tighter smile. "I'm the father, *and* Kanako's support person."

"Right, then. Follow me."

"Now you've gone and done it," Kanako hissed when the woman was out of earshot, tugging on his hand. "She *recognised* you."

"So?"

"So, she'll *tell* everyone!" Kanako's eyes were wide.

"Kanako." He moved his hand to her shoulder. "I'm not ashamed of this baby. Are you?"

"No!" Kanako slid her shoulder out from under him, holding one hand protectively over her belly. "But it's *private*," she whispered furiously, blinking up at him.

"Right. Understood." Daniel shifted gears in his head. This

wasn't just about him anymore. "Sorry," he added, briefly touching his fingers to hers.

Daniel made it his business to strike up a conversation with Helen, the technician, as Kanako got comfortable on the raised bed, asking if she had children of her own and listening attentively to her spiel about her twin girls.

"This is my first time," he admitted, so I'm looking for all the advice I can get on how to make it a smooth ride for Kanako."

Both women turned to him in surprise.

"Well, that's good to hear." Helen began manoeuvring her equipment into place. "For obvious reasons," she blatantly sized him up, "This is probably going to be a large baby, and Kanako will need a lot of rest. Day snoozes, taking it easy. Keep her fluids up, and gentle exercise only." She turned to Kanako and her voice took on a more direct tone. "*No* heavy lifting, and *regular* meals." Turning back to Daniel, her tone gentled. "She needs to remember to put her feet up and let someone else do the hard work for a change. Any sign of spotting or pain, and you should call your midwife right away."

"Okay," he agreed. All of that was doable, except… "Do we have a midwife?" Turning to look at Kanako, he noted she was still fidgeting nervously with her clinic gown, even as she nodded.

There was still something bothering her; something he hadn't addressed.

"Kanako's a very private person, so we were hoping you'd be able to keep this quiet for us? Not all of our family members know yet." Daniel smiled at Helen.

"Oh, of course." The woman flushed, patting Kanako's arm conspiratorially. "Whatever goes on in this room remains between us."

Kanako clearly began to relax, just as Daniel's own nervous tension reached its zenith. Helen had rolled up Kanako's clinic gown, and he watched in fascination as the technician applied a little pressure to each side of the tiny swell around her navel.

It was the most surreal moment in time.

His child was growing under that sweet belly-button, warm and toasty inside Kanako's body.

"Let's have a listen to the heartbeat," Helen murmured to

Kanako, and they shared a private smile before she turned to get the gel.

Kana smiled up at Helen, delighted when she picked up the little 'swish, swish' of the busy heartbeat.

So comforting, so grounding.

Daniel made a strangled sound. His eyes were lit with fascination, and he placed a hand on a dry spot to the side of her belly.

"*Hajimemashite aka-chan*. I'm your Daddy." He introduced himself with a catch in his voice, bending to drop a kiss next to his fingers. The sweetness in the gesture snapped a thread of control Kana had been holding onto with a very tenuous grip.

She'd had the support of Sam, and her family, but for the most part Kana had felt so very alone throughout this journey. Against her own wishes, her traitorous eyes began to pool again.

Tears trickled down her cheeks, silently at first, until her body built itself up into uncontrollable, raking sobs.

The ultrasound technician stood quietly by, then leaned forward to touch a hand to Kana's shoulder. "I'll give you two a moment alone," she said soothingly, wiping off the cool gel with tissues before leaving the room.

"Don't cry, sweetheart."

"Don't you 'sweetheart' me Dante D," she sobbed, turning her face away from the gentle look on Daniel's face that made her want to howl even louder.

"But you are my sweetheart, little swallow." Daniel traced his finger over the small tattoo on her hip, just visible above the stretchy waistband of her jeans. "I missed you," he whispered, leaning forward to bury his face in her hair on the pillow, before turning to murmur softly into her neck, "everything about you."

"You said you weren't looking for complicated." Kana sniffed, trying to gain traction over her shaky voice and waving a hand over her bare belly. "This is complicated."

"No. If I recall correctly, it was *you* who said you weren't looking for complicated." Daniel pulled back, took her hand in his, and brushed her knuckles with his lips. "Complicated is beginning to sound pretty good to me. I want you in my life, Kanako, complicating the hell out of everything. The farm's empty without you," he stated, looking into her eyes. "*I'm* empty without you."

She desperately wanted to believe him.

Being with Daniel had at times been absurdly lovely, but the incredible highs had been closely accompanied by soul-destroying lows. His hot and cold moods had been as unpredictable as they had been hurtful. Being with Daniel would no doubt eat away at her self-esteem, just as her relationship with Ken had done.

Kana might've been nutty enough to try and weather that, because against her better judgement she was still bonkers about the man. Just being in the same room with him had solidified that point. Over him? *Not*.

She could admit to herself she would've jumped at some kind of reconnect if it hadn't been for the baby... But what would that kind of treatment do to a child?

"A baby's not something you can change your mind about later, Daniel," she cautioned, a great stillness mounting inside her as she considered her options. "You may well lose interest in me down the track, but that could destroy a little person. They wouldn't understand it was their mother, not them you were leaving." She stroked her slightly sticky belly, the movement calming, giving her stronger purpose.

Daniel ran a rough hand over his face, clearly trying to get a grasp on his emotions, and hold them in check.

"I'm never going to change my mind, because I've never been more sure of anything. But you don't believe that, do you?" He spoke in a low voice.

Kana smiled with all the softness she had left in her, trying to take the edge off her answer. "No. I'm afraid not." She took the time to wipe the wetness off her cheeks and push herself a little more upright on the bed.

"I didn't handle this well. I didn't play it right." Daniel groaned, jumping up to pace the small space like a caged animal. For the first time since Kana had met him, he seemed to be at a complete loss. "I can see why you thought I didn't care about you. I pushed you away. I was an obnoxious bastard." He stopped to place both hands on his hips and contemplate her.

Dishevelled, and feeling less than presentable with her clinic smock pulled up to her bra and mascara more than likely tracking down her cheeks, Kana edged the cotton slowly back down over her thickened waistline.

She returned Daniel's stare with as much poise as she could muster.

"You're highly addictive Kanako. Being with you is like taking a hit, and that scared the shit out of me." Daniel scraped his thumbnail along his jawline, back and forth. "I want to make it up to you," he stated, raw determination apparent as he sat down next to her and drew both of her hands into his. "I acted like an asshole, I know, but that's not who I really am. Let me prove it to you? I want to see you. Please."

Kana considered the seriousness in Daniel's hazel eyes, trying to gauge if he was really wanting this, or feeling that he should, due to the baby.

"I won't hold any animosity towards you if you decide you want out." She spoke slowly as the idea settled in her head.

He would get cold feet eventually. She was sure of it.

"But make it before the birth, okay? So the child knows it's not their fault." She double-checked to see Daniel understood. "I'm due in just under seven months—"

"You'll give me seven months?" Rather than unhappy with a deadline, Daniel seemed to be over the moon about it.

Kana shrugged. "Sure. I mean, I don't know how often we'd see each other with you down there and me up here. Maybe the odd weekend. It would give us some time to sort out how we want to play it with visitation and stuff."

"Visitation?"

"You know. If you or your family wanted to see the child."

"*See* the *child*? Kanako, I want to be with you," Daniel insisted, his smile gone. "I know Christchurch is home for you, you have Obāchan and your parents here—your friends. But I figured I could get a place nearby and if you were up for it later, if you trusted me, you might consider moving in?"

"In *Christchurch*?"

"Sure, why not? You like it here, right?"

"What about the farm?" she exclaimed, shocked.

Daniel shrugged. "It's just a house."

"That farm is *not* just a house," Kana disagreed vehemently. "It has a heart and soul, like a living being."

"I wouldn't sell it," Daniel promised. "It'll always stay in the family. I just wouldn't be living there on a day-to-day basis. I should probably put the wheels in motion to put it in a trust for the kids."

"You have other children?" she managed to choke out.

That hadn't been in his online blurb.

"Not yet," Daniel grinned, touching his fingertips to the cotton gown overlaying her belly. "Just this one, so far."

"So, to get this straight." Kana blinked at him. "You're thinking about moving to Christchurch to be near the baby?"

"To be near *you*, Kanako." Daniel took both her hands in his. "I love you."

She exhaled swiftly, Daniel's unexpected words bringing a sharp pain with them, like a sneaky knife thrust under her ribs.

Direct stab to the heart.

"You don't have to say that." Kana pushed back on his hands, urgently removing herself from his grasp. She clutched the sides of the mattress instead, giving herself some semblance of strength. "I'd rather you didn't say that. Ever," she reiterated in a mutter, shell-shocked.

"I *do* have to say that," Daniel moaned, his eyes meeting hers. "It's all I can think about. It eats me up inside, every day you're not with me. I didn't know anything about you switching cars, so I thought you were with Baka-Ken every time his work vehicle was parked at the annex. He told me at the gallery you were still married, that you'd taken a break, but were going to make another go of it; try for children. I wanted to kill him. I wanted to slit his gloating throat." Daniel laughed, but it was mirthless, and aimed at himself. Putting his forehead into his palms, he rocked forward. "I'm such an idiot. I saw you with him… It seemed feasible, so I took his word over yours. I've never thought of myself as a jealous person. I'm not envious of what anyone else has. But I realise now I've just never had something to be jealous about, until you."

Ken had said *what*?

"Oh Kenneth, you *bastard*," Kana murmured, as the timing of what had been Daniel's most confusing mood-shift began to dawn on her and it all started to fall into place. "He saw the magazine photos, and decided to claim something back. Either me or the car." She twisted her mouth wryly. "He got the car, but it sounds like he couldn't actually stomach the thought of me being happy with someone else, after all."

"And you *were* happy with me, weren't you?"

"For a time, yes." She could honestly say that.

"I don't blame Ken. I felt the same way." Daniel looked across at her, his voice subdued. "I called you to tell you about your locket, and the misunderstanding with the car. I wanted to apologise about the photos, and the way I treated you. I was going to ask for another chance; ask you to consider coming back to Wānaka, for the remainder of your grant at the very least. But Obāchan told me you were pregnant, and living with some guy called Sam."

Kana made an involuntary sound in the back of her throat, and Daniel continued to stare, eyes searching.

"I was ready to fight him to the death, too." He smiled a little crookedly, with more than a touch of self-depreciation. "Get rid of him by whatever means necessary. Until I realised he was a she." Leaning across, he stroked one finger down the length of her cheek. "Canines shouldn't worry you, Kanako. You've got Sam, and she's the fiercest guard dog I've ever come across. I answer to her if I hurt you."

"That sounds like Sam." The smile tugging at her lips chased away the tremble.

"Sweetheart." Daniel delivered the banned endearment with what appeared to be heartfelt tenderness. "I'm not going to hurt you."

"Because you're afraid of Sam?" she returned lightly.

"No, because I'm in love with you."

The look in Daniel's eyes made Kana catch her breath, and begin to doubt her earlier conviction. Could he actually be?

"We'll see," she whispered.

"We'll see, meaning you'll consider this? Consider me?" Daniel stood, taking both her hands in his again, eyes alight.

What choice did she have?

"Yes, but not necessarily here."

"Anywhere. Anywhere is fine," Daniel assured her earnestly.

"Okay, then."

Daniel squeezed her fingers so tightly she yelped.

"Sorry, sorry." Daniel released some of the tension on his hold, raising her hands in turn to kiss her knuckles in apology. "For everything," he murmured.

Dropping one of her hands to pat at his pockets, Daniel dove in and came out triumphant. "I was hoping…" He placed a very familiar stone centrally on her clinic smock, right over her belly button. "We could start again from Ruby Island. Like a new beginning. You and me."

Kana looked down with some surprise at the beautifully carved double koru she'd had commissioned for Daniel's birthday.

Reaching down, she traced the spiral out from the central meeting point.

"It came full circle," she whispered. "You gave this to me on Ruby Island."

"Yeah. That day was something special."

"It was."

Kana looked up to meet Daniel's eyes, the shared memory as warm as the sunshine that had kissed their skin.

"I was all in by then." Daniel's teeth flashed white as he smiled.

"Were you?" To be honest, it had probably been her own point of no return, too.

"So far gone I couldn't think straight," he assured her. "I wish I'd told you under those willows what you'd come to mean to me."

Kana cleared her throat. "I need to warn you. I come as a package deal. Obāchan's with me now," she added seriously. "We're still working on visas and the like, but wherever I go, she goes."

"I get that." Daniel's smile turned into a grin, still holding her fingers in a semi-crushing grip. "How would you feel about helping me look at some rental properties tomorrow?"

Daniel's eagerness to get underway was almost comical, and Kana couldn't contain her laughter.

With it, a large part of the pressure lifted.

She was inviting Daniel Dante back into her life, and the perilous high of it was almost as intense as jumping out of a plane.

EPILOGUE

February

"Daniel-kun has purchased *niwatori*." Obāchan used a mixture of Japanese and English when she entered through the backdoor from the courtyard, her smile almost as wide as her face.

Kana had a miniature cotton singlet up to her nose, and was in the process of inhaling the fresh scent of summer sunshine. She blinked across at her grandmother from her seat at the farmhouse dining table, temporarily distracted from rolling tiny socks into pairs and folding swaddling muslins.

"He *hasn't*," she refuted in an undertone.

In answer, she was handed Obāchan's cell phone with a flourish.

"Great Buddha! He *has*. I hope Halfback doesn't think they're a tasty new breed of rabbit," Kana worried aloud, idly flicking through the photos of red hens of varying shades, scratching happily next to the distinctive corrugated-iron walls of the annex.

Obāchan chatted away in Japanese about fresh eggs for breakfast as she moved around the now familiar kitchen, putting the kettle on and organising cups with a spring in her step.

It'd only been six days since they'd all made the move back down to Wānaka, and Daniel had been unrelenting in his mission to make sure Obāchan was as excited about the shift as Kana was. On each and every morning since they'd been home, Daniel had ensured there was some form of welcome gift for her grandmother.

Chickens now, including a henhouse and a large enclosed run. How the hell had he managed that in less than a week? The man was nothing if not determined.

Sighing, Kana moved the pile of washing aside, then leaned forward to flick through some older photos. There was one of the annex lounge, redecorated with a large roll of tatami matting, tasselled floor cushions and a low table for Obāchan's tea ceremonies. Kana could imagine her grandmother preparing *matcha* there; the soft whisper of stiff silk sleeves, and the swish and tap of the bamboo whisk on hand-thrown stoneware.

Daniel had set up the annex as her grandmother's private space, replacing the bed with a westernised futon and organising the shipping of her personal effects from Japan. He was endeavouring to make the transition as painless as possible, in spite of the fact the shift had been Kana's idea.

She swiped back to the photos of today's hens.

"What's this one?" she squinted at the small screen, trying to make out a blurry block-shape in the final photo. Obāchan was a terrible photographer, possibly due to the fact she couldn't remain still for the space of two seconds.

"I thought you'd never find it!" Obāchan crowed. "Your *subarashii* new kiln has arrived." She fairly danced back across the hardwood to look over Kana's shoulder, glowing at the picture on screen.

"What new kiln?" Kana frowned.

"*That* one," Obāchan insisted, pointing to the blue blob on the screen. "It took six of Daniel's rugby men to get it into the studio." She had a definite twinkle in her eye now. "I stayed to watch. Made sure they got it into the right spot." Holding up a bony arm, she mimed pinching a bicep, though she had very little of her own to speak of.

"Bloody hell. A new *kiln* now?" Kana had to get down to the barn.

Pushing out of her chair, she glanced anxiously at the baby monitor, then the clock.

"Ruby's been down for half an hour, and she's due a feed when she wakes up," she began explaining.

"No problem. You go," Obāchan laughed, clearly expecting to be left in charge.

"You should have about thirty minutes grace, but it's anyone's guess." Kana was yanking on her Ugg boots as she spoke. "She changes it up to keep me on my toes, the wee madam…" she trailed off. Thinking of Ruby made her boobs ache. "There's a bottle of expressed milk in the fridge."

As if sensing she'd been mentioned, the baby made a soft snuffling sound in her sleep.

Both women turned to stare at the monitor on the kitchen bench, holding their breath until all was silent again.

"I'll phone you down there if she wakes grizzly and I can't settle her." Obāchan smiled serenely. "Or maybe you'll hear her bellowing from as far away as the barn if she really means it," she added with a chuckle. "Go."

Kana went.

They'd agreed on staying in Christchurch for the birth. That was a no-brainer, as the hospital was the best in the South Island. But if they'd stayed any longer in the city where everyone wanted a piece of them, Kana would've gone stark-raving mad. Her itch for Wānaka had grown stronger by the day after Ruby's birth, until finally she couldn't stand it anymore.

"I miss the studio in Wānaka," she'd complained to Daniel. "I miss the air. I miss the colours and the privacy. I need to go back and work there."

"It's Mum and Clem's wedding next month, so you can get a fix then," Daniel had smiled softly, and her heart had squidged like warm putty at the view of him ambling around the lounge of their Christchurch rental property, his big hand gliding over Ruby's tiny back in gentle circles. He was supposed to be trying to get a burp out of her, but the nearly one month old had fallen asleep in her favourite spot after her feed—draped over her daddy's solid shoulder.

Kana had stalled to watch.

Father and daughter had formed an undeniable mutual

admiration society, and the sweetness of it brought a lump to her throat.

"No. That's not what I meant. I want to go now, and I don't want to come back."

Daniel had turned to her then, all other movements ceasing.

"To live?" His brows had been raised in query, and she'd thought she'd seen a glimmer of excitement in those earthy eyes.

"Sure, why not? You like it there, right?" She'd mimicked Daniel's original argument for moving up to Christchurch to be with her. "Besides, we'd be doing Papa a favour by separating Mum and Obāchan." Breastfeeding was thirsty work, and Kana poured herself a second glass of water and downed it before continuing with a touch of humour. "Though the farm's a little further than his stipulated 'walking distance.' "

Daniel had laughed, stopping mid chuckle when their daughter stirred, her tiny fists balled.

He'd resumed the gentle pacing, and Ruby's little body had released a huge belch before slipping instantly back into snooze mode, her dark cap of hair looking unbelievably fine and wispy next to her father's stubble.

"We'll fly them down as often as they want." He'd spoken in a whisper. "But judging from the fireworks between your mother and Obāchan last night at dinner, different towns might be just what's needed to soothe family relations."

Daniel had never pushed Wānaka as their home, though Kana could see he was really excited about the prospect. Maybe if he *had* pushed, she would've balked and run a hundred miles in the other direction.

Not even maybe. Definitely.

Kana hadn't trusted Daniel, not initially, and she'd been incredibly tentative about stepping into a relationship with yet another strong-minded male.

Especially with a ready-made family on the way.

But Daniel had slid into the weave of her Christchurch life with surprising ease, and proved himself loyal time and again. Through the media circus, family squabbles, the birth—everything.

Kana knew it wasn't just Obāchan Daniel thought he had to win over with the changes at the farm. There was evidence in the carefully tended orchard, with new flagstones under the re-painted grape arbour, and a little silver hook for her locket to hang while she practiced yoga. Also waiting for their arrival had been a flower garden in honour of Daniel's Nana Nona, and his first child.

Daisies, lilies, irises, poppies, white standards, and a beautiful creeping ruby rose.

All of that was lovely, but it was the crib that made Kana really feel like she'd come home; the family heirloom Poppy had dressed in fresh white cotton, waiting patiently for its cherished new occupant.

Halfback must've sensed Kana coming, and came to meet her before she was halfway down the drive. He trotted up beside her and shoved his wet nose into her hand, as was his custom now.

"What's going on, eh?" She stroked one of his velveteen ears as she continued towards the barn. "Daniel on another mission?"

She'd expected a truck and a lot of activity, but it was just Daniel sitting on the concrete step with his back against the barn door, sunning himself. He rose when he saw her, and strolled up to meet her.

It never failed to kick her heart rate up a notch, that smile of Daniel's that lit his eyes in a slow, lazy twinkle. He was one hell of a stunning man.

"I hear you've been busy?" she quipped.

"All in a day's work, my sweet *tsubame*." Sliding his arms around her waist, Daniel bent to drop a kiss on the side of her neck before kissing her lips. He'd settled on calling her that a month ago, the evening after she'd been given the all clear from her doctor and they'd been lying naked together in bed, rosy and flushed from lovemaking.

Daniel had leaned across to stroke a finger over her tattoo, and named her after the little swallow.

She hadn't told him not to.

In fact, she'd grown rather fond of the endearment.

"Mmm, you smell like sunshine and mischief," she murmured against his mouth.

"Come and check my mischief out," Daniel invited, clearly excited and drawing her towards the barn door.

The light was dimmer inside, but the new kiln stood unmistakably pristine within the well-utilised studio, and it was *huge*.

"Merry Christmas. It's a bit late, but—"

"Buddha's *belly*! Twenty-nine inches?" she squeaked.

"I figured your work's getting larger and larger." Daniel hesitated. "It's what the Canterbury Potters recommended." His voice sounded a little strained, and she realised with some surprise he was actually nervous about her reaction to this top-of-the-range appliance.

"I *love* it."

"You do?" Daniel breathed out again when she threw herself at him and squeezed tight. "I thought you might want to start fresh. Clean slate." He lifted her up to his height and she slid her legs around his waist and kissed him, hard.

Daniel groaned as they deepened the kiss, and walked her slowly back against the wall.

She'd been half expecting him to tire of her pregnant, then post-birth body, but rather than the novelty wearing off, Daniel seemed pretty enthusiastic about her extra curves and mounds. For the first time in her life it really was necessary for her to wear a bra everyday, though with Daniel in the house, it spent as much time coming off as it did going on.

'Afternoon naps' had taken on a whole new meaning, and the couple stole time whenever they could within their crazy schedule as new parents.

Getting the vague feeling she was being watched, Kana opened one eye. Two bulky forms loomed behind Daniel on the workbench, one fierce-faced, and the other sublimely happy.

"Daniel Dante!" She pulled back from him. "How much did you pay Clem for the Yin and Yang dogs?" she demanded.

"Four times what he paid for them," Daniel conceded. "He drove a hard bargain, but I wanted them for my office."

"I see. And Daniel gets what Daniel wants." She poked fun at him. "That's quite a mark-up though, especially considering Clem's soon to be family." Poppy and Clem's lakeside wedding was less than a week away.

Though Kana continued to fuss, the bluster had gone out of her, and her voice had taken on a dreamy tone. When Daniel nibbled along her collarbone, her thought processes became anything but direct.

"Clem was thinking maybe he could commission another set, and I told him commission was your new favourite word," Daniel murmured into Kana's skin, the rasp of his bristles setting her nerve endings tingling.

"Mmm… This has got to stop, Daniel."

"What?" His head whipped up and the kisses ceased.

"I mean, *chickens*?" Kana laid her forehead against Daniel's and contemplated him at very close range. "Really?"

Daniel laughed, and her heart skipped a beat in a corresponding move. "Whatever makes Obāchan happy." Sinking his face into her hair, he inhaled deeply. "Whatever makes you happy," he murmured on the exhale.

"*You* make me happy," she replied with complete honesty. "You're the guy who took me skydiving."

"Yeah, I'm that guy." Daniel pulled back to search her face.

"I lost sight of you there for a while." She fought to find the words to explain. "I wasn't sure if you actually existed. I thought maybe I'd made the best parts of you up."

"And now?" Daniel's frown pulled his eyebrows together, and Kana was reminded of Saffy's name for Daniel's fierce concentration face, 'Jet-lagged Uncle D.'

"Ah, well." She ran one fingertip down the side of his cheek, then stroked away his frown lines with her thumb. "Now I'm absolutely *positive* I did," she teased.

"I'm real." Daniel placed her back on her feet, taking both her hands and settling them on his chest. "See? And I'm not going anywhere."

"I love you, Daniel," Kana said, and the words slid out as naturally as the air she was breathing. "More than I can say."

Daniel squeezed his eyes shut for a moment before answering with quiet tenderness, "I love you too, Kanako Nichole Janssen. More than I would've ever believed possible."

Kana knew she'd made Daniel wait too long to hear the words, but she'd needed to be absolutely sure, for both Ruby and herself. Because love wasn't just a statement, it was a promise of intent, and Daniel had more than proved his.

Pulling her tight to him, Daniel swung one arm under her knees and the other under her shoulders, lifting her close to his chest.

"It was the kiln that tipped the scales, right?" he joked, wearing a small, private smile that blossomed in Kana's heart like a blush-pink lotus.

She laughed. "It's the fact you know me, and back me, one hundred percent."

"And?" he prompted, eyes glinting.

"*And…* you smell good, make beautiful babies, have truly lickable abs, and show exemplary taste in both life partners and kilns."

"I knew that kiln would be worth its weight in gold," he murmured, nuzzling near her ear. "Is our sweet *musume* sleeping?"

"Uh-huh." Kana nodded, content beyond her wildest imaginings. "Obāchan's watching her."

"D'ya reckon we've got time?" Daniel eased back to raise his eyebrows at her, and there was definitely another large dose of mischief lurking in those hazel eyes.

"Oh, I reckon so. But you're only getting lucky if you bolt the barn door." She smiled up into his laughing face, and sent up a small prayer of thanks to Buddha, and every Shinto god in existence, for this man's mud-loving Nana Nona.

The artist in residence position set up in Nona's name had led Kana directly to Wānaka, and straight into Daniel Dante's arms.

THE END

WANT MORE?

Thank you for reading Ruby Island. Read more of the Otago Waters series with Cam and Shal's story in Mako Bay, and Adele's journey in Lake Taimana, both available now on Amazon.

For information about about new books, sign up for my newsletter at www.stephanie-ruth.com, and I'll send you a short-story prequel to the Otago Waters series, Scent, Not Sensibility.

I hugely appreciate your help in spreading the word about my books, including telling your friends. Reviews help readers find books, too. Please review Ruby Island on Goodreads, BookBub, Amazon, or your favourite site.

Turn the page for an excerpt from Lake Taimana.

1

TAIMANA - DIAMOND

The hardest naturally occurring substance on Earth.

———————

James readjusted the package under his arm with great care, and considered the likelihood of detonation. The contents themselves weren't remotely explosive. Not in physical terms.

Could still blow up in his face, though.

Changing his mind, he backtracked to settle the well-wrapped box on the passenger seat of his rental car, and locked it. A hug wasn't the kind of reception he was expecting, but for some reason he needed his hands free and unencumbered when he finally saw Adele Montague again.

Fergus, not Montague, he had to keep reminding himself. Adele had taken her maiden name back after the divorce.

James shifted his shoulders in discomfort.

She might not be home. It wasn't like he was expected. He could well be interrupting, asked to come back another time or told to bugger off altogether.

Adele's place was a cottage-style bungalow, with a standard white rose guarding each side of the porch steps. Nothing grand or showy. A welcoming scent. A home.

Knocking firmly on the front door, James began to wish he had something tangible in his hands after all. He fisted them by his sides, then unfisted them—shoved them into his pockets, then yanked them out again. They were resting uneasily on his hips when the woman who still sizzled up every salient thought in his head opened the door a crack.

"James?" Adele eased the door wider to reveal her whole, unbearably tempting person. Her eyes were wide and startled, crystal-blue like the lake he'd just glimpsed on arrival into this poky New Zealand township.

"Dell." His stunning wife.

Ex-wife.

"You're in Australia." There was some confusion in Adele's statement—in the fingers fluttering at the base of her throat.

James offered her a half-smile. "Clearly, I'm not, though."

"What are you *doing* here?"

"I came to deliver your jewellery box."

"But, I sent a letter with instructions." Adele leaned a little further out onto the porch, her eyes shifting towards his rental car. Searching for what, exactly?

The scent of Adele's favourite hair product reached out to him, teasing. Tropical rainforest, with a hint of coconut. Light, fresh, and achingly familiar.

Unfamiliar was the flash of silver at the curved indent of her nostril, the tiny stud adorning her freckled nose, reaffirming the fact things had unquestionably changed.

Adele glanced back at him, then away, catching him staring. "I sent your lawyer my postal address."

"I decided to deliver it in person."

For a man who'd been unsure of a door slammed in his face, this wasn't such a bad reception. His ex-wife was fiddling with her hair, drawing attention to those strawberry corkscrews and making his own fingers itch to rummage and furl. She looked so damn pretty in her T-shirt and jeans, gnawing on her bottom lip.

"But, why?"

To see her. Just to bloody see her. Get her out of his system, once and for all.

Yeah, not likely.

James shrugged. "I had some business come up in Otago, and the diamond is five-carat."

"Right, the diamond." Adele looked down at her bare feet and wiggled her toes. There was silver there too, in the form of a toe-ring. It effectively hid the slim scar she'd been left with years ago, after a particularly nasty bluebottle sting. "I didn't think about that. But a secure courier—"

"It's great to see you, Dell," James interrupted.

"Is it?" Adele shook her head faintly. "I haven't—"

"I couldn't—" They both spoke at the same time, adding to the awkwardness.

He should've bought her flowers. Why didn't he think to do that? Bird of Paradise, her favourite. Big, bold and structured. Or lilies, the brighter the better.

Were her favourite. Once.

Things changed. People changed. It'd been five long years, after all.

"Go ahead," Adele offered, waving a hand in his direction.

"Ah, I was just going to say I couldn't get a park on the street, so I've pulled in behind your cleaner. I hope that's okay?"

"My cleaner?" Adele leaned forward, once again checking out the unevenly matched cars parked up the shingle driveway, nose to bumper.

There was a much older, heavily logoed cleaner's vehicle in front: Spic'n'Span home cleaning and property management services. Apparently 'elbow grease' was their middle name.

James wasn't sure it was advisable to use the word grease in a cleaning slogan, given the fact it evoked the image of, well… *grease*.

Adele began to laugh, a small chuckle that curled James' toes. Warm and mirthful. "Oh, James." She wound down to a tight little smile. "That's *my* car. I clean my own place." She waved a hand to incorporate the house behind her, and James belatedly recognised the Spic'n'Span logo on her T-shirt. "And a bunch more."

"Oh, right." When they'd first met, Adele had been working as a legal secretary for a high powered law firm. Admittedly part-time due to being a solo mum, but a million miles from domestic help. "You, ah… You enjoy that line of work?"

Adele's lips flatlined, and she stared James down for a moment before replying.

He quashed the urge to take a step backwards.

"Oh, absolutely. It's a joy getting down on my hands and knees and scrubbing other people's porcelain. My dream job." Adele's caustic tone was wince-inducing.

"Company car though. Bonus," James quipped, attempting to scramble to higher ground.

"Management perk." Adele's demeanour remained cool, as did

her eyes. "It's an honest living, and it keeps mine and Saffy's heads above water."

His ex-wife hadn't invited him in, and didn't appear to be considering it.

James cleared his throat and tried a new tack. "I thought it might be less of an intrusion if I came when Saffy was still at school. She tells me she finishes at three?" He smiled, knowing full well it would take more than a stretch of his lips to win Adele's trust back.

They'd been through the mill and back during their short marriage, and with so much left unsaid, James wasn't expecting anything other than reservation from this woman.

Adele raised her eyebrows in lieu of answering.

"There's some paperwork that goes with it; a couple of things for you to sign. But we can do that out here, if you'd prefer?" He wouldn't ask for an invitation inside, but he wasn't above hinting.

Again with the cool stare. The sunny afternoon had begun to morph into a distinctly cold front.

Adele's visible shock on opening the door to him had been compounded by James' lack of finesse in handling their meeting, and he wasn't sure how to proceed from here.

He'd thought he was prepared to see her again—had talked himself into a reasonably calm state—but everything about Adele threw him off his axis. Whenever he opened his mouth, she seemed to take another metaphorical step backward.

"Just give me a moment." Turning to stride back to the car, James unlocked it to remove his briefcase and the package he'd carried as hand-luggage from Sydney. Returning to Adele, who'd remained resolutely in the doorframe, he offered her the sizeable box.

One Meiji period lacquered jewellery box, with nine hand-painted interior drawers in excellent working condition. All of its owner's original contents present, and accounted for... Bar one.

Adele didn't advance to take the package as James had expected, and he hesitated. She too seemed undecided, blinking at him from her half-in, half-out position in the doorway.

"You don't want it?" He lowered the box slowly, nonplussed.

He'd gravely miscalculated. Through everything, he'd thought this would be the one item that still meant something to her.

Of course Adele wanted the jewellery box. It was the man holding it she could've done without ever laying eyes on again.

It was a little surreal seeing the great Aksel James Montague at a loss. In both business and personal life he always appeared to be in charge and in control, moving swiftly and confidently in whichever well-researched direction he chose. Adele had no idea what had possessed her ex-husband to hand deliver her personal belongings to the deep recesses of this Otago lakeside town, but for once, the C.E.O. looked well out of his depth in his expensive suit pants and business shirt.

"You could give it to Saffy," James ventured.

"I will *not* be giving it to Saffy." Presenting her nine-year-old daughter with an antique of this value? No way. It belonged to Adele.

Still, she couldn't seem to bring herself to reach out and touch the package in her ex-husband's hands—her memories suddenly too real, and too raw.

"No. Right." James drew back slightly, and she could see she'd offended him by the upward thrust of his chin. He tucked the box awkwardly back under one arm. "Of course not." He cleared his throat. "I have the independent assessment; the credentials to authenticate…" he trailed off. "You could sell it, Dell. Buy yourself something nice."

No. Neither could Adele see herself ever selling this particular piece.

It was the only thing she could be certain James had personally chosen for her, because she'd been with him at the time. And it stood as a reminder her she hadn't been completely bonkers to believe marriage to a virtual stranger had held the potential to work. No matter what her family had thought of the idea, she hadn't been totally nuts to rip her small daughter from everything they'd called home, and relocate to Australia to be with James.

Not stark-raving mad in the beginning, anyway.

Adele had seen the Japanese jewellery box at an antique market on her honeymoon in Venice, and was unable to walk past it.

God, what a romantic city. The pure ridiculousness of its existence, perched precariously on its sinking foundations, was enough to draw in the lovers, the writers, and the artistic dreamers. The staunch beauty of the old buildings, pride unmoved by flood and sunken wealth, still appealed to Adele like no other.

So paradoxical sitting amidst the battered old European treasures and junk, the Meiji box had been meticulously made, and carefully maintained. The time and workmanship given to the painting of the central pheasant alone would've sold Adele on it, but the tiny brass handles and hinges on the concealed compartments pulled at her inner child, too.

The price, once converted, was astronomical. Adele had bought used cars for less. She hadn't even bothered attempting to barter the seller down, and had walked on.

Unbeknownst to her, her brand new husband had crept back and arranged for both payment and delivery to their little boutique hotel. And she'd cried, because the action was so sweet; so thoughtful and attentive.

Adele sighed. She had no tears left for James. Not for the man standing before her offering this priceless box full of unwanted memories. No longer as a symbol of enduring love, with whispers of romance from faraway lands, but as some kind of olive branch.

"I guess you'd better come in, then," she conceded ungraciously, considering how far he'd travelled to hand-deliver her personal effects.

James could've sauntered off the set of a Yves Saint Laurent photoshoot, and it wasn't fair he presented so well, when Adele was currently sporting the dragged-through-a-hedge-backwards look. He caught her eye as he stepped over the threshold, close enough to brush against her arm and send a shockwave clear down to the soles of her feet, making her wish she'd done something with her hair this morning other than just running her fingers through it.

With James' heritage and colouring, the flaxen hair and quick-to-tan Nordic skin, you'd expect blue eyes. But her ex-husband's irises were a bright bottle-green, and the unusual combination had always hit like a hoof to the gut.

Adele huffed an irritated breath out from between her lips, not particularly appreciating the view, nor her body's ridiculous reaction to it. Not even a little bit.

Lake Taimana is now available on Amazon

TE REO MĀORI - MĀORI LANGUAGE GLOSSARY

Aotearoa – New Zealand

E hoa – friend, partner, spouse

Haere mai – come here

Haka – cultural dance

Harakeke – flax

Hongi – to press noses in greeting, share breath

Kaihana – cousin (loan from English)

Kaihanga – builder, maker

Kaimoana – seafood, shellfish

Kāmana – Australasian crested grebe

Kia ora – hello, good wishes, thank you

Kiwi – native flightless bird, New Zealander

Koha – contribution, gift, donation

Koru – curl, coiled shoot

Mānuka – dense native shrub, white flowers

Marama – moon

Māori – indigenous people of New Zealand

Nau mai – welcome

Otago – southeast area of South Island. Originally *Ōtākou* denoting the marae

Papatūānuku – Earth Mother, God of the earth

Rākau – wood, stick, tree

Ranginui – Sky Father, God of the sky

Raranga – weaving, plaiting

Rua – two
Ruru – morepork, small native owl
Tane – man
Tāroaroa – tall, long
Taimana – diamond
Te ao Marama – the bright moon, full moon
Te Reo – the language
Toetoe – large native grass, feathery plumes
Wānaka – township and lake in central Otago

NIHONGO - JAPANESE LANGUAGE GLOSSARY

Aka-chan – baby, infant

Anata – you

Anata no – your

Anata no ban desu – it's your turn

Arigatou – thank you

Asa – morning

Asa-gohan – breakfast

Baka – stupid, idiot

Ban – turn

Chan – suffix for a familiar person, or child

Chotto itai dake – only a little sore

Desu – is

Desu ka? – is it?

Douzo – please

Douzo yoroshiku – best regards, please take care (of me)

Eigo – English

Eigo wa wakarimasen – (I) don't understand English

Fūjin – Shinto god of wind, often depicted as a devil

Futon – mattress

Gaijin – foreigner

Gohan – cooked rice

Gomennasai – I'm sorry, my apologies

Gozaimasu – polite form of is

Hai – yes

Hajimemashite – glad to meet you (for the first time)
Hiroshima – city and prefecture, Chūgoku area
Hiroshima-ben – Hiroshima dialect, brogue
Hokkaido – prefecture, island in the north
Honshu – central island, main province
Houkou – direction
Itai – pain, soreness
Itai desu ka? – is it painful?
Jikan ni seikaku na hito – always on time person
Kanji – Chinese character
Kansai – region - Osaka, Kobe, Kyoto, and surrounds
Kewpie – brand name
Kimono – traditional clothing (full length)
Kirei – pretty, beautiful, lovely
Kirei desu ne – beautiful, isn't it.
Kirei desu yo! – it's so beautiful!
Kiwi ja nai desu ka? – you're not a Kiwi?
Ka – spoken question mark
Korekara – from now, in the future
Korekara mo yoroshiku – please take care (of) in the future
Kun – suffix for junior, master, boy
Matcha – powdered green tea
Ma ma – so-so, sometimes, sort of
Mamonaku – soon
Mamonaku migi houkou desu – turn to the right soon
Migi – right
Moshi moshi – hello (on phone)
Motto – even more, longer, further
Musume – girl
Nagano – city and prefecture, Chūbu area
Neko – cat
Nigiri – rice ball with seafood
Nihon jin – Japanese person, people
Nihon jin desu ka? - are you Japanese?
Nihongo – Japanese language
Niku – meat
Nippon – Japan
Niwatori – hen, chicken

Obāchan – grandmother
Ohayo – morning, early
Ohayo gozaimasu– it is early, good morning
Okonomiyaki – savoury pancake with cabbage base
Onsen – hot spring
Osaka – city and prefecture, Kansai region
Raku – low fired pottery
Samurai – warrior (Edo period)
San – respectful suffix after name
Sashimi – raw fish
Sayonara – goodbye
Sensei – teacher
Shinto – indigenous spiritual belief of Japan
So desu – it is so, correct, that's right
Subarashii – glorious, excellent
Surimi – minced fish
Sushi – made with vinegar rice
Takoyaki – chopped octopus cooked in batter-balls
Tokidoki – sometimes
Tokyo – city and prefecture, Kanto region
Totemo – very, exceedingly
Totemo yasashii ko desu – (she's) very tender
Tsunami – swallow
Tsugi – next, following
Yamada Keisuke – name: Keisuke Yamada
Wakarimasen – (I) don't understand
Wasabi – Japanese horseradish
Yasashii – tender, kind, graceful
Yen – Japanese currency
Yo – spoken exclamation mark
Yoroshiku – best regards, please take care of (me)
Zouri – traditional thonged sandals

ACKNOWLEDGMENTS

Firstly, to my Master Potter, Gael, where would I be without your expertise and ever-welcoming studio? And to my mother's good friend, Margaret Riley, who nurtured my love of clay very early on. Thank you both. There is nothing to compare to this glorious mud.

Aotearoa is a stunning backdrop, and I'm proud to call it home. However, the cultures here are as diverse as the people, and I can't claim them all as my own. Thank you to Fiona, Heperi, and Ranui, for your time and invaluable suggestions in Te Reo Māori. Thank you also to Saori and Shinobu, for your insight and corrections with regards to Nihongo, and for being so gentle in pointing out everything I have forgotten. Arigatou gozaimasu!

To Aaron, who had the difficult task of explaining the intricate ins and outs of rugby, kia ora e hoa tane, and my deepest apologies. The haka is where my comprehension ends.

As always, I couldn't have published this book without the input from my ground crew. Lyssa and Melissa, I'm so grateful for both your editing skills and support, and to Mel for wading through the publishing mire with me. Fiona and Megan, your continued enthusiasm for everything I give you to read makes me confident enough to move paper mountains. Without a doubt my band of loyal ARC readers are second to none!

And last but definitely not least, Ruth, who walked me through everything pregnancy that I was too muddle-brained to notice on my own, personal journeys. Aroha nui.

A great many people have helped steer my waka as I wrote Daniel and Kanako's story, but any errors remaining are mine, and mine alone.

ABOUT THE AUTHOR

An award winning contemporary romance novelist and short story writer, Stephanie Ruth lives in the South Island of Aotearoa, Te Waipounamu, with her husband, three children, and an ever-expanding array of animals. If it doesn't have a happy ending in some form, Stephanie's not writing it. Ruby Island is her second novel, and the second book in the Otago Waters Series.

You can find her on Facebook @stephanieruth.nz, Twitter @ruth_writes_nz, and Instagram @ruth_writes_nz.

Sign up to her newsletter and receive exclusive access to short stories, prologues, epilogues, and cut scenes on her website www.stephanie-ruth.com

ALSO BY STEPHANIE RUTH

Otago Waters' Series

Mako Bay

Ruby Island

Lake Taimana

Taniwha Creek (novella)
- Valentines in the Vines Anthology

Add a Splash of Love (short stories)
- Otago Waters' Anthology-

Independent Short Stories

Hair and Now
-Rising Heat Anthology-

Between Friends
-One Kiss is Never Enough Anthology-

Printed in Poland
by Amazon Fulfillment
Poland Sp. z o.o., Wrocław

33681693R00201